PREYING FOR SALVATION

Seventy, eighty feet high, the Wood-wose moved with a strange clockwork gait. The long arms darted out in front, huge hands reaching for the men.

Gort was picked up and stuffed into the giant mouth while wailing in horror. Jaws chewed on him before the hunters' astonished eyes.

The thing smashed Porosh into a jelly with a blow from a fist the size of a door. A servant in white fell into a fetal ball on the ground. A foot stamped the servant flat.

Rifles were firing by then, but even as puffs of fiber and dust blew off the monster, it kept killing. Revilkh followed Gort into the thing's snapping maw; vigorous mastications took place, a few indigestibles were spat out, including Revilkh's saliva-coated binox.

By Christopher Rowley
Published by Ballantine Books:

GOLDEN SUNLANDS

STARHAMMER

THE VANG: The Military Form

The Fenrille Books:

THE FOUNDER

THE WAR FOR ETERNITY

THE BLACK SHIP

THE FOUNDER

Christopher Rowley

A Del Rey Book

BALLANTINE BOOKS • NEW YORK

A Del Rey Book
Published by Ballantine Books

Library of Congress Catalog Card Number: 89-91792

ISBN 0-345-33175-3

Manufactured in the United States of America

First Edition: December 1989

Cover Art by Stephen Hickman

1

A.D. 2435. DAY 20. EIGHTH MONTH.
OBERON'S EYE SPACE HABITAT. URANUS SYSTEM.

THE SCHOOL WAS DELIBERATELY DESIGNED TO LOOK A THOUsand years old. Ivy clung to pseudostone, windows and doors were arched. Faux chimneys thrust from the red-tiled roofs.

A ten-year-old boy wearing a gray jacket, brown shorts, and boots, raced across the junior quadrangle. He rounded the corner, passed the long colonnade called the Arches, and ran into the junior common room at full tilt.

"Run for your lives everyone, Tariq's on the rampage," he announced. The boys lounging by the door stood up in immediate alarm.

"Uh-oh," someone gulped.

"It's total warpath, he's got a bat," said the bearer of bad news.

The ten-year-olds by the door scattered.

Someone told Dane Fundan at gym, "Tariq's in a rage, he says he's gonna do you."

"Me?" blurted Dane, a skinny twelve-year-old from the famous family.

"Yeah, well, didn't you write your name on the inside of Tariq's study door?"

"What? I don't write my name anywhere, thank you."

"Well someone did, and Tariq's gone into one of his fits. You know how he gets."

Dane Fundan was left to tremble. He'd dreaded this possibility since the day Wagner Fundan left school and took his protective strength with him.

Now, as a result, Tariq Khalifi was a colossus of terror standing astride the lives of the boys at the Reserve, the renowned private school for the difficult children of the very wealthy. Tariq and his gang of thirteen-year-olds were in the Upper Shell. They'd failed the standard examinations and were being crammed for the secondary exams, their last chance to get on track for either Chesk or Nippon secondary.

Tariq, his cousin Revilkh, and Johan Smits were the core of the group. Ostentatiously wealthy, rude and boisterous in classes, rebellious and wild outside them, they were well on their way to becoming proper adolescent hellions.

Tariq Khalifi had an especial hate for all Fundan boys. He had lost many fights with Wagner Fundan.

As a result, Dane spent that afternoon's free time hiding in the boot closet. Where old Grary cleaned the young masters' boots for them.

Old Grary was a simpleton. The school legend had it that he'd killed a girl in his previous life. It had been his second murder, so he got cerebro-reduction treatment.

Another story, equally popular, was that old Grary was actually the dimwit, bastard son of Senior Teacher Deitz. The mother had been the wife of the former Headmaster, who had committed suicide thirty years ago.

While old Grary watched porno video in the corner of the dark cellar that was his home, and drank beer and occasionally masturbated, Dane shivered inside the boot closet and tried not to watch. Old Grary dribbled a lot when he masturbated.

Eventually the bell rang for evening supper. Everyone had to attend for roll call. Dane slipped out of Grary's dark domain and sneaked along the Arches to the quadrangle.

This was a dangerous point. Open ground that might be under observation by any one of Tariq's cronies. But it had to be crossed to get to the mess hall.

Dane started across. He heard a cry that rang down the corridor behind the arches. He started to run, but a figure stepped out in the doorway to the mess hall.

"No way through here, Fundan." It was Revilkh, carrying a short crank bat. Hoskins and Tae Wo were behind him.

Dane skidded leftward but found Johan Smits blocking the escape to the gym and the main building.

"You're not going anywhere now, you little bastard," a voice behind him hissed. He turned and found a red-faced Tariq, also wielding a crank bat.

"You're a daring one, aren't you?" Tariq said while he swung the bat about, making vicious little swipes in the air. "Wrote your bloody little name in my study, didn't you?"

Dane felt his mouth go dry. Five of them. He couldn't fight them, he had to outrun them.

2

"No, I didn't."

"No, you didn't?" Tariq roared. "Then what's it doing there now?"

"I don't know, Tariq."

"Don't tell lies, you scumbag Fundan. I know you think you did something funny, well now you find out how I feel!"

"I didn't do anything, Tariq. Why would I? I mean, is it reasonable to think that I would?"

Tariq's face broke up with a weird kind of glee.

"Is it reasonable . . ." he mocked.

"What's it think it is?" Hoskins sneered. "Thinks it's an attorney, does it? Thinks it can talk philosophy, does it? Look, little bug, you've had it. You're gonna get squashed."

"Yes," Revilkh said. "We're gonna remember this one for a long time."

Dane turned and ran in desperation, across the quadrangle to a little door that went down into the cellar. If he could get to it first, he could get to old Grary's domain. Past that and he might find a patrolling teacher. Mr. Deitz was on duty; Tariq wouldn't dare do anything in front of old Deitz.

He reached the small door a few strides ahead of Johan Smits, who led Tariq by a similar distance. The door was open. He was through and down the stairs and running for his life when Smits threw the crank bat at his legs from behind and he stumbled and fell.

Smits was on him the next moment with a kick that missed his crotch but did sink into his thigh.

Dane lashed back with his own legs from the floor and scrambled to his feet when the bigger boy fell over a sack of garbage, trying to avoid his flashing boots.

Dane ran on, although his left leg felt numb. Tariq was close behind now, and old Grary's door from this side turned out to be locked.

In despair Dane ran on down the passage to the drive. But he knew that the drive was a dead end. It simply ran between the main building and the twelve-foot-high outer wall, all the way around to the front gate and the holly bushes that grew there. The wall itself was boy-proof. No one had ever escaped.

Dane heard boots crunching on the gravel behind him. Tariq, Smits, and Revilkh were hot on his trail. With an impending sense of doom, he staggered on, around the main building and past the front steps.

3

He stopped, sobbing for breath, beside the holly trees, run to ground.

The pursuit drew around him.

"You can run, you little shit, but you can't run forever." Tariq swung the crank bat at him. Dane dodged.

Revilkh ran in from the side and grabbed him in a head-lock.

"Got him!" Hoskins yelled with glee.

Tariq kicked Dane's ankles and he fell. Smits and Tariq took hold of his legs, Revilkh held his head, while Hoskins and Tae Wo grabbed his wrists.

"One, two, three," they chortled. On "four!" they hurled him into the dense holly bushes.

Dane fell through the spiny vegetation, scraping hands, knees, and forehead. He struck the ground hard enough to knock the breath from his body.

His tormentors were roaring with laughter.

"One, two, three, *four!*" Revilkh bellowed, slapping his hands together in time. The Khalifi brothers did a jubilant dance together, celebrating victory over the Fundan enemy.

Eventually Dane crawled out again. There was blood trickling down his cheek from a scratch on his forehead.

"That boy is very messy!" Tariq snapped in an excellent imitation of old Deitz.

"The untidy boy is not the boy I like to see!" Smits replied, also in perfect imitation of the dreaded Senior Master.

"Exactly!" Tariq said, pushing Dane down to the ground again.

"No fight left in him, eh?" Hoskins shouted in delight.

"One, two, three, *four!*" the bigger boys cried as they swung him again into the holly bush.

Once more he crashed through spiny leaves and branches, slammed into the trunk of a tree, and fell slowly through the branches to the ground.

It took a while to regain his feet, but when he did, he staggered out and stood there gasping for air.

Something was happening at the front gate. A black limousine had appeared. The gate opened with an electric *whirr* and the limousine drove smoothly up to the front steps of the main building.

It stopped. A man in a gray frock coat climbed out and stood on the steps, watching the boys by the holly bushes.

"What's he want?" Smits snarled.

"Look out, there's old Deitz," Revilkh exclaimed as the front doors opened and a tall figure appeared.

"Oh shit," Tariq muttered.

"Yeah, just when we were having some fun," Revilkh grumbled.

Dane had his breath back. He was filled with a blind, dreamlike anger. The bullies weren't even looking at him.

He snatched Johan Smits's crank bat and cracked it hard over Revilkh's head.

Revilkh went down with a thud. Tariq whirled around.

"By the blood, showing some spirit, are you?" Tariq raised his bat.

Dane tried to kick Tariq in the crotch. The bigger boy dodged, cursing vilely.

Dane's dander was up now, he didn't stop. He swung the crank bat hard against Tariq's bat, and both bats broke across the handle.

Now it was fist to fist. Tariq had forgotten himself, was lost in a wild state of rage.

"He's mine, leave him for me!" he snarled, and moved in with his arms windmilling punches.

Dane fought more coolly, picking off Tariq's wild blows, dodging one roundhouse right and then sticking a straight left right into Tariq's nose.

Tariq stopped dead with a squawk of dismay. Blood ran from his right nostril. Dane waited, in position, as taught in his karate class.

Tariq charged him again and this time got in a blow to Dane's shoulder, then got his arms around him and went for a headlock.

Dane kept his head and punched Tariq in the crotch. Tariq vented an explosive breath, and Dane kneed him in the behind and popped his head free from the bigger boy's grip.

Tariq gave a scream of rage and charged once more, but Dane dodged a wild punch, stuffed Tariq in the solar plexus, and dropped him to the ground.

Tariq lay there gasping for breath while the other boys stared. Tariq was the biggest, toughest boy in school. They had never seen him humiliated like this.

Revilkh had regained his feet. He found his crank bat. "The little bastard! Let's get him!"

Reanimated, the four advanced on the one.

A sharp, adult voice floated over their heads. "Hoskins,

5

Khalifi, Tae Wo, Smits. What do you think you are doing?"

They froze. Old Deitz was there. Old Deitz had them square in his sights.

Old Deitz was advancing on them with his characteristic stride, measured, implacable, terrifying to those with a guilty conscience. His voice rolled before him, bearing a bracketing volley of pitiless sarcasm.

"Ah, both of the Khalifi brothers are present, but Tariq appears to be playing in the gravel. Tariq continues to skirt the issues of maturity, does he not? It looks as if my detention class will be considerably fuller in the coming weeks. Tariq will perhaps learn some of the limitations that infantile behavior can lead to. Yes, Tariq, I foresee many hours that we shall spend together in the coming months."

"Ah, sir, I think I can explain," Hoskins began.

"Do you, Hoskins? Do you really?" Deitz inclined his head. "If I allow you to, however, and you fail to 'explain,' as you put it, I shall double your detentions."

Hoskins gulped.

"Do you still wish to 'explain,' Hoskins?"

"No sir."

"Hoskins, I do believe that a semblance of intelligence has finally awakened within the thick carapace of your skull." Old Deitz beamed.

The man from the limousine was approaching. He, too, possessed the look of a hale and healthy man of late middle age that was so common among the spacer population. He was actually 105 years old, standard terrestrial time units. Still, he retained a firm grip and a steady tread.

Old Deitz noticed that the distinguished visitor was standing right beside him. "Boys, you have the honor to be presented to Edward Fundan. Stand up straight and be a credit to the school."

Edward Fundan! Their eyes registered shock. The Prince himself was here.

"Hello, young fellows," the Prince said with a pleasant, musical-sounding voice.

Nervously they bobbed their heads.

Standing behind the others, Dane Fundan still had a trickle of blood running down his cheek and soaking into his gray school jacket.

"I'm actually here to see that little chap." He pointed to

6

Dane, who stared back dully, eyes filled with shock rather than understanding.

"A very messy boy I'm afraid, Your Highness," old Deitz said with the very tiniest of smiles.

Edward Fundan returned it with a wintry grin. "Yes, but a game one, Senior Master, a game one."

2

PRINCE EDWARD FUNDAN HAD ACHIEVED MUCH IN HIS LIFE-time, but of late he had begun to appreciate more than ever the swift passage of time. Time had become very precious, because his final project was upon him and he knew he could not live long enough to complete it. His enemies in his family were going to kill him.

He had conceived of this last project a long time before, when he was still a young habitat builder, still scrambling for backing among the financiers of the outer planetaries. Back then it had been the dream of a young man with far to go.

Now it seemed beyond his reach, and this thought galled him terribly, because he saw that without it, all his work was wasted and Clan Fundan must fall, along with all the other proud clans of the spacers, cut down in ruinous warfare.

Edward had a magnificent information-gathering network. The jewel in its crown was an agent code-named Optimor, who operated at a high level within the Earth bureaucracy.

Optimor's information provided only the gloomiest projections of the future behavior of Earth's World Government with regard to the offworld colonies and habitats.

The only way to avoid the coming wars was to flee the solar system and make the great jump into the beyond. But to build the huge ram scoop, with anti-matter drives for initial start up, was not only enormously costly, it was a direct challenge to Earth and its social-union government which proclaimed itself the true arbiter of all human affairs.

Even in Clan Fundan there were traitors. Predictive soft-

7

ware now gave him only a limited time for survival.

And so he had turned his attention to his grandson, determined to forge a weapon that would span the generations and carry forward the building of the great ship, the *Founder*.

Edward's son Maxim had had none of his sire's spark. He'd spent a dissolute life in the demimonde of leisure that consumed most of the great families. Begetting an heir was the first thing Maxim had ever done that Edward found remotely worthwhile.

Edward had few children during his life. Two daughters who died on Mars, then much later his son, from a liaison with Semeri Okisi, the artist who had affected much of Edward's late work. Since Maxim had turned out to be worthless, Edward had reconciled himself to the end of his line.

Then had come the birth of a grandson. Edward watched with consuming interest.

Of course, Maxim had proved utterly incapable as a father. Edward might have moved earlier, but he was stopped by the implacably greedy nature of Dane's mother, Messaline Vesko. Messaline was a skilled practitioner of "Cleopatra's grip," and with it she kept Maxim on a rein for long enough to give him an heir. Then as Maxim drifted away, Messaline had clung tightly to the boy, to ensure that she was well-treated by the Fundan bank.

Eventually, however, she tired of mothering, and of Maxim and his stuffy family, which was so difficult about money, which she always felt short of. She sent the boy to the Reserve and threw herself into the gaudy charivari of the high life on Oberon's Eye.

It took Edward two years to get the matter through the Fundan family council and get Messaline's allowance cut off. The council was the seat of his clan-enemies' power, and a place where he was at his weakest.

But without her allowance, Messaline faced poverty and humiliation.

When she'd come to her senses, Edward had been there, and in a single, swift transaction, he gave her enough money to see her well off for a century in exchange for all parental rights to the boy.

Edward then withdrew the boy from the Reserve, which he judged to be very much the wrong school for him. Dane was flown on a private shuttle out to *Fundan One*, where he moved immediately into his grandfather's household, a magical enclave of power, wealth, and style. Coming from the hard regimen of the Reserve, where brats were hammered into men or monsters, Dane found the change liberating, intoxicating. It was as if he had been taken up into a film fantasy, where anything he might think of and want was placed before him.

But there were rules. Edward placed much store by sets of rules, including the three E's: Education, Effort, and Energy. The first of these was the most important, and Dane was made to understand that if he applied himself to it, his grandfather would be pleased and would continue to let Dane live at the center of power, inside Castle Fundan itself.

Castle Fundan bestrode its own deck on *Fundan One* habitat, the queen of the fleet of Fundan habs in Uranus' outer system.

Fundan One was a nu-urban miracle of planning and cultured modality. Somehow, despite the presence of more than four thousand people per square mile, *Fundan One*'s ambience was that of a low-density suburb. The attention to "ma" was strict; order, serenity, and a subtle discipline were everywhere.

However, despite the overall modernity of the thinking that lay behind the habitat's social and financial success, Edward had built himself a mansion set within the exterior of a medieval castle, a luxury anachronism of the most fantastic kind for a Fundan.

The population of *Fundan One* was stable, long-lived, and sophisticated in its pursuits. Schools were lavish and small, golf courses equally lavish and large.

At this time the blue triangle and the words "Fundan Made" were a mark of quality with few equals. The Fundans were among the wealthiest, the most powerful, of all the outer planetaries. They were old-time Oxygen Princes, then space-line owners and hab builders. An ancestor, Compton Fundan, had even been executed for space piracy in the inner belt during the early 'Roid Rush.

More recently the family companies had become known for superior design in the manufacture of thousands of technical items. Something that was Fundan Made would never break down, nor would it become obsolescent before its time. Fundan space-suiting, Fundan vac-seals, were the ultimate.

Now living on Fundan space, Dane attended Chesk, the ultimate Fundan school.

At the end of the school day Dane bid his friends good-bye and returned to his grandfather's world.

In a great room decorated in faux-Victorian wood and velvet, Edward conducted business. A pair of antique Sony flatscreens were the only visible concession to the world after A.D. 1900.

Edward wore suits of white silk, with brown shoes and shirts of Fundan blue. Edward had never forgotten his roots. An original street map of the city of Toronto hung on a wall in an indestructible frame. A painting of the Fundan Gerontology Clinic was on another wall. The painting was a Mazoli, done from the original color photograph of the clinic taken at the grav well by Talbot Fundan himself in A.D. 2058.

In this room Dane would sit quietly in a corner, having tea and scones while being privileged to witness the wheeling and dealing. Edward bought and sold shares and securities all over the system, from Uranus Prime back to Tokyo itself.

Frequent visitors included Jebediah Bones, a skilled merchant banker, and Dego Manute, another banker, who had a villa across the park from Castle Fundan.

The business day usually ended with the ringing of an ancient brass bell, the "Tiger Cat" bell.

Then came dinner, served in the hall, with portraits of ancient Fundans looking on from the walls. Dane was allowed to sit at table. Dane was also allowed wine, but not the brandy that would follow it.

After dinner there would be billiards for ten spots a point, or a poker game, or backgammon. Dane was allowed to play billiards and backgammon, but only to watch the poker.

"Too soon for poker, boy. But I want you to watch, you can learn a lot about human beings from the way they play poker."

On other evenings Edward dismissed his court and sat alone with Dane, playing chess. As they played they talked, and Dane learned much about his world and his place in it.

At every turn Edward worked to instill in his protégé his own genius for the hunch, for the canny move.

And at times Edward saw to it that the boy was drugged and brought down to a room where he was probed by the psych-softs in the house A.I.

He was probed and then programmed, with lines of ancient doggerel which were the secret key phrases to Fundan softwares.

10

"Tiger Cats and Maple Leafs, and Blue Jays in the summer, that's what we are, boy."

At the Chesk school Dane discovered a natural interest in economics and the history of technological design. He took electives in constructon physics and organization studies. He did well enough in all these to earn a school commendation.

For his fifteenth birthday Edward took him to Leisure City, a restricted pocket hab famous for its casinos and high life.

The cronies were along, of course. Mr. Bones was the terror of any casino's blackjack table. Corvallon, Bakuven, and Manute were ragers for craps, and in the wee hours they all retired to the exotic sex saloons.

Dane was allowed to play blackjack until he'd lost a thousand credits, then he went to watch his grandfather play baccarat.

Later there were iced champagne and beautiful young women with exotic hair colors, one of whom, a gentle girl with long pink hair, assisted a tipsy Dane into his hotel room and undertook to educate him in sophisticated sexuality.

After that weekend Dane found he had crossed an invisible line. He was no longer considered a child.

"You'll be a man soon, boy, and you'll have a man's work to do. That's why it's important you take as much as you can from your time at Chesk. I'm going to need you soon, to work with me on building the ship."

Dane wanted nothing more, then or ever.

"This is an age of mass misperceptions, you see, boy. This system has fifteen billion living in a greenhouse hell down there at the bottom of the grav well. Out here we've got twenty million living high and free and thinking that this is the natural order of things. Well, they're wrong about that, I can tell you. And someday soon those billions down there are going to reach out and shake the money tree."

"Why, Grandfather?" he had said.

"Because they have no other choice. They've overwhelmed their planet's resources. They're going down, and they'll reach out to drag us with them, if we're still here."

Now Dane was set to work with the new A.I. that had been spun to operate the great ship.

"This is *Founder*, boy. It is young in places, but it contains all that my father's A.I. knew and all that his father's knew. It knows you well too."

"Hello," the *Founder* said in a warm, masculine voice.

With the A.I.'s tutoring, Dane became adept with most aspects of Fundan software.

Edward chuckled. "Regular Hamilton Tiger Cat of a boy, I always said so."

On his sixteenth birthday Edward took Dane to another room, a secret room in a vault beneath the castle. Here were kept a set of Kunushu computing cubes, a meter on a side, black and glistening.

"You will stay here until you have absorbed the innermost codes and know them by heart."

From that point Dane moved directly into the project. He became Edward's roving agent, plugged into the *Founder* at every level.

The years went by and the great ship grew. The engines were finished, the hab sector was completed, powered up, and initiated with atmosphere and biotics. The project approached its climax.

And then, in Dane's twenty-fourth year, this all came to an abrupt end one evening when Edward opened a new box of cigars and extracted a Zimba panatella. He was sitting out on the terrace, watching the deer frolic in the waining light and sipping a spritzer with Jebediah Bones.

This particular cigar, however, was the result of many year's worth of effort by his enemies to penetrate his guard.

Edward took down an antique lighter, U.S. made, and lit the cigar. He took one whiff and died, poisoned by an acute nerve toxin hidden in a tiny pellet in the cigar's tip.

3

A.D. 2447. DAY 10. THIRD MONTH.
FUNDAN ONE, URANUS SYSTEM.

EDWARD'S DEATH WAS ATTRIBUTED TO A FAILURE OF HIS ME-
chanical heart, and his personal physician later retired from
practice to a surface villa on Oberon's Eye. Even before the
death of the Prince was announced, a certain youth, employed
by the Fundan Messenger Service, disappeared without trace.
This mystery was never officially solved.

Once Edward's funeral was over, his enemies within the
family moved. At their head was Dane's great-aunt Agatha.
She summoned Dane to her villa at the opposite end of Fundan park from the castle.

It was Agatha Fundan's greatest moment of triumph. She
pronounced the sentence with relish.

"I am now the senior of the family. I have suspended Edward's will. It is a document riddled with imbecilic nonsense.
It will be set aside in the courts."

At twenty-four, Dane was almost a century younger than
Agatha. He was naive enough to think there was still reason to
fall back on. This, despite his grandfather's assurances that it
was absent among his relatives.

"But Great-Aunt, if you suspend the will, we're going to
have endless difficulties with the financing."

Agatha had the look of extended medical, fashionably
emaciated, with hair transplants and skin smoothing. She
chuckled, amused, revealing perfect white teeth in her long,
tight-skinned face.

"I can imagine, but you'll just have to cope somehow,
won't you?"

He stared at her. Grandfather had always said Agatha and
Luther and the rest of the controlling clique on the family

financial board were stupid and treacherous. But he'd retained a youthful trust in older people and now found that trust ripped away, just as Edward had predicted.

"Look," he protested, "the ship is half built and we've sunk a lot of capital into it. What's the point of causing problems now?"

Aunt Agatha smoothed her knee-length pleated skirt.

"I don't know. It's not exactly my problem, you see."

"But—" he spluttered. She raised a hand to stop him.

"No, my mind's made up, I'm not letting you have another credit. You're cut off."

The words seemed to throb in the air. It was the end.

"Not a credit more, it's over. Your days of parasitizing our family's wealth are finished." Agatha's voice had hardened.

"To finish the *Founder* was my grandfather's single remaining wish."

"I'm sorry, you can forget all that. We buried Edward's pretensions along with the rest of him."

"I am his heir, it says so in the will."

"The will is ridiculous, it will be overturned in family court."

"You have no right to do this!"

"Don't talk to me of rights, I have every right to do what I must to protect the fortunes of Clan Fundan."

Dane looked past her out the window at the ginkgo trees that grew in her garden. He drew no inspiration from them.

"You will destroy our family by this act. You don't know what you're doing."

"Not another credit, by the breath in my body I swear it!" Her eyes shot daggers.

"You're blind"—he felt a dam bursting inside him,— "absolutely blind." Bridges were burning behind him. "This is just so foolish, so tragically stupid."

Her face reddened. "Why, you insolent puppy!" She was beside herself. "Get out! Get out at once! Before I—" She reached for her walking stick and swung at him, knocking over her tea table and sending cup and saucer shattering to the floor. She screamed for her guards as he backed away.

And thus he left Agatha's Grecian villa. In the boat, crossing the lake, he'd looked back with eyes that felt hot and hard in his head.

The clan elders had closed ranks against him, and there

14

was nowhere he could appeal this decision, except to the System Court. A judgment might take years.

Dane supplied the sad cello music for himself. The villa's graceful white walls and orange tile roofs sparkled on its little island. The willows and ginkgos gave shades of green to the composition. The lawn on the villa's spinward side was a flash of emerald. It was all incomparably sad.

He knew then that he would always remember this moment, no matter what happened.

Then the boat turned into the canal and the villa disappeared from view behind a big American beech that grew on the promontory. It was over, Edward was gone. Everything was very bleak.

But they were far from finished. The *Founder* would fly; Dane knew what to do.

He let go of Edward in his mind, consigning the great man to the past.

A line of Fundan spacer doggerel rose in his mind, from an antique ad for Fundan breathing systems.

> In the dark so hard there's no one to hear,
> every breather must breathe his last . . .

4

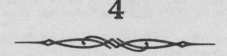

EVENTS MOVED QUICKLY AFTER THAT. DANE HAD TO WORK fast to find loans to keep the *Founder* in progress. The family council worked against him with a great deal of spite and pettiness.

Castle Fundan was emptied of Edward's possessions while the will was tied up, and they were auctioned off.

At the last moment Dane was told that among other things, Edward's tall, dour manservant, Alter, was to be sold. Since Alter was a Fundan Made clone, he had no rights unless they were specifically given to him. Of course, in Edward's will they were, but the will was being set aside.

Dane would not stand for this, and he bought Alter himself and gave him hab rights immediately. Aunt Agatha tried to prevent the transfer of such rights, but here she overreached and the family court ruled in Dane's favor.

Still, finance was the overriding difficulty. Huge sums of money were required for the completion of the ship.

Jebediah Bones contacted him in the second week. It was the first time they'd spoken since the funeral. Jebediah urged Dane to meet with him, at his cousin Adelaide's apartment.

Dane could ill afford the time. His life was a constant round of phone calls and on-screen meetings with banks and finance houses. The *Founder* was enormously expensive.

Still, Jebediah could not be ignored, he was Edward's closest advisor.

Dane rode the transit car that wound along the length of the habitat to his cousin Adelaide's neighborhood, a section where the corridors were disguised as streets and the apartment buildings were separated from one another by gardens artfully lit by mirrors. Lavender ficus and microbeech grew in tubs at every corner.

Adelaide answered the door to her apartment.

It was a small place; Adelaide was not one of the moneyed Fundans. She was Dane's quarter cousin through a daughter of the Natural Fundan line on Mars. Dane had known her for three years, since she had begun working on the *Founder* project for Edward. She had assisted on the financial side. Dane had been Edward's point man for the project construction, and so he and Adelaide had often had cause to work together.

Adelaide had the typical Fundan look: tall, blond, Noram, with a small nose and wide-spaced blue eyes. It was the look that was sometimes referred to as "Minnesota Fundan" by very old members of the clan.

Her apartment was furnished in minimalist style, some lo-frames, a couch, a small white table. Shelves overloaded with tapes, readouts, and general stuff filled up the walls.

Jebediah Bones rose up from one of the lo-frame chairs to greet him.

"Good to see you, boy, hope you're bearing up under the strain."

At that moment Dane wasn't sure if he was or not.

"You wanted to see me, Jebediah?"

"Yes, my boy, your grandfather told me to make some preparations for this sad moment. He was a farsighted man, your grandfather, but I'm sure you're aware of that."

Dane nodded. "He was. I wish I were more like him. I didn't think we'd really get to this point."

Bones smiled, his long toothy face shifting to accommodate it. "You refer to Luther and Agatha, I take it?"

"I'm afraid so. It will take years just to get them into System Court. I can do nothing at the family court."

"Yes, we are cut off from the family capital now. But all is not hopeless. Edward put aside some money for you in my keeping, and I have the account numbers for you whenever you want them."

"Thank you, Jebediah."

"There is at least twenty million credits there."

"That's all?"

Jebediah grinned mordantly. "Twenty million credits isn't enough for you?"

Dane laughed with him.

Jebediah grew solemn. "So, you will have to abandon this crazy project. Give up the starship. You can have a good life, though, you are financially secure."

Dane flashed him a dangerous look, pure Edward.

"Jebediah Bones," he said in his best imitation of Edward's manner, "I will finish building the ship if it kills me. The *Founder* will be built!"

Jebediah's face broke into a weird smile. "Good, good, Edward was right about you, I always thought so myself. You're a stern young man, Master Dane, a little harder than I thought you might be. And that is good news, because I have one further task to discharge for your grandfather."

"What is that Jebediah?"

"I am instructed to ask you a question."

"Oh yes?"

"What assets do you have? Things he might have given you."

"Mmm, forty shares in Fundan Bank Control, plus my portfolio in general stocks. Then there's bonds and promissaries. I own some floor space on Deck Thirty-four, and a space boat and a small tug company, Dane's Tugs. I bought it when I was eighteen. Never made that much money, but it was fun."

Bones was nodding as if gazing at an internalized list in his head.

"Yes, all correct. Altogether you are worth a bit more than half a billion. And you have positions in several funds that Edward set up in the last year of his life. But that's not it. I am particularly charged to inquire about holding companies."

"Other than Fundan bank, I can't think of anything, except, well, I own something called Grandson Savings. When I was sixteen he set it up for me, it was my first company. But it just holds some titles to phony companies. I think it was a practice thing. We bought and sold cheap stocks with it, but I haven't looked at it in years."

Bones's face lit up. "Ah-hah, there we have it. Grandson Savings, is it? Doesn't it strike you as odd, young man, that I, who knows everything about your grandfather's accounts, should never have heard of that one? Give me an index number, will you?"

Dane checked the memory in his wrist unit and gave Jebediah the number. Adelaide called up her computer terminal, and Bones put a call to the central data base and soon had a schematic of Grandson Savings Corporation.

It was very simple. Grandson Savings Corporation was a holding company with controlling shares in a couple of other companies. In both cases Grandson Savings held a hundred percent of the voting shares.

One of these companies, Lancelot Investment, was simply a file name, it had been inactivated years before. The other, Farstar Corporation, owned a number of properties.

"Interesting, I do detect Edward's hand in this," Mr. Bones purred as he examined the business schematic.

"Now to 'Farstar,' another name with which I am unfamiliar," he said. "We shall have to continue our search."

Most of Farstar's holdings were in empty shells, named after the Knights of the Round Table. Then there was Merlin Investments, which led to four other companies. When these were investigated, they led on into a maze of others. Gradually the holding companies faded into design and production companies. Companies that actually did things, with employees and even offices.

Eventually Bones looked up. "At last, I see where it is heading."

Dane and Adelaide were intent on the screen, which was

now split between forty-two windows, each with a corporate schematic.

"You do?" she said. "I'm baffled. These are all little design shops, situated on Obe's Eye, for the most part."

"You see that one?" Bones pointed.

"Ramus Rheological Ices?"

"Yes. Now, that is a name I know. They pumped the weird-ice for the *Founder*'s habitat torus."

"The ship?" Dane exclaimed.

"Of course!" Adelaide said. Her fingers flew to the keyboard; more schematics appeared.

"Electro-Rheo A.S.!" Bones shouted, pointing to another new company on the screen.

"You own fifty-one percent of Electro-Rheo A.S.!" Adelaide said in delight.

Dane sat down suddenly.

"Electro-Rheo is the prime contractor on the ice cladding. We've dealt with them for years."

"You never knew it, my boy, but you owned them all along." Bones pointed to more and more familiar names that were finally coming into view.

"These are all the big contractors working on the *Founder*, unless I'm very mistaken," Dane said, a little awe in his voice as he realized what Edward had done.

"What does it mean?" Adelaide said.

"It means I own the means of building the ship, everything except the Fundan tech sat, which belongs to the family bank. All we need is alternate financing and we can carry straight through with hardly any interruption."

Dane felt the grand purpose stir within him once again, and with it the excitement. "It means we can still build the ship!"

5

SLUMPED IN A CHAIR, IN HIS SHIRT-SLEEVES, UNSHAVEN, DANE Fundan slept the uneasy sleep of exhaustion. In front of him, ignored, were a half-dozen screens. Across them ran a flickering blatter of numbers. Reports from the solar system's money markets, all of them, from Tokyo Nikkei to Luna Net to the Beltwide, they splashed up in pastel indices, the financial pulse of humanity.

In his dreams the fantastic and the all too real blended in a nightmarish swirl. He walked a beach of pink sand, beneath a silvery-blue sky. He carried a rifle, and he lifted it to his shoulder. Through the sights he saw himself, and the others, Adelaide, Melissa, Tobe Berlisher, working the phones.

The scope tightened. The cross hairs of the analysis soft worked into the probabilities. Inwash from the markets blazed on the screens as they surfed the waves of numbers.

They worked around the clock, making money, raising loans, keeping the *Founder* alive. They worked like machines, dream machines, with metal faces and green-lit eyes.

Their problem was terribly simple. Without access to Edward's enormous credit positions, they could not buttress the really big loans they needed.

Meanwhile the *Founder* orbited Uranus and devoured credit like some monstrous interstellar money hog, gulping down six- and seven-figure numbers with every delivery of raw materials.

Faces, Fundans, prominent members of the financial community, floated across his view. Their eyes mocked him. The questions reverberated. How could he be sure the ship would fly as fast as he claimed? Who was this Professor Borvik? A mad exile from the Mars Physics School, that's who. Why was he in exile? Because nobody there believed his theories either.

Wise-eyed cynics, they brought up the Tau Ceti "expeditos" of the ancient generation. "They'll get there in three hundred more years!"

"Those that survive the defreeze."

The Dane in the dream protested: "The M-sun margin balls in every direction have colonies, small ones, but they're there."

"There are no Earth worlds, none within a lifetime."

"But we have the new engines, we can achieve greater speeds than the old expeditions."

The doomsayers grew brutally jolly. "Engines will blow up. Big bright flash half a light-year out, like the Nippon ship in 'twenty-three."

"Awfully sad, really, but, will advance the cause of science, eh? So much human plasm in the spectrum like that."

Dane shook his head, he opened his mouth to shout that they were all fools, all blind, all lost. Then they were gone, their faces blowing away across a flat silver plane.

Edward appeared, wearing a dark pinstripe suit, sitting on the terrace with the park behind him.

Edward had just shown him the secret reports from the inner system, from ancient Earth itself.

"We keep agents there who scarcely look like human beings, boy."

Dane was only fourteen.

"What is Gung An Bu, Grandfathaer?"

"Public Security Buro, boy, the rulers of the inner systems."

"Who are they?"

"Social Synthesists, every one of them."

"What is Social Synthesis, Grandfather? Why do you hate them so much?"

"They killed my father, boy, put him and his woman out the airlock of their own home, just like that." He snapped big fingers in front of Dane's face for emphasis.

"But why?"

"Called him an enemy of the Synthesis, that's why, boy."

"What's an enemy of the Synthesis, though, Grandfather?"

"You are, boy, along with every single breather in this system. Now move, my bishop is pinning your knight pawn, so don't bother looking there."

But instead of chess pieces, another dream memory surfaced.

Edward was sitting in his black oak chair, with the black cat called Nemo sitting in his lap.

"There's only one option open to us, boy, only one, and there's only a certain amount of time left to us to take it. If we wait too long, they'll have political control in Uranus system and we'll never make it out."

"Yes, Grandfather."

"You'll have to save our family from themselves, boy. They won't listen to me, and I won't last long enough to finish, but you will. They don't want to recognize the obvious, but they're going to wake up one day and find that the Gung An Bu is so heavily infiltrated into their world that they don't control it anymore."

And on the computer screen, cunningly hidden in the polished walnut desktop, Edward showed him the workings of the World Government, the power system on Earth. He called up grafix depicting the spread of the control net, leaping from Earth-Luna to Mars, to the Jovians, to Saturn's cities, and ultimately to Uranus itself.

A brown stain of control nets, all linked to the nerve centers in New Baghdad and Beijing.

Dane would never forget.

Suddenly a hand stirred his shoulder, he awoke. Alter was leaning over him.

"You must awake, young Master. Your meeting is in a few minutes. I let you sleep as long as possible."

"Thank you, Alter." He had been unable to get Alter to stop calling him by that title, although he had been able to persuade him to accept his freedom.

There was coffee waiting; eagerly, he reached for it.

6

THE MEETING WAS IN DANE'S OFFICE, IN THE HEART OF THE *Founder*'s financing group. The usual faces were present—Adelaide, Mr. Bones, Tobe Berlisher, and Melissa Fundan-Sogorov, a high-speed Martian Fundan who had risen rapidly under Dane.

There was a somewhat melancholic feeling to the meeting. The sense that they had won every battle and lost the war had been growing for a while.

Dane had dug a bottle of vodka out of the chiller, poured shots all round, even to Mr. Bones, who rarely partook.

Nobody could think of a good toast.

Melissa downed hers in a gulp and set the glass down. Dane reflected that Martians were Martians; they'd inherited something strong from the ancient Russians.

"So what's next?" Melissa said.

"I was afraid you'd ask that question," Dane replied.

"Well, someone had to."

"It looks like we're in trouble." Dane toyed with his glass; the vodka was wearing a few splinters off the vile mood he felt descending over him. But there was no way out of this.

"We have contracts coming up for the power-ice framework and shielding supports," Adelaide said in a quiet voice.

"That's right," confirmed Tobe Berlisher, "the legal work arrived yesterday."

"And we still have to go to the Hong Bank, very shortly, for another loan."

"We don't have enough for the Hong Bank note," Bones said.

"We can't get enough, for sure," Dane agreed. He poured another shot of vodka.

"All right." Dane pushed himself back from his desk, arms wide. "Skull session, what do we do? I'm open to suggestions."

Melissa was first, as normal.

"Piracy. Just fund a Jolly Roger in the outer belt."

"Piracy?" Dane nodded, surprised. "Go back to the family roots, eh?"

Bones guffawed. "That would be a good idea."

"It means we'd obtain a quick supply of mega credit," Melissa said.

"So it does, and we do have the perfect ship."

"You have the *Compton Fundan* in Oberon orbit, don't you?"

"Yes, Adelaide, exactly."

"I should point out . . ." Tobe said in a hesitant voice,

"Yes, Mr. Berlisher," Dane purred.

"There are risks involved."

"Yes," Dane sighed, "there are. So we must consider this

23

carefully. Say we hold up some well-off 'outers,' what kind of payoff do we foresee?"

"One, two macros," Melissa said.

"So, a relatively small payoff, not enough to finish the ship, and pretty intense risk if the Belt Police show up."

Melissa's round face grew impassive. "It was just a suggestion."

Tobe was next. "I have an idea. Why don't we take them on in Probate Court? You are Edward's designated heir. You have the will, put it to the test."

"The courts." Dane pursed his lips. "Get back access to Edward's money. All the money we'd need. Good payoff, what's the problem?"

Tobe blushed,

"Well," Tobe's pink face became even pinker, "there is the time factor."

"Yeah, it'll still take three years to get them into the System Court."

"Certainly makes the option less than ideal," Adelaide said.

"You have an idea, Addy?"

"Yes. We know the G.B.s wouldn't let the System Court find in our favor, anyway, they'd find some way of slowing everything down for decades. I think we have to go begging."

"Begging!" Dane exclaimed, as if the idea had never occurred to him.

Melissa cracked her glass down on the desk again.

"We could try the Kempongs," Adelaide said. "Maybe even line up some Zaibatsu money."

"We could try them. We wouldn't get anywhere, but we could try them."

"I have some predictions that are better than that."

"Oh?"

"Fifty percent shot with the Kempongs right now. They just moved heavily out of Noram bonds, ahead of the fifty-year crisis cycle. They have a lot of liquidity. Dir Kempong is friendly, we talk."

Dane nodded. "I think you'd be right, except for one thing, the politburo meeting last month in New Baghdad. Kladus Menget was missing. Lu Dzong is ascendant. One-system extremists like Wei and Gosolov were voted on to the junior politburo."

"Menget just vanished, then?"

"I'm afraid so, the last voice of moderation is gone."

"What happened?" Tobe said.

"Lu Dzong had him shot."

Their faces had grown very solemn. This was information from Edward's secret agent, his mole in the World Government.

"Optimor?" Adelaide said, eyebrows raised.

Dane made no reply.

"They'll try to stop the ship," Melissa said.

"They certainly will." Dane picked up the bottle again. "So I'm afraid normal banking channels are out. Wei is buro chief of the G.B. offworld unit. The Kempongs won't dare to help us now."

Heads dropped, despair in the air.

"But we still have one option left. Not a good one, but one I think we can play."

Their eyes drilled him. He had something up his sleeve, it was in his voice.

"There are wealthy bandits in this system, just like there are wealthy bankers. If we can't get anything from the bankers, we'll go to the bandits." Dane poured more vodka with a grin.

"Who are you thinking of?" Bones said.

"The Khalifi."

The shock showed on their faces.

"But they're . . ." Adelaide groped for effective adjectives.

"Buccaneers? Outlaws? Pariahs? They're all those things, and they're also very rich."

"But they're the sworn enemy of Clan Fundan, Merzik especially, and that crazy son of his, Tariq."

Dane nodded. "Merzik is certainly not the man I intend to visit. As for Tariq, well, he is a mad dog, no doubt about that, but I know about Tariq from way back. I think we can handle him all right."

"Then who, dammit?" Bones growled, unhappy with this thought of dealing with ancient enemies.

"Ibrahim Khalifi himself, the old man."

"But," Melissa mumbled, "he hasn't been seen in ten years."

"The question is whether he's alive, isn't it?" Bones said.

"He's alive. He says he'll see me."

Awe came into their eyes. How had Dane penetrated the veils surrounding the reigning sheik of Clan Khalifi?

"How?" breathed Adelaide.

"Surprisingly simple. I asked Prince Ras Order, who likes to swing around the hab circuit. Trade shows, gambling, anything that takes him out of the monotony of home. I know Ras Order from Chesk, where we were friends. It turns out that Ras Order actually works for Ibrahim. So he asked the old man, and the old man said yes, come see him in person."

"He wants to see us?" Adelaide said.

"When do we go, then?" Melissa said.

"We're on the ten-hour shuttle. We meet Ras Order at arrivals in Rimal City fifty hours from now."

7

THE SANDS OF THE RIMAL STIRRED IN THE ENGINEERED BREEZE; micrograins streamed from the crests of the dunes. The sun projection was a hot white ring, blazing harshly in the center of the blue-white "sky." And yet, despite the aridity of the scene, the breeze was incongruously soft and laden with the scent of the nearby forest, a lush hunting preserve.

Indeed, they could hear the hunters' guns behind them, taking a toll on cultured boar, lion, and deer. The guns fired low-velocity plastics but employed a charge that gave a thumping loud bang with each shot.

Every so often the gunfire thickened into volleys as fresh animals were driven on to the guns by the beaters.

On they rode, through the artificial sand dunes on beautiful Arabian ponies provided by Prince Ras Order, who led the procession alongside Dane Fundan. The illusion was total. But for the ring-sun, the observer would have sworn he was on a planet, not a fragile space hab made of energized ice.

Ahead, across the dunes, lay a strip of well-stocked birch thicket. Hawks hurtled through the air above, in pursuit of white doves stirred up by the beaters. White feathers showered down, catching the sunlight.

Behind Dane and the Prince rode Adelaide and Melissa, all on similar, magnificent Arabian horses. Behind them came Tobe Berlisher, feeling very plump and pink, on a gentle gray mare. Behind him came a Khalifi bodyguard, Amesh, a silent tower of man, nearly seven feet tall, built on a Herculean scale, riding a horse with Shire genes. Dane had been required to leave Alter behind on board the shuttle; only Khalifi bodyguards were allowed on Khalifi habitat. The absence made Dane peripherally uncomfortable. No one could be sure that the Khalifi were trustworthy, they signed no System covenant, they ignored diplomatic protocols.

But if Dane was uncomfortable, Tobe was petrified. For a start, he had never ridden a horse before in his life. He found the exercise more difficult than he had imagined, even though his mount exhibited a sweet disposition and was quite happy to be out and on the move, toward the water she smelled up ahead. Her eagerness translated into an urge to trot, which gave Tobe palpitations.

The young Fundans, he'd observed gloomily, rode with considerable authority and experience. Once again he felt that line that was drawn between them. They were of the family, within it and protected by its enormous wealth and power. He was just a law-school graduate, albeit a good one.

They mounted the lee face of a major dune. Tobe clung to the pommel on the big western saddle they'd given him.

When they reached the top of the dune, they paused. The dune was one of the tallest, and from this spot they could see back across the Rimal to the green forest line.

Another volley of gunfire echoed ahead.

Tobe stared around himself in awe. To create the Rimal desert, the hab engineers had artificially desiccated a twenty-square-mile sector of the Khalifi habitat. At the center of this arid zone was this pocket sea of dunes, fifty crescents of white silica, which blew back and forth, two miles this way and two miles that, in the artificial winds.

To this bizarre extravagance the Khalifi family elite, an all-male group, came to ride, to hawk, and to sit in tents of traditional black while conducting horse trading and other manly business.

"How can they get away with this?" Tobe had asked Adelaide quietly, out of Prince Ras Order's hearing.

"The Khalifi are not believers in our mode of civilization,

27

Tobe. They do what they want on their space. Only male family members have any political rights."

"But Khalifi City teems with others. It hardly seems an Arab city, in fact."

"Most of them would live somewhere else if they could," Adelaide replied.

They rode on, and soon they could see their destination, a row of black tents, a dozen in all, set up by a grove of palms. Men on horseback were in motion farther away. In the foreground a small crowd of figures in the white of the servant class were clustered around an olive-gray truck.

Tobe felt as if he had ridden a time machine back to some ancient era of savage whimsy and royal eccentricity.

On the level ground past the dunes the mare decided to run, excited at the thought of the water ahead. Tobe was unable to restrain her, and was carried on, ahead of the others, into the tents, where laughing servants caught the reins and brought her to a halt. Finally, a perspiring Tobe was helped out of his saddle and escorted to Ibrahim's tent.

He was waiting by the entrance when the others rode up and dismounted smoothly. Prince Ras Order had a loud chuckle over Tobe's embarrassing lack of riding skill. The Fundans were not amused. The look on Adelaide's face made Tobe wish he could vanish into a hole in the ground.

The wizened figure of ancient Ibrahim was waiting for them inside the air-conditioned cool of the tent. Ibrahim sat on a low-set platinum throne studded with emeralds and rubies. Black cushions were arrayed on the floor around it. The air was scented with rose blossom and coffee. Dimly visible in the low light, behind the throne, stood retainers and enormous slave guards with bare chests and golden armbands.

"Welcome." Ibrahim inclined his head very slightly. A faint smile played across his lips. They were all aware of a keen, intelligent gaze from those dark, luminous eyes. Ibrahim was said to be one and a quarter centuries old, but still firm in the mind, with no trace of senility.

"Thank you, Khalifi Bey," Dane said. He and Ras Order took seats close to the throne. The others were made to sit farther back, almost out of earshot.

"You are not of Arab blood, my friend," Ibrahim said with a sunny smile, "so I will spare you the customary, long-winded salutations that we heap upon one another in my family. But I will insist that you have some coffee with me."

Small cups of bitter black fluid were distributed. Tobe looked to see if Dane drank his. Dane did not. He held up the cup but made no move to drink from it.

Ibrahim noticed this and gave a forthright chuckle and elaborately took a sip from his own cup.

"See," he gestured with a withered claw of a hand, "it is safe for a Fundan to drink coffee while in the tent of a Khalifi."

This sally provoked muffled laughter in the shadows. Ibrahim snapped his fingers for quiet, but a wicked smile lingered on his lips.

Dane took a tiny sip of the coffee, then set it down.

Ibrahim nodded. This one was a real Fundan, the classic model, quite like Edward had once been. He composed himself. There was no need to feel nervous. His position was unassailable.

"So, Dane Fundan has come to visit me, the enemy of his grandsire. I find this most interesting, an illuminating example of our saying that 'all lost horses find their way home, even the ones we never loved.' "

Ibrahim took another sip from his cup and continued.

"As a matter of course, I have followed your career quite closely, my young friend. I know that your grandfather took a large hand in your education."

Dane nodded. "Yes."

"Then you will be a keen student of human history, I am sure." The dark eyes seemed to bore into his.

"To some extent."

"Always in human history it has been the creative activity of small groups, usually outcasts, hated by the majority, that has propelled the race toward progress. Do you believe this?"

"Yes."

"Good, I like that. All the powerful, creative cultures have begun with small, peripheral groups, surviving on the margins of established civilization. Think of the early Greeks, or the Arabs of early Islam, or the colonists of North America. All these were cultures where men took great risks for glory. It is a truism, to succeed at greatness, one must risk all."

Ibrahim paused and nodded to himself, lost in some private reverie for a few seconds, then snapped back.

"And you, my young friend, you are very much an outcast now, I believe."

Dane found his gaze pinned.

"You need much money, do you not?"

Dane still said nothing. Ibrahim went on, still smiling; the Fundans had always been so stiff, so forthright. "Fundan Made" was such a fitting sobriquet. A family of engineers and bankers and builders, no grace, no artistry, Caucasoid clods. Fundan Made!—it would be their epitaph.

"And so, I am faced with an interesting problem. Should I join in your project, to risk capital and life on this flight into the unknown?"

Dane spoke. "You were given the contents of certain espionage files, many years ago. My grandfather told me this."

"Yes."

"Then you know that it is only a matter of time."

Ibrahim shrugged and spread his hands widely. "Some say we can develop weapons to protect ourselves from them."

Dane shrugged dismissively. "We cannot fight them, you know that. We will lose because we will be penetrated from within. Already fear of the Gung An Bu constrains us."

"We could invest in powerful weapons and threaten Earth itself."

"We might attack them with projectile weapons, they would defend themselves with the orbital laser systems. I doubt that we could overwhelm those before their main fleet arrived within range of this system and forced our surrender. But the question is academic. The fear of the G.B.s would prevent us from ever arming in the first place."

Ibrahim chuckled, he knew the truth of this. "So the only option remaining to us?"

"We must finish the ship and escape. It is our last chance. A second ship will never be built."

There was a pause. Ten, fifteen seconds ticked by in silence.

Ibrahim weighed the moment. It was time. The Khalifi had done well in the home system. But now it was time to go on to their destiny, for there were entire worlds to be ruled in the interstellar vastness.

"I think you may be right, young man." Ibrahim's dark eyes danced with unreadable magic. He clapped his hands for more coffee, "But tell me this first, how did your recent maneuver on the Beltwide pay off?"

Dane struggled to prevent his dismay from infecting his voice. He hesitated only briefly.

"Quite well, thank you." And how the hell did the old Khalifi know about that!

Ibrahim chuckled merrily. "Some of us made a killing, you know."

Now they knew who it was who'd hammered the big water market down with puts against their calls last week!

Adelaide, Tobe, and Melissa exchanged stunned looks. Melissa flushed. Security was her province, and it sounded as if they had been penetrated by a Khalifi agent.

"And you recently bought five percent of a small company called Callisto Cryo-Bacto, I believe."

Enough of this. Dane put down the coffee cup.

"You seem to know a lot about my business dealings."

"Yes, young man, I do. It is my business to know these things. But humor me, tell me what you did."

Dane stared back at the old man with stubborn eyes, then relented.

"Well, yes, we did buy five percent. The new strain they've developed offers a radical improvement in efficiencies for ice handling."

Ibrahim chuckled. "Yes, it does. But I have decided to buy the entire company, you see. My family is heavily invested in macreterial genetics. This upstart product would damage our business. I have already acquired forty-six percent of CCB. I want your five percent as well. Then I will be able to suppress the new strain."

Dane struggled with himself.

"And what do we get in return for this?"

Ibrahim smiled again, his dark eyes unknowable. "You will receive goodwill. And a certain amount of financial assistance. Together, we will finish your ship."

"A rather large 'certain amount' in this case, I should warn you, Khalifi Bey."

"You will find that we have a deep purse, my young friend. Credit will not be our problem, you can count on that."

Dane shook hands on it, with the feeling that he had placed his own head beneath a guillotine and that it was only a matter of time before the blade fell.

8

THE AZRAQ PALACE WAS AN ARCHITECTURAL MARVEL. A sculpture in man-made marble, with four soaring corner towers capped with sky-blue, onion cupolas. These surrounded the central dome, itself covered in blue tile, and gave the ensemble a floating elegance that made the place a legend. Indeed, the Azraq was grouped in the Great Seventy buildings of *Leewenook's Syntropic Digest.*

As a mark of high honor, Ibrahim had thrown a party for Dane Fundan on a terrace that circled the dome and gave views across the topmost deck of Rimal City. Under the engineered evening light the spires of mosques across the city were outlined in orange. Golden beams illuminated the trees in the parks and reflected off the windows in the apartments in the downtown section.

The guests circled amid the hubbub of conversation, crisscrossing the blue tiled floor, upon which were reproduced the words of the Ninety-third Sura of the Quran in flowing Arabic script half a meter tall.

Did He not find thee an orphan and give thee a home?
Did He not find thee in error and guide thee to the truth?

Ibrahim received selected guests in a corner, on a throne roped off and guarded by the giant warrior slave Amesh.

Dane and the rest of his group worked the party. They wore silk blazers in Fundan green, with gray slacks and white shoes.

Dane had noted the repeated phrases on floors and walls and asked their meaning. Ras Order translated for him with a very slight, sly smile. Dane understood at once. Dane was meant to think of himself as the supplicant here.

There was no power behind the green jackets, not here—this was Khalifi habitat. There were few who were not aware of Edward's recent death and the setting aside of his will. Dane was in difficulties with his family, his enormous project seemed in trouble, quite possibly he was headed for a quick oblivion.

Still, Ibrahim's surprise invitation had brought out a large crowd from the wealthy elite of his habitat kingdom. Here were water brokers, bond salesmen, bankers, and dealers. Dress was of the new formal variety, the men in sober suits of dark colors with white shirts, brightly striped ties, and English shoes with thick soles, laces, and toe caps. Women wore dresses in similar dark shades and cut very close, but with a hint of austerity. Fashionable hemlines were climbing above the knee again, a problem for the oldest women, those beyond eighty who were still looking forty, because it was in the thighs and the buttocks that you really started to lose it when the time came, despite all the arts of extended medical.

Ras and Dane patrolled together, hunting finance for the *Founder*. The mood they met among the guests was complex, a blend of excitement and fear, tinged by curiosities, large and small.

First of all there was the matter of Ibrahim's return from ten years' exile in the Rimal.

Ten years in hiding, and now he challenged the Gung An Bu. Everyone knew that independent interstellar expeditions were not encouraged.

Still, the party was the social event of the month and one that would be talked about endlessly in months to come. Everyone was very intent on being noticed. If Ibrahim was going to go down in flames during the near future, they wanted to be able to say "I was there" to their incredulous friends.

Simultaneously, however, many of these same people were quietly terrified of the growing threat they perceived from the secret activities of the Gung An Bu.

As a result, Dane and Ras Order had polite, evasive conversations with Nipponese bankers, Khalifi princelings, freelance ice billionaires, and even Dir Kempong, the queen of the gigantic Kempong Yin Hang, the largest bank in the outer systems.

Most of them were more eager to gossip about Ibrahim than to hear about the *Founder*. Everyone listened politely, asked a wondering question or two, and then fell quiet. Some even appeared genuinely moved by Dane's earnest tone and the offer of a ride out of the solar system. People were always trying to sell them something, usually just a bunch of boring numbers. This was at least romantic.

"A new world, a new Earth, just four years away!"

Escape from the growing encroachment of the World Government was on many minds. The nightmare word "taxes" had begun cropping up more and more in ordinary conversation. People were selling up and taking raw space way out in the Neptunian system. It was as far to Neptune and Triton as it was to Earth, and out there rich people could be safe from taxes for a while longer. Maybe a lifetime.

But the power of the Earth government reached out among these people, and they knew it. The Gung An Bu had agents everywhere.

Thus there was a risk involved in seeking to escape. And would there be freedom from the G.B.s out on Neptune? And if there really was, how long could it last?

As yet the G.B.s were said to be having a hard time getting informers into the ranks of the Khalifi administration. The Khalifi were skilled at security techniques. The Khalifi were also just as ruthless as the G.B.s.

But the G.B.s were said to riddle the society of the lower decks, and where else did you get good servants? Thus everyone's proud feeling of independence from Earth and the dreaded Social Synthesis was compromised.

That Ibrahim dared to challenge the G.B.s suggested to some that incipient Khalifi megalomania had claimed another great sheik. Feelings were bitter among the more frightened.

"He should have stayed where he was and bred horses, that's what he liked to do."

"Besides buggering little boys."

"Oh, you make so much of that, it's only rumor."

"It's true. They smoke hashish and then do what comes naturally to them."

"Now, let's not get too nasty, shall we? Ibrahim is 137 years old, they say. You know as well as I that sexual function doesn't last that long."

"He courts death, and he risks our lives as well."

Thus the underlying mood was sour, the bright chatter empty.

Dane and Ras Order finally turned away from the last group of wealthy investors, ice skimmers from Miranda. Dane was feeling distinctly depressed. No one was biting.

Ras Order was unconcerned.

"You worry too much. This exercise is not really to raise money. This is to show that Ibrahim is investing in you. That you are under his protection."

"Fine, but who's protecting Khalifi Bey?"

Ras Order laughed. "Ibrahim is quite capable of protecting himself, you will find." Ras Order went on, with his smoothest smile. "Besides, Ibrahim loves this kind of project. Remember, Ibrahim was an engineer. He built habitats. He designed this very palace for his mother Yasmina. I think he is in love with the sheer grandiosity of your ship."

Ras Order was Ibrahim's most potent agent. Unlike most of the ruling Khalifi, Ras Order was charming and personable.

Finally Dane shrugged. "Yes, I suppose you're right. Anyway, I'm sure that Ibrahim understands the real situation. I know that my grandfather gave him access to the Optimor reports."

Ras Order's eyebrow rose slightly. "We know our peril, you can rest assured on that score."

Suddenly the Prince stiffened. Dane saw two tall figures ahead, both in the black robes of the desert dweller.

"Uncle Merzik!" Ras Order hissed.

That was the older man, Merzik Hussayn Khalifi, brother of Ibrahim and blood enemy of the Fundans. He had a face like Ibrahim's, long and pointed, except that his beard was streaked with gray.

The younger man had to be his son Tariq, Dane's old enemy, who now gave Ras Order and Dane a frankly physical, insulting stare.

Dane hadn't seen Tariq in twelve years or more, and indeed it was hard to see the boy he'd known in this heavyset man with the dark eyes and bad complexion.

Tariq had not aged very well. His features had splayed out into a gross caricature of those of his youth. His lips had thickened and his skin had coarsened. He wore the black robes that were the family hallmark, over jodhpurs and riding boots. And in Tariq's case the boots were for real and he really had ridden a horse to the palace from his air-conditioned tent in the artificial desert of the Rimal.

How many of these wealthies owned so much as the tenth share of a living horse!

Dane returned Tariq's steady glare with an amused stare,

then dug down for his best salesman's smile and extended a hand in friendship.

"Tariq, it's been a long time, eh?"

Tariq ignored his gesture, continued to glare.

Ras Order clucked, "Tariq, why this objectionable melodrama?"

Tariq's head swiveled, lips contorted in a small snarl.

"What? You dare to open your mouth, Ras Order, you who are now a slave of the Fundans?"

Ras Order hesitated a second and then laughed at this absurdity.

"Tariq, for heaven's sake, stop this and behave yourself. Ibrahim himself is your host!"

Tariq shifted his weight; Dane noticed that he'd not gone to fat.

"I spit on the name 'Fundan.'" Tariq spat loudly and eloquently on the ground.

Ras Order's eyebrows rose.

Dane chuckled. "Well, some things don't change then, eh? We always did think Tariq was an imbecile and a boor."

Tariq muttered an oath and spat again on the tile floor a little closer to Dane's shoes.

"I will kill you, Fundan dog, as I should have done long ago."

"Tariq, you forget yourself!" Ras Order snapped.

Tariq and Merzik glared back. Tension rose to a dangerous level. Dane marveled, Tariq had become even less pleasant in the adult form than he'd been as a larva.

Suddenly Merzik relaxed. His eyes crinkled, a smile broke the expanse of beard. He laid a hand on his son's forearm. Tariq became still.

"Well, you are a grandson of Edward, then," Merzik said with an oily smile.

"Yes, I am."

"Still besotted with your mad project?" Merzik's voice carried an unpleasant undertone.

"Mad? How so?"

"You disturb a delicate equilibrium that underlies our position in this system. You attract the wrath of a very powerful enemy."

"So you are prepared to submit to rule by Earth?"

"We will not submit to anyone's rule." Merzik's dark eyes

seemed to glow. "Earth is far away and can be easily satisfied. Why should they make the effort to rule us unless we arouse them unduly?"

"One-system extremists are rising in the politburo."

"Bah, they are one and a half billion miles away. They will not bother us." Merzik scowled, jabbed a finger at Dane. "Unless idiots provoke them with their silly schemes."

Merzik turned away; Tariq continued to glare. Dane shouted to Merzik's back, over Tariq's shoulder. "Taxation levels on Mars are going up to twenty-five percent. They call the new taxes 'Earth Bonds.' I call them chains."

Tariq thrust him back angrily with a powerful shove in the chest.

"Back, Fundan dog!"

"Get your hands off me!" Dane pushed Tariq's hands away.

"You dare to speak to my father like that! I will chasten you, here and now."

"What happened to you, Tariq? They send you to charm school after you got thrown out of Reserve?"

"Now!" Tariq had thick veins standing out in his neck. He lunged at Dane.

Instinctively Dane evaded Tariq's wild blow and then dropped into position. His gym sense took over.

Tariq peeled off his robe to reveal a bullet-proof vest in pale blue meltmar, zippered to his chin. He raised his fists and came on.

Tariq had learned some kick boxing somewhere, but it was of the flashy school, and he wasn't in good enough shape to pull it off well.

Dane easily countered a kick. Tariq attempted a swirling back kick, but Dane looped away long before it arrived.

People screamed and scrambled to get clear. A table went over with glasses crashing to the tiles. The rest of the crowd goggled.

Tariq was the new wild beast of the Khalifi clan, and he seemed more obnoxious than most of his kind. Here, he seemed to have completely forgotten himself.

Tariq circled Dane, panting a little, but whether from the exertion or just the desire for blood, Dane couldn't be sure.

"I should have stamped on you like a bug long ago!" he bellowed.

At last Amesh was visible, shouldering through the crowd.

Dane evaded another rush by Tariq, cut to his left, stuck out a foot, and succeeded in tripping the Khalifi as he went past. Tariq sprawled in an undignified heap before the crowd. He got up spitting with rage and produced a whippy little stiletto from within his vest.

With a shriek of hate, Tariq hurled himself at Dane.

Dane darted to the side, Tariq slashed, reversed, and came on with a mad light in his eyes. Dane was trapped against a wall of people. They drew back, but too late; a woman fell, a man went down over a table in a crescendo of breaking glass, and Dane almost lost his balance.

Tariq had his shoulder. The knife slashed through Dane's jacket and shirt. He felt the sting down his back and twisted away to evade the next cut, pushing blindly through screaming people.

And then Amesh arrived on the scene. He threw his massive form between Tariq and the Fundan.

"No, Master, you may not fight him here."

"Out of my way, slave!"

"It is forbidden."

Amesh wielded a small shock baton. Tariq considered it, for a second. For a moment he trembled on the brink of assaulting the giant, and then he thought better of it. Amesh was more than his match. That way lay nothing but humiliation. He dropped the knife, turned on his heel, and marched out of the party. His uncle followed shortly afterward.

Solemnly, Amesh gathered up the knife and put it in a tube that he sealed and removed.

Adelaide and Melissa crowded around Dane.

"Are you all right, boss?"

Dane concentrated on breathing.

"Just incredible, these people," Melissa said, examining his shoulder.

Beneath the jacket was a shallow cut about two inches long that had soaked a patch three inches across with blood.

"Jacket's ruined, boss."

Ras Order's face was filled with horror.

"I think I'll have to have this attended to," Dane said quietly. "Can I leave you to carry on here?"

"My apologies for this incident," the Prince said. "My cousin is mentally disturbed. I am afraid that my family will have to take steps some day to put him under psychiatric care."

Dane snorted. "My Prince, excuse me, but Tariq's been in urgent need of psychiatric restraint for twenty years. Problem is his father is Merzik, and Merzik likes Tariq the way he is."

Ras Order wore a troubled frown. "It is a problem that my family must face sooner or later. Merzik has raised a monster with manners and habits worse even than his own. Tariq likes to kill. I have heard it said that he even fights slaves, for the thrill of killing them. They fight unarmed, of course, and he has a sword and a knife."

"Boss." It was Adelaide. "You better get some attention."

"Yeah, I'm coming."

Impulsively, Dane collared a passing waiter and grabbed a couple of glasses of champagne. He downed one in a gulp and then sipped the other more slowly.

The party had returned to itself, the hubbub renewed, but now with a fiercer buzz. Ibrahim's madness had ignited Merzik and Tariq. What would it portend? Civil war? Anything was possible among the hot-blooded Khalifi.

At the entrance Dane noticed that a woman was watching him from a group standing nearby.

She was gracefully slender, even elfin, with large, luminous brown eyes. She wore a black silk suit and had shoulder-length dark brown hair. Her nose was a little too large for beauty and her cheekbones too high, but there was something fascinating about her, some delicacy, some hint of remoteness.

"Hello," Dane said on another impulse.

"You fought well," she said with a serious face. "Are you hurt?" Her hair was perfectly lustrous. He felt a sudden, strong attraction.

"No, it's nothing much, just a scratch. It was hardly a fight. I never touched him."

She smiled. "Yes, I was so glad. Tariq is such a bully. It was time someone stood up to him. But I think he will never forgive you for the humiliation, Mr. Fundan."

"Please call me Dane." He felt unaccustomedly gawky.

"All right." She smiled again. He thrilled to it. He felt as if that smile were a privilege conferred upon him.

A shadow fell across them. Ras Order purred, "Ahh, yes, I wondered if you two would run into each other. Dane, I see that I must introduce you to my sister, Leila. She is our most distinguished family rebel. Leila is contratradition. Rather an outcast, I'm afraid, as far as the palace is concerned."

Dane found the eyes mesmerizing. She was like a bird, intensely graceful and delicate. But the eyes clearly reflected a formidable intelligence.

She showed none of the deference normally accorded the Prince by Khalifi women. She would not accept Ras Order's description of herself either.

"I wouldn't say I was an outcast, Ras. I'm an exile. They come after me about once a week. Either it's my grandparents or it's my brothers. Why won't I 'stop it' and 'behave myself.' Why won't I come back to the palace?"

"Oh, you prefer the desert?" Dane said.

She laughed, shaking back the lovely glossy hair. "No, not at all. I live in the city, on the Mulkhdar, near the Budayin."

So the Princess liked to live on the wild side. Dane immediately grasped the nature of her rebellion.

"She could be living here, amidst unsurpassable beauty." Ras Order raised his hands to the loveliness of the palace. "But she prefers to live in a warren of slums."

"Things are more real on the Mulkhdar. And besides, I see you there often enough, Ras, along with all my other brothers."

Ras Order sniffed. "It is not a place for you to live."

She laughed. "I'm sorry, Messire Fundan, my brother is like the rest of them, clinging to ancient ways. Women must be protected and veiled and all the rest of that rot."

"And you, I take it, don't hold with any of that."

"Of course not."

She noticed the blood staining the back of his green jacket.

"You *are* hurt!" she exclaimed. "Someone must see to that." She sounded quite genuinely upset. The woman's concern was intoxicating. Dane recognized the symptoms of an intense infatuation, and he found no will to resist it.

"Yes, I'm on my way. But later I would like to see the Mulkhdar and even the Budayin. We have nothing like that on Fundan habspace."

This brought immediate response from Ras Order. "I wouldn't advise it. The Budayin is a dangerous place. There is little rule of law."

Dane smiled. "But your sister virtually lives there. It cannot be that dangerous. And besides, there doesn't seem to be much rule of law inside your palace. If that's your concern, I'm surprised you don't live on a safe hab, like *Fundan One*."

Ras Order sniffed and looked away. Dane laughed out loud, but when he looked back, Leila was gone.

He felt a profound sense of disappointment.

9

THEY MET IN A PLACE CALLED BOSS'S BAR, ON A SIDE ALLEY off the avenue Mulkhdar. Inside it was all faux leather and brass and dark, quiet booths.

"So you came?" she said, sounding quite indifferent to his presence.

She was wearing a green silk suit with a simple pearl necklace.

"Well, I . . ." He hesitated. Her mood seemed very different from that of their earlier meeting. But he had come, and without guards. He tried to joke, "I guess I'm ready to see something new and unusual."

He failed, her eyebrows arched. Coolly, she said, "Oh, are you, now? Well, let's see about that, shall we?" She seemed annoyed, as if it had been a mistake to invite him.

They rode an escalator down to an executive level, a wilderness of white walls, with offices, banks, small eating places crowded along the main corridor. There was a hush, white noise blanking out the human buzz. The floors were carpeted in green spa-turf.

Here they set out upon the Mulkhdar, a broad avenue that wound sinuously through the decks of the habitat.

Oriental ideografix jammed the walls in dark areas. They seemed to float out of nothingness, there was no sense of up or beyond, everything either electric color or utter black. Zombie cities, lit by electric flowers that encapsulated human wants, needs, desires.

They passed through a crowd that was pressed so close

together that involuntary contact was inevitable. It was like a sports crowd, packing into the Spectrohome on Obe's Eye for the basketball championship. Dane had never experienced anything like it on Fundan habitat. This kind of density was deemed psychotraumatic by Fundan Doctrine and hence was illegal.

The side streets were a maze of bars, casinos, and brothels catering to every imaginable sexual urge. The crowds themselves reflected the complex genetic paths humanity was taking in the outer satellites.

The Saturns were the most garish; Dane saw Titan Orangers, some Blue Adoni, and some Pinkees.

Leila suddenly turned off the crowded thoroughfare, heading up a dark, narrow alley surrounded by overpopulated tenements with people sitting out on balconies and fire escapes.

Dane's Fundan-raised instincts were atingle. There was an element of claustrophobia in this scene that he found hard to ignore.

Leila ducked beneath an archway and they emerged on a narrow street. Ahead loomed a pair of giant doors, curving up to block off the end of the street.

Leila walked up and knocked on one of the doors. Dane was amused. Leila had given up her position as a Khalifi Princess, but apparently she had not abandoned all the habits of the ruling family. She chose to live in the lower depths of the Khalifi world, but she lived in a place as big as a palace anyway.

A security camera scanned them and then a small door within a door opened to admit them to a white-walled corridor with a greenish light and an antiseptic smell.

They followed a man in a set of light green overalls down the corridor to a room floored with gray linoleum. Several people, sitting at desks, jumped up to greet Leila with obvious affection.

The place was bare but for office furniture and wall charts. It had the unmistakable atmosphere of an office. Dane's forehead furrowed.

Leila introduced Dane and exchanged a few formal pleasantries in English-based interlingua, but these people spoke Arabic among themselves, and so he was soon groping for a word here and a word there as she chatted.

But he now understood, at last, that he had seriously misjudged her. This was not some palatial apartment building, this was an orphanage, a school, and a hospital.

He could hear the sounds of children a few rooms away, a lot of children.

"Orphans," she said, "and runaways. We have eight hundred of them in here."

Dane was stunned. Precious children, abandoned by their parents? On Fundan habitat children who lost both parents would be adopted within minutes. The right to have children was precious, not commonly allowed, except, of course, for high-placed family members.

And "Orphanage"! That was the Reserve's nickname, a big place filled with unwanted "rich brats and bad boys," as one TV report put it.

And the walls of the Reserve floated into memory. And with the walls came a rare memory of his parents. Maxim taking them on an outing, a picnic in the Canada park. His mother, Messaline, complaining the whole way about the smell of the ponies, and stopping to be sick behind a spruce tree because she had one of her "absolutely fucking vicious hangovers" again.

The walls came back, locked around the rest of his childhood. Yes, Dane concluded, he knew some of the pain in that word "orphans."

Leila finished signing herself into the volunteer's book, scheduling classes in aerobic exercise and dance for the following week.

Then she turned to Dane.

"That's all I need to do here right now. Would you like to see our children?"

The experience was surreal for Dane. Mute with tension, he followed her through the brightly lit rooms, ending with a gymnasium. The odors of antiseptic and too many bodies were strong. And everywhere they went there were children, bright-eyed and noisy with barely muffled giggles.

These were children that had been rescued from the streets, had glimpsed the life in the abyss and were obviously grateful for the good fortune that had placed them in the school.

The place was walled with their bright, aware little eyes. After a while Dane found it suffocating. He wanted to get out.

Finally they paused in a corridor behind the gymnasium.

"Why do they allow these things?" he said.

"What things, the school?" She was startled. Fundans were conservative, she knew, but surely not enough to object to a

43

school for these disadvantaged, abandoned children?

"No, orphans, runaways."

Ah, he was just naive. She relaxed.

"This is Khalifi habitat. The protection of laws is for the people of the tribes alone. If you are not of the Al Quyyun, then you have no rights except residency right."

It was appalling, so barbaric that it sounded just like some of the cruder Synthesist propagandist descriptions of the pirate habitats of the outer systems.

"That's like synth prop, raw. No wonder the Khalifi are outlaws."

His words seemed to annoy her.

"Not because of this school, you idiot. Sometimes I wonder who's the blindest in this system; there's a lot of competition."

He stared at her. "What do you mean?"

"You Fundans, you're all so smug and secure. You think everyone lives in similar security. Well, you're wrong. I'll have to show you, I guess."

They left the orphanage and strode on into the Budayin. Every corner contained some bizarre affront to Fundan senses.

Beggars, amputees who'd lost limbs to space-suit breaks while working on exterior hab maintenance, called out from the shadows for alms. The worst, though, were the children. Street urchins abounded, some as menacing little pickpockets and thieves, others as helpless sex objects, kept in what were virtually cages on the sidewalks.

Dane gestured to some of these as they passed. The proprietor, a gigantic black man with decorated front teeth, tried to interest Dane in his wares. Dane drew back with a hiss.

"What the hell is this?" he said to Leila.

"Sex for sale, in the time-honored way. It was like this on Earth, they say."

"But those are children!"

Leila gave him a blank stare.

"Look, my friend, this is Khalifi habitat. It conforms to the human norms, not to your pious 'Christian' culture. Human beings have traded in children as sex objects since the beginning of recorded history. My family has little interest in the tenets of the west. They belong to the older record—they're Muslims, but bad ones, like ninety-five percent of all the Muslims there have ever been. They feel no compunctions about these things."

44

"The culture of the west brought a lot of good into the world."

"It also perfected war, invented nuclear weapons and modern genocide."

Dane was startled by the vehemence of this outburst. Behind the polite surface this Princess was seething with what sounded like Synthesis politics.

Ahead, more brilliant bursts of neon announced a street lined with large bars. Crowds of sharply dressed young men high on stimulant drugs milled around the doorways. The young men sold an incredible array of exotic poisons that were illegal everywhere, and generally not widely available. Certainly not on Fundan habspace.

Leila drew him into a bar, under the sign of a giant locust. The young men in the shining suits receded behind them. Inside everything was dark, hushed, with vid screens for the customers blazing like bright jewels up above the bar.

Dane exploded. "That is unimaginable. You have children out there, and those thugs are selling junk drugs, that stuff is deadly."

She simply stared back at him for a moment. Didn't he understand by now? Well, everyone said the Fudnans were pretty remote, they'd been in their own-built space too long. Then she moved on, past the bar and into a small theater area with tiers of seats rising around a square pit sunk in the floor.

She chose a pair of seats that shared a microtable halfway down the aisle.

A waiter in white appeared and took an order for two Sinoise beers.

Dane ran a finger under his collar. The bandage on his back was itching slightly, he felt hot and uncomfortable.

How was he doing with the Khalifi Princess? Not so good, it seemed. He just hadn't ever seen anything like this, not in the Uranus system.

Leila Khalifi knew this dark region inside out, it seemed, and obviously she could tell how inexperienced, even naive, he was. What must she think of him? he wondered. A lumbering dolt? A well-fed "cauk" with all the shallowness exhibited by so many in his wealthy old family?

While these thoughts preoccupied him, Dane examined the scene before him with distinct unease. The pit was at least eight feet deep and floored with white tiles. He could see a number of doors and hatches that punctuated the dark brown walls.

"What happens here?"

"Watch," she said.

10

THE SEATS FILLED UP QUICKLY. A GROUP OF MEN IN BLACK robes were soon giggling loudly nearby. The smell of kif wafted through the rows.

The waiter returned with their order. The Sinoise was cold and clean. Dane sipped it quickly.

A loud chime sounded and was repeated and slowly speeded up. More men, and some women, flowed into the seats. An expectant buzz of conversation went up. A group of Chinese men took the seats next to Leila and Dane. From them a buzz of gambling chatter arose as they bet among themselves and with the house through the punch pad inset in the table.

A door opened in the pit, throwing a bright yellow light onto the opposite wall and floor. A cage was maneuvered half into the pit. A door in the cage was pulled up and three robust little animals were released.

Dane stared at them. They were dogs, but of a breed he was unfamiliar with. They were of various colors, one black, another dark brown, and another streaked black on brown. They were short-legged, tubby little beasts equipped with big heads and heavy jaws.

"What are they?" he said.

"Pit bulls."

His eyes narrowed.

A small hatch opened about six feet up in the wall of the pit. The dogs responded with a few urgent barks. Another dog was thrown out among them. It was a long-haired toy, with a high yippy bark and a fluffy tail.

The crowd convulsed with laughter.

The pit bulls converged on the toy dog and literally tore it apart in a whirl of shrieks and snarls that spread scarlet stains all over the pit and themselves.

The laughter never slackened.

Dane stared about himself with appalled eyes.

Another door opened, another cage was half pushed in.

In the cage was a man, dressed in a black bodysuit, padded in the crotch and round the wrists and ankles. He was spotlighted, and in that light his face could be clearly seen. He was a young man—in his late twenties, perhaps—and he was terrified.

The cage door opened and the man jumped into the ring with the dogs.

With a chorus of growls, the dogs attacked. They knew what they were doing, it was crystal clear. Each dog tried for a different leg or arm. They fought as a team.

The man kicked and struck with his fists to keep them back. His kicks were successful for a while, but they were never hard enough to actually kill these dogs; and these dogs, unless killed, would never stop coming.

After a minute the man was obviously tiring.

A dog seized one ankle. He bent down to pick it up and pull it loose, but another dog got one of his wrists and held on. He was pulled down. The third dog worried at his arm and then crunched down on the elbow. The man screamed, a thin, desperate cry, and struggled to his feet, hurling one dog away to carom off the wall with a thud.

This dog bounced onto its feet and came straight back.

The man's arm was bleeding profusely. He punched the black dog that gripped his right calf, to make it let go, but it wouldn't.

The other jumped and bit into his thigh, and he toppled over again with a shriek.

Dane turned away, horrified. The dogs made horrible noises, the man's screams were nerve-wracking as he thrashed and fought for his life.

His good arm was held at the wrist. Another dog was up on him and worrying at his throat. The man's screams cut off into gurgles.

The crowd was roaring; the Chinese men were on their feet with stopwatches in their hands. Then the big chime sounded again and sped up the scale to its climax and the bout was ended.

47

Dane's mouth was dry. Desperately, he gulped the beer down. His pulse was racing, he felt dazed, unable to decide what to do.

Three men in padded white suits, carrying short shock rods, entered and drove the dogs off their prey. The dogs were quite insensitive to pain. The shock rods sparked again and again on their hides before they were finally driven back into their cages.

Only then did a medical team emerge, wearing light green oversuits. They examined the fallen man briefly, then loaded him onto a stretcher and bore him away.

The audience seemed massively unconcerned. Casual conversation, gambling, drinking, continued unabated.

Leila avoided his eye. She stared off into the middistance. "Look at this, understand it well, and then go back and deal with Ibrahim," she seemed to be saying.

Another chime sounded. The doors opened again. This time a pair of women, in tight blue and red bodysuits, were to fight with padded clubs. Dane tried not to look as the thuds and gasps rose from the dismal spectacle.

The crowd cheered loudly, revelling in this stuff. He turned away in utter dismay. Leila was watching him.

"This is disgusting. I want to go."

"So soon? The show is only beginning."

"Why are they doing this?"

A thud was followed by a shriek and a tumble. More thuds came, with screams.

Leila said, "Who, the bar? It makes money, of course."

"No. Not the bar, the people, dammit!" He felt very close to losing control.

"They are doing it because they have been convicted of property crime. The choice is either this, or a sentence on the maintenance squad for the hab exterior. Lot of radiation out there. Always the chance of a suit accident."

The big chime rang out, the bout ended.

Dane gulped his beer.

The next bout had two blindfolded men armed with short, weighted bats. They swung their bats vigorously, missing wildly and making contact quite accidentally. The crowd roared.

A bat connected with a head, blood sprayed the wall and the first row. The roars grew in intensity.

Dane stood up. "I'm leaving."

She made no resistance, just followed him out.

48

Dane's hands were shaking as he fumbled in the pockets of his borrowed jacket for a pack of tranks. The boys in slick suits circled him, offering their deadly wares, but he ignored them.

"That's murderous, brutal barbarism!" He turned on her. "How can your family sleep? Don't they know what goes on down here?"

She shrugged. "For the most part they don't know and they don't want to know. I have had it explained to me as all being part of the price that has to be paid for keeping their habitat open to all comers. We do not reject people who can only afford the bare minimum. We accept all refugees. No other Uranus hab can say that."

Dane acknowledged, uneasily, that *Fundan One* had sky-high floor prices.

"But why this horror? I still don't understand."

She gave him a look of mock scorn.

"What, you want my family to pay for such expenses as police and courts and prisons? Why should they pay to repair what people do to each other? These people are infidels, they mean nothing. They are given cheap entry right, cheap residence right. This is cheap justice, what more do they deserve?"

"I need a drink," he said.

"You just had one."

"What? That beer? I mean a real drink."

Dane had to have Khalifi money. This was the only route open, since most financing centers were afraid of the project.

He had no choice, the *Founder* had to be finished. He would die before he would ever give that up.

"All right, we go there." She pointed to a small streetside bar.

Dane felt the shakiness in his guts subside a little as he worked on a large vodka.

"Freeze, but that was pure evil. Your family has a lot to answer for."

She sipped another Sinoise. Her smile conveyed a mix of emotions. For a moment he thought he read pure hatred in her eyes. And then something like respect appeared, but her eyes were blank, and when she spoke, her voice was almost toneless.

"So, you find it easy to condemn us. And yet you are now under Ibrahim's saddle. How does that go with your new opinions? Now you've seen how his world is operated."

Dane shook his head slowly. "I don't know, I honestly don't. I'm Fundan, that means a lot to me, and this is evil, this dishonors all the system."

He winced at his own words. "But I have to finish my ship."

"And thus you will sacrifice your honor for your dream?" She shrugged. "More waste. You chase an impossible dream."

"What do you mean?"

"You pursue a forbidden goal. The age of independent space travel and exploration is to end. The Social Synthesis is to be attempted throughout the solar system."

Suddenly struck by an alarming thought, he asked, "Are you a Synth? Do you believe that?"

She looked at him for a long moment. "Is it important to you?"

He stared back at her. What the hell could she think? He was Fundan.

"No," she said, dropping her gaze. "It's impractical. It remains a dream, human beings are not cooperative animals. But that will not stop it from being attempted."

A familiar warm anger rebuilt itself within him.

"You're saying that we can no longer rule ourselves, that we have slipped under the rule of the Earth without even knowing it."

She sipped, made a wry face. "Yes. It was inevitable. We have too much, they too little. Such inequalities stir the hidden depths of the human soul. Social Synthesis is just another in a long line of philosophical responses to the agonies of civilization."

"We have to escape, we have to. We can't allow all human freedom to be snuffed out."

She laughed, but kindly. "How well-meaning you are. You know, I believe you have a good heart, and you are a handsome fellow. I like you. But you're naive if you think you will be allowed to finish building your ship."

"With Ibrahim behind me, I can do it."

She smiled, but without mockery. "What about the Gung An Bu?"

"Ah, the dreaded G.B.s. Well, actually they do pose a problem, but the odd thing is that there isn't much they can do once we have the money and can buy the ice. We've completed most of the ship's systems, we just have the engines and the propulsion mass to build."

"They will attack you in space."

"With what? The Earth fleet is in the inner system. It would take weeks for it to get here, and by that time there would be a state of war. They're not ready for that."

"Are you so sure that the other habs would fight to protect you from the Earth fleet?"

"They would have to, or else surrender their own sovereignty shortly afterward."

"I think you face a lot of troubles, my friend." She put her beer down.

"We can handle anything they might try to throw at us short of a major fleet. All we really need is the money to finish. That is why Ibrahim is essential."

"Ibrahim will steal your ship in the end. If you manage to finish it."

He shrugged. "I'm resigned to that. As long as those who want to can escape, that is all that matters. I will have fulfilled the plan."

Her eyes had softened. "Another hopeless idealist," she murmured. "I always seem to find them. I wonder why that is."

She kept her eyes on his.

"I like you," she had said. His mouth had gone dry for some reason. The blood pulsed in his temple so loudly that he wondered if she could hear it too.

"Where do you live?" he said after a while.

"We take the elevator at the next corner. I have two rooms; my building has some nice people and some not so nice people."

"You live here, then, with this crowding?"

"Of course. Where else would I live? Up in that archaic palace with those monsters like Tariq? He threatened to kill me when I was thirteen and I refused to wear the veil in public."

Dane absorbed this. Finished the vodka.

She smiled. "So, you've made your choice, then."

"I have," he said. "Let's go to your place."

11

LEILA'S PLACE WAS TWO ROOMS, EACH ABOUT FOUR METERS across. One room was entryway and kitchen, the other was sleeping and living. She had a window, and the view you'd expect from the fourth floor on an interior courtyard.

She didn't have much furniture. It was futon living, with floor pillows and inflatable storage packs. There was a comfortable deformer chair, a glass-top table, and the wall screen. In the entryway room there was an overstuffed closet. Clothes spilled across the bed, and the tables too.

"You've lived here a long time?"

She shook her head. "Let's not talk."

Instead she reached for the top button on her blouse and undid it. The barriers broke, releasing a hot ocean of feeling. His arms were around her. Her lips came up to meet his. There was a spark, something very strong, too strong to even think about.

They had made love then, with considerable energy. They took their time about it. It was the first time in a long time for either of them, and though neither was fully able to articulate to themselves why they were so attracted to the other, there was a passion between them that blazed with the desperate fire of the lonely and the stressed.

When it was finally wrung out of them, they slept soundly, for several hours.

When Dane awoke, his wristwatch was flashing to indicate he had phone messages. He pressed the watch to his ear.

It was Adelaide. There was an emergency on the Fundan tech satellite. An effort was being mounted by Agatha Fundan and some other family leaders to seize control of the tech sat. Currently the sat was controlled by the Systembank, which generously allowed Dane Fundan liberal use of it. Dane had forty-five staffers berthed on the tech sat. In effect, he was using half of the facility.

He groaned in protest. It was the third hour of the morning. He wanted to stay where he was. For days perhaps.

Quietly he pulled himself to his feet. Leila moaned softly and turned over. For a moment he admired the smooth curve of her flank, the delicacy of the thigh and leg outthrust across the covers. The temptation to stay almost overrode his will to duty. But the *Founder* rose up in his mind like some half-finished moon of his mind's eye. There was no escape. After a few seconds more he turned away.

He splashed some water on his face, swilled more around his mouth with clenzer, and then pulled on his slacks, shirt, and jacket.

He whispered a message into her beeper, left a phone number, and set it, flashing green, on the floor beside her.

Outside her door he paused, unsure of the route back to the palace. Adelaide and the others would be working on the emergency in their suite at the Azraq. He wanted to join them as quickly as possible. The tech sat had to be saved—without it they could never finish the *Founder*.

He looked both ways on the first street he came to. Bright lights, plus the public sodium cobra-heads, filled the distance. The crowds were undiminished. He stopped a tall, pale man wearing a shiny blue coat. The directions to the deck elevators were complex. Dane did his best to memorize them.

He found that while the crowds were still thick on the Mulkhdar, on the sideways there were few people about at this hour. Since the Mulkhdar meandered sinuously from side to side, he pushed through the side streets where possible.

Somewhere, on one side street or another, he became aware that he was being followed.

A glance back showed two figures trailing about twenty feet behind. The next time he looked, they were still there. He turned the corner and accelerated.

He looked back and saw they had matched his increased speed.

At the next turn he began to run.

He jogged to the end of a long alley between tenements and emerged onto a street of garden walls.

His pursuers were no longer in sight.

He turned; this was a right turn, as he recalled it. The deck elevators were close by now. He entered the passage.

There was someone waiting there, a tall figure that he

barely glimpsed before a shock rod swung down and struck him across the side of the head.

The hot "spat" knocked him off his feet. Things went fuzzy at the edges. Dane looked up. Two figures were bending over him. One of them fired a gas spray into his face. Oblivion followed almost immediately.

Consciousness was slow to return. For a long time he hovered in a twilight region. Dimly he perceived a flat floor, upon which he lay. Later he was carried somewhere. Then everything was dark again.

Finally he awoke. Someone was jabbing him in the side with a foot. He struggled to sit up. It wasn't easy.

His jacket was gone, he was covered in perspiration. It was very hot and humid, wherever he was.

"Wake up, Fundan dog!" The foot jabbed him again, in the back.

He swung around, tried to stand up.

Rough hands grasped him by the neck and the arms. They hauled him to a kneeling position and held him there.

He looked up into Tariq Khalifi's grinning face. The dark eyes were pools of hate.

"Now, Fundan animal, you will run for my amusement."

Dane shook his head. Was this some bizarre nightmare? If it was, he'd like to wake up, please.

A short whip slashed across his face.

"Wake up, dog, when I speak to you!"

Dane was fully awake now. He glared back and tried to shift away from the grip holding him down.

Tariq snapped his fingers. A door opened and a man brought in a quartet of heavyset dogs on thick leashes.

The dogs broke into a horrific howling and barking as they were allowed to sniff Dane and take his scent. They snarled and snapped at him when he looked at them. They were large dogs, with much the shape of pit-bull terriers.

"These are manhounds, Fundan. I bred them myself. They love to hunt a good man, someone who gives them a good workout. I love to watch them hunt. You will give us a good hunt, won't you, Fundan?"

"Tariq! You're crazy, you'll never get away with this."

Tariq laughed. The dogs bayed and drooled. Tariq turned on his heel.

The men who were holding Dane down pulled him roughly

to his feet. One of them used a knife to cut his clothing to ribbons.

Virtually naked, he was thrust out a door into a dank, humid tunnel, flagged in wet stone.

A dim orange light came from up the tunnel. The door closed with a slam. He heard it bolt behind him.

Tariq's mocking voice broke in on some hidden audio speakers.

"You had better start running, Fundan, the hounds will be released in two minutes."

12

DANE RAN, HIS BREATH RINGING HARSH INSIDE THE TUNNEL'S laminated walls. The only light came from palm-sized panels at head height, and a lot of them weren't working. It would be a nasty place to die in.

Abruptly the tunnel took a ninety-degree turn to the right. Orange blurs diminished into the distance for a hundred meters or more. As he ran he noticed he had begun a long, slow descent.

Gradually a dank, jungly smell filled the air. The floor continued to slope gently downward, and then he noticed that the lights had begun to curve leftward, the corridor entering a wide spiral. It curved on, out of sight, and then suddenly a brighter, whiter light appeared ahead.

The light intensified. It was coming through a doorway that opened in the left-hand wall of the corridor. When he reached it he found the source of the smell. Inside was a jungle of stubby palms, growing in a white-walled corridor thirty feet wide with ceilings twenty feet high. The entire ceiling glowed with diffused sunlight, bounced down from the hab mirrors.

Somewhere far behind him he heard a door clang open. A chorus of barks echoed faintly down the walls. The hounds were loose.

He ran into the forest, dodging around trees, evading undergrowth.

Progress was slow; in fact, it was nightmarish work. The undergrowth included little thorn bushes. The palm fronds could cut like knives. Thorns raked his legs.

He tripped and fell into a rubbery-leafed bush. Under the leaves were sharp spines that jabbed him along the arms and shoulders. Blood ran down his arms as he got back to his feet.

And behind him the sound of the dogs was much closer.

He stumbled on, running where possible, clambering where he had to.

Abruptly the corridor turned right and went down a step and there was a pool of water spread before him, from wall to wall.

The water was dark and forbidding. Slime covered the walls of the tank, tall water weeds grew along the sides. He plunged in and swam across.

As he hauled himself out on the other side, he felt something flap against the skin of his thigh. He looked down and gave a great cry of disgust. Brown leeches, each three inches long, were fastened here and there to his legs. In fact, they were all over him.

With little cries of horror he tore them off himself and hurled them to the ground.

A sudden uproar echoed behind him. The dogs were already in the jungle corridor. He turned and ran on, taking desperate strides among the thorns.

Abruptly the corridor turned right and presented him with another tank of slime-surfaced water.

There was nothing for it; he swam the tank. The dogs were swimming the first one.

Not long after that he found a rough stone wall, five feet high, built across the corridor. He scaled it and soon found another lying across the way. They became a feature of the jungle, every twenty meters or so.

After the twelfth he was exhausted, barely able to haul himself over.

But from the sounds they made, he could tell he had put some distance between himself and the hounds; they weren't as good at climbing walls as he was.

From here he discovered that the vegetation was thinning out. Prey and hunters were expected to run full out on this stretch. He jogged.

The corridor turned right again and climbed. At the top of the incline was another stone wall, this time ten feet high. There were footholds and it was easy enough to climb. For the dogs, however, it would be an impossible task, he was certain.

He was equally sure that this was not the end of the chase. Tariq had designed this whole mad place. He had not built it to allow his victims an easy escape.

From the top of the wall there was a view down a long, long slope. Here a savanna flora was predominant, with dwarf acacias among tall grasses.

On he went, pushing himself as hard as he dared.

Then, through the trees, he saw the head of Tariq. He marveled at it as he approached. The carver had done excellent work, capturing perfectly the straight Khalifi nose, the heavy eyebrows, and even the sneer of mad arrogance in those thick lips.

How many poor wretches had been here before him, in his state, to contemplate this godlike enormity? Tariq Khalifi's megalomania writ large in stone.

The dogs were coming. He moved on, past the great stone head.

The trees ended. Ahead of him the corridor was carpeted with nothing but grass for a hundred meters.

Was this the killing ground, then? Was this where the dogs usually ran down the prey?

There was nothing to do but run, and so he jogged forward with the breath coming hot and hard in his chest.

There was a terrible fatigue working its way through his body. Not even the "Endurance," Chesk's ten-klick cross-country run, had been like this.

And then he reached the next turning in the corridor, to the right once more, and he looked back up the long slope.

He could see the top of the high wall, and on it a black figure. This figure was suddenly joined by a second, smaller, four-legged figure that jumped down. Another dark shape joined the larger one on the top of the wall. The barking of the dogs became much louder immediately.

Tariq! The hunter with his hounds. He had set the wall as a dog-proof obstacle on his personal hunting course. It gave the prey a chance to prolong the hunt. After all, Tariq had built the course to give himself some exercise, some challenge. It was pointless if the sport were too easy.

Dane turned and ran on, through the dwarf acacias. The ground was damp, there was grass beneath the trees. The minutes wore on and he kept going, but he was unable to greatly increase his stride.

The sound of the dogs was definitely getting louder now, and there was another sound, shrilling above the hounds, the cry of the hunter's horn. Tariq wanted him to know that he was hunted by man as well as hounds.

He took another turn and ran through short grass toward a stand of acacias.

The dogs set up a terrific noise suddenly. They saw him! The hunting horn brayed excitedly behind them.

Dane tripped over his own feet. He staggered, almost fell, then recovered and ran on toward the trees. The dogs were terribly close now, every second would count.

They broke out of the trees and into the grass, their quarry in full sight, and they began baying as they closed in for the kill. He heard them coming, claws spattering gravel.

The trees were just ahead. On the outskirts of the copse was a twelve-foot trunk, relatively smooth. Dane leaped into its lower branches and began to climb.

The dogs were right behind him. They lunged upward in desperate leaps. One snapped its jaws within an inch of his heels. Frustrated, they milled around the base of the tree, baying for his blood while he clung, exhausted, to the branches.

A minute or so later a figure in a powered space suit came up. Inside the bubble helmet he could see Tariq's face quite clearly. Tariq smiled, waved, and spoke through the suit's communicator speakers.

"At last we have you treed! Well, it has been a good chase you have given us, Fundan. You came three-quarters of the circuit. My congratulations on a good showing."

Tariq called the hounds back with short blasts of a whistle note from his suit speakers. The hounds were reluctant to obey, but finally did so. Tariq leashed them and tethered them to another tree. Then he positioned himself beneath Dane and unslung a hand weapon with an oversized barrel.

"Aren't they enthusiastic, eh, my beauties? How they want you, Fundan. But they must wait a while yet, you are *my* prey first."

He fired the gun, and a web of gummed netting flew up and over Dane. A strong cord trailed behind it. Tariq jerked hard on the cord and pulled Dane out of the tree.

The dogs went mad, lunging wildly on their leashes.

The fall was hard. Tariq approached. In one suit mitt he held a miniature circular saw, its blade spinning. Dane rolled away, tried to get to his feet. The gummed filaments were constricting, movement was difficult. Desperately he pulled the netting off his head and shoulders.

Tariq's suit brayed the hunter's horn.

Dane was finally on his feet. Frantically he pulled away the sticky strings. They clung to his hands, a mass of them constricted around his waist. But his arms were now freed and the last string around his legs was broken.

Tariq attacked. Dane moved sideways and almost fell into the reach of the hounds.

The dogs brought him up sharp, with growls and choked hisses. He lurched away from them. Tariq came on.

Dane staggered into the strand of trees. Tariq followed. The netting trailing from Dane's waist caught on a low branch and tore away when he fell. Tariq blundered into it and the netting wrapped itself around him. Tariq was forced to pause to free himself.

Dane stared back in terror. He needed a weapon, anything that he could find. He looked frantically about.

He glimpsed a damaged tree branch. It was as thick as his arm and quite heavy. He yanked on it, dragging it down with his body weight. The branch sagged to the ground, pulling the tree down with it. It remained attached. Desperately he tore at it with one foot up on the trunk, a faint scream coming from his throat. Abruptly it snapped and he went down in a heap with it in his hands.

Tariq had freed himself and was coming. Dane got to his feet and turned to confront him with the branch held like some primeval club. Tariq gave a great, amplified caw of laughter.

"The resourceful prey! Good sport you have given us, Fundan. But now you must pay the final price. Come, I wish to spill your blood before I feed you to my hounds."

Tariq lurched forward; Dane swung with the club. The powered knife sliced through the end of the branch and powdered wood flew in the air. Tariq laughed again and slashed back and forth with the knife. Dane withdrew, the limitations of his stone-age weapon all too evident.

He scrambled backward, then lashed out high with the branch. The plastic bubble top of the suit, that was the only weak spot! But Tariq ducked, and he missed by a meter or more. Tariq laughed again and rushed him, blade whirring.

Dane changed tactics and grasped the branch as if it were a spear. He drove it home two-handed against Tariq's chest just as Tariq ran onto it full tilt.

The heavyset Tariq fell backward with a harsh exhalation from the suit speakers. He wobbled for a moment, and Dane swung the branch hard against the helmet bubble.

The helmet cracked. Tariq gave a cry of outraged fear.

He swung the knife hand wildly. Dane ducked, almost lost his footing, and felt a tree against his back. No escape now, and Tariq came on with a scream of triumph. Dane dropped to one knee and braced the branch like a lance. Tariq slashed at it and missed, and Dane speared him again. Tariq lost his balance and fell over with a wail of dismay.

The power knife bit into a tree trunk and stuck, spitting wood chips into the air with a nerve-biting screech.

Dane brought the club down again on the helmet. The bubble cracked, and then broke like a crystal egg.

Tariq struggled to get to his feet. Dane brought the branch down again. The rest of the helmet shattered and the wood struck Tariq's head.

The Khalifi Prince staggered, pitched over an outstretched root, and fell heavily to the ground.

Dane dropped onto the back of the power suit, unzipped it and tore it half off Tariq's body.

A set of tools dropped free. Tariq was making swimming motions. Dane kicked him brutally hard in the crotch. Tariq gave a gasp and doubled up in agony.

Dane worked him over, looking through the suit for weapons, but there were only the circular blade and a pyramidical key matrix of purple glass.

Dane held up the matrix. "What does this open?"

Tariq made no reply. Dane kicked him a couple more times. Tariq rolled onto his belly and tried to stand. Dane kicked him down again.

"Answer me, what doors does this open?"

"I will never tell you." Tariq rolled over into a fetal crouch.

Dane believed him. He didn't care to linger in this hell hole. He looked for something with which to immobilize Tariq. Finally he stripped the gummed netting off the bushes. It had lost much of its stickiness and made a good, strong string. He used it to bind Tariq's wrists and ankles.

Then he took stock of the situation. Tariq had said he was three-quarters of the way through the obstacle course, so to reach its end it would be quicker to go ahead than to go back.

The hounds continued to rage, straining at their leashes. Dane raised the powered knife. At the press of a stud the blade whirled. He contemplated killing the dogs then and there, but decided not to. He was just too weak, too exhausted emotionally. The dogs howled, and he turned and shambled away from them.

He jogged, then slowed to a walk. He felt a wave of dizziness pass over him and he nearly fell. He leaned against a tree for a minute and slowly fought down the nausea and fatigue that threatened to overwhelm him.

He went on. A few minutes later he reached the grand finale of the obstacle course, a series of stairways, each step a meter high, which wound around on themselves as they climbed out of sight above.

He stared at the stairs. They were meant to finally break the spirit of any specimen who managed to get this far. Here he would climb, weakly and slowly, until the dogs caught him at last and pulled him down.

He stared around him in despair. He could never climb those steps. Then his heart leapt as he caught sight of a mark on the white wall of the corridor. A red box was indicated. He staggered across to it and pressed the purple matrix into a recess inside the red box.

With a hiss a door slid open in front of him. He stepped through it and the door hissed shut behind him.

He stood in a blank access corridor, ceiling and walls in raw puffcrete, floor covered in blank tiles. The passage went about twenty feet before ending in front of an elevator. The car was waiting, the doors open. Dane stepped in and the doors closed automatically. The elevator rose smoothly, and when the doors opened again, he stepped out into a bare gray-walled room lined with equipment racks.

A set of hooks was lined along one wall. An armored space suit similar to that Tariq had worn was hanging on one of them.

13

DANE LISTENED CAREFULLY AT THE DOOR. NO SOUNDS PENE-trated from the interior. He examined the mechanism; it accepted the key matrix. He stepped through as it opened.

The next room was an office, with two desks set opposite each other. From the racks of video and print on the walls, Dane assumed it was a hard-copy library.

A door at one side opened onto a small washroom with a shower and washbasin. On the other side of the room was another door with a matrix lock.

He moved on. Through the next door he found an office corridor, carpeted in green, with white walls and office doors every twenty feet.

He slipped cautiously along this corridor, eyes scanning for any movement.

Another door sealed the corridor's far end. This door was made of synthetic wood, with oak finish and brass fitments. There was no lock. Dane paused. The offices around him were silent. Whatever this door led to, it seemed to signify a change of landscape. He imagined a wider space, a central office. Beyond that would lie a perfectly normal hab deck. Out there he could escape to the palace.

He pulled the door open a crack to see a lobby. No one was in sight. He started across, but the outer door opened without warning and three short men and a taller woman with a sharp, angular face pushed in.

"Excellent, we are just in time!" the woman said.

The men stepped forward with grim, eager expressions.

There was no time to think, barely time to fight. Dane slashed with the power knife. The men backed away. They circled him, feinting. He kept the knife whirring in their faces.

To his horror, he heard the woman speak into a wrist commo and heard Tariq's unmistakable voice squawk from the same device.

"Take him alive!" was Tariq's command.

In consternation, Dane realized his mistake. Tariq had used his suit commo to raise the alarm. Dane cursed himself for his stupidity in thinking that by smashing the helmet he had destroyed the communications capability of the suit. If he'd been thinking clearly, he would have searched the suit more thoroughly and destroyed the rest of it.

A man pushed a chair toward him. He slashed at it and the knife sheared half the back off. The man retreated. Another man hurled sofa cushions at him. The knife cut them in half as they came, foam shreds scattered in the air.

Then the woman threw a large, metal desk ornament. It struck him on the side of the head and he staggered.

The third man launched himself low along the ground. Dane slashed, but hesitantly, afraid to kill, and the man tackled him around the knees. Dane went down. Another man kicked the knife away. They dropped on him. Punches rained down.

The woman screamed, "Stop it, you fools! That is for the master!"

The blows stopped falling. The men eyed each other sheepishly. They got up. They dragged Dane to his feet.

"Hold him tight!" she commanded, and pulled a scanner from her pocket. Her eyes were dark and angry.

"Why are you doing this?" Dane whispered while blood ran down his face from a cut on his forehead. There was another on his lip. He had a black eye coming too.

"Shut up!" she said.

Coldly, she examined him with the medical scanner for a second or two, then pulled out a dispenser pencil and treated the cut on his lip. While she did it, she tore into the men holding him up.

"Damn fools, you'll get us all in trouble. Just what we need, to mess him up before the master gets him."

She left a medtab on his forehead and pointed to the synthetic oak door.

"All right, bring him to the master."

In despair, Dane felt himself lifted and carried toward the door, unable to resist.

The woman pulled the door open, they pushed him into the corridor.

A voice cut the air behind them like a knife.

"Let him go, now!"

The men turned. Dane felt their confusion, a woman's voice.

Then he glimpsed Leila. She was holding a handgun with both hands, training it on the men just a little unsteadily. Reluctantly, they released Dane. He staggered, went down on one knee.

The woman snarled and tried to draw a weapon of her own from within her jacket. Leila fired. Dane dived for the floor as explosive pellets winnowed the space above him. The woman was hurled down the corridor, where she bounced and came to rest against a computer cabinet.

Someone was screaming, but it wasn't her.

Dane struggled to his feet, staggered toward Leila, who was standing on tiptoe with one hand held to her mouth. She was white as a sheet, but still holding onto the gun.

The screams had stopped.

Sullenly, the men backed off, hands raised. They turned to confront the wall, as ordered.

"Thank you," Dane whispered.

Leila's eyes were wide, staring. "We're not out of this yet," she stammered. "You hear those alarms?"

It was true, there were alarm tones whooping outside the offices.

Dane opened the front door and found a large open space, the exterior of a commercial deck. The alarms continued. Sunlight shafted down a central atrium, glass-walled offices and shops lined the walls.

Figures were running toward him. Lights swiveled down from farther away. He slammed the door.

"No way out there."

"How did you get here?" she said. She was trembling.

"Through the back."

"Show me."

Dane led her down the corridor, pausing to pick up the dead woman's handgun.

The men remained in the front office, hands on their heads until the door closed, whereupon they slipped out the front door. This was up to armed guards now.

Dane and Leila reached the equipment room, found the door to the hidden passage leading to Tariq's private hunting preserve. They ran down the passage to the elevator.

Ominously, the elevator was not there. Dane put his ear to the elevator door. He heard, faintly, the barking of dogs. The hairs on the back of his neck rose at the sound.

"They're coming." Taking Leila's hand, he pulled her after him back to the library room.

They were trapped. It was hard not to panic a moment later when the elevator arrived on that floor with an uproar from the hounds.

"What in the world?" said Leila.

"Manhounds, Tariq's killers. He must have got free."

There was the crunch of a door lock blowing open. Armed guards in battle armor appeared in the doorway at the far end of the corridor. Leila whirled and fired the rest of the clip in her gun. Shots ricocheted wildly along the ceiling and walls. The men in the door pulled themselves back to safety in the outer office.

Dane meanwhile investigated the other side door, which had a matrix lock. His fingers were trembling so hard he found it difficult to press the matrix accurately into the socket. At last the door slid open.

"In here," he called. Leila poked her head inside.

"It's a dead end."

Dane looked back to the outer door. He'd forgotten to lock it. Abruptly it was wrenched open and the hounds were struggling over each other to get through the gap.

Instinctively Dane shoved Leila through and activated the door. It snapped shut on the jaws of the hounds.

The room was a box, lit by a single orange glow panel. It echoed with the outcry of the dogs just outside. The prospect was horrifying, but there was nothing in this small room except a narrow metal ladder that rose in the center and vanished into the murk above their heads. There was no ceiling in sight.

"Now what?" she said.

"We climb, I guess," Dane said, and started up the steps, his thighs fairly creaking from the effort. After two steps he paused to put the key matrix into his mouth for safekeeping. This freed up one hand; with the other he hung onto the gun.

Leila followed, and they ascended into the darkness. The door behind them began to resound with heavy blows as the guards tried to break it down.

The climbing was slow work. Dane became terrified that he might simply black out and fall. The dogs would tear him to pieces in the darkness down there.

After twenty-five steps he came to a matte black ceiling. Outlined in a red glow, though, was a matrix socket. He juggled the gun to get to the matrix key clenched between his teeth. The gun slipped, clattered on the step, almost hit Leila in the face, and fell to the bottom.

"Watch out!" Leila said.

"Sorry," he said with a shiver.

With a shaking hand he pressed the matrix into the socket. A small purple light came on next to it, and then a heavy pair of bolts slid aside and Dane was able to push open a trapdoor. It moved easily on powered hinges.

Light seemed to explode into their darkness.

Dane pushed the hatch all the way up and gazed out, virtually blinded by the brilliant light of the blue-sky illusion of the open hab surface.

He took the last few steps and rolled over the edge of the hatch and onto hard, gritty ground.

There was a loud explosion down below as the door was blown open. Smoke swirled up the ladder. Dane turned to help Leila but found that she was already diving over the edge. She landed lightly on all fours and got to her feet.

"All right?"

"All right," she said, dusting herself off. Then they froze as they heard the howling of the dogs at the bottom of the ladder. Dane flipped the hatch over and slammed it shut.

He stared around himself at the miraculous expanse of the Rimal. A handful of thornbushes grew around them. Off to the left in mid-distance were the sand dunes.

Dane looked back to the top of the hatch. The upper surface was camouflaged with ochre dust. Unless you knew it was there, it was hard to even see the outline of it in the ground. However, there was a distinctly visible matrix socket. Tariq had been thorough about the placing of locks. Dane inserted the purple matrix and heard the electric bolt slide home.

"What do we do now?" she said.

"Try to reach Ibrahim."

"Yes, of course. Not even Tariq will dare to attack you there."

"Question is, where is Ibrahim?" Dane gestured to the emptiness of the artificial desert.

"Over there, I think," she said, and pointed to their right.

Straining, he finally made out a line of black shapes, almost lost in the heat haze, situated beyond the end of the dune sea.

There was a thump on the underside of the hatch. Then another. "We'd better get going," Leila said, and started to jog.

Dane wearily set out to follow.

They were barely halfway to the tents when they heard an explosion behind them. They looked back in time to see the hatch being blown thirty feet into the air. A thick cloud of smoke roiled out of the ground.

"Uh-oh," Dane said.

They tried to run faster, but Dane found that he simply lacked the strength. He was truly spent. The best he could manage was a loose, shambling walk.

Half a minute later there was an uproar of horrific barking, and looking back, they could see three, then four, small forms speeding across the artificial desert toward them.

Leila swung up her gun and pulled the trigger, to no effect —her clip was empty. With a cry of despair she dropped it.

Dane looked toward the black tents, now clearly visible a few hundred meters ahead. He was ready to fall, unable to stagger, let alone run, any farther.

A column of dust was visible, with a dark speck beneath it. The dust was moving, coming toward them very quickly.

"It's all right, Leila, someone's coming," Dane croaked.

Leila glanced up and then redoubled her efforts. She grabbed Dane by the hand and dragged him along, forcing him to wobble along on rubber legs.

Dane looked back as he staggered. The hounds were in full course and they were already close. It was going to be a very near thing.

But the dark object beneath the dust was close enough for them now to identify as a sand buggy with the giant bodyguard Amesh at the wheel.

A terrifying few seconds ensued as the dogs closed to within a hundred meters of them. The sand buggy slid to a halt in a cloud of dust. The door burst open and they staggered into it as Amesh kept the engine roaring. The dogs were right behind, tongues out, teeth shining. Dane and Leila hit the seats and slid across them. Amesh slammed the door shut even as dogs cannoned into it with sudden yelps of fury a split second later.

The buggy roared as Amesh accelerated back to the line of tents. The hounds barely paused before setting out in pursuit, falling behind but determined as ever to catch their prey. As Tariq had said, they were unstoppable.

In front of the tents Amesh brought the buggy to a halt. They were helped out by servants in the white uniforms of slavery. The servants pointed to an armored gun buggy from which a machine-gun barrel projected.

They staggered forward and found Ibrahim, wearing a wide-brimmed sun hat and a simple brown jelaba, sitting in the gun seat. Ibrahim greeted them with a cheery wave.

"You have survived, my friend. Well done. I knew you had a good chance of coming through alive. Especially with my remarkable, great-granddaughter on your side."

"You knew? What are you talking about?"

But Ibrahim had adjusted the guns to bring the cross hairs down upon the hounds, still doggedly pursuing their prey, and getting quite close to the tents now.

Ibrahim aimed carefully, and then the machine gun stuttered briefly. Dane marveled at how quiet the thing was while a fountain of bright-red plastic shell casings flew up in the air. Two hundred meters away the manhounds disintegrated violently.

Ibrahim stopped firing.

"You have flushed my enemy out of his lair, my young friend. Now I will be able to draw his fangs for good."

"What do you mean?" Dane was staring out to where the poor damn dogs were no more. Leila had looked away; she had her face in her hands. Dane reached out and folded her in his arms.

When he looked up next, he found Ibrahim watching him and smiling in a way that was almost eerie.

"Yes," the old man said, "Tariq has overreached himself. He has broken our most sacred rule. He has brought conflict to the Rimal."

The Khalifi had their own rules. Do what you want, but don't do it in their private desert.

A servant handed him a can of chilled soda. He slugged half of it down before stopping for air.

Ibrahim was chuckling and rubbing his ancient hands together with undisguised glee.

"Now I can order Tariq restrained, you see. I can even force him to be kept under observation for psychiatric testing. Merzik will have to become more pliable. Congratulations, young man, nothing can stop us now!"

Dane was too astonished to protest. Instead he voiced his immediate concern.

"The G.B.s?"

Ibrahim laughed. "I can neutralize the G.B.s for long enough."

"How?" Dane gulped.

Ibrahim wore his most mysterious smile. "Your grandfather had his spies. I have mine. So, you can stop worrying. We shall build your ship now. It is a certainty."

Servants came to assist ancient Ibrahim out of his seat and down from the armored gun buggy, while Dane looked on from what felt like a face of stone. Somehow Ibrahim had used him to draw Tariq's fangs. Had Leila set him up? He couldn't believe it. Or had their meeting simply formed a fortuitous link for Ibrahim's chain of plans? Was he just some dim-witted pawn in internal Khalifi power struggles?

Ibrahim took his arm.

"Come with me, young man. You look like you need a bath and some clean clothes. In my tents we have all necessary facilities. And when you are ready, we will talk. I have many questions to ask you."

14

A.D. 2451. DAY 2. FOURTH MONTH.

The *Founder* was moving out-system.

Reaching out to the great ship as she picked up speed were the last few passengers and video signals from the inner system.

Meanwhile, far back in the inner system, the rebellion on the old L5 hab *Atlantis* was over. And, of course, the viewers in the outer systems were getting the whole story. Of course, by then it was old news, and the termination video was truly horrifying. Suicide squads of shock troopers, from the gene vats of Beijing, cut through the airlocks and blasted their way in.

Deck by deck they worked through the old American-built

habitat. After two hours the defense collapsed and the remaining population surrendered.

Five thousand preselected politicals were weeded out immediately and marched to the airlocks. There they were shoved in, in groups of fifty at a time, and voided into space.

When the TV rehash started, Dane switched off with an angry curse. He stared at the wall for a long, long minute.

The worst of it was the weird sense of helplessness he felt. He was so irrelevant in this catastrophe that it was unbearable.

And besides, what could he have done for those who didn't want to be saved?

They were the ones who had chosen to ignore the cardinal rule taught all the descendants of Talbot and Emily Fundan. To stay free of "Government by Others" and the "Imposition of Taxes," the family would always have to keep moving outward. The governments they had left behind them would always hunger after them.

The Fundans on *Atlantis* had the choice all along. Any of them could have left before it was too late.

Dane had been raised with a near-mystical reverence for all things Fundan. This made the sense of defeat and helplessness seem overwhelming now.

Unsought memories bubbled up to the surface. Like that of the very first day at the palace, with Edward, after leaving the Reserve and shuttling to *Fundan One*.

Dane had been shown into a warm room of red velvet, Oriental rugs, leather, and brass. He'd had a mysterious hot drink called "beef tea" and had then played three games of chess with Grandfather. Two French defenses and a vicious Ultra-Benoni—Grandfather was the first person Dane had ever met who was better at chess than he was.

"What's the color we like, boy?"

"Green!"

"Right, green for the Earth we left behind. Green for the money that's still in our hand. Green for everything that's fine and grand."

Edward had a little green pillow, which was always around him. It was his "luck." It was stuffed with thousand-dollar bills. The real thing from Earth. Edward had often promised to give him the "luck of the Fundans" on his death. Like so many other things, it had been withheld by Aunt Agatha.

The scene faded from his memory. The frustration returned. Without conscious thought he pulled a bottle from the chiller and made himself a stiff drink.

It would be hellishly easy just to keep drinking, he thought, and he struggled with the idea.

He couldn't go back. He'd improved so much in recent months. He couldn't let himself slip back to it. Not like in those weeks after the Khalifi took the ship away from him. When the wheel snapped loose and spun away into the dark.

Back when they had just begun the *Founder*'s sneak-away power-up. A year ahead of schedule. When Earth was behind the sun.

Right then, before he was ready to fight them, the Khalifi had taken control. Old Ibrahim had set the new rules.

Then they'd forced him to accept the Purple Class of accommodation, which gave privileged passengers fifty square meters of space apiece.

Many Cabin holders were demoted to the Seats. But Khalifi gunmen under Amesh's command enforced this edict.

Dane had resigned, and they'd taken over. A couple of Fundan hotheads had even been killed trying to assassinate Ibrahim.

Jebediah Bones had been killed next by a bomb that may have been meant for Dane. Alter had disappeared soon afterward, and no trace of him had ever been found.

And there had been nothing Dane could do about it. He'd been reduced to a "consultant." Although he held meetings with Adelaide and Melissa, and sometimes with Berlisher, there was little point to them.

He was just a Cabin passenger, an irrelevancy. And to Dane that had been a terrible new thing in his life, because he had lived for the *Founder* since he was fifteen years old, and had circled close to power ever since.

The chilled vodka tasted good, too good.

He caught himself staring at the bottle in the chiller.

He was saved by the bell; the door chime rang as Leila sailed in wearing a new denim suit. She had been to the market enclave and was carrying a bag with fresh vegetables, wine, and freshly grated Parmesan cheese for the pasta.

"We eat in tonight, darling," she announced. "We watch Sillueta on Jade channel. My friend Maillou is going to be on. Later we're going to the reception, you remember that, I hope?"

Dane reached out to her with the passion of a drowning

man. For a long time he held her close. He was visibly shaking from the rage and the frustration.

Leila smelled the alcohol and suffered a pang of sick disappointment. He'd been so much better just recently. But soon she could feel the old, self-lacerating torment upon him again.

He was a man, she told herself for the thousandth time, and men were possessed of fragile egos, and poor Dane's ego had been kicked around mercilessly for two years now by the Khalifi. Slowly but inexorably the situation had been crushing him.

In the early days he'd seemed to come apart right before her eyes. The vodka came out of the chiller faster and faster. He became obsessed with controlling what little of the ship he had hung on to.

Tormented by dying love and horrible guilt, she stayed and struggled with him through the worst of it.

She tried to relax him.

"Dane, darling, don't let it get to you. It's over, there's nothing you can do."

He winced in her arms, then pulled away.

"Did you see the news of the end of the rebellion?"

"*Atlantis*? No, I didn't know. I . . ." She groped. She didn't even know the rebellion was over. It was shocking, somehow. She had never thought that the World Government would seriously make war on the spacers. "*Atlantis* gave up? I can't believe it, they would never surrender. I don't understand."

"No, they didn't give up, not until the storm troopers got inside and took control. They were conquered, deck by deck. They destroyed estates wholesale, burned the chateaux."

There wasn't much she could say. Leila had always said this moment would never come. She had always hoped that the Social Synthesis was a different movement from previous race-improving, moralistic, sociopolitical creeds.

Automatically, to give herself something to do, she swung down the little stove unit from its place on the wall. She'd picked up fresh pasta and sauce at the spaghetti shop.

They were supposed to go out later, to a reception given by her friends, the Sillueta artists. The reception would be held in an Atrium restaurant. She wondered if she should cancel.

She had also bought the bottle of wine. Which posed a quandary, because Dane would drink some, and if his mood turned down, he might drink a lot of it and get drunk. If he got drunk, she didn't want to be escorting him to the reception. If he got drunk, she didn't want to be going anywhere with him.

He followed her to the galley.

"You know the *Atlantis* was the first free habitat?"

He wanted to argue, another bad sign.

"Darling, everyone knows that. Americans built it, right?"

"Yeah, and my ancestors, Talbot and Emily, they went there. They were among the first ones, the original spacers."

She was suddenly seized with a desperate urge not to talk about the old Fundan family. When Dane got drunk and maudlin, it was often to the sounds of the tales about the old Fundans and how nobody had ever dealt fairly with the Fundans, who always dealt fairly with the rest of the world.

"Right," she said, "Talbot and Emily. They sold up their part of the family business, hospitals in Toronto, right?"

"Yeah." He sensed her attempt to contain him, to deflect his raging tirade, but he refused to be turned aside. "They owned gerontoclinics all over Ontario and Michigan. But they knew what was coming."

She threw pasta into hot water. Decided to try and change the subject.

"I saw a woman in the market, a woman with a child."

"So? There are lots of women down at the market, all the time."

"This woman was begging."

Dane snorted. Leila was always exaggerating these things. Begging! Aboard the *Founder*? Impossible.

"Begging? Oh, come on!"

"Dane, you don't understand what's going on on this ship."

"Now, Leila . . ." He was getting angry.

"It's true. I've seen it in the market, there are lots of people going hungry, lots of people are sick. Down in the Seats."

"Look, they're lucky they've got seats."

"They're sharing the seats. You have no idea what's going on. You stay in here, locked away from it all."

"The shared-Seat problem was something we dealt with a long time ago. Ibrahim promised me there would be no more Seat share-selling."

"Ibrahim's promises are worth less than the air he uses to give them with. You should know that by now!"

"Look, I just watched them push five thousand people out of the airlocks of *Atlantis*. People from my own family were there. So I'm not too concerned right now about people who are getting out of this system alive, all right?"

73

"What?" Her eyes had gone round.

"Five thousand people, summarily executed. Francesca Fundan was one of them, my oldest living cousin."

"Oh my, I . . ." She was stunned. She turned to embrace, to comfort him. But he would not be comforted long, and soon moved away. She watched as he poured himself a glass of wine and took a seat at the tiny dining table. With a moody expression he watched the news rehash while she readied the pasta, the salad, and the sauce.

They ate in silence at first. Then Dane made a great effort to be pleasant. They chatted smoothly enough for a little while, but then Leila forgot herself and returned to the sore subject of the Seats.

"I'm afraid it is true, Dane. In some sections there are people on the floor."

Dane refused to believe it. Couldn't allow himself to visualize that, not aboard *his* ship.

But Leila saw the people from the Seats in the marketplace. She saw half-naked, dirty children, and other people who were plainly hungry.

"There are gangs down there, Dane. Thugs who are employed by the Khalifi to find sex objects for Ibrahim's friends. They take seats whenever they want them and force the rightful owners to stand or sit on the floor if there's room." Her knowledge put an edge on her voice.

Still smoldering from the *Atlantis* horror, Dane snarled a curse and then gave a cynical shrug. "So what? They're getting out, aren't they? This is the last ship for freedom."

"There are going to be deaths down there, Dane. Deaths that could be prevented if more people were given accommodation on the Cabin decks."

That again. Dane felt weary even thinking about that subject again. He launched into a tirade.

"Look, you know perfectly well that that is a hopeless cause! The people in cabins paid for their places. How do you plan to compensate them? These are the people who paid up years ago, when there was no guarantee the ship would ever be finished. They had faith. And there are lots of families in the cabins too. Don't they have any rights? No, it's impossible."

She remained unconvinced.

"Darling, I know you don't mean to be so hard, I know that if you would only come down and see what things are like in the Seats, you'd see that something has to be done."

Dane knew he couldn't face that.

The Seat passage had been an area of difficulty since the beginning of the project. Four years to the new world, four years living out of a seat five feet long and two feet wide. Dane's own Fundan-hab conditioning made the idea of this kind of constriction quite horrifying.

But from the beginning it had been the only way to accommodate the hordes of people they'd known would eventually beg for passage out-system. Because the *Founder* would be the last ship crewed by free spacers.

As it was, there were people doubled up throughout the Cabin deck. Dane was with Leila, Adelaide and Melissa were sharing.

The Seat problems were beyond solution, like anything that had to do with human beings, as far as Dane could see. Dane belonged to the simpler world of engineering. Designing to meet the demands of performance, coping with stress and material fatigue, ice freeze, and energy lattices.

People, on the other hand, were just defiantly immune to planning and designing. Because of Khalifi greed, some passengers might die on the floor from acceleration affects.

It didn't have to be this way. The *Founder* had been designed to accommodate all its passengers in safety and relative comfort.

His phone priority code flashed on the wall unit. Dane stared it at a moment, shocked. He didn't get too many calls these days, especially not on the priority-code line.

He picked up with his wrist unit, routed the video through the main TV screen. To his surprise, it was Great-Aunt Agatha Fundan. She was pale, her eyes wavering.

"Young man, I have an urgent requirement from you." Her voice was a husk.

"Great-Aunt, where are you? I didn't think you had shipped aboard."

She glared, then her eyes seemed to go out of focus.

"Young man, despite our past, uh, disagreements, I want you to know that I have decided to forgive you. I am aboard a private shuttle, closing within ten thousand kilometers of your ship."

It was Dane's turn to stare, speechless.

"What I require, young man, is accommodation, or a berth, or whatever you call it, upon your ship. I require a full salon, two bedchambers, a kitchen and scullery, full reception area, and some office space. In addition to myself, I have a personal staff of three, for whom accommodation must also be found."

Dane gulped at the fantastic insouciance of the woman.

"Well, Great-Aunt Agatha, I'm afraid that won't be easy. I don't have the power to provide you, or anyone else, with that kind of space. Perhaps I can get a seat or a seat share, that's all that's left. All Cabin space was taken up long ago."

"What? This is a Fundan-built ship. I am the oldest living Fundan. I exert my familial right to come aboard and be accommodated!" Agatha's face had flushed red; her eyes seemed to protrude from her head.

"Great-Aunt, this *was* a Fundan-built ship. Perhaps you don't remember, but you suspended all financing more than two years ago."

She stared back blindly.

"This is now a Khalifi ship. They even wanted to change the name, but I stopped them."

"What does that matter? Enough credit had been drained from our reserves as it was, it was time for others to contribute."

Dane smiled thickly. Bizarre emotions pulsed in his breast.

"The financial reserves of the family." He sighed. "How unimportant they seem now, eh, Great-Aunt?"

She blinked. Grandfather had always said Agatha was more stupid than malicious.

"What?" she gurgled. "What are you talking about? Listen, I am on course for docking within two hours. I must have some kind of accommodation ready. Surely you can find me a cabin, at the least?"

How to explain to this most obdurate and willfully ignorant of all the elder Fundans? How to tell her that because of her blindness, Dane was almost powerless to help her or anyone else.

"Great-Aunt, all I can do is to call Prince Ras Order Khalifi and beg him for a seat or a seat share. For your personal staff I doubt that I can get even that. They will have to return to *Fundan One*. The ship is full."

"A seat? What does that mean?"

"Exactly what it says. A seat for a four-year voyage to the New World, where you'll be safe from the World Government."

"Just a seat? This is ridiculous, there must be something you can do. You built the ship, damn it!"

"Great-Aunt, let me call Prince Ras Order. Hold on for a few moments, will you?"

With visible poor grace, she acquiesced.

Ras Order picked up in a darkened room somewhere in his Purple-class suite. Someone played a sitar nearby. The Prince had been smoking hashish, Dane could hear the excitement in his voice. A girl would be dancing for him.

"Dane, how good to see you. It has been a long time, my friend. What have you been up to?"

Dane tried to ignore the cruelties unleashed in his mind by these words. Ras Order meant no harm, he was just stoned.

"I've been, well, I can't say I've been busy, damn you. But you know all about that."

Ras Order smiled, a little wistfully. "Yes, of course."

"I need something now, Ras."

"Speak, my friend. Whatever it is, I will provide it if it is in my power to do so."

"My great-aunt Agatha has decided she wants to ship out. I need to get her a seat, and some seats for her servants."

Ras Order's eyes grew calculating, a little distance entered into his voice.

"All seat allocations have been made. There are, in theory, no vacant seats left."

"In theory, but Ibrahim has some, doesn't he?"

"Well, yes."

"Can't he give me two? One for my great-aunt and another for her staff."

"I don't know, I will ask. One moment."

The screen flickered. A view of the Rimal of old was shown. The sound of the sitar continued, playing through a quiet, reflective passage. Twenty seconds passed and Ras Order came back.

"Yes, Dane. I have two seats for you. They're on deck Fourteen, Orange level."

"Thank you, Ras."

"Dane . . ."

"Yes, Ras."

"These are the last seats I can get you, or anyone else. Ibrahim made that plain to me just now."

There was no reply that Dane felt fit to make.

He punched up Agatha's signal.

"Great-Aunt, I can help you."

"Good, that sounds much better."

"I have managed to get you two seats, one for yourself and one for your staff to share."

"Seats? I require a cabin."

"The seats are on an Orange level, that's good, because the Orange levels have the best shower and toilet facilities."

"I am not sitting in a seat for four years."

Dane stared back at her. He had kindled a goodly portion of what pride remained to him to obtain these seats. And she was too good for them?

"Have it your own way, Great-Aunt. There are at least fifty thousand other people who will be happy to take your place."

Agatha bit off the harsh words in her throat. Some vestigial self-preservatory instinct came to the fore.

"One moment, young man, I will take the, ah, seats."

"You will? Well, fine. Have a good voyage, Great-Aunt, I expect I'll see you in the New World."

Dane punched across the seat numbers and the authorization codes, then he switched out. For half a minute he simply stared at the screen. Somewhere deep inside there were terrible sobs; a weird kind of agony suffused his mind.

Leila came from somewhere, Leila was there.

15

WITH NOTHING TO DO, THE VOYAGE TO THE NEW WORLD WENT on far too long for Dane Fundan. His drinking increased, despite several attempts to quit.

Slowly, month by month, things began to slip. He was cold to Leila while sober, alternately passionate and angry when drinking, finally stupid and sad when drunk.

Desperately, she tried to retrieve him, but he would not see doctors, he would not take medication.

Spectacular two-day binges became frequent. He could not

stand the feeling of uselessness that hung over him whenever he was not drinking.

He could hear Edward's voice in his dreams. "Go to it, boy! You've got it in you, regular Hamilton Tiger Cat of a boy!" Sometimes he imagined he heard the voice in his waking moments.

He got in a fistfight in the Atrium restaurant. For some reason he felt he had to fight the Khalifi security guards when they came along to restore order.

Ras Order had him released on that occasion, but he made it clear that it was the last time. Dane could expect no further favors from the Khalifi elite.

He drank in his cabin after that. Months went by. He behaved badly. He struck Leila on more than one occasion. She thought her heart would break some days, on others she felt suffocated beneath sediments of sorrow and anger.

And yet Leila also felt a new life quickening in her womb. She was pregnant. That knowledge made her desperate. But Dane was beyond reason now. Sometimes when he'd had just a few drinks, he became strange, took to conversing with himself, ignored her entirely.

So she never told him, and one day she was gone.

She took a tiny space on the Purple level. Ibrahim had not used his personal allocation in the harem section; there was a room.

It was a humiliation for her to be there, of course, but she endured this for the sake of privacy.

Dane got drunker than ever within hours of her leaving. Months went by.

Leila stopped calling, and began to systematically cut herself off from the social world she had shared with Dane.

Dane drifted through binges and short bouts of abstinence during which he would roam the decks, half crazy with melancholy. He had already lost contact with everyone. He hadn't seen Adelaide or Melissa in many months. He was finally alone, although he spoke to the Prince in his dreams.

One day he wandered unsteadily into the pub in the Atrium and fell over a table. After drinking vodka all day, he had decided to go out for a few beers. He assaulted a man who cursed him for knocking over his drink.

The security team took him away, struggling.

He awoke in a cell with a couple of other offenders picked up in the public spaces of the ship.

They were examined by a brisk young team of medics and psychs. Dane was certified sane and sound. He was sent up before the Magistrate on a charge of public intoxication.

The Magistrate for the occasion was Merzik Khalifi. The Khalifi dispensed justice in majlis style, quickly, directly. Each elder brother took the job in turn.

Merzik greeted Dane with an eerie smile. He listened to the charges and the evidence. Then he removed Dane's Cabin status. Since the cabin was a gratuity extended to Dane by the *Founder* Construction Administration, it could legally be sequestered by the ship's administration.

Dane's possessions were impounded to general luggage and he was sent down to the Seat section with a ticket for section 25 on Green deck.

The Seat sections were a shock. Most seats had been double or triple sold. People were huddled on the floors of the aisles and corridors. Others roamed aimlessly. Most were heavily tranked, their gaze blank, the faces slack.

Seat 187D was occupied by a henchman of a burly thug named Fogo, who worked for the Khalifi in administering the Seats. When Dane waved his ticket stub and remonstrated, Fogo's thugs appeared and drove him off with kicks and blows.

Dane roamed the aisles in helpless rage.

But eventually he found a tiny space, in the crevice beside a fire-fighting equipment locker where it bulged from the bulkhead in a short corridor that connected two Seat sections.

There was just enough room to sit or to lie, with his back against the locker and his feet stretched along the wall.

Bewildered, dazed, Dane sank into a comatose depression.

He was shaken awake by rough hands. Fogo towered over him in a tight gold shirt, blue pants, and white boots.

"What do you want?" said Dane.

Fogo was a heavyset individual with long arms and a barrel-like chest. He had an evil smile and a bald skull decorated with tattoos.

"I want half your water, three-quarters of your food." He growled happily.

"What?" Dane said stupidly.

Fogo reached out a massive hand and grabbed his shirt front.

"Water, food, got that, fool? I'm talking your allocation.

You new here, this is Green deck, here we have different rules."

"You can't have my water, or my food," said Dane.

Fogo grinned. "Oh, really?"

They fought, but Dane was out of condition. Fogo beat him senseless and dumped his body in the elevator to the waste-recycling sector.

"Good-bye fool, now you're going to be food for everyone!"

At the hab sump the attendant checked Dane's body and found him still alive. He was sent to the hospital.

The broken bones in his face were set and repaired, the cuts stitched up, and then he was back on Green deck.

There was nowhere to go to except his crevice by the fire-equipment locker.

Fogo came to see him every day, usually accompanied by Zenise, Fogo's female, who pushed a little white plastic water tank on wheels, in which she collected Fogo's tribute from the section. Zenise wore skin-tight zipsuits.

Dane was forced to surrender his water and food.

In a gesture of "leniency," Fogo allowed him to keep half the food. The other half went into Fogo's buckets.

Food on Green deck was three large meal platters a day made with some skill by the Fundan-designed food processors. There was always enough for a comfortable satiety. The Fundans knew the value of keeping passengers full and therefore peaceful on interminable space flights.

Giving up half of the ration still left enough for one to survive on, but it was a meager survival.

Dane still had credits at the ship bank. Thus he could afford to buy back some food from Fogo's stall, which was set up in what had been designed as the exercise chamber for the deck section.

Dane discovered that Fogo was not alone. Khalifi-sponsored cliques ruled and abused every Seat section.

Since he had nowhere to drink but the bars and restaurants of the Atrium, and since with Seat status he had only very limited time in the Atrium, it became difficult to keep drinking. Any vodka brought back to the Seats was an invitation to Fogo to show up.

In desperation, Dane took to drinking on the elevators, riding up and down, taking occasional sips on his bottle.

But somehow it was a very different experience being drunk in the Seats, compared to being drunk in his own cabin.

81

For a start, his crevice in the passageway had to be defended.

After his first drunken blackout in the Seats, he found he'd been stripped of his clothing, right down to his shoes.

With considerable embarrassment he made his way into the Atrium and bought fresh clothes. A khaki-colored one-piece suit, double-layered cotton and porcryl, new one-piece floor shoes.

He returned to the Seats and found his crevice occupied by a teenage youth. He evicted the youth, who slouched away with ill grace.

He crouched in the crevice and surveyed the situation.

Fogo stomped past, grinned and nodded at him.

"They be serving lunch real soon, don't miss my share, eh?" The coarse laugh echoed behind him.

Dane considered living like this for another two years, until the *Founder* reached the New World.

His eyes were wide in the semidark, staring but unseeing.

16

DAYS PASSED. DANE DRIFTED IN HELL. HE SPENT WHAT TIME he could in the Atrium. He rode the elevators, along with many other seatless people. Those who had been dispossessed by the Khalifi.

Every shift a few bodies were shipped to the sump dump.

Slowly, Dane came out of the alcoholic haze. He began to work on his body, exercising against floor and bulkhead.

Zenise spotted him doing push-ups.

"You think you can make yourself hard enough to challenge my Fogo, eh?"

She strutted past him in her skin-tight clothes. "You delude yourself, you will find Fogo will not be so damned merciful the next time."

He continued to exercise, but moved to the gymnasium in the Atrium, where he bought time on the machines.

His face grew thin and haggard. His body grew hard. However, he did not recover entirely. Something inside had broken. He spent long periods just staring into the semidarkness, eyes vacant.

Faces drifted through his thoughts, Edward's, Alter's, old Jebediah Bones's. Most often it would be Leila, and tears would start from his eyes.

Fogo, unfortunately, was easily bored. And Fogo's ilk were not allowed in the Atrium.

So Fogo would roam the crowded corridors and seek out prey among the weaker passengers. Quick shakedowns and brutal little beatings were the usual result. Fogo referred to it as, "my exercises!"

Dane, in his misery, drew Fogo like a carcass draws flies.

Fogo would bring all the boys, and Zenise, and they would bait Dane, and chivvy him out of his crevice and push him around a little. Dane fought back to the best of his ability, but he was outmatched by impossible numbers.

"Dance for us, Fundan!"

He was surrounded by their hot, beady eyes.

"Dance! Dance! Dance! Dance!" they crowed.

Dane's eyes slowly filled with madness.

He visited the Atrium and stole a knife used to pare lemons at the bar. He ran from the bar with it hidden in his pocket, his mind sizzling with fear and rage.

Back in his crevice, he prepared himself.

Fogo and the gang soon came. Fogo had been drinking a little, he was in a cruel mood.

"All right, Fundan, you're going to dance for us today!"

The others chuckled together, an evil sound. Zenise was carrying a whip.

"Let's flog the Fundan and make him dance!" she cried.

"Hah! I like that," said Fogo. "We'll really make him jump! Strip the shirt off his back!"

The men came forward. Dane pulled the knife; it gleamed in his hand. He slashed at them in the air with it.

They fell back, their arms up, with cries of dismay.

"The bastard's got a knife!"

"Where'd he get that! Send him to the Magistrate!"

Fogo leaped forward, his long arms whirling.

"Beat the shit out of him, Fogo," said Zenise.

Fogo gave a mirthless chuckle. "She always like it when I do that!"

The henchmen had recovered their courage and were grouped behind their leader.

Fogo outweighed Dane by twenty kilos, he was two inches taller and heavier all over.

Dane kept the knife between them.

"The knife thrower needs no handholds, attack with the point of the knife, riposte with the blade." Alter's words floated into his mind from the depths of memory.

Fogo sensed something different about the Fundan. He shifted cautiously.

"Oh-ho, we have a hot one today, boys! I say we have a little fun with him!"

Fogo approached, his big hands at the ready.

Dane attacked, striking for Fogo, with the knife like a rapier before him.

Fogo's evasion was cramped by his henchmen. Dane struck lucky and got the knife into the meat of Fogo's shoulder. A red stain spread across Fogo's golden shirt.

Fogo vented a scream of woe. This was not supposed to happen!

The henchmen swung feet and fists toward him. Dane jumped back, slashing with the knife.

He caught one fellow across the ankle with the blade and elicited a howl.

Fogo was urging them on, and Zenise was screeching insults from the back, but the men were less and less interested in facing that knife. They held off, and Dane backed away.

After ten meters there was a side passage that connected to the next corridor. He ran down it and turned into the next corridor.

Zenise was there. She swung her heavy whip at him, but he caught the whip in his hand and yanked her off her feet.

He knelt briefly on her chest and held the knife to her throat. At its touch she froze, eyes wide.

The henchmen were coming, Fogo behind them. Dane slipped a ring of key tabs from her belt, then ran down the corridor until he found himself outside Fogo's purloined room. He tried the various plastic keys until a blue one opened the door. He stepped in and locked it behind him.

A few seconds later Fogo's henchmen were beating on the outside. With many dire threats they informed him that mighty Fogo was being treated for his wound and would soon be back. Then they would force the door and kill him.

Dane took a deep breath and sat down on a chair made from the former exercise equipment. Fogo's room was lined with shelves made from food trays and rectangular sections of the lining materials taken from the public hallways. On these shelves was stacked a fortune in freeze-dried food.

A pair of beds, stolen from a cabin, had been wedged in the corners. There was stolen video equipment as well, quite a haul, in fact.

Fogo would be back soon. Dane was trapped. When they got the door open, they would make sure to beat him to death this time before he vanished into the sump dump.

There seemed no way out. Even with the knife, he couldn't take on Fogo and the henchmen, especially now that he'd lost the effect of surprise.

Dane looked down at the floor, which was covered in black and white hexagonal tiles. Would this be the end?

Something caught his eye. In the corners of one tile, in the center of the room, were inset three tiny green triangles.

A hatch!

Dane flung himself down beside it. Of course, this space was on an intersection of major corridors. There were often maintenance hatches at such points.

Desperately he sought to recall the exact sequences that were required for these particular hatches.

Green deck, the seventh deck—that was it, the seventh deck.

He pressed one of the triangles seven times in quick succession. Then he waited a second; it lit up.

Dane's heart soared. He pressed it again seven times and then waited. Nothing happened. Sweating, he pressed the next triangle over, but just once.

It lit up. His pulse pounded. He pressed the next one, but twice, and it lit up, and he whistled in relief and continued. Child-proofing code had been a feature on all these maintenance hatches. Nothing was more insidious than bored passengers, and ships had been lost as a result.

The hatch opened with a faint hiss. Colder air wafted in, with the smell of insulation and raw puffcrete. Dane stared down a narrow ladder into a claustrophobic adit, seven feet by three.

He looked around him, his eyes fastened on some water jugs, and he grabbed four and dropped them through. They survived the impact. He cleaned a shelf of freeze-drieds and shoved them through.

Then he climbed down the ladder and found a Fundan Made logo gleaming on what was the ceiling of this passage. He pressed it seven times and the hatch hissed shut.

After stuffing the freeze-drieds into his clothing, he gathered up the water jugs and started off, heading to his right, where he vaguely imagined there might be a wider passage than this inspection adit.

He shivered in the cold, dry air. The only light was provided by occasional green triangles. There were miles of these passageways, a labyrinth surrounding the passenger spaces.

Dane trudged on, heading into the deep tunnels.

17

MAIN DECELERATION WAS OVER, FOR WHICH EVERYONE WAS very grateful. New World enhancements were on every screen. Blue oceans glinted beneath white spirals of cloud. The primary, BD4455, their new sun, was a bright blaze directly ahead.

While spirits were boosted by these developments, rumors were running like wildfire through the Seats and Cabins.

The Khalifi were said to have decided to keep the entire New World for themselves.

In four years of whimsical, authoritarian rule, the Khalifi had made few friends among the oppressed passengers. Few doubted that such an enormity was beyond the Khalifi. If there was an upper limit on Khalifi greed, it had not yet been demonstrated.

A group calling itself the Committee for the Rebellion was meeting every day on Orange deck in a space cleared of all Khalifi monitoring devices.

Anti-Khalifi feeling had lead to the systematic smashing of

listening devices all over the Seat decks. Attacks on Khalifi themselves had occurred in the Atrium.

As a result, the Khalifi had locked themselves away on the lavish Purple level. They'd placed their guards around the elevators.

Unfortunately, a lot of people down in the Seats were no longer completely rational. Four years of close confinement had taken their toll. None of them had ever been poor, none of them had ever been treated like this. They thirsted for revenge.

"We want out! We want out!" resounded the cry in the Seats. The remaining Khalifi thugs were forced to wield violence on a more or less continuous basis to keep their rule intact.

At the meetings of the Committee the atmosphere grew explosive.

In Dane's absence, since he was presumed dead a year before, Adelaide had taken over as "leader" of the small group that had once administered the construction of the ship. As representative of that group, Adelaide attended the meetings, with Tobe Berlisher to assist.

Fifty people had shown up for the latest. The ten representatives of the Cabins were seated behind a cafeteria table, while forty Seats were standing on the other side of it.

"All we want to know," said Astrod Benenki, a tall florid woman from Orange deck, "is when do we start the takeover?"

"Yeah," some of the others chorused.

Astrod needed little encouragement. "It's time the Cabins stopped stringing us along. I think that you're really hoping the Khalifi will decide to include you in their master plan so you can dump the rest of us."

Part of the truth at last. Tobe glanced along the table; the Cabin people shifted uneasily. These meetings were getting out of hand. The Committee had begun in the Cabins, but now the founders seemed to be losing control to these awful people from the Seats.

Another hothead, Kasok from Green deck, pushed to the fore. "You're all just wetting your pants in fear of them!"

That galvanized the Cabins at last.

"It's all very well to shout nasty names at us, but have you thought about the consequences if you try a revolt and fail?" It was Armego Butte, representative from an ancient asteroid family.

Kasok snorted in disgust. "Cowards."

"They can turn off the air anytime!" Adelaide said quietly.

Kasok turned to her, weighing her words. "Yeah, they can, but we have to make sure they don't get the chance."

"Don't you see what you're saying!" boomed Armego Butte. "You haven't thought this all through, you damned red hots!"

"Cowards!"

"You won't be satisfied until you get us all killed."

"Cowards!"

"Idiot," roared Armego. "If all you can do is yell one word over and over, maybe you should resign."

"Don't tell me to resign, you bloody aristocrat!"

"Cut the crap, Kasok!"

"You want to try and make me?"

"I don't know where Kasok gets the right to call someone an 'aristocrat.' You were one of the richest men in the Uranus system yourself. You just didn't buy into the ship in time to get a cabin."

"Look, Ms. Fundan, I don't have any quarrel with you, so just let's forget that stuff. I just want to know when we're going to do something!"

Kasok turned to stare back into the mob behind him.

"I'm just tired of sitting down there being terrorized by the damn water thieves."

"Yeah!" roared his supporters.

Adelaide stood up and waited. After a few moments they quietened. They had all learned that she spoke with a practiced, professional wisdom. By attending every meeting, she had earned everyone's respect.

"Look, let's not waste the time we have."

There was a general murmur of assent. Kasok shut up, Armego sat down. Adelaide had the floor.

"We can't do anything effective without planning, extensive planning, but everyone's too busy yelling insults to even think of working together cooperatively. What are you proposing, Kasok? We blow the hatches to Purple deck, and then what? How do you intend to deal with Amesh and the rest of them? Those men are genetically-bred killers."

There was a silence.

"All right. Some of us have been working together, so if you and Astrod will keep quiet for a little while, we'll take a report on progress so far."

Astrod colored. There were appreciative murmurs behind her.

"Sony Chung," Adelaide said in introduction.

Sony was in her mid-twenties, a slight woman with a merry face. She had a prepared statement in her hand.

"Report on Crossbow and Slingshot Project," she said.

Astrod's jaw fell open.

"We have tested three models of easily-made crossbows, assembled from reworked support rods taken out of the ventilation ducts. We have found that the second of our designs worked best, and copies of that design are being made now and will be available shortly for everyone who wants one."

Tobe grinned. Adelaide had walloped the opposition again.

Sony Chung went on to describe ways of manufacturing slingshots from strips of elastic floor matting, plus methods of making bolts for the same from corner protectors on small doors and hatches in the public-access areas of the Seat decks.

The meeting concluded with a vote of thanks for Sony Chung, Adelaide, and Berlisher. A subcommittee was organized to prepare lists of volunteer fighters from the Seats.

It was determined that they would concentrate their plan on just seizing the Khalifi control center, which in effect was Ibrahim's private suite.

The meeting broke up in a buzz, and they filed out to the corridor.

They were confronted there by Fogo and a gang of his fellow Seat bosses carrying Khalifi-issued shock batons.

The scene dissolved into chaos punctuated with the hot zaps from the batons and screams of pain.

Tobe used his briefcase as a weapon and a shield, taking several thwacks from the batons as he tried to protect Adelaide.

"Don't crowd me, Tobe," she said as she seized the outstretched hand of one of the thugs and swung herself into him with her knee up.

He went down with a gasp. Tobe held off another attacker, his briefcase zinging under the lash of the shock baton.

Adelaide had the fallen thug's baton. She stuck it in the face of a squat fellow who was yanking Astrod Benenki's hair while crushing her to the decking with his foot.

Then she was swatted on the shoulder herself and knocked off her feet. Tobe slammed her assailant over the head with the briefcase and pulled her up.

"Come on," he croaked. "This way."

They ran back down the corridor; more thugs were coming. Outside the door, they passed Kasok's unconscious form, then they were around the corner, and the sounds of screams and blows, and the hot zapping of the batons, receded.

18

IN TOTAL DARKNESS A SPACE-SUITED FIGURE DRIFTED DOWN airless corridors in the no-grav section to a dead end with blank walls. Small suit lights on the chest and helmet turned up and picked out a graphic in Fundan design code on the end wall.

Hands in clumsy gauntlets broke out the thigh pack and removed a small mechanics platform with delicate robot arms at either end.

A jack from a wrist outlet plugged into the oblong platform's interface. The arms activated, tools were removed from the platform's magnetic enclosures.

A wall panel was pried open. Cutters clipped through fasteners. The panel was peeled back, exposing a hole in an interior cavity.

The figure disappeared headfirst into the gap and emerged inside a hangar for shuttle ships.

It approached one of the shuttles. Again the platform was put to use and a maintenance port on the shuttle's upper side was opened.

The robot arms sliced open the seals, cut the fasteners, and tugged out the ship's backup microcomputer. The figure in the dark connected the computer to a power pack it wore on the other thigh. The Fundan logo lit up bright blue.

Satisfied that the unit was working, the figure in the suit

placed the microcomputer inside a carrying case. Then it re-sealed the maintenance port.

The figure drifted back down the corridor, pushing the carrying case ahead. It reached the high intersection, turned, and vanished into the darkness.

On the Purple level, in his lavish suite, Ibrahim Khalifi held a restricted majlis. Only the High Brothers, Merzik, Faruk, and Feisal, had been invited to attend. All their advisors, even Prince Ras Order, were left waiting in the outer chamber.

These men, with an average age of 111 in terrestrial standard years, now sat in a semicircle around a Fundan Made view screen of standard type.

Ibrahim was showing them some amusing video clips of the fighting outside the meeting of the Committee for the Rebellion.

On the screen Fogo and his thugs were clubbing screaming people with their shock batons.

Faruk bellowed with laughter at the sight of a fat woman rolling back and forth on the floor while several men beat her with the batons.

Feisal and Ibrahim giggled. Even Merzik's wintry countenance cracked open in a brief smile. The woman's pale, jelly-like face was perfectly hilarious in close-up as she wailed to a rhythm of hot zapping.

"These infidels think they can conspire against us with complete impunity?" Feisal said, with a snort of contempt.

"We have been too gentle with them," Merzik grumbled. "From the start we should have ridden them hard, to wind them, to break them, to show them we are the masters." Merzik slapped his fist into his palm for emphasis.

Ibrahim sighed. "If we had ridden too hard, they would have risen against us long ago."

Merzik chuckled, looked to Feisal and Faruk with baleful eyes.

"They could have tried. I would have crushed them."

Ibrahim smiled. "We would have had no end of trouble. But now we are in almost the perfect situation."

"Bah, what do you mean?" Merzik's brows furrowed.

"I mean that once we are in orbit about the New World, we will have the maximum leverage on the passengers. We will control their access to the planetary surface, and that planet will be very close by, so close that they will be unable to resist the urge to set foot there."

"There is much wisdom in what Ibrahim says," Faruk murmured.

"Yes," Feisal said. "I agree. Merzik, you forget how easily a man may be broken in negotiations when what he wants is too close and too important to him."

"They will be like horses impatient to reach water they can smell."

"Willingly they will accept the positions we offer them. Willingly they will work for us."

"They will chafe at the bit, they will give us nothing but trouble."

"But Merzik," Feisal said, "we need them. We need the scientists and the engineers. We need willing laborers. You aren't suggesting that we do everything ourselves?"

"Feisal is right, we must maintain a relationship with at least half of the passengers, we need that many for a viable colony."

Merzik grunted, unhappy with this. "I still say we should arrest all these troublemakers and put them out the airlock."

Ibrahim raised his hands in horror. "Merzik! Please. Why waste these people? They are a precious resource."

"We do not need them! We can take the women and breed better people, anyway. We do not need a lot of infidels with western genes. Or Japanese! You wish to live with those monkeys!"

"Merzik, aren't we being a little too, ah, parochial about this?" Faruk murmured.

Feisal tittered. Merzik threw them a thunderous glance.

"You would let your daughters rut with such creatures?"

Faruk rolled his eyes. "No, of course not, but—"

"I demand that the only males we allow to the surface be castrates, except for our own selected breeders."

Feisal sniggered again, and apologized. "I'm sorry, Merzik, but that's not an idea we should publicize any too soon, eh? What do you say? Eh?"

Faruk laughed out loud.

Merzik glared back at them from lowered brows.

"It's not funny, you fools!"

"We cannot exist alone, Merzik," Ibrahim said in a reasonable tone. "What would you have us become, a people of inbred half-wits and freaks?"

"We can vary the genemix in the laboratory. We have little need for out-family breeders. We certainly don't need rogue males let loose among our women like stallions in a herd of willing mares."

Faruk guffawed once more. "Merzik, what are you afraid of? I didn't think anyone as old as yourself could care about the pleasures of women. Is there something you haven't been telling us? You have found a way to put a charge back in your balls?"

"You insult me!" As always, prickly Merzik was at odds with the more cheerful Faruk.

"Now, my brothers." Ibrahim spread his hands between them. "We are too old for duels, and too valuable. Without us, nothing would get done."

On this the four High Brothers could agree, if on little else. Feisal nodded sagely and added. "If it had been left to anyone else, we'd still be in the old system."

Faruk and Merzik had subsided to mutual glaring. Then Faruk gave an amused snort.

"But really, my brothers, the idea of the infidels lusting after our women is ludicrous. Think of Aunt Rekshiba, who would want that?"

"I would rather fuck my goats than Aunt Rekshiba," Feisal said with a giggle.

Ibrahim was not about to smile. Ibrahim was always careful with his brother's dignity. Merzik's face expressed his disgust.

"We have other problems," he growled.

"Yes, indeed, we do." Ibrahim grew serious once more.

"The G.B. filth is aboard," Merzik said.

"Is this true?" Feisal said with eyes widened in alarm.

"It was," Ibrahim said. "We thought that one had been planted in the maintenance squad, and we dug that one out at flight initiation. Under the surgery we got some clues to individuals placed higher up in our organization. Those we took care of shortly afterward."

"You promised the most rigorous search!" Faruk exclaimed.

"The G.B.s are subtle, as you know." Ibrahim paused, clearly unhappy. "Alas, we found another, this time a shuttle pilot. He has been probed. We think he is the last."

"Ach, we are undone." Feisal shrugged in despair.

Ibrahim waved a hand to calm them.

"No, not nearly that bad."

"What about in the Seats?" Merzik snapped.

"We screened the Seats. They were easy to screen because they had full and detailed records. It is from the lower economic groups, the scientists, that we face danger."

"I still think we should have done without them," Merzik groused.

"My brother, how many physicists are there in our family? How many engineers or construction experts? You know as well as I that we must have these people if we are to build our New World."

"Back in the home system we did not have to entrust our family's fate to such genetic filth."

"We could not remain in the home system and retain our independence. The World Government made that crystal clear. You saw the intelligence I received from Edward Fundan."

Merzik shrugged. "Yes," he conceded.

"Which is why you decided to join me on this voyage in the first place, I believe."

Merzik sighed unhappily.

"Anyway, as to the problem of the would-be rebels, here is what I think we should do." Ibrahim drew them in with a gesture to his screen.

19

THE NEW PRIMARY WAS A YELLOW G5 STAR. SEVEN PLANETS, none larger than Neptune, made up the system. It was the third of these planets that the *Founder* approached.

Miraculous blue oceans, a single brown continent, entranced everyone aboard the great ship.

Now the shuttles unshipped and the ground-break teams dropped to the surface.

In the Seats and Cabins the Committee for the Rebellion met again and again, to little effect.

Events were slipping out of control. The Khalifi had postponed any discussion of a timetable for the disembarkation of the passengers.

In addition the Khalifi had put a block on all information coming out of the ground break teams. All they released was monotonous video of the massive trees that covered the New World's single, enormous continent.

To many in the Seats it was beginning to look as if the worst fears concerning the Khalifi were coming horribly true.

The Committee had few weapons, and fewer opportunities of using them. The Khalifi were locked away on their interior deck, and their guards had control of the ship's facilities.

The Green-deck gang had a plan of their own, but they refused to share information now with the committee. At the meetings there were endless debates on the morality of Green-deck "splitters."

Adelaide tried to maneuver as best she might. Somehow they had to hold on to the peace, and if they couldn't do that, then they had to be at least partly armed, otherwise they didn't stand a chance.

What weapons were available to her, Adelaide put to use.

And so a work group was assembling crossbows and bolts in one secure cabin. A chemistry group was making super elastic for bowstrings in another.

And elsewhere another kind of weapon was at work.

In a tastefully decorated cabin on the science section of the Purple level, a young woman with a matronly figure and shoulder-length dark hair made love to the elderly Administrative Coordinator for the science-service ground-exploration projects. Afterward she cradled him to her breasts and listened solicitously to his stories about his work.

Hideo Tagomi had many complaints.

Melissa Fundan had done many things for the family cause, but she had never done anything that made her feel as strange as this cold-eyed seduction of an old man.

If old Hideo hadn't been one of the most diffident men alive, in the sexual sense, she doubted that she could have done it at all.

But by persistence she had gained access to a wealth of secrets. Along the way she had even consolidated a position as one of his advisors, with an access card to the science section of Purple level.

Her intelligence reports had been gratefully received by Adelaide and Tobe. Through her they had learned of the first moves in the Khalifi betrayal of all their hopes when shuttles had been commandeered by the Khalifi princelings.

Hideo complained long and loud about this practice. On one occasion he was particularly incensed.

"They are more bold than ever!" He sat up, agitated, eyes wild. "I can hardly get a shuttle free for ground-break resupply. I have a team on the north coast that is two days overdue for pickup. They are running out of food."

"What can be done?"

"I am at my wits' end, I tell you. I have complained until I am blue in the face, and they pay no heed."

"Did you try calling on Prince Ras Order?"

Hideo closed his eyes and clenched his fists.

Melissa cuddled him to her again, her hands stroking his neck and shoulders.

"You're tense again. These neck muscles are going to be agonizing if you don't let me relax you."

"I have called the Prince. It is so humiliating to have to deal with them, they are so arrogant!"

"What did he say?"

"Oh, the usual things, says he'll bring the matter up in the next majlis. But that may be days from now, and besides, Ibrahim himself is guilty! He commandeered a shuttle for his agents to examine the site of his planned palace."

Melissa remembered the Prince very well, in part for his attempts to get her into his bed.

Hideo was still tense, shivering with the efforts of repressing something. There was more, something worse, she knew the signs by now.

She began to massage his back, deftly working on the connections of the neck muscles to the shoulder blades, where he always had the worst pain.

"You're all in knots back here, you poor thing."

Hideo could not hold it in any longer.

"They are the worst people I have ever had to deal with. Never in my life did I imagine I would experience anything like this."

"I understand."

"I told Ras Order that it is vital for the morale of the science service that he take care of this. If they don't stop it, soon the word will get out and I don't know what we'll do."

"But the word has got out."

Hideo hesitated, as she'd known he would, and then slowly, bitterly, shook his head.

"No it hasn't. The damned Khalifi are running shuttles now for their goddamn hunting expeditions!"

Melissa paled. "That is forbidden, surely, in the ship covenant?"

"Of course, of course, but I tell you I have seen it with my own eyes. Tariq Khalifi himself, with some of his friends, took a shuttle to the surface for about eight hours. When they came back they brought dozens of dead animals that they wanted irradiated in the laboratory. To kill microorganisms. I said no, of course, and they went storming off to bully Wa Ching, and he let them do it."

"That is terrible," Melissa murmured while the wheels of her mind spun fast.

Tariq Khalifi was aboard. A well-kept secret, then. And a terrifying thought. After all that Ibrahim had said about Tariq, and the promises that Tariq would be left behind in the Uranus system, he had lied. The truth was, Tariq was one of them, they could not leave him behind against his wishes.

"I saw the animals, dozens of them, many species, alien animals, some large, some small. All had been shot, some many times. I was made unwell. Felt colossal loss of face, had to go to the toilet to be sick. It was horrible, horrible."

She petted Hideo down again and relaxed him to the point where he finally dozed off.

Satisfied that he was asleep, she rose and showered, then dressed and left.

She rode the elevator to the Cabin deck and went immediately to Adelaide's cabin. She found that it had been torn apart again in the constant search for listening devices. There were fresh holes in the walls, more bulky scramblers were stacked in the corners. The light fixtures were out, dangling on their retainers. Adelaide and Tobe were busy analyzing screen data.

The news from Hideo was received with grim faces.

"Ibrahim lied to us about even that," Adelaide muttered.

"Poor Dane," said Melissa. "This desecrates his memory."

"Yes," Adelaide sighed, and hugged herself. "It also means

that the Khalifi are probably going to attempt to lock us all out. It's just as the pessimists predicted, the Khalifi really intend to ignore the ship's covenant. They're going to grab the New World."

"How can we stop them?"

"I don't know, I'm afraid to bring this information to the committee."

"There'd be an explosion," Tobe Berlisher said. "We have to sit on this for as long as we can."

"But won't they find out eventually? I mean, Hideo was not the only person in the science section who saw this. This news will spread, and when it does . . ." She spread her hands.

"It will confirm the worst fears. The Seats will explode in rebellion." Adelaide sounded dispirited.

"All our work will be wasted, the Seats will riot and the Khalifi will feel justified in doing their worst."

Melissa pressed her hands together.

"We have to go to the end-game maneuver we discussed."

They paused; this was their ace in the hole.

Adelaide nodded. "If we do, we have to succeed. We won't get a second shot."

"I have examined the designs of that section. I'm sure I can handle the circuitry work, and if anything comes up, well, I'll have Hideo along. Hideo understands the workings of those systems very well."

Before parting, they held hands together. "Be careful," Adelaide said.

When she got out of the security elevator that connected to the science section, she checked for Hideo's whereabouts on the section monitors and found he was at a meeting of ground-break supervisors in the Admin Center.

She headed for Hideo's office, which was just down the hall from the center.

Along the way she glimpsed a line of figures at the jungle suits of a ground-break team. One figure at the end of the line caught her eye for some reason, and she looked again, but it was gone.

20

GROUND TEAM 8 DROPPED FREE OF THE SHIP ABOUT FIVE hours late. The long wait had done nothing for their nerves. They watched the world below grow closer with tight eyes and dry mouths.

Headed up by a thirty-five-year-old field scientist named Flecker, the team consisted of six scientists and four "breakers."

Randolf Flecker had been in the *Founder* science program for many years, having joined as a young man right out of university. He hoped his team would perform well, although he had misgivings about some members, like Im Sohn, the dainty little ecologist, and Trudi Guvek, the overweight entomologist.

There was also the new man in the breaker team, Strang. Breaker Daichuk broke a foot in final training. Strang was the replacement, and Trask was given point. Strang was a man of very few words, a tall, gloomy fellow with dirty-blond hair and the looks of one of those old Noram spacer families.

Flecker put him down in his own mind as a Khalifi plant. There had to be at least one of them on the team, and Strang might well be a Smits man. The Smits and their band of families in the High Vaal Free State had worked for the Khalifi for centuries. They looked like this, too, blue eyes, blond hair, tight faces with harsh planes.

If that was the case, then it looked as if he was not just a plant. Strang most certainly had orders to kill anyone who might cause trouble or spread sedition.

Further speculations on Flecker's part were cut off just then, as the shuttle rammed into the first atmospheric turbulence and Flecker, like everyone else, was tossed up into the webbing, grabbing instinctively for the rails.

"Hang on everyone," whispered the voice of Shekushib the pilot. "Gonna be rough for a little while."

Static howled on the commo and things jumped around as they hit another rough spot. Im Sohn gave a little shriek. Tarf Asp, the soil specialist, bellowed in fear. Then something in the rear gave a heavy thud, and abruptly they hit a calmer region and everyone got their breath back.

The turbulence continued, but at a less jolting level. Flecker turned his thoughts forward to the mission ahead of them.

They were to land at a coastal site, unload their equipment and supplies, and then set up base camp. From there they were to negotiate a way through twenty-five kilometers of the alien jungles to a high point from which they were to survey the region.

On the face of it the mission seemed simple. But Flecker knew enough now about the New World to have grave misgivings.

Right from the start there'd been problems for every ground-break mission. The terrain was uniformly described as "difficult." But getting around proved to be the least of it.

Ground Team 2 had taken the first casualties when two members were killed and partially eaten by carnivorous animals that resembled outsized terrestrial baboons. Since then everyone had carried weapons.

Then Ground Team 3 had died en masse, killed by a horrible fungal disease contracted while exploring an inland swamp.

After this horror every team had worn breathing filters and taken daily boosters of a potent antifungal drug.

Subsequently, Ground Team 5 had been attacked by predacious insects of a species that built enormous nest structures on the forest floor. These insects were now regarded as a major hazard.

All in all, the New World was getting an evil image among the ground teams.

The sheer physical dimensions of the place were also intimidating. Ground Team 7 had crossed a river that was ninety kilometers wide, at a point more than two thousand kilometers from its mouth. This river was the size of the Earth's Amazon, and there were sixteen other rivers that were similar in scale.

Ground Team 6 had dropped into the equatorial mountain range. They'd quickly confirmed the astonishing beauty of the terrain. Enormous mountains that topped 55,000 feet clawed the sky all around them. Amongst these mountains they found occasional high river valleys, along the bottoms of which grew forests of small trees with leaves so dark they were almost black.

Now a major reconnaissance of the coastal regions was to be undertaken. Teams 8, 9, and 10 were dropping to three selected sites on the southern coast of the belt continent. They were to be followed soon by further teams who would set up the first permanent camps.

Team 8 was assigned to explore a promising region on the eastern side of the vast delta of Team 7's Nova Amazon. After landing on a sandy promontory, they would move inland to the top of Prominence 46, which had been measured as reaching a height of two hundred meters.

The good news for Team 8 was that the fungal disease was reportedly absent from coastal regions. And the landing site itself was free of the dominant megaflora that seemed to cover just about every other square centimeter of the land space and made landings hellishly difficult.

Despite these reassuring reports, everyone had equipped themselves with full breathing gear and filters. Nobody wanted to follow Team 3 in succumbing to the entomogenic fungus.

. . . turning into a sodden heap of mushrooms.

The shuttle was turning again. There was a sudden chorus of "aahs" in the cabin. Flecker glanced up at the big view screen at the front of the passenger cabin.

They were down below the clouds now. In the distance was a large smudge of dark green. Beneath them glittered the enormous southern ocean, with crests of white sparkling along the wave tops.

A lump rose in every throat. This was it, this was the New World.

All at once they were struck by the awesome mass of it. Whatever else was true about this place, it was absolutely not human-made. This was a world, not a habitat. To lifelong spacers this was a strange sensation; "planet sense," it'd been called. It was slightly overwhelming, even frightening. They were left dazed, faces slack, eyes staring.

The shuttle arrowed down, braking on tertiary chutes, swinging in toward that heavy smudge of land.

Now they could make out a coastline. Rocks flecked with

foam passed below, extensive sandy beaches became visible.

A jungle of green arose beyond that and stretched away into the distance on all sides but one.

In that direction the green was slashed by the mouth of the river. Dotted across the waters was a necklace of sandy isles that pointed to a jut from a far headland that extended toward them.

"A single continent, so fascinating," Im Sohn commented aloud.

"So fascinating it's driving the plate tectonics people crazy," old Tarf Asp replied. "They've been trying to model the processes for months, and they're not getting anywhere."

"I can't see the problem. The New World isn't Earth, why expect it to be exactly the same?" Flecker said.

"Still haven't been able to model it."

"It's like a belt buckled around the planet at the equator," Im Sohn said.

"Perhaps it's because there are two moons," Guvek, the plump entomologist, said.

"Sure there's two moons, but there's still less mass out there than Luna. Nobody's come up with enough tidal energy to affect continental drift to the necessary extent," Tarf Asp grumbled.

"Well, it's certainly beautiful to look at," Im Sohn said brightly, "whatever the problem of the computer modeling."

"It's beautiful from up here," groused Trask, the point man on the breakers' drop team, "but I bet it's gonna stink down there."

"It's ninety-five degrees Fahrenheit down there, people," said Guvek, who was sweating at the mere idea of it.

"The humidity is gonna be awful high too," Im Sohn said. "At least ninety percent in our target region."

"Just as they warned us," Tarf Asp groaned.

Ahead was the peninsula, a ribbon of sand, vegetation growing down the spine. Beyond it loomed the headland, beyond that another headland, and beyond that more.

To their left stretched a great sea of green vegetation. To their right the ocean occupied everything to the horizon.

The shuttle approached the shoreline and hovered over the sands of the peninsula until the computer calculated the best of the available sites. Then it rode down on the vertical booster and sent a booming challenge thundering across the tree tops.

When the thrusters cut off at last, the stolid mass of the jungle hurled the sound back in muffled echoes for a while and then a great silence fell upon the world.

Small fires were crackling in the undergrowth nearby, and thin plumes of smoke whirled up and blew away.

The whine of the shuttle's airlocks began. Steps were run forward with a crash, and the breakers hit the dirt in a star pattern around the ship. Each man wore a lightweight one-piece of tough spylo and carried a sixty-caliber assault rifle capable of firing either explosive or piercer loads. In addition, each wore webbing for grenades, flashes, and flares.

They faced out onto a peaceful scene. The air was warm and sticky. The river flats were a stretch of deserted gray muck, and at low tide, under the hot sun, they stank. The burning vegetation stank too.

"Hey Trask, you were right," yelled a hefty breaker named Bosun. "It does stink."

Across a quarter-mile stretch of slate-colored lagoon was the nearest forest. Shaggy green titans thrust up two hundred meters or more into the sky. Beyond them were others even mightier.

"Would you look at those things," Trask muttered.

Everyone stared. The trees were incomprehensibly huge. They raised shaggy canopy to the heights of large office buildings.

"Never saw anything like that before," Tarf Asp said.

Flecker licked his lips. There was something ominous in this landscape. He shook his head. Nothing in his experience was preparation enough for this. He felt dwarfed by these monstrous plants, which appeared like an army of occupation from some outlandish empire of the vegetative.

With a whine the cargo doors cracked open, and soon the scientists brought the ground vehicles down from the belly of the shuttle. The vehicles were ATVs with eight-hundred-horsepower hydrogen-burner engines atop giant "ground gobbler" tires. They carried five passengers plus their water and supplies.

While the techs, Kuiper and Greer, inspected the ATVs, the scientists started unloading supplies.

Flecker circled the perimeter of the position. No one had anything to report yet except some flying insects and a couple of things that might have been birds about a kilometer off-shore on the ocean side.

Up the sand spit the vegetation thickened into a forest of the small trees with green-black leaves.

On the ocean side great combers beat upon the shore and a salt spray rose to tinge the warm air. An offshore wind gave some relief from the sun's heat, but everyone was already feeling uncomfortably hot and sticky in their suits.

Flecker paused beside Corporal Bentri, the commander of the breaker squad.

"Ninety-seven degrees Fahrenheit, just like they predicted," Bentri said.

"What's the humidity again?" Flecker said.

"Ninety-one percent."

"No wonder it feels so disgusting."

"Get used to it, this is home now."

"Yeah, right. Soon as we put up a dome."

"Hey!" came a shout on their right, toward the ocean.

They looked up in time to see something long and brown break the surface of the water and come down with a loud slap.

"Time to go fishing!" Bosun chortled.

The scientists were soon grumbling as the physical labor set the sweat running down the inside of their brown spylo one-pieces. Especially uncomfortable were the breathing masks.

The scientists were supposed to do their own grunt work at this juncture. None were happy about this. Tarf Asp dropped out after his second trip down the ramp underneath one of the white crates of food. Geologist Hundu sat down shortly after and refused to continue. Flecker was forced to take his place, and he was soon bathed in sweat from the effort.

Eventually they were done. The scientists collapsed in the shade cast by the shuttle and guzzled water from their flasks.

"It's too damn hot for this kind of work," said Trudi Guvek, who was already squishing in her boots.

"I agree completely," Im Sohn said, "too damn hot."

"Get used to it, ladies, this is the New World," Tarf Asp said.

The shuttle crew, cool and collected in their space whites, emerged from the air-conditioned interior of the ship to get the receipt signed by Flecker.

"Everything looks fine from our side," Shekushib said.

"Perhaps a little warm," Norgil, the subpilot, said.

"Yeah," Flecker said, "I'll bet." He thumbed the contract and gave the recorder back to Shekushib.

"Okay, so now can you move your stuff out of the way please?" she said.

"What?" Flecker said. "We only just finished moving it."

"So you'd better move it again, then, because we're going to raise this bird in twenty minutes."

"That's the launch window," Norgil said with a blank face. Flecker looked to the scientists.

The scientists were unhappy. Their equipment, their tents, their food and water, it all had to be moved again. The ATVs had to be loaded and driven. It was ninety-seven degrees Fahrenheit and very humid.

"Hey, get some of the damned breakers to help, why don't you? That's a lot of stuff we got here," Guvek called.

Corporal Bentri heard that. "Hey, you were briefed, like everyone else. On first landing breakers are to stand in readiness while science staff make sure supplies and equipment are cached and made operational."

"To hell with you, Bentri," Guvek snapped. "What is this, we going by the rule book now?"

"So what are you suggesting? You want my breakers to be loading stuff instead of standing guard and protecting you?"

"Come off it, Bentri, we're perfectly safe here, anyone can see that."

"Hey, while you people are arguing, my time is wasting," Shekushib snapped. "We have orbital liftoff in nineteen minutes, so you'd better not be around here, or you're gonna be a lot hotter than you are now, okay?"

Pilot Shekushib stumped back up the ramp to the airlock.

"They wouldn't do that, would they?" Bosun said.

"You wanna risk it? All pilots are crazy, don't you know that?"

"Come on, Guvek, get it moving!" Flecker said.

With much complaint the scientists got to their feet and began humping the equipment and food supplies.

The ATV engines started up again with a roar when all was loaded. Trask drove the A vehicle, with Flecker beside him and Bosun and Kuiper in back.

They'd only gone about three kloms landward along the

sand spit when the ground shook as the shuttle's main jets ignited and the ship rose up on pillars of fire, tilted, and then fired main boosters. A cloud of hot exhaust roared across the sullen waters of the lagoon and the shuttle headed skyward.

The ATVs rumbled on, into the alien thickets.

21

GROUND TEAM 8 HAD A LONG, HOT DAY OF IT BEFORE THEY finally reached the almost invisible slopes of Prominence 46.

Working around the huge roots, which had an average thickness of ten meters, was an obscenely difficult job. The ATVs whined and groaned all day as they climbed over the lesser roots and crashed down again into the pits between. For every kilometer's worth of progress on the map, they covered six in detours.

Fortunately, the ATVs virtually drove themselves, since everyone inside was too busy concentrating on just staying in their seats to be able to control a moving vehicle.

Flecker had been forced to abandon the mission's predetermined schedule. It was absurdly optimistic, thought up by blue-eyed Fundan engineers who had never set foot on a planet.

Flecker was now simply praying that the ATVs would hold together long enough for them to get to Prominence 46 at all. The gearbox on the third car was making ominous noises.

By this time Flecker was also riding with a thick coat of slime covering him from the chest down. At an early river crossing he'd stepped out of the ATV to see why it was getting bogged down in the shallows of the stream. He had promptly sunk into quicksand up to his waist.

Flecker had tried to shrug it off—it was muck, and muck was what you had to expect if you were a field scientist. But it was peculiarly pungent muck, and it took a long time to dry in the damp, humid conditions. And after a while it was another miserable source of irritation in what ought to have been a wonderful day, his first day in the alien forest.

Just when he thought he was getting seriously depressed, they had their first brush with the much discussed social insect.

Driving into a rare open space between the roots of giant trees, they were halted by a radial arrangement of fins made of dried mud five meters high.

Unwittingly they had driven right onto the roof of one of the gigantic nests.

Almost immediately three-inch-long soldiers with black bodies and scarlet abdomens were climbing all over the ATVs and running in the windows with an audible clatter of oversized mandibles.

In the subsequent panic, Flecker had suffered a nasty bite. On Earth he'd been exposed to Virginia hornets, and even the hideous stings of Paraponera clavata, the giant ant of Central America, but neither of those stinging insects had the power of these alien soldiers.

Flecker was relatively fortunate too. Many were in much worse shape. Those in the second car had suffered the worst, because of poor, hapless Guvek. She'd rolled down a window and leaned out with a collection net in an effort to capture some specimens.

Guvek had readied her net, earnestly swished it down. Then she'd let out a piercing shriek and dropped the net as if it were red hot. She stabbed the window control with urgent gestures. Unfortunately, it was too late.

Confusion broke out in the car, which sped off, veered wildly around a root, and crashed into a patch of enormous fungi. Screams emerged from it, and then it raced off again away from the nest.

It took almost an hour before they'd killed every last insect in Guvek's ATV. These bugs were wary and very tough, their bodies encased in thick plates of chitin. They had to be hammered hard with boot or gauntlet to be sure. And one wanted to be very sure, because their bites were like sudden, hot needles, and they could bite through any single layer of spylo.

Guvek's preference for a lightweight one-piece had completed her undoing. It took them another thirty minutes just to calm her down, bandage her up, and put her back in her seat.

She was already beginning to puff up in the most alarming fashion.

Eventually, after everyone else had been given shots of antivenin, they'd moved on.

They stopped again for lunch. A brief affair of sandwiches eaten hurriedly, inside the ATVs.

Then they'd slogged slowly ahead to reach Prominence 46, from which they were supposed to get a view of the entire estuarian region.

When the computer finally informed Flecker that they were at the top, he pulled over and stopped the lead ATV. He clambered out, favoring his right arm, where the sting had ballooned up.

The other cars ground to a halt; people got out.

Flecker felt a peculiar sense of helplessness for a moment.

There was nothing about the spot that suggested they were on top of a hill. The huge trees grew right up the slopes. All around them rose the same mighty trunks, spaced about two hundred meters apart. Above was a vault of leaves, from which the afternoon light filtered down in tones of dim, mud green.

A tangle of vines and pale pink megafungi grew in thick patches on the forest floor.

Past the nearest trees rose other huge trunks, and beyond them more, and beyond them more of the same.

Flecker climbed out his side, Trask out the other.

"This is the hilltop, then?" Trask said in a bleak voice. "This is what we came all this way to see?"

"The computer says this is the top of Prominence 46."

Trask looked upward with gloom-filled eyes.

"So now we have to climb a tree if we want to see anything."

Flecker glanced up the length of the nearest tree, undaunted.

"Looks that way. We'll have to get out the climbing cradles. Shouldn't be that bad. I've used them before, just never on anything this big. Really, they're pretty easy once you get the hang of it. We should be up there in no time at all."

The breakers moved to unpack the climbing equipment lodged in the trunk of the lead ATV.

Poor Guvek's face was a brilliant red, her neck grotesquely swollen and puffed up.

"We mus' stop now, pitsh camp," she mumbled through swollen lips.

"We will," Flecker reassured her, "this is it, this is the top of Prominence 46."

"Good, mus' sleep now." Guvek was ready to fall over at any moment.

The order to pitch camp went out. The breakers pulled out the pop tents to inflate them and then pegged them in position. Wun and Strang set up the heat plates, and Bosun got some water boiling.

Flecker and Trask strode up to the nearest tree and examined the problem.

Im Sohn joined them. She, too, sported a shiny red blister on her cheek.

"This is too bizarre, I do not understand."

Flecker was preparing to fire the rocket-propelled line lifter into the tree canopy above. He grimaced as he strained to lift a safety latch imposed on the line feed. "I don't know why you'd say that, it's just a completely alien ecosystem, and we've only been working on it for a few days."

Im Sohn did not smile, she seemed dazed. She muttered, "But that's not it, I mean."

"What do you mean?" Flecker said.

"Well, where are all the dead trees and the fallen trees and the saplings? Have you seen many?"

"A few, not many," he admitted with a shrug.

"How can that be? Any natural ecosystem must be an untidy place with a certain amount of dead material that's in the process of being returned to the soil. But here all the trees seem to be mature adults."

"Maybe these trees live a long time."

"But you'd see dead and dying ones, you'd see young ones, you'd see sick ones. It's as if someone culled out all the sick ones, all the dead ones."

Im Sohn gave a deep sigh. "And then there's the problem that everywhere we go there is just this one tree, a single species. This is nothing like any forest I've ever heard about. I mean, this is like some damn monoculture, a field of corn, or a rubber-tree plantation."

Flecker stared around at the enormous forest. The immensity of it was intimidating, spooky. It was almost as if these enormous trees were watching *them*.

He shivered a moment. "I don't know," he said. "It's not

the way I had imagined it, the videos didn't do it justice."

"Whole damn place is amazing. Drive all planet-sci people crazy," Im Sohn said.

Trask chuckled. "That ain't that hard, you know, they're already halfway there."

Im Sohn did not smile.

Flecker fired the line lifter and the bob went soaring upward and was lost in the green murk. It snagged there over a high branch. Flecker activated the automatic return feature and it extended clippers to cut itself loose and drop back to the ground, pulling the line over the branch.

To the line they attached a cord of tough spylo which was then pulled up and over the high branch. A climbing rope of reinforced spylo was then welded to the cord and hoisted aloft.

After a few snags they finally got a second rope over, tied to the first, and erected the first climbing cradle.

"Who's first?" said Trask, who clearly had no desire to be the one selected.

Flecker grinned. "I am."

With practiced ease he sat down in the seat and activated its power winch to haul the cradle up the rope. Attached to the bottom of the chair were three more lines.

In a minute or so he was just a moving dot high up in the canopy branches, with the lines playing out beneath him like bright red threads.

Eventually the communicator crackled with Flecker's voice.

"I'm on the branch here," he said. "It's about three meters in width. There are sub branches. I guess they're what you would call twigs, except they're a meter across. There's a low population of epiphytes and parasite plants, a few clusters of flowering things, but not enough to give you the impression this was a rain forest."

"Let's have some pictures," Im Sohn said.

Flecker got his videocam working and the ATV monitors lit up with a good view of the branch. Flecker dropped the weighted boblines over the far side and they dropped through the green.

He patrolled the length of the branch, pausing to lens plants and insects, of which there were a multitude.

Flying things the size of small birds whipped past the camera's eye like occasional colorful bullets.

"I've got an animal here," Flecker said suddenly. The camera caught a sinuous little fur bearer with bright green eyes and a wicked-looking mouth. It was in the process of devouring an insect. They watched it eat while it kept its eyes riveted on Flecker.

The jerking legs vanished into the animal's mouth at last, and then the creature washed its paws, giving Flecker and the camera one last glance before vanishing into the low, shrublike growths that grew along the median of the branch.

"Insectivore, I'd say. Size of a mink."

"How about a view of the surroundings, can you see through the canopy?"

Flecker grunted, then lifted the camera high and turned it 360 degrees. Trees, branches, leaves filled the view.

"I was afraid of that," Bentri said.

"We'll have to go farther up," Flecker said. "I'd say I'm in the lowest rung of the canopy here. Bring up the line gun and some coils of spylo."

Bentri, Kuiper, and Im Sohn rode up on climber cradles.

From Flecker's branch they spent a fruitless hour attempting to shoot a line over a branch set much higher in the canopy. But every shot fired sent the bob careening off the intervening branches. Twice it grew too tangled to retrieve and they had to cut it off and fire another.

They noticed that the sun had begun to set. In the high canopy long, golden beams of light were caroming through the branches. A cooling breeze blew in from the ocean.

Flecker was eventually forced to give up for the day. They were all exhausted anyway. In a sullen mood, he rode with the others to the ground.

There they found that dinner was warming on the heat plates, and soon the delicious smells of sizzling protein patties and toasted buns were wafting into the evening air.

Everyone except the stricken Guvek gathered around the cooking plates.

Bosun, Trask, and Kuiper were enjoying dinner. Strang was nowhere to be seen, and Wun was working on one of the ATVs.

"Not as easy as you thought, then?" Trask said with a sly little grin. Trask had been waiting for the uptight little forestry expert to run into trouble.

Flecker ignored him, munched his food. He was filthy, soaked in perspiration and mud.

"Tomorrow," he said. "We'll get to the top tomorrow."

"Oh, for sure," Trask murmured.

The others gave weary shakes of affirmation. Soon afterward they dispersed to their pop tents and sleep.

22

DUSK HAD FALLEN BY THE TIME THEY FINISHED THEIR EVENING meal. In the short tropical twilight there was a hush. Then a nighttime chorus of animal cries began. Not far away were some creatures with particularly loud voices, who wailed in uncanny imitation of men dying in agony.

The exhausted ground breakers were once more given notice that they were no longer in a sterile, human-made environment.

Eventually the creatures quietened and Team 8 sank into a welcome oblivion.

This relatively happy state of affairs lasted until the beginning of the third hour after dark.

A sudden outburst began in one of the tents. There was shrieking and bellowing. Blinking, with bleary eyes, people struggled to life. The shrieks redoubled in fury with every second.

Flecker jumped out of his tent with his pistol drawn, ready for anything.

And then a pop tent opposite him exploded as Bosun charged out the door, ripping the stops. He danced and wailed while beating at his body with both hands.

With a plangent wail, Im Sohn emerged from her tent. She thrashed and twisted with convulsive gestures.

There were gunshots, more screams, the whole camp in an uproar.

Trask appeared, naked but for his boots. "Damned bugs, all over the fucking place!" he screamed.

"Bugs." Flecker gaped and saw Strang was there, grim and silent.

Flecker felt something on his pants leg and brushed at it with an instinctive gesture. It was on his hand in a flash, and then a sting of excruciating power bit into his wrist.

With a curse he dislodged the thing. Then he saw dozens of them scurrying across the ground.

Without thinking, he opened fire and sent ricochets winnowing through the tents.

By a miracle, no one was hit.

Strang wrenched the gun out of his hand.

Cursing, screaming people had hurled themselves to the ground. Now they gave vent to loud complaints.

"Don't shoot!" Im Sohn screamed, dancing in place.

"Who the hell is that shooting?"

"Damned maniac, you can't shoot these things!"

"Shut up, let's see if we got casualties."

"No time," the normally silent Strang said. "Look." He swung his lights over the area where they'd prepared their meal. A boiling mass of the insects was at work.

Then the beam cut on into the darkness and revealed a moving multitude of small bodies. They were surrounded.

The rest of the pop tents began to collapse as the insects cut through the inflatable ribbing. As they went, the tents made spectacular firecracker bangs and whistles, which gave a counterpoint to the cries of human rage and pain.

Another soldier was running up Flecker's boot and he was forced to bat it away. He crushed another with his heel. More were coming, many, many more, excited to battle rage by the smell of their smashed fellows.

"What do we do?" Im Sohn screamed. Soldiers climbed on Guvek and she sprang suddenly to life and bounded away.

Flecker stared around him wildly. He did not know what to do. He was on the verge of mindless panic.

Im Sohn started screaming in a new timbre as soldiers got onto her bare legs.

Flecker swiped at the insects on her skin, but they were horribly quick and would try to cling to his hands, happy to bite anything that moved.

"Get into the ATVs," screamed Strang, who was yanking open the door on Number 1.

Bentri sprang to the door of Number 2 and they thrust the befuddled Guvek inside.

"Hurry!" Strang yelled. Flecker gaped for a second, then

113

sprang toward the nearest car. Strang was already inside, gunning the engine.

Tens of millions of the scurrying insects had arrived. The entire campsite was submerged in them.

"Look!" Im Sohn said, pointing in horror.

The tent with their supplies, all of their food, was completely invisible now.

"Get me the fuck out of here!" someone screamed.

Cursing, struggling, swatting at the demonic insects, they roared out of the camp and headed for the nearest open space between roots.

Strang sped a hundred meters away and then jammed on the brakes. They all stumbled out, still cursing and slapping.

The second ATV skidded to a halt beside them. Bentri and the others got out and repeated the process, slapping and stamping, cursing the while, with occasional shrieks of pain.

"Where's the others?" Flecker said suddenly.

They looked up. The third ATV had failed to appear.

"The gearbox!" Kuiper said in dismay.

"They didn't make it out!" Trask said.

"Who didn't make it out?" Guvek mumbled, her speech slurred by painkillers.

"Someone has to go back!" Im Sohn exclaimed. "We can't just leave them, they'll be killed!"

"What can we do?" Tarf Asp said.

Flecker stared back toward the ruins of the camp. Car Number 3's lights were on. Members of his team were trapped back there. Did that mean he had to go back and rescue them?

Flecker thought he would prefer not to. He stood rooted to the spot.

"The radio!" Strang said, breaking the spell. "Call them."

"Of course." Flecker came out of the daze and punched up his communicator.

"Three, come in, this is Flecker."

The response was immediate.

"What the hell kept you? The damn car won't start and the bugs are all over us."

"Did they get inside?"

"A few, damn you, hurry it up. They're eating away at everything that isn't made of metal."

"Right." Flecker was nonplussed. He looked up. Strang was close by, staring into his face.

"Hold on there while we try to work out a plan of action,"

114

Flecker said. His mouth felt dry, he was sweating freely.

"Hold on? Try? You'd better do better than that or we're dead."

Flecker dropped his commo.

"How the hell can we help them?" Bentri said.

"Can' go back," Guvek said. "What if we los' 'nother car?"

"Oh no, don't say that, we have to do something. We can't just let them die in there!" Im Sohn wailed.

"Sometimes you have to sacrifice a few to save the majority," Bentri said.

"True!" Trask said.

"But who are you to make the choice?" Im Sohn said shrilly.

"I made no choice. The third car was broken down, a twist of fate."

"Better try to call in a Rescue Squad," Bentri suggested.

"S'good idea," Guvek agreed.

"Meanwhile lets get the hell out of here, there might be more of those bugs," Trask said.

Flecker stared at them. They were making the decision for him.

Strang moved, slipping into the second ATV while no one was looking.

"Get out of the car," he told Guvek.

"Who're you orderin' around'?" she complained.

"You. There won't be room for you and the others. I'm going back to get them."

"Hey, wait a minute," Bentri said. "If you get stuck in there, we'll lose two ATVs instead of one."

Strang gave him a disgusted look.

"That's right," he said while he started the engine and put the car on manual. "So you'd better pray I make it out again. Call them back, tell them to wait until I give 'em the signal, and then tell them to make it damn quick."

Strang turned the ATV and sent it back into the camp at top speed.

The place was awash in insects. A soft roaring of insect movement filled the air.

ATV 3 was besieged. A swarm of workers gnawed on the tires and flexiseals around engine openings and the edges of the doors.

Strang jerked to a halt beside Number 3. In his lights he

glimpsed the terror-struck faces of the trapped men.

"Well, you finally came back for us!" exclaimed a voice on the radio.

"Let's keep our heads now or we may all die right here."

He opened the side doors on the count of four.

The other ATV's doors opened. The men jumped out and leaped for the open doors of Number 2.

They cannoned inside, scrabbling over one another in their haste.

With them came a dozen or more soldiers. Determined slapping and small screams of pain echoed inside.

The doors shut. Soldiers swarmed on the windshield. Strang hit the wipers and drove back out of the camp as fast as he dared.

He pulled to a halt beside Flecker and the others.

"The bugs got everything else."

"Yes." Flecker stared at him with something akin to awe in his eyes.

23

AFTER A HORRIBLE RIDE THROUGH THE NIGHT THEY REACHED the shore around dawn. Their calls to the *Founder* brought no immediate response, however. All shuttles were busy. They were to dig in and hold on and use their emergency-ration packs.

Conditions were terrible. The stings brought on fevers, and they had run out of antivenin. Most of them had lost their breathing masks and were at risk of catching the fungal disease.

The morning wore on. Biting flies were attracted to them and had to be fought off with insect spray, which was also running low.

"You know something," Trask said loudly. "They can take my share of the bloody New World. It ain't worth it."

"Yeah, Trask, we heard you," Bentri said.

"Yeah, shut up about it, Trask, we all got bites."

"Watch out, more of those damn flies."

"I am so hungry, I could eat anything, I think."

Strang emerged from ATV 1. "Shuttle coming in," he said. "I'm picking it up on the ATV nav-radar."

A shout of relief went up.

"Well, it's about goddamn time," Trask said.

Eventually a silvery point appeared in the sky. It swung out over the ocean and then curved back in to the peninsula.

The sight of the shuttle was enormously reassuring. Several of the breakers were on their feet cheering and waving. Then the retros cut in with a boom and the scene was hidden in steam and gas.

A few minutes later, when the last exhaust gas was blown clear, the shuttle's doors opened and ramps slid down to the ground.

The breakers jammed into the ATVs and drove slowly down to the shuttle, now parked on the beach.

Figures were in motion around the ramps. Men advanced to meet them. With shock they saw that these were Khalifi guard clones, who waved them to a halt with imperious gestures.

"Halt! Park the cars!" shouted one giant with a rifle in his hands.

"Hey, we got seriously wounded people here, what are you telling us?"

"You wait for next shuttle. This shuttle is Khalifi shuttle now."

And it was true, out of the shuttle came a group of men wearing jungle suits and Khalifi headdress. They jumped into ATVs and headed up the sand spit. They halted beside Team 8's pair of battered ATVs and two rather portly figures got out.

They sauntered over to Flecker's car window and pulled down their breathing masks.

"Officer," began the lead one, a fleshy-faced fellow with thick lips and closely set eyes, "what are the conditions inland? Have you spotted the game?"

"Game?" Flecker said in wonder.

"Yes, Officer, such as the baboonoid. We are especially fond of the baboonoids. Such courage they have, they will charge right onto the guns!"

"Really..." Flecker muttered, rendered almost speechless with anger. "No, we didn't."

"A pity, we are in need of some sport."

"How dare you do this!" Guvek said. "How dare you divert a shuttle like this! Don't you realize that we've been wounded! We need immediate medical attention!"

Not in the least fazed by her complaint, the Khalifi princeling rounded on her. "What is your name, woman?" he snapped.

The big guards moved closer. Somebody cocked his weapon with a click.

Guvek ducked back inside the ATV, the window rolled up.

The giant guards were aiming at the ATV's windows.

"Tariq!" the other Khalifi said. "Don't."

"But, my friend, why not? She is a troublemaker, it is quite clear. She should be eliminated, don't you think? And besides, it will encourage the others to behave themselves."

He scowled at the breakers standing around the first car. "Dogs, you are in the presence of your masters! Remember that!"

"Come on, Tariq, don't be so upset by them. We need them still. Come on, leave them, let's get to the hunting!"

The one addressed as Tariq whirled around with an inarticulate oath and stamped back to his own ATV.

Slowly the guards lifted their weapons and shifted back a few paces.

Flecker took a deep breath. In the back of the ATV Strang and Trask released the triggers on their own guns.

The door to the Khalifi ATV slammed and all three cars roared off in a cloud of dust.

Ground Team 8 went back to waiting for a relief shuttle.

Hours passed. The alien sun crawled to its zenith and then started down again and the day passed into afternoon.

Distantly they heard the sounds of gunfire, a few shots, then a fusillade.

After a few minutes it stopped altogether.

"Sounds like they got some action," Trask grunted.

Flecker stared off inland.

To recover any shred of pride, he had to face the Khalifi, here and now, and punish them for this abuse of the science service. But to do that meant accepting possible death.

He swallowed, his mouth dry. He didn't want to die. He

118

resolved to keep his complaints until later, until he somehow got back to the ship.

An hour or more later they heard the whine and sputter of the returning ATVs. Finally, in a cloud of dust, the hunters roared past with a number of dark, furred bodies tied over the roofs.

The Khalifi drew up beside the shuttle and posed for video recordings of their triumph.

Flecker observed the scene through binoculars.

Eventually the Princes tired of their triumph and rode up the ramps into the ship. The bodies of the fallen baboonoids were plastic-wrapped and stowed in the hold.

A few minutes later the shuttle's ramps retracted, the doors closed, and the engines ignited. The shuttle lifted off smoothly, swung away out to sea and began to climb and accelerate.

The members of Team 8 watched it go with bitter eyes.

The afternoon waned slowly, the sun sinking toward the western horizon. Team 8 suffered in moody silence.

At last another shuttle appeared, swung in, and came to a booming landing on the peninsula.

Wearily, with aching bodies, the breakers gathered themselves and trudged up the ramp.

24

LEILA KHALIFI RODE THE ELEVATOR DOWN TO THE CABINS THE day after the lifting of the "siege." She disguised herself as a prostitute in a sexily-cut suit of psuede with black high heels and fishnet stockings. The guards never gave her a second look.

They met in Adelaide's cabin as agreed, Leila, Adelaide, and Melissa.

Leila sensed a new maturity in the younger women. Without Dane to lead them, these two had taken charge of affairs themselves, and their experiences had caused them to grow. Leila had to admit she envied them.

Adelaide had recently intensified the security systems. Null-zone generators and senso baffles were all around the wall. In the center of the room they generated an area where sound and video surveillance was impossible. There they converged, standing in a circle.

"Good null zone here, Adelaide," Melissa said, after a check with her wrist unit.

"All my own work," Adelaide said. "Though, to be honest, Tobe helped a lot."

"You're sure we can't be overheard?" Leila said.

"This is as good a null zee as you're going to get." Melissa said. "Believe me, I've generated a few."

Leila raised an eyebrow. "Then what we say will be kept among us, alone."

Instinctively, Adelaide and Melissa exchanged a look. Did Leila mistrust them? They were Fundan, she was Khalifi, after all.

"Well . . ." Adelaide began.

"You need my help, is that it?"

Adelaide jumped right in. "Yes. We have to get an audience with Ibrahim. We have to start negotiations over the grievances of the Seats, or else . . ."

"The long-forecast rebellion will erupt?" Leila shrugged. "I'm afraid that's been anticipated for a very long time. I don't think Ibrahim is having too many anxious moments worrying about that little charade."

Adelaide and Melissa exchanged another glance. She was a Khalifi Princess, after all.

"But many people will die if there is a rebellion. We have to stop it," Adelaide said sweetly.

Leila nodded slowly. Had she begun to behave like the rest of her family?

"Yes, you're right, of course." She looked up, "What can I do?"

"Can you take us to Ras Order? We can talk with him. He always seemed like a sensible man."

"Yes, Ras is a sensible fellow, which is very unusual for my family, but you know all about my family, don't you? You've studied us for years."

Adelaide smiled weakly, struggled for a reply. "Well, yes, I suppose. Force of circumstances, really."

Leila managed a smile. "Not the most pleasant subject, I'm sure. And no doubt you know of my humiliation, my, uh, punishment for having lived with Dane."

Melissa felt her eyebrows rise without volition.

What had they done to the wayward Princess? With the Khalifi, anything was possible. Everyone knew horror tales of the barbarities imposed on Khalifi women.

"Oh yes, my dears, here I am, a Princess of the blood, and I have been given this miserable little suite in the harem quarter. You can't imagine what an insult that is! No one will see me, I am an outcast."

Melissa sniffed; well, it wasn't that bad.

"Well, perhaps we can imagine it," Adelaide said calmly.

Leila nodded. Perhaps they could. The Fundans had been brought low of late, it was true. They were not the haughty Fundan clan of old, which had lorded it over the Uranian system.

"Yes..." Leila paused, gathered herself. "Anyway, it's been ages since I last saw either of you."

She stopped, struggling with something, her eyes suddenly troubled.

"How is he? Dane, I mean."

Adelaide and Melissa exchanged a glance. Had she not heard?

"You mean you don't know?"

Leila shook her head. Adelaide swallowed, then told her.

"Dane got in a fight on Green deck with Khalifi-backed thugs. They killed him and threw his remains in the sump."

Leila went white. She raised a trembling hand to her lips. Tears started from her eyes.

It was obvious that Leila still loved Dane. And it was also clear that she was very out of touch, living in the soft cocoon of wealth on the Purple level.

"No, I didn't know," Leila said in a choked voice after a few moments. She sucked in a breath. "Excuse me, I hadn't expected that."

"I'm sorry," Adelaide said. "I thought you knew. It happened more than a year ago."

"No, I..." Leila felt a tear trickle down her cheek. There was a long, embarrassed moment of silence as she sobbed quietly.

"No one tells me anything, I'm afraid."

Leila herself was surprised that she still could be hurt by

121

Dane's demise. She had thought she'd forgotten him, just another man, another hopeless, ruined man.

Eventually she recovered enough to go on.

"My apologies, but you must understand that this has been a considerable shock to me."

"We understand," Adelaide replied. "I regret that we did not inform you at the time. We were not in touch back then, and I was sure you would have been told by someone else."

"Alas, I have very little connection with my old life. I am virtually a prisoner, and besides . . ." She paused, gray-faced. "I had given up hope that Dane could be saved. It had just gone too far."

She couldn't finish.

Again they waited out the silence. Leila finally spoke again.

"I'm sorry, we have little time, we should get on to other things. I will save my grief for later, when I am alone."

Adelaide eyed the woman. She had never fully understood her or the reasons she had been drawn to Dane Fundan, of all people. They were so dissimilar, almost always at cross purposes. But Adelaide had always been aware of the power of the love they shared; she'd seen that it was fierce, elemental. At the time, she'd been envious of it.

"All right, I will speak to Ras Order. But Ibrahim is another matter. Ibrahim sees very few people."

"He must hear us out! We can't allow a war to break out!"

"Ibrahim may not think it so important. He anticipates negotiating from a position of unassailable strength."

"Perhaps we can persuade him otherwise."

"I doubt that it is possible. However, if anyone can help you, it will be Ras Order."

Adelaide looked down at her hands.

"There is more?" Leila said.

"Yes," Melissa said. "We have little but rumors to go on, concerning Ibrahim's plans. Any real information would be helpful in our calculations."

Leila shrugged eloquently. "I imagine that I am the last person in the family that Ibrahim would confide in, but as to his intentions, I do not think they are hard to discern. The Khalifi will take possession of the New World."

"All of it?"

"Everything. Only the pliable, the sexy, the obedient, will be allowed down to the planetary surface."

"You're sure of this?"

"It is common knowledge, even where I am, in the harem quarter."

"Things are often known in the harem before anywhere else, I've heard," Melissa countered.

Leila turned toward her with a bitter smile. "That, my dear, is true of the classical harem, but the Khalifi brethren are long-lived these days, too old for sex, anyway; the harem trades only in low-level secrets. So if I know this, we can be sure it's general knowledge on the Purple level."

"What will they do with the rest of us?" Melissa said.

"My guess is that the ship will be maintained as an orbital prison. The unwanted will be kept here indefinitely."

"They are that confident in their ability to keep control?" Melissa said.

"Wouldn't you be? They have upward of fifty purpose-bred guards. These men are well-armed and well-versed in their weapons. By maintaining control of the hub, the brethren have you all in the palm of their collective hand."

"They can turn off the air whenever they want."

"Exactly." Leila gave Adelaide an appreciative glance.

Melissa held her tongue. There was a way, perhaps, and she and Adelaide had already mapped it out, but she would not speak of it here, not in front of a Khalifi.

"No," Leila continued, "it is hopeless. Your rebellion will be crushed, and then Ibrahim will have his excuse."

"Then it is even more important that we try and speak to Ibrahim and prevent this rebellion from taking place."

"I understand. We must try, there are many lives at stake."

Later, when Leila had left, Melissa turned to Adelaide. "It is time we looked at our final option," she said quietly.

Adelaide's face grew thoughtful. Did they have no other choice?

Melissa grew impatient, as was her way. "Come on, Adelaide, we can't hold off any longer. The Seats are gonna blow any moment now. They're bound to lose, and then it may be too late."

"Yes, all right, but it is a risk."

"We can't be afraid to fail, not now. I will go. Hideo will accompany me."

"You're sure of this."

"Hideo will do it. I will make him if I have to."

123

25

PRINCE RAS ORDER RECEIVED ADELAIDE IN A SMALL, DARK room at the rear of his suite. He had little to offer her, however.

"I understand your reasons for coming to see me, and I commend you, but I'm afraid that what you ask for is impossible."

"Why? I only want to talk with Ibrahim. Surely he can see the need for avoiding bloodshed!"

"Of course, Ibrahim is a humane ruler. But he is constrained by the wishes of his brothers. He cannot appear weak."

"Weak? By preventing considerable loss of life he will appear weak? I'm sorry, I'm just a Fundan, I don't understand that kind of thinking."

"It is Merzik's thinking. Merzik is of the old school, he emulates our most famous rulers in the past."

"Pirates, asteroid bandits? Your family's past is filled with evil deeds, grim treacheries."

Ras Order smiled again. "Well, perhaps some would see it that way, but in my family those were glorious times."

"But Merzik is only one voice. What about the others? What about Faruk and Feisal?"

"They are torn both ways, but each is beholden to powerful interests that cannot be represented at these meetings."

"Oh? And what might they be?"

"For Faruk it is his grandmother, Qalima. She thinks much like Merzik. In Feisal's case it is his wife and her mother. They own nearly a third of the Master Stock in the exploitation combine."

He saw her bafflement. "Yes, I know we have left the home system behind. But our family continues to organize its affairs through our traditional corporate structure."

"Exploitation combine . . ."

The words chilled Adelaide. The Khalifi did plan to steal the New World, just as Leila had said.

She sagged in her seat. "Then there's nothing we can do to stop it. And after a few hundred people have been killed, then what?"

Ras Order wore a troubled frown.

"I am afraid that Merzik has succeeded in imposing a harsh strategy as regards treatment of the passengers."

"What? What are you saying?"

"Well—" He hesitated, then brought forth a sound baffle, which he clicked on as he leaned across to whisper, "You might as well know the truth. Prepare yourself for the worst."

Adelaide trembled.

"The defeated passengers will be examined and a rigorous selection will be made. Only the most, ah, useful will be accepted as colonists for the New World."

"What about the rest?"

"They will remain in the Seats, indefinitely."

"And the rebels?"

"The most troublesome will be killed, the rest, well, they will serve out life sentences."

"You can't do this! These people gave up everything for the *Founder*."

Ras Order hushed her. "Believe me, my family can do this. They do not subscribe to your notions of civility."

Adelaide stared at him. The Prince regained his smile, raised his voice a little.

"For yourself, of course, I am sure that something can be arranged."

Adelaide continued to stare. The Prince tented his fingers under his chin.

"Perhaps if you will reconsider your response to my offer, I can find a place for you in my own household. That way you will be guaranteed a place on the New World."

Offer? What offer? Adelaide opened her mouth to ask, and then the memory crashed home. Ras Order suggesting that she accompany him to his bed for an interesting bout of hashish and sexual relations, during her first visit to the Khalifi habitat, years before. In what now seemed another life.

She swallowed, her throat suddenly dry and hard.

"I'm sorry, I cannot do that, I . . ." She was unable to finish.

Ras Order's dark eyes were hypnotic, compelling. Adelaide could only stare back at him like a wounded animal.

After a long moment the Prince spoke. "Believe me, I'm very sorry too."

He sounded perfectly genuine, which only made it more horrible.

She got to her feet unsteadily, and somehow—maneuvering by remote control, perhaps—made her way out of the Prince's suite.

She barely spoke when she got back to her cabin. Tobe looked up from the reports he was working on and found her crying by her bed.

Tobe went to her, put a tentative hand out to her shoulder.

"Adelaide, what happened?"

He could barely hear her response.

"She was right, Leila was right about everything she said."

Tobe paled. Adelaide broke into tears again and suddenly reached out to Tobe with a convulsive gesture and laid her head on his shoulder with her arms around him as she sobbed.

Tobe, who had loved Adelaide from a distance for so long, discovered emotions too complex and strong to be withstood. He found himself crying and laughing at the same time, and wondered if he might be going insane.

On the surface of the New World Camp Two presented a scene that seethed with activity. The "big push" was on, and the entire ground-break force, plus most of the engineering staff, were at work building the camps.

Every couple of minutes the ground shook under the crack of dynamite charges as the "stumpers" did their work.

Bulldozers, concrete spreaders, cranes, and assemblers roared and chugged, some under robotic control, others under direct human supervision.

Between the big machines moved the people, in colorful one-piece suits, intent on myriad tasks as a small city arose on the heights above the southern ocean, not far from the estuary that Ground Team 8 had first investigated a few days before.

A pair of silvery domes, each forty meters across, was the centerpiece of a burgeoning grid of puffcrete cubes, roofed with plypress made from the giant trees. Puffcreters, shaped like giant onions in matte green, chuffed beside the beach. A plypress plant exuded huge clouds of smoke nearby.

Beyond the buildings and streets, the saw teams were clear-cutting the alien forest.

Ground-break teams had been pulled off the science survey, which, in effect, lay in ruins, and recruited to work the saws.

These saws had blades twenty meters in length, and they were barely large enough. Cutting the trees was arduous work. They gushed sap, jammed the saws constantly.

But they were only made of wood, and the saws were steel. And another forest giant would slip and fall with a ground-shaking blow upon the ground. Vines snapping, smaller trees collapsing, fragments flying wholesale, these trees died with considerable majesty.

When they came on one of the gigantic nests of the hive insect, they sent robots in with demolition charges to open the nests up, then they mortared them with gas shells. It was time-consuming work, and the consumption of insecticides was so high, a plant was being rushed into production at Camp One.

The Khalifi designs for their new palaces called for a great deal of wood. Accordingly, the trees were cut into lengths and widths, and great stacks of these were being built up on the seaward side of the camp.

Behind the tree-trim teams came the stumpers. These trees left stumps that were enormous and filled with thick, sticky sap. It took many heavy charges to reduce them to pulp and fragments that could be dug out by machine. The machines became gummed with the sap after a short while and required cleaning. Special units had been formed whose sole task was to clean off the sap.

The blasting, the cutting, the rumbling of dirt movers, went on day and night as the Khalifi drove their workers to complete the camps in record time. All the camp details, like the machinery, had been designed by the Fundans, but instead of putting the new buildings to scientific use, the Khalifi were preparing them as temporary residences.

Ibrahim had accelerated the colonizing program. Roads were being cut out to nearby hillsides, where further clearings were under way for the palaces. The Khalifi were eager to stretch their legs. They also wanted to put distance between themselves and the fighting they knew was imminent aboard the ship.

Fortunately, it had been rather easy to recruit more fighters from the ranks of the ground breakers. The Khalifi could laugh once more. The dogs would even fight each other for the chance to become slaves!

Ground Team 8 had been broken up after its first and only scientific mission. Now Flecker led a team of stumpers, which included some of the old ground team. In the assembler robo-frames he had Trask and the taciturn Strang. The frames had three-hundred-horsepower engines and were used to wield drills to sink ten-foot holes in the stump wood.

Into the holes Flecker and Guvek placed explosive charges. Im Sohn then tamped home the charges with a long rod.

Working in quarter sections, they smashed stump after stump, leaving each as a four-sectioned crater filled with smithereens to a depth of fifteen feet.

In the prevailing hot, humid conditions this was hard enough work, but the Khalifi had instituted a speed-up, so that everyone worked two eight-hour shifts in every twenty-four. All were exhausted as a result.

For poor Flecker there was the added effect of mental confusion. His hatred of the Khalifi had become obsessional. He had dreams in which he killed the Princes one by one, in horrifying ways. He had other dreams in which the process was reversed.

Following Team 8's catastrophic expedition to Prominence 46, three members had been hospitalized and the team officially terminated.

Flecker's storm of complaint to Hideo Tagomi got him two days in the cooler. Then he'd been released, still white, still shaking with anger.

He heard about the two female biologists who'd been abducted by Khalifi guards and whom the Khalifi refused to give up. Then came the rumor that there had been the loss of an entire expedition to the highland valleys.

Flecker knew now that the Khalifi intended to rule by the application of the oldest human methods, virtually unchanged since the days of ancient Sumer. They intended to plant their feet upon the necks of the rest and to keep their feet there forever.

At any moment Flecker expected to be arrested. Then he imagined they would space him out the airlock. So when the accelerated camp-building program was announced, he was amazed to find that he was still regarded as an officer by the Khalifi. He was ordered to return to duty and was immediately assigned to stump-demolition school. There he learned about the equipment that had been hurriedly designed to meet the problem of the gargantuan tree stumps.

A few days later he found himself assigned to lead the 14th Stumper squad, and shortly afterward found the other remnants of Ground Team 8 sent to join him.

Now Flecker sweated as he scrambled across the stump face. He wore lightweight spylo clothing, but it was near midday and the temperature was in the nineties, so the sweat ran off him and pooled in his boots.

He reached the next set of bore holes and dug in his pack for another set of hexadylak blast caps. Each of the buff tubes was the size of a man's thumb and carried the explosive power of a kilogram of dynamite.

Carefully, he inserted the charges.

Im Sohn was behind him. She hefted her tamping rod, made of reinforced spylo, and drove the charges firmly home.

Flecker was already at work on the next set of holes, which were placed on the other side of a jagged rip piece as tall as a man and jutting up from the stump face.

When he'd finished, he climbed down from the stump face and flicked up his commo mike.

"This is Fourteen calling for permission to fire. Hello, Central."

The radio crackled awhile, then the voice of Garuda, the stumper controller, came in loud and clear.

"Permission is on hold there, Fourteen. That's stump 624, sector two, everybody got that?"

The radio crackled again.

"Okay, Fourteen, this is how it is. Tree team on your left will need a minute or so to clear their equipment. Hold on."

The stumpers took the opportunity to move farther back from stump 624. All around them, for a square mile or more, the huge trees had been felled. Heavy machinery was at work on the remains.

To their immediate left, men in bulky motor frames were moving saws away. To their right, two hundred meters away, a pair of huge robot diggers continued to clear a crater.

The stumpers took shelter behind a husk of bark the size of a small house. Strang and Trask climbed out of the assembler frames to join them.

"This gonna be the last stump on this shift?" Trask said.

"I think so," Flecker said with a glance at his chrono. "We only have a half hour left, by this."

"I can't wait. I'm exhausted."

"We're all exhausted."

"Yeah, Trask, shut it, will you," Guvek said sourly.

The radio crackled again. "You have clearance, Fourteen. Fire when ready."

Flecker hit the switch and the charges blew with a heavy thud that shook the ground. A second later a hail of pulp and fragments of wood came down upon them.

"I don't know how much more of this I can stand," Flecker said when it was over.

Strang gave him an inquiring look.

"I mean it," Flecker said.

The blast was over. The stench of charred sap and wood blew across the scene.

"Okay, Fourteen," the radio blared. "You're in for now. Twenty-one is taking over on your sector."

"Where do we bunk this shift?" Flecker said. "They told us at the last place we wouldn't be going back to Camp Central."

"I've got you accommodations in a new dormer. Follow yellow-tag lane to red-tag sector control, they'll give you instructions there."

"Red-tag sector control? Where the hell is that?" Flecker said.

"New designator for what used to be the second-equipment strip."

Flecker recalled that name. "All right, I know *that*—in the canyon there, near the cliffs?"

"Yeah. Get going."

They strode slowly back through the smashed forest. Around them the air was filled with dust, fragments, and insects that hazed to gold in the light of the setting sun.

26

AFTER WANDERING THROUGH THE TRUCK PARK THEY FOUND red-tag control center in a big green inflatable overlooking a canyon that ran down to the lagoon behind the sand spit.

The place was in chaos. People milled around tables of harassed administrators who directed them to this address or that. Workers wrestled with the wiring, plugging in phones and screens. Yellow and pink forms were scattered on the floor.

"We're the Fourteenth Stumpers," Flecker announced when he reached the head of the line.

After a half-minute review of a large book filled with forms and loose papers in profusion, someone thrust him a yellow slip.

"Here, go down the canyon road."

And so they found themselves trotting down the canyon road toward some gray dorm buildings erected on the lower slopes.

Beyond these, a bulky new puffcreter loomed beside the lagoon beach like some giant baby of green matte metal.

Red lights winked like eyes on its upper rim. A green light flashed furiously from the chemprocessor in its belly. It sent a heavy, hot chuffing sound into the night air along with the thick smell of raw puffcrete.

Trucks collected the crete from the hopper and climbed the road up the canyon with engines revving.

A seven-foot clone guard in black spylo and boots called them to a halt.

"You are new stump team, correct? Fourteen?"

Flecker assented.

"Good, I am Garmash, I keep order here. You will follow easy rule. Do job, eat, sleep. Do nothing else. If you do, you displease Garmash. It is not good to displease Garmash, you understand?"

Glumly they followed Garmash into the dorm. The place had been constructed out of gray modular units of plypress, then sprayed down with puffcrete and a toner. There was a strong smell in the air from the toner chemicals. The metal fittings still had plastiwrap on them.

"Oh no," moaned Guvek, who hurriedly covered her mouth when Garmash turned an ominous eye on her. Garmash wore a habitual tight-eyed scowl.

There were no cubicles, it was all one room. The toilets and showers were unisex.

"Not even a curtain for the shower stall? This is not fair!" lamented Im Sohn, who sat down on a bunk and burst into tears.

Flecker stared at her. Compared to everything else the Khalifi had done to them, this was relatively minor. But Im Sohn had drawn the attention of Garmash over it.

"Pretty girl unhappy with nice new quarters?" Garmash stood at the end of her bunk. Im Sohn gave a little scream and curled up in a fetal ball.

Flecker leaned over Im Sohn, grabbed her shoulder.

"Get up, keep quiet, you'll get yourself killed."

A massive hand grasped his shoulder and pulled him roughly out of the way.

Garmash wore an odd smile. He pushed Flecker onto another bed and turned back to Im Sohn.

"Maybe pretty girl come with Garmash? Garmash have good ration card, can get you things you like."

Garmash reached down for her, but at his touch she reacted quickly and jumped up with her back to the wall.

Garmash smiled at her. "Now, pretty girl, you come with Garmash, yes?"

"No," she said, shuddering.

Garmash lost the smile. His eyes hardened again.

"You not want ol' Garmash?"

"No, thank you, I don't. I don't want anyone."

Garmash pondered this for a second. "Ah," he declared, "you not want anyone. I understand. Later you want Garmash. Good. I will see you later. Be sure to shower, I like you clean. Understand?"

Garmash laughed heartily, swung his head to left and right. Something about the look in Flecker's eyes upset him.

"You look like subversive!" the giant growled.

Flecker swallowed. He'd seen men beaten in public by the guards; they terrified him.

Garmash scowled down at him. "Subversive activity is not allowed," he growled.

"Yes," Flecker said. It was best to always agree with them. Anything else could have unpredictable results.

Suddenly Garmash grabbed Flecker's shirtfront with a big hand and lifted him off his feet.

"You better make sure you understand that."

"Yes, I understand."

Garmash set him down, sniffed, then strode away.

When Garmash was gone, they dropped their gear and collapsed on their bunks. There was a chorus of groans, then Guvek shed modesty, stripped and ran for the shower. She discovered that it ran only cold water and voiced loud complaint.

"I'd be careful, Guvek, if I were you," Trask cautioned when he joined her in the shower. "He might hear you."

"They have no right to treat us like this. I am a trained entomologist, I have important work to do."

"Yeah, yeah, well, I guess you may get back to it one of these days. If the Khalifi decide it's worth it. Personally, I had my fill of the native flora and fauna on our last trip."

Trask soaped himself, trying not to look at Guvek, who still sported angry red scabs from the insect stings she'd suffered on Prominence 46.

Im Sohn was crying on her bunk.

"What is it?" Guvek said as she pulled a fresh spylo lightweight over her shoulders.

"I am tired and dirty and I want a shower and I have to go to the toilet and I cannot do these things like you, naked in front of others."

Guvek flushed slightly. "My dear, in the circumstances, I would rather be clean and comfortable. I guess modesty will have to be put aside for a while."

"I cannot do this," Im Sohn said with a little shriek. "I cannot expose myself to others."

Guvek shrugged. "Suit yourself, then, I'm going to see what's cooking in the galley."

Trask and Strang returned from the showers and began dressing. Strang dressed quickly and followed Guvek to the galley.

There was a long counter set in the outer room of the dorm building. A couple of cooks were ladling out a fish stew and some nutriveg. Both were severely overcooked. Nonetheless, workers were seated around the room, eating their rations with intense concentration.

Garmash was absent. Strang queued up, received his ration, and sat down at a table.

Flecker joined him a little later. "This is slop," he said bitterly.

Strang nodded.

"They treat us like animals," Flecker said. "I am at the limits of patience. I cannot take it anymore."

Strang gave him that same questioning look again. "This place is probably bugged," he said unexpectedly.

Flecker was shocked. Strang rarely spoke. He stared at him, but Strang did not look up again.

They finished the meal in silence. Outside, Strang drew Flecker to one side.

"It is not wise to draw attention to yourself like that."

"You sound very certain of this," Flecker said.

"I have reason to know."

Flecker heaved a sigh. "Well, if you're right, it makes our situation all the more hopeless."

"There is going to be a rebellion aboard the ship."

"Everyone knows that."

"Things may change after that."

"If the rebels don't get themselves killed. They don't have much hope of beating the Khalifi."

"They may surprise the Khalifi. Who knows?"

Flecker shrugged. Strang fell silent again. Flecker returned to their quarters alone and flung himself down on his bunk.

But his thoughts were a torment, and after a while he pulled himself off his bed and stalked out into the night.

Darkness lay on the canyon slopes. Above glittered the first stars. A cool breeze was blowing in off the ocean.

Flecker strolled down the path. The puffcreter chuffed quietly as a new load was mixed. Two-thirds of the way down the canyon another path went around the puffcrete complex and onto some sand dunes.

Flecker strode that way, intending to visit the dunes along the lagoon shore. The path was steep initially, but soon he reached the crest and began descending into the dunes.

The puffcreter was behind him now, and ahead lay the lagoon, wreathed in mist. To the left the sand spit formed a low barrier to the ocean. Lights gleamed there from the landing field.

Flecker walked along the margin of the lagoon. An enormous piece of driftwood had beached itself there. As he got closer, something scuttled off the wood and splashed into the lagoon. He felt the old thrill reawaken. Alien life, alien world, the idea that had driven him all his life.

Later he heard a loud slap on the water, but whether this was connected to the previous incident he could not tell.

A stumper blast cut the peace of the night with a heavy thud. Somewhere farther off a big saw started whining high and shrill.

With a shrug Flecker continued walking along the shore, heading toward the peninsula.

He had gone about half the distance when he caught sight of someone else out walking on the dunes. This person was about a hundred feet ahead of him and unaware of his presence, being to landward with the lights behind him.

A moment later Flecker was startled to see that the other night stroller was Strang.

His curiosity aroused, Flecker followed Strang down the beach to the point where it joined the sand spit.

Strang crossed the rocky little inlet and scrambled up the side of the sand spit. He climbed over a four-strand security fence and disappeared through the vegetation.

Flecker followed and found that a square building with lights on the far side stood close to that fence.

He watched as Strang approached the building and opened a small door in the rear. Flecker waited, his mind whirling with questions, and twenty minutes later Strang reappeared. He slipped away from the building in a furtive manner and disappeared into the vegetation.

Shortly afterward he returned over the fence at the same spot and continued back the way he had come, toward the big puffcreter at the mouth of the canyon.

Flecker followed, his mind boiling. Impelled by rage, he caught up, and Strang turned to face him. Strang wore an expression of dismay. Flecker's suspicions were confirmed.

"You're a spy for them, aren't you? A filthy spy! You just went back in there to give your daily report, didn't you?"

"No."

"You disgust me."

Strang said nothing.

"Answer me, I demand that you answer. You pretend to be our friend and then you go off and report everything we say to the Khalifi."

"Wrong."

"No, damn you, I followed you, I saw what you did." Flecker's temper disintegrated. He swung a roundhouse right at Strang.

His punch missed its target. Instead his wrist was seized and pulled and he toppled over an outthrust hip to land with considerable force upon the sand. The breath went out of him with an explosive grunt.

While he lay there unable to breathe, Strang walked away without another word.

Flecker struggled to sit up, still gasping, thoughts racing in mad profusion.

He'd been dumped unceremoniously on the sandy beach. He seemed to have failed all around.

He was a field scientist, he told himself furiously, he had to be able to take the rough with the smooth.

It was just that there seemed to be an awful lot of rough to take just now.

Slowly he got to his feet, dusted himself off, and then lurched over the dunes until eventually he climbed to the top of one and sat down to absorb the unearthly beauty of the scene.

A piercing whistle rang out behind. The puffcreter flashed and began dumping another load into its trucks. The chuffing was interrupted by the wet sound of tons of raw crete squirting into the tanks.

Flecker stared at the mists. Life seemed a bitter experience. The Khalifi could not be defeated, they had riddled the work force with their agents.

Strang had warned him not to talk, and Flecker had trusted him as a result. What a naif he'd been! And then Strang had gone to report on him to the Khalifi.

Next, Garmash would get the orders and Flecker would be dragged out and put to death.

Flecker put his head in his hands. There seemed to be no

way out. He could not imagine surviving in the jungle alone. The Khalifi ruled everything else.

Another noise intruded as the chuffing of the creter subsided somewhat. At first he thought it was an animal growling somewhere nearby, but after a while he noticed distinctly human qualities to the sounds. He got to his feet and then investigated the gullies in the dune on the inland side.

In the second gully over he came on a desperate sight.

Im Sohn was bound hand and foot. Standing over her was Garmash, naked. With urgent gestures he ripped her spylo one-piece, then sank to his knees, seized her by the hips, and began to use her most forcibly. Despite the tight gag, Im Sohn emitted a piercing shriek.

Flecker discarded reason and charged. He dove onto Garmash's back and swung down with both fists together.

Garmash was knocked onto his side, and with an explosive oath, rebounded to his feet. Flecker faced him across the bound, weeping figure of Im Sohn.

"You bother me," Garmash growled.

"Leave her alone," Flecker said, surprised that he was able to actually speak. His knees were knocking together.

"She is mine. You are mine too."

Garmash came forward, sweeping out a leg in a massive kick. Flecker jumped back, but with tremendous agility Garmash swung around and struck with the other leg in a reverse.

Flecker fell down, got back up, and Garmash was upon him. A huge hand seized him by the back of the neck. Another hand slapped him sideways.

Flecker staggered back, stunned. Then he bunched and lashed out with a fist.

He surprised both of them and landed a stinging jab on Garmash's nose.

Garmash roared and lurched forward. Flecker ran a few steps backward. Garmash came on.

"Garmash do you good for that."

Flecker twisted aside from a punch, ducked another, tried to block a third, without much success. Garmash swung a backhand that knocked him right off his feet.

Flecker's face stung and his head rang as he watched in stunned horror as Garmash reached down and picked him up by the front of his spylo.

Garmash pulled back for another huge slap.

And suddenly gave out an odd grunt. Flecker was dropped on his back.

Garmash pulled around. He had a tamping rod of reinforced spylo thrust into his back like a spear.

Strang stood there. He kicked Garmash hard in the crotch. Garmash doubled up and took a knee in the face. Garmash went down, still trying to pull the spylo rod out of his back.

Strang put a foot on the giant's back and leaned hard on the spylo rod, driving it in like a harpoon.

Garmash struggled up, hurled Strang back by main strength, but was now transfixed by the spylo spear which protruded a good six inches from his chest.

Strang then dove to the sand as Garmash yanked out his sidearm and fired a burst that clipped the edge of the dune.

Flecker staggered forward and hung himself over Garmash's gun arm, pulling it down. Garmash kept firing and put three bullets into one of his own feet.

He screamed and hurled Flecker away with a convulsive gesture. The gun came back up and Flecker stared into his own death, when Strang leapt out of the dark with a rock that he brought crashing down on the back of Garmash's head.

Garmash toppled, slowly at first, like one of the giant trees.

After a long moment of silence, Flecker found his voice. "Thanks, you saved my life."

"Likewise," Strang said.

"We'd better see to Im Sohn."

"Get rid of the body first. Khalifi better not find it."

Strang heaved Garmash's shoulders up. Flecker took the big man's legs. They were very heavy.

They carried Garmash up the beach to the big creter. The machine's crew was out of sight of the motor buckets. With a heave they managed to get Garmash up onto the lip of one of the buckets, and then slowly the giant body toppled inside.

A minute later they saw the bucket lifted and emptied into the feeder. Instantly, Garmash's body became part of the hot flux.

"Now we must rescue Im Sohn," Flecker said.

The creter flashed. "You go," Strang said. "I have some arrangements to make." He turned on his heel and strode away back toward the sand spit.

27

FLECKER WANTED TO CONFRONT STRANG AGAIN THAT NIGHT, but he never saw him return to camp. The effort it took to carry poor Im Sohn to the medical lab consumed his remaining strength. He barely made it to his cot before he collapsed.

When he awoke, it was to find Guvek shaking him. Her breath reeked of instacaf.

"Get up," she said. "We've been reassigned. We're on a road team today."

Flecker sat up, still groggy, and found the rest of the team dressed and ready.

He saw Strang at the door, but as Flecker got to his feet and called out his name, Strang slipped outside. The others began following him.

"Strang?" Flecker said again.

"He's been very talkative all of a sudden," Guvek said. "Our mystery man, you know."

"Yes?" Flecker said.

"He came in this morning with the new orders, told everyone to get up and get ready to leave."

Flecker shook his head. New orders? He stretched. He was covered in bruises, the left side of his head extremely tender. Strang was the source of constant surprises now.

"Im Sohn?" he said after a moment.

"Won't be working today, she's in the psych ward."

Flecker thought of Garmash and shuddered. After that experience, the cool isolation of a cot in the psych ward, pumped up with sophisticated tranquilizers, had a definite appeal. Im Sohn would probably need days to recover. Flecker decided he would try to visit the little ecologist when the team got back to camp.

He pulled on his boots, grabbed his equipment, and was ready.

Guvek snorted in exasperation. "Flecker, you're forgetting something."

"What?"

"Breath mask, we're heading inland."

Flecker shivered. He'd almost forgotten. He returned to his bunk, pulled out the mask, and checked the filters. None were pink, so he snapped it shut again and slung the mask on his utility belt.

He followed Guvek out and found a personnel carrier waiting for them.

Behind the personnel carrier there was a cart loaded with the assembler frames and the saws themselves. The big saw blades jutted out beyond that.

Inside, Strang was sitting beside Trask in the front row of their six-seat section. Flecker squeezed in between Trask and Strang.

"What's going on?" Flecker said.

Strang gave him a hurried glance. "Road team, reassignment."

"Yeah, but what's really going on?"

"We're going upcountry. Going to be hot."

"Come on, Strang, let's have it straight. What the hell are you up to? You some kind of provocateur?"

Strang's face was still. "No," he said quite calmly.

"What? What the hell is going on?"

Strang tensed, struggling with himself. Finally he whispered back, "Look, keep it down. I've debugged this truck, but I can't vouch for everyone on those other teams."

"All right, but you are going to damn well tell me what's going on around here." Flecker dropped his voice to a whisper.

Strang was unmoved. "Not yet. Look, enjoy the ride, I'll tell you what I know later."

Strang got up and moved to the back of the carrier.

And Flecker had to be content with that. He sat back in his seat and gazed out the window as the carrier droned up the dirt road hammered out of the forest by the ground breakers in the past few days.

To either side the dark hush of the alien jungle continued.

Several bridges were under construction along the way, puffcreters and block lifters at work. But only one was even half completed yet, so the carrier was forced to zigzag up and down the river valleys, fording the streams where they were shallow enough.

Soon, however, they passed a huge clearing. For more than half a mile in any direction the trees were down. Hundreds of them lay on their sides like beached ships. Among them the saws whined shrill and high.

The feeling was suddenly completely different. This cleared space, with access to the sky, lifted hearts after the stygian gloom beneath the trees.

In the center, where the trees had been chopped up and cleared away, construction machines were already at work. Scaffolding cloaked the beginnings of massive walls. Diggers and shovels were burrowing foundations into the ground.

Around them a colorful profusion of tents, sheds, and inflatables had sprung up. Men and women, mostly in slave white, moved about, intent upon their tasks.

The Khalifi weren't wasting any time in building their palaces. Already the outlines of the world they planned were becoming clear. In their huge palaces they would rule like feudal lords. Around the palaces, in their work compounds, would live the essential work force. Everyone else would either be peasantry or prisoners up on the ship.

During the three-hour ride, they passed two more similar clearings, although neither was as advanced in construction.

Finally they reached the road head and disembarked. The roar of activity was familiar. Three big saw teams were at work. Behind them came cutters and stumpers. Bulldozers and dirt graders were churning the muck where the stumps had been pulverized.

The 14th Stumpers were assigned bunks in a trailer set back from the machines.

But before they could visit the bunkhouses, they were expected to complete a shift of work. The team they were replacing had left hours before; they were late, stumps were waiting.

Flecker looked around for Strang, but he was suddenly nowhere to be seen.

The 14th Stumpers went into action. Stumper charges shook the ground every minute or so.

Trask and Flecker wore the assembler frames and hammered the long spikes into the stump face. Guvek placed charges and then tamped them in herself.

141

Stump by stump they followed the saw teams into the jungle.

Thus passed the day, with no sign of Strang.

Flecker was in an agony of suspense. The Khalifi must have noticed the disappearance of Garmash by now. They would also find that the 14th Stumpers had been reassigned. Flecker could think of no way to escape.

What would he say to the Khalifi investigators when they came? What might Im Sohn have said already?

Flecker had been as vague as possible about Im Sohn when he'd brought her in. She was incoherent and unable to respond to questions.

But the Khalifi would investigate the med lab in the search for Garmash. They might question her.

However, the Khalifi guards had still not made an appearance by the end of the shift. So Flecker lurched gratefully back down the new-made road, to the bunkhouse trailers.

The evening food was a stew, served with the inevitable gray-green nutriveg. He tried to get more.

"We discourage the gulpers," said one of the food servers, a group of men and women in slave white. There seemed to be more and more people wearing this humiliating costume, proclaiming them to be property of the Khalifi family.

People from the Seats were accepting slavery as a ticket out of the orbital prison? Flecker was horrified.

The future seemed intensely bleak. Lifelong oppression beneath the Khalifi heel.

Flecker wandered out. The road was lit up with bright mercury beacons every hundred meters. Their harsh light cut through the soft alien night.

It also summoned enormous insects out of the alien night. Things that zoomed in like missiles. One came booming in at high speed and slammed straight into a nearby lamp, which exploded.

Somebody let out a whoop, someone else took it up.

"We got flies again tonight!" yelled a voice.

Flecker felt a touch on his arm and turned to find Strang waiting there.

"Where have you been all day?" Flecker snapped.

Strang spoke in a whisper. "I've been busy, things are starting to break open."

"What is going on? You haven't told me yet."

Strang looked around them, then pulled Flecker off the

graded road. They stumbled over some piles of dirt and into the darkness between two enormous roots. Finally, in almost complete darkness, Strang turned to him.

"The Khalifi are going to be tested very shortly. The rebellion is about to blow."

"How do you know this?"

"I was on the ship today. I only just got back from the camp."

Flecker jumped. "How do you get to be on the ship today? Why weren't you here, blasting stumps with the rest of us?"

"The Khalifi have made careful plans. I think they will overcome the rebels."

"I still don't get this. How are you free to travel around by yourself? You must be working for them."

This seemed to arouse Strang a little. His voice tightened.

"I will not work for them, ever. Of that you can be assured. I know the ship's systems, the controls, the computers."

"Then you're a Fundan, I thought so from the first time I saw you. I thought, there goes a Noram from the old days, must be one of the old families."

"It does not matter who or what I am. All that matters is that we must defeat the Khalifi."

"But how?"

"You will see. I want you to come with me. I need a another person, but it must be someone I can trust."

"You don't know me."

"I have watched you since we were assigned to climb Prominence 46. I believe I can trust you."

"What are you offering?"

"The chance to stop the Khalifi."

"Sounds like a good chance to die."

Abruptly a splat of something wet and sticky dropped on Flecker's head. He ducked away.

"What the hell is that?"

A strong smell like cinnamon was in the air. More stuff splattered down.

Strang was shining a light up on the tree bark above. More of the sticky, viscous fluid was visible there, dripping down through the thick, shaggy-textured bark.

"Must be sap," Flecker said, peering up at the tree.

A pattern of horizontal stripes was visible in the bark of the tree. The stripes were black and possessed an oily sheen. They were a foot wide, perhaps, and five to ten times that long.

"What's that?" Flecker said.

"I don't know, but I saw it on some of the trees near the road by the camp. Marks like big zippers or something."

"An infection of some kind, a fungus perhaps?"

Strang peered up at the marks. They extended to a height of one hundred meters or more.

"I don't know," he said. He turned back to Flecker. "What are you going to do? Whose side are you on?"

Flecker didn't hesitate. "I'm with you."

28

SLOWLY, STEP BY STEP, THE REBELLION SPUTTERED INTO LIFE, driven on by acts of Khalifi stupidity.

The first real event was a small riot in the Atrium when two drunken Khalifi Princes simply seized a waitress in the restaurant and began forcibly to drag her away toward the elevators to the Purple level. People rose to help her, and the princelings' pair of guards drew their shock batons and swatted people down. With a growl of rage and desperation, all the people in the Atrium rose and hurled themselves upon the guards and their royal charges.

One of the guards was killed, both the Princes were severely beaten, all were hospitalized with severe injuries.

The Khalifi reacted with rage. A force of ten guards appeared, smashed up the restaurant, beat the manager to a pulp, and then withdrew, uttering dire threats.

Soon afterward the Khalifi began offering rewards for the names of those known to have participated in the riot.

Then a young man who had fallen foul of the fierce young Prince Hasta was killed in his cabin by a squad of four members of the Planetary Legion.

The Cabins rioted again, and the Khalifi sent more guards, who tried to clear the Cabin level entirely.

At this point Adelaide Fundan was forced to commit the force of crossbow archers. Within a few minutes three guards were shot down and the Khalifi withdrew their forces.

The Khalifi were riven by rumors; these begat fear. The great family, with its retainers and slaves, jammed the exits of the ship as everyone decided that the unknown terrors of the planetary surface, dangerous insects or not, were less worrisome than the warfare they knew was about to break out.

The Khalifi high council was unable to even slow this stampede. They dithered, unsure whether to strike back hard immediately and perhaps be forced to kill many, even all, of the people in the Seats.

The fiercely-expressed opinion among the younger men was that it was too soon to resort to ultimate force. Ibrahim himself met with a delegation of younger Princes, men in the thirties and forties of life. The young Princes had little power in the family, except when they united entirely on an issue, and on this issue they were united.

Ibrahim held off; the Khalifi guards stayed out of the Atrium and the Cabin level. No mass retribution took place. An electric tension began to build in the Cabins and down in the Seats. Seven thousand people awaited the final battle.

Then a Khalifi engineer discovered that the surveillance systems in the Atrium and Cabin levels had been tampered with. A sophisticated fogger system had been feeding randoms to the checkers. Computer-generated images of the Atrium, scrambled speech sounds—none of the pickup had been real for weeks.

Ibrahim's only fear had been the loss of cybernetic control of the ship. At the worst, he was sure, he had but to close the elevators down and stop pumping air to the Seats and the Cabins and he would break the rebels. But if he lost control of the computer net, then the ship itself could become vulnerable.

Then, to confirm his fears, the engineers discovered more tampering. Unreported software patches, right in the nexial programming areas of the ship A.I., *Founder* itself.

The A.I. was unaware of the changes, nor did it have any log of when they had been inserted.

Ibrahim ordered the seizure of anyone thought capable of this kind of espionage. The A.I. itself pointed out that the most likely suspects were Fundans.

Ibrahim had long awaited a thrust from the Fundans. They had been so easily defeated, and then they had sunk into such a fawning submission to the will of the Khalifi that Ibrahim had suspected some deep, subtle game was in play.

Ibrahim had even interrogated some older family members, but found to his surprise that they were genuinely, sublimely ignorant.

The Fundans had lived soft lives for so many generations, they had lost their edge. That drive that made them princes in the Asteroid Belt was gone. The Fundans of Edward's generation were not like him, and he was dead.

Ibrahim breathed a sigh of relief. Then he ordered all Fundan computer experts arrested at once. A few were found, some from the hardware divisions, some from software teams. The interrogations with drugs and mind probes began. But even the most rigorous investigation produced no culprits, although it did clarify how someone might have attacked the A.I. without its knowing who or when.

"Fundan Design Codes"—they were everywhere, programmed into all the ship's software. As ubiquitous as the Fundan Made blue triangles.

Of course, the Khalifi ordered the ship's A.I. to be purged and rebuilt as soon as they completed their takeover.

But Ibrahim had neglected to consider refashioning all the rest of the ship's software library. Once again he felt old Edward's shadowy hand: "By using some of the higher codes, an intruder could disarm the *Founder* A.I., could override doors and other controls."

They checked, and sure enough, there were odd little discrepancies.

A dozen shuttle seats had been misappropriated for unknown passengers.

Something weird had been going on for several weeks, perhaps longer, in terms of airlock usage. Some emergency airlocks on the roof of the hub section had been used repeatedly without authorization.

Ibrahim ordered Red Alert status for his entire network. Guards were ferried up from the surface.

A serious Fundan player was at work, someone who knew the high-level design codes. A search was ordered for all Fundans involved with the construction of the ship. All were to be arrested at once.

The mass invasion by the guards into the Cabin level on a foray to capture Adelaide and Melissa Fundan produced the final spark that lit the rebellion.

The crossbow program had made more than a hundred

weapons. When the guards came, they were attacked at once. Two more guards were killed. Shotgun fire ripped up and down the corridors. Casualties mounted until the fifth guard went down with a bolt through his throat, and the Khalifi pulled back.

The guards were too precious to waste.

Adelaide Fundan was taken down to the Seats for safety. On Green deck, Kasok called for immediate attack. Within twenty minutes it had begun.

With a sharp series of booms, homemade explosive charges blew holes through the structural wall between the ceiling of the Cabin level and the Purple level.

Six assault teams of twenty men each broke through and carried the struggle to the Khalifi. Wielding swords made from flooring strips, and firing slingshots and crossbows, the assault teams penetrated the lavish apartments of the Khalifi Princes. Screaming women fled from the harem as Kasok lead a team of Green-deck bravos through the floor.

A half-dozen Khalifi were taken prisoner and dragged below. Several princelings chose to fight and some were killed, others left wounded and even mutilated.

But as the teams from the Seats rampaged on through the Purple level, they discovered it was largely empty. The Khalifi were in the hub or already en route to the surface.

They were looking forward, to their New World. They had new homes to build, farms and estates to map out and stock. A whole world to build, a world of their very own.

29

HIDEO HAD DONE HIS BEST TO STAY OUT OF TROUBLE. WHEN Melissa first turned up at his door, he had said no. But she pushed her way in anyway, and after checking the null zone she'd set up, she produced a pair of collapsible space suits from inside her pack.

"I'm staying here with you, Hideo," she'd announced.

"The rebellion's going to start any time soon, and you and I, we've a job to do."

"What are you talking about?"

She had told him then.

"I need you, Hideo. Adelaide and I couldn't access any of the files guarded by *Founder*. We don't know anything about the layout of the hub section and the connectors to the airlocks. You have to get me a floor plan."

Hideo shivered involuntarily. "If the Khalifi found out I had done this, they would have me boiled alive and fed to their dogs."

"Then they must not find out. You can access the data."

Hideo refused. Melissa remained adamant. "For me, Hideo—do it, please!"

Hideo had finally given in. He dreamed up a dummy project, an addendum to the Fundan-designed Shut-Down One program. Completely unnecessary "shrouds" were now to be designed for the optical ports in the hub section. Hideo set up a dummy subcommittee which was entrusted with the job. A schematic of the hub section could then be requested by this subcommittee.

Hideo sweated over the wording of the request and sent it in through remote control of a terminal in the science-section administration room. He could almost feel the boiling water at his toes as he tapped the keys.

All went well at first, and he pulled down a menu for the hub data base from the science-service data net. He pushed through to the grafix section and tried to pull down a grafix set of the hub.

At this point there was an automatic security check, but Hideo overrode it with his priority code. This was the most dangerous moment.

The screen flashed, then the menu vanished.

Hideo trembled. He had tripped the security net. Would they arrest him?

Then another menu came up, with options for ending the security override. It was not a security menu; there were dozens of options. It did not have a Fundan Made logo, nor any other brand. There was no way of telling where it had come from or how it had been inserted into the resident software. He investigated, poking around the options menus, and found something called "Interrupted Dataload Override." He entered that, and after a momentary wait received the floor plans of the hub.

He dumped a copy and disconnected.

Hideo's breath was tight in his chest, there was perspiration on his temples and his legs felt very shaky.

But Melissa gave him a huge hug, and Hideo swelled with a pride the likes of which he had never known.

From that mistaken pride he had doomed himself to this!

Crouching in a maintenance well under the floor of the hub section, listening to the heavy boots of Khalifi guards right above. The guards had been there for hours, and might be there for hours more. Hideo already felt faint from lack of food.

He and Melissa had been three-quarters of the way to the dorsal docking section. There they'd intended to infiltrate one of the dozens of airlocks that opened to the shuttles in the docking bay. They'd reached a point where they just had to cross a series of rectangular rooms, each filled with equipment bolted to the floor, to reach the access tube to one small air-lock.

Halfway across a room stacked with machinery they'd heard guards approaching. Doors boomed open nearby. A klaxon was wailing.

The rebellion had finally broken out.

Hideo had almost fainted with the fear.

Fortunately, Melissa didn't hesitate for a second. She pulled a floor ring up and yanked open a narrow hatch in between pallets of machinery.

"Get in," she'd ordered, pushing him down inside, then jumped in on top of him and pulled down the hatch.

There was barely enough room for both their bodies, but they were trapped there, and there was no knowing for how long.

The rebellion was blazing. A dozen Khalifi youths had been seized and dragged down to the Seats.

They had been stripped, mocked, beaten, and hung up by their heels.

Kasok had opened a line to the Purple level.

"Get me Ibrahim," he demanded.

The face of Prince Ras Order appeared on the screen.

"Your request for an audience has been rejected."

Kasok laughed, confident that he held the edge.

"Listen, asshole, tell Ibrahim to start talking or we're gonna be sending him some Khalifi heads."

Ras Order's face darkened. "That would be a foolish mistake," he said. "You will place yourself in blood feud with my family. I warn you that this is not something to undertake lightly."

"Don't give me any of that crap. What the hell are you gonna do to us that you haven't already done? Tell Ibrahim to start talking or else."

"I repeat, do not harm the young men you have so wickedly taken captive. Cut them down. Return them to us."

"Why the hell should we?" sneered Kasok. "Be real."

Ras Order's eyes flickered. "We shall turn off the air to the Seats."

"Go ahead, damn you. They'll be the first to suffer."

Ras Order did not reply for a few seconds.

"Be that as it may, we shall turn off the air refreshment at once unless you surrender, completely and unconditionally."

"Surrender? Are you out of your mind? We have hostages, why should we surrender?"

"The air is being turned off now. Within one hour you will be begging me to replenish."

"But what about your young men?"

Ras Order assumed a diffident expression. "They will die like heros for our family, I am confident."

"I can't believe I'm hearing this," Astrod Benenki said.

"Drag that one here!" Kasok shouted, pointing to one of the unhappy princelings, dangling from the remains of an overhead luggage locker.

Burly members of Kasok's group pulled the youth down, lugged him over, and set him in front of the screen.

"The Prince says that you will die bravely."

"No!" wailed the youth, whose light brown skin was marred by purple bruises. He begged for his life. "Do not forsake me!"

Prince Ras Order sniffed. "It would be more seemly for you to comport yourself with dignity. You are Khalifi, of the blood, behave like it."

"You cannot leave us to die among these pigs!"

"Silence."

"They have tortured us!"

"You will face your end with courage and dignity, do you understand?"

"This is easy for you to say, you are not down here. I cannot describe the filth we are having to endure."

Kasok shoved in front. "You better get Ibrahim."

Ras Order's voice was frosty. "I have given you Ibrahim's response. He expects them to die with dignity."

The contact cut off.

"No!" the youth screamed, his fellows hanging from the ceiling screaming with him.

A few minutes later two squads of guards, a dozen in each, attacked the Cabins through the recently-blown holes leading to the Purple level. They dropped canisters of antipersonnel gas into the corridors and moved slowly and cautiously to take control of the central section of the Cabin level. Elevators to the Seats were sent down with gas canisters smoking.

The speakers blared throughout the ship, "Air circulation has been turned off for Seat decks Orange through Green."

Seven thousand people faced the end of hope.

30

THE GUARDS HAD LEFT, FINALLY. HIDEO WAS CERTAIN OF IT; he'd heard no booted feet for at least twenty minutes. No equipment had whirred or clanged for longer yet.

He nudged Melissa with his thumb.

"What is it?" she said.

"They've gone."

"You're sure now?"

"I will risk my life on it."

"All right, you will indeed, let's go."

Together they heaved up the maintenance-hatch panel and emerged onto the floor of the equipment room.

The machinery was gone, the room empty. To Melissa it suddenly seemed enormous, a huge wasted space.

"Which way?" Hideo said.

Melissa checked her wrist unit. "This way." She ran.

They checked the doors; they were unlocked.

Outside they found themselves in a near-featureless corridor that curved out of sight on both sides. They took nervous little steps down the corridor, but met no one, and eventually reached a set of elevators.

The elevators were open.

"They are confident, aren't they?" Melissa marveled at the seeming lack of security control.

Hideo, on the other hand, was so scared he was shaking, and he thought he could hear his own heart thumping loud enough to wake the dead.

"I'm not sure I want to go in there," he said.

"No way back now, Hideo, you know that," she said lightly, and pushed him in and hit the button.

They went up, fast, and were soon weightless as they hit the hub, at the center of the torus.

The elevator stopped, the door opened, and protex webbing intruded to catch passengers drifting too high, so Hideo was gently guided out the door by the web belt.

They floated down the corridor. Melissa showed him how to travel in no-grav, bunching feet together, holding oneself stable on walls and ceilings. Hideo slowly got the hang of it.

At last they reached a pressurized emergency hatch. Melissa opened it with a Fundan patch code.

On the other side was space.

For Randolf Flecker life held no more surprises. Recruited by Strang in the battle against the Khalifi, he'd had a thorough introduction to Strang's methods.

First they rode all night in a purloined ATV. Then they slipped aboard a shuttle using false ID tags Strang had produced.

As the shuttle closed on the *Founder*, Strang signaled him to the rear and opened an emergency door with a small blue key. Inside was an airlock with two space suits ready for use.

Curious people in the back rows watched them briefly, then turned back to the view on the main screen of the *Founder*, which was very close now.

There was hardly room to pull the space suits on in the little airlock, but Strang assisted with practiced skill, and when he'd sealed the last seal, he popped the hatch and they were spat out of the shuttle along with a small cloud of vapor and gas.

Flecker had never spacewalked before, and he tumbled wildly for a few seconds until Strang steadied him and pulled him into a stable position. Strang maneuvered with small wrist and ankle jets.

Flecker gulped.

He was in close orbit around the *Founder*. The vast bulk of the particle shield was to one side, the glittering torus of the life-support zone on the other.

The shuttle was edging slowly toward the docking bay in the hub, where red flashing lights beckoned it in.

The New World hung below, vast and blue, with white clouds spiraling across the great oceans.

Flecker realized that Strang knew his stuff when it came to no-grav maneuver.

Their orbit decayed rapidly, and they spiraled in toward the sweeping curve of the particle shield, to a point very close to its rearmost edge. Utter darkness lay beyond that.

Flecker felt a surge of panic. Surely there was some mistake? Shouldn't they be heading for the life hab, where there was air and light and warmth?

But Strang had clipped a line to Flecker's belt and released his arms. For a moment Flecker spun helplessly around, then he was looking straight into the sullen, dark mass of the shield, and he spread his hands out as he impacted gently and rebounded.

Strang had stuck a sucker to the smooth rock of the shield and was working his way along the surface to the edge. The line attached to Flecker's belt now tightened and tugged him along behind. He swung out at the corner edge and was then reeled into the darkness behind. Eventually he saw Strang illuminated by the small amount of starlight that penetrated between the shield and the life hab.

The inside and "rear" face of the shield was cut with a radial pattern of grooves, six feet deep and wide.

Strang pulled him close and pointed inward, then his attitude jets gave a slight puff and he headed away, moving toward the center of the rear of the particle shield.

Strang seemed to know where they were going. Flecker felt the tug of the line and was towed along behind him.

31

ADELAIDE AND TOBE WERE SPECIAL PRISONERS. PULLED OUT of the herd, they were taken to Ras Order's personal quarters.

In a lounge of white, black, and leather, they were served mint tea by a blond slave girl in a skimpy costume.

As the girl walked away, Adelaide reflected on the vast chasm that separated Fundan from Khalifi.

Then Ras Order was there, striding in with grave mien beneath his white headdress. The black robes were of the finest silk, jewels flashed on his slippers.

"So," he said, taking her hands in his, bending his steady gaze down upon her. "You have finally come to us."

Tobe shifted uneasily behind her. Ras Order flicked him a glance.

"And you, young man, you have survived without injury?"

"Yes, Prince, but Adelaide needs to rest. Is there somewhere we might shower and relax?"

"Most certainly, you shall inspect the place yourself. We shall make plans at once to find both of you quarters at the New Palace. It will be quite magnificent eventually. An entire city is being mapped out for it."

"You are moving fast, then," murmured Adelaide.

The Prince nodded enthusiastically. "Yes, under Ibrahim's wise guidance we are moving very quickly indeed. The entire schedule has been accelerated."

"And building palaces?"

"Yes, each of the new palaces will house several hundred people, you understand."

"And the rest?"

"Ah yes, well, there will be houses for them."

Ras Order snapped his fingers loudly. The slave girl appeared.

"Clari, conduct the young man to the showers, then show him the quarters you have prepared for our guests."

154

The slave escorted Tobe away. Only when he was outside the door did Tobe realize that Adelaide was not with him, that they had been deftly separated.

"Come." The girl beckoned him to follow. A stern-eyed clone guard, seven feet tall and brutal of countenance, was watching them. The door was closed; there was nothing to be done about the separation. He resolved to be quick.

When they were alone, the Prince turned back to Adelaide. He sat down beside her, too close.

"Adelaide, you should not have waited so long to come to me," he said with a wickedly sincere tone.

"Ras Order, I—"

He raised his palms. "No, don't say it. I know. I was too intemperate on our first meeting. I admit it. I was inexcusably rude, and I demeaned myself in your eyes by my behavior."

Adelaide's face turned cool and thoughtful.

"But now you are here, and I beg you to reconsider your earlier rejection."

"What are you saying?" Adelaide felt herself cringe inside.

"Why, what do you think? Become my bride."

She felt her cheeks flush, but whether it was from rage or the humiliation, she wasn't entirely sure.

"You want me to join your harem, isn't that it?"

Ras Order laughed. "I think the harem is a concept that carries a grossly inflated reputation in the world outside my family."

"You mean you prefer the company of your bioengineered sex objects?"

The Prince laughed again, a little more tightly this time.

"Now we do indeed enter a realm of philosophical contention. Many are they who claim that the best woman is one of our simple beauties, a Clari or an Anji. But, of course, those who claim this are forgetting that woman is more than a machine for sexual pleasure. She has a mind of her own, the perfect female half of the totality that is human life! Thus, the most satisfying experience is always that obtained with a woman who wishes to join with us with all the strength of her free will and mind. At least, this is how I think."

Adelaide nodded. "And so, you are quite a liberal in your family."

The Prince nodded, beaming. "I am liberal in my ways,

155

indeed, very liberal." He threw back his head and laughed again.

She stared at him, all too aware that she was in his power. The rebellion had failed, as she had known it must. And unless Melissa's long shot hit the jackpot, Adelaide knew her future would have to be negotiated with this man.

"So, once again, I will ask you. Will you consent to join me as my bride?"

"I will have to think about this, it is too soon." She wanted to spit in his sly face.

"Ah, so, always the same with you Fundans, eh? Always you are so difficult." He clapped his hands together, stood up and paced back and forth. "Now, of course, you expect me to find you accommodations in the palace, which is difficult since there are so many other claims upon the space available. But for this you will give me nothing. Such is the bargain you place before me, is it not?"

"Look, I cannot help my feelings. I was raised to find things like those slave girls of yours an abomination, and I still do. Khalifi barbarism disgusts me."

The Prince sniffed. "Ah, so." He rolled his eyes to the ceiling and resumed pacing. "Fundans, so difficult, so difficult."

He turned upon her suddenly. "You may find such attitudes will change after you have lived awhile in the New Palace without honored status. As my wife you would be entitled to all the privileges of rank. Without such status, things will go differently. You will see."

The door opened suddenly. Ras Order spun around to find Tobe Berlisher, hair wet, pushing into the room.

"Why are you not in the showers, young man?" said Ras Order with irritation.

"What happened while I was gone?" Tobe said to Adelaide.

"Nothing, Tobe, it was nothing."

Tobe grew alarmed by the deadness in her voice. "What happened, what did he try to do?" He was getting pink in the face.

"Tobe, it was nothing." Adelaide tried to prevent an explosion.

The door chime sounded once more.

"Now what?" Ras Order said. He snapped his finger and the door opened.

Adelaide gasped.

It was Ibrahim himself.

"Sire, I am honored," Ras Order said.

"My Prince, greetings. I am here to ask your captives some questions."

"They are guests, Sire."

Ibrahim chuckled. "Well, well, well, we have Fundans as guests."

Tobe could easily imagine Ibrahim ordering such "guests" to be toasted for breakfast.

"That sort of status can, of course, be changed," Ibrahim said. "Some may start out as guests and end up as pests!" He cast a merry glance Tobe's way.

"Still, I will honor your gift of hospitality. But I do request the opportunity to ask them some questions. Right now, if you don't mind."

Ras Order blinked. Ibrahim had no love of formality, but this seemed immoderately abrupt.

"Of course, of course, at once." The Prince realized something very important was in the air.

Ibrahim looked around himself for a moment, and Ras Order looked to his slaves and pointed. The Clari and Anji clones pushed a chair forward and the ancient ruler sat down.

With another click of his fingers, Ras Order sent the girls away and ordered the null-zone generator on.

Ibrahim sat directly opposite Adelaide. "Now, my dear, I want to talk to you about some odd little developments that we have recently uncovered. I speak about some interference we have detected with the ship computer controller."

His eyes seemed to bore into her. "Who might be responsible for such things?" Ibrahim beamed at her suddenly, reached forward, and patted her hand. "Tell me and I will reward you well."

Adelaide's thoughts were in a whirl. What was this interference the old man referred to? And who could possibly have gained access to the *Founder*'s memory banks?

"I'm sorry," she said, "I just don't know." And then she could hold back the rage no longer. "And anyway, you are responsible for so many unnecessary deaths now, that I wouldn't tell you even if I did know."

"Now, now." Ibrahim waved his hand in disgust. "I do not wish to argue philosophy with you."

"It is not philosophy, it's lives that have been lost because you broke the covenants. You have blood on your hands!"

Ibrahim was dismissive. "These were quite unimportant lives, I'm afraid. We do not need them."

Adelaide confronted once more the certainty of the Khalifi family in its own innate superiority to all other people.

Ibrahim continued. "The work on the A.I. was very fine. Detailed programming, by someone who knew intimately the details of the organization of the A.I. softs."

Adelaide shrugged, relieved. "Not me. My computer skills are limited to financial marketing. I know virtually nothing of design codes or Fundan programming."

"I did not accuse you."

"It doesn't matter, I know very little about these things, they were never my area."

Ibrahim had an unpleasant smile.

"I think you know more than you wish to admit. This young man, I assume he knows much of these things too?"

Puzzled, she said, "But Tobe knows nothing about such codes either. He was our legal aide. Ask him about the legal network and he can help you, but of these design matters, I can assure you he will know no more than I do."

"Hah! So you say. We will ask the young man some questions, and perhaps we will have him put to the torture to make sure we get the answers we need."

"He knows nothing! He cannot help you."

"We shall see."

32

THE KHALIFI EXODUS CONTINUED. THE PALACES ROSE IN THE forest and Khalifi poured into the suites as fast as they were built. Squabbling over apartments became a major headache.

Around them the work teams sweated under the hot sun in a haze of puffcrete fumes and dust thrown up by the huge vehicles that churned across the building sites.

The Khalifi, clad in the traditional black silk, sat out on

air-conditioned balconies, sipped mint tea and watched the work in progress.

And, of course, the saw teams continued to cut trees. The jungles had been cleared in great swaths for miles around each of the palaces.

Fields were being laid out. Soon a newly recruited agricultural force would be at work sowing them with the selected grain crops. A small petrochem plant was in production down by the coast. Oil had been discovered in two large fields, quite close by. Wells were already producing a million barrels a day.

From the petrochem plant came a steady outpouring of insecticide. The communal insect of the new world, already being called the "chitin," was a major pest.

Above, aboard the *Founder*, only the old men remained, with half their guards. The rebellion was crushed, but they were taking no chances. They did not plan to move until their own suites were completed.

Indeed, Ibrahim was too embroiled in the riddles surrounding the *Founder* A.I. to think of leaving.

And then, right in the midst of the interrogation of Tobe Berlisher, Ibrahim received an urgent message from Merzik, asking him to visit at once.

Ibrahim found Faruk and Feisal waiting for him. A moment later Merzik appeared. "Welcome, my brothers," he said, drew them into another room, and switched on the light.

They stared, shocked rigid, with mouths open, at an alien being, a biped, standing in a tall cage in the center of the room.

It was the size of Amesh, with large orange eyes and the muzzle of a bear or lion. Short gray fur grew over most of the body, with longer fur trimming the shoulders.

And above those eyes was a relatively large cranium. This was no mere animal! Most shocking of all were the clothes, made of finely-worked hide, and the moccasins on the big feet. She wore an apron worked with beads and small red feathers. This was belted at the waist, and from the vest hung several pouches.

It was obviously a she—there were unmistakable breasts beneath the apron.

The creature hissed to itself and said something in a guttural tongue.

"What is this?" Ibrahim said at last, marveling.

"An intelligent alien life form," said Merzik. "We captured

159

it in the equatorial region. They have been spotted in several places there, usually in high valleys."

It suddenly grabbed the bars of its cage and shook them furiously.

"It seems upset at your treatment of it," Faruk said.

"It was captured only with great difficulty."

"How numerous are they? Why have I not heard of this before?"

Merzik shrugged uncomfortably. "There was a report, a ground team in the equatorial region found them. However, on their return a shuttle malfunction took place. None of the ground team survived an emergency depressurization in orbit."

Ibrahim chuckled. "So there are no witnesses, eh, Merzik?"

"I did not say it."

"Hah-ha. Rarely have I seen you attempt such subtlety."

Merzik scowled. Ibrahim continued speaking. "Merzik, I imagine, thinks we must exterminate these lovely creatures."

"Of course, they can challenge our right to take the New World."

"But to whom shall they apply for aid? They are probably nontechnological, that much is obvious from the creature's garments. Nor have we detected any radio signals or even any electric lighting. They cannot threaten us physically."

"If word of their existence leaks out and is transmitted back to Earth, then we would not hold full legal title to the New World."

"We would be outlaw once more. So what?" Feisal said.

"Quite right, Feisal," Faruk said. "And this time we would also be forty light-years distant from any of their so-called authorities."

"We will not be so fortunate forever. Eventually there will be more ships."

"Not if the Gung An Bu has its way."

"Ach," Merzik said, "the World Government is undergoing a Stalinist phase. Already new pharaonic figures emerge. But you know how cyclic Earth's governments are. Eventually new technologies will seep through and improve the economy, the social pharoahs' day will be over, and Earth will look outward again."

"And so?"

"So these creatures must never have existed. They must be expunged completely, utterly."

Feisal shook his head with distaste.

"Look, you dolts!" Merzik grew irritated with his brethren. "Do you think that when the Earth sends its own expedition here, they'll come at our technological level? If they can wrest the title to our planet away from us, they will, so we must have absolutely no taint to that title. This is our world, we were the first here and we shall always rule here. But we will have to do so by force of legal norms. Otherwise our rule will last a hundred years or so and we will be submerged by the tide of submen that will flood over us."

"You exaggerate, my brother."

"Not so. Consider Mars. Once the Russians opened the doors to free immigration, they were swamped within a century. The Russians are now a small minority on what was once their own planet."

Faruk sneered. "Bah, if you call a dozen domes a planet worth having."

"Besides, the Russians breed for extinction, their free women and other filthy concepts. We will breed more vigorously," Feisal said.

"That is disgusting!" Merzik roared. "We must remain pure of blood, we cannot submerge our essence in the common genetic ruck!"

"Now, now, Merzik, let us not squabble about such things," said Ibrahim, who had locked eyes with the female creature and was entranced. "These creatures are beautiful. We shall have to study them carefully before we make any decision about their future."

Merzik's scowl intensified. "Bah, it is as I feared. You have become a soft-eyed sentimentalist with old age. You must move aside and let me take control of our family's destiny."

"Really," Feisal snorted. "Merzik, I am surprised at you. You know that Ibrahim hasn't a sentimental cell in his body."

"Hasn't had one for ages," Faruk seconded.

Merzik ignored them. He kept his gaze on Ibrahim.

The creature suddenly gave an angry cry and shook the bars of the cage once more, then released a long stream of voluble syllables.

"I would say," Feisal said, with a sly grin, "that she is cursing us and our ancestry in no uncertain terms."

Ibrahim laughed. "I think you're right. An enchanting creature—we shall have to investigate these creatures thoroughly." Ibrahim turned to Merzik.

"My brother, listen to me, please—"

"No, Merzik. We shall not exterminate them, we shall make friends with them."

"How can you make friends with that!" Merzik shouted. "It is an animal!"

"And are we not animals?"

"Of course not, we are divine instruments of Allah's will upon the cosmos."

"Oh, yes, I had forgotten your views on that," Ibrahim murmured.

Faruk groaned aloud. Merzik flashed him an angry glance.

"Enough," Ibrahim continued, "I have made up my mind about this. I will take control of this creature. It shall be shipped down to the surface and we will study it, and more of its fellows as well."

33

ALTHOUGH HIDEO HAD THOUGHT HIMSELF QUITE ADEQUATELY terrified before, the terrors aboard ship seemed insignificant once he was outside. Melissa tugged him behind her as she maneuvered with attitude jets.

Ahead loomed the mass of the particle shield. He felt like a grain of wheat about to be ground by a millstone. He clung to the line with the frozen strength of panic.

He was outside the ship!

The thought iced his brain.

Fortunately, Melissa had not been idly boasting when she'd claimed to be an expert in no-grav maneuver. She'd taken her weightless rescue training up to the Bronze Star. She deftly maneuvered the pair of them with the aid of her jets and the safety line connected to Hideo's belt.

Once again he realized how little, really, he knew of the girl.

When Hideo looked back, he caught the flashing glare of a slice of the New World visible beyond the bulk of the life-support torus. There it was, the planet of his dreams, which now seemed more like the stuff of nightmares.

Then Melissa fired her braking jets and Hideo swooped past her, taking the tether line with him. She gracefully maneuvered out of his way and then was pulled on, but more slowly, toward the inside surface of the shield. She braked again, slowing herself and Hideo still further.

There, ahead of them, a darker pocket loomed. And within it came occasional gleams as light reflected in from the hub.

They entered the dark pocket, and Melissa flashed a light ahead. Hideo shivered as he saw what they illuminated. A turning hab surface, with FUNDAN MADE stenciled on the outside.

Then they were approaching the small hub, about ten feet across. There was power; the small approach lights around the hub airlock door were winking in red and blue.

Melissa used the secret key code to open the airlock.

They slid into the brightly-lit cavity and it automatically pressurized. Then the inner door opened.

The interior was dark, lit only by tiny emergency lights set in the ceiling.

"There's atmosphere," Melissa said. "So far so good."

Nearby they found the entrance to the access tube, a dark hole sunk in the floor. Nothing but the sound of a distant ventilator hum broke the chilly silence.

"Lo-grav to hi-grav descent coming up. You remember what I told you?"

"Keep your handholds," muttered Hideo.

Melissa went down first, pulling herself along the no-grav rail. The approach tube was narrow, centered by the rails. Soon they had reversed approach and were climbing "down" on the handholds on the rails. The gravity increased quickly, and they turned to use the spiral staircase.

They emerged from a narrow door into the interior of the microtorus. A warren of narrow corridors in Fundan spaceline style confronted them. The rooms were unfinished. There were walls that were merely studs and wiring, others with half the panels in place. Colored leads and wires dangled down from the ceiling in such profusion, they made a virtual jungle of bright reds, yellows, and greens.

But all these rooms were perfectly empty. Melissa breathed a sigh of relief. The Khalifi had not seen fit to occupy this place. It had been decommissioned, its computers taken down.

She pulled off Hideo's helmet after depressurizing her own. Now to confront the big question. How far down had the computers been degraded in here? If they had been physically removed, she was sunk.

She headed for the ramp to the outermost deck, where the computers and the command module were centered. Hideo followed.

Right by the ramp a door stood ajar, and as she drew level with it, an arm stretched out holding a small handgun.

"It's a low-velocity weapon, plastic loads. It can kill you, but it won't bust the outer skin of the hab." The voice was wound tight with tension.

"I know what it is," Melissa said with considerable bitterness. Failure, and so close to their objective. She felt a pit open up in her; she could barely breathe.

She backed away. Hideo stared, aghast.

But the man who emerged from the hidden doorway was no Khalifi guard. He was short, less than six feet. He had red hair and the look of early middle age about him. He was wearing an emergency suit much like their own.

Melissa felt a breath of hope. Maybe there was still a chance.

"Who are you?" she said.

"I'll do the talking," he replied. "Move ahead of me, go in the door I just came out of, both of you."

The gun was made of clear plastic, and he held it in both hands now, trained on her face. There was nothing Melissa could do.

She entered the indicated room, designed as an office but never completed. It was stark, bare, and there were no holes in the walls or ceiling.

"All right, you wait here."

Melissa spun round. "At least tell me who you are."

But the door closed as a small light went on.

She had only Hideo for company, and he was on the brink of a heart attack from fright.

34

THE RING CONTINENT OF THE NEW WORLD FEATURED AN enormous range of mountains that marched along the equator itself. In these mountains were high valleys which were home to a native life form that called itself the fein.

In the high valley of Kanwa Ibli lived one Igi of Yamuka, a fein of the Ukala, a "widepath" kin group.

Kanwa Ibli was a green wrinkle in the center of the Hokkh, the "Knuckle of Delight" in fein lore. Normally Igi was a joyous fein, filled with good cheer. But a grim tragedy had fallen upon him, and Igi was a fein possessed.

He had recently been mated with Kyika of the Inko, another widepath family well-represented in Yamuka village. They were blissfully wed.

One day while they were out together, gathering glob glob fruits, tang berries, and tubers in the forest of Yamuk, a strange noise filled the air above them. A shining craft containing sky demons appeared.

It swooped down to land and sky demons emerged who fired projectile weapons at the two fein. The fein hid themselves, but were driven out of concealment by a metal demon thing and forced to flee.

Igi lead Kyika down a steep-walled canyon, seeking to escape in a direction that would lead the sky demons away from the village.

However, the sky-demon craft appeared again, flying up the canyon toward them.

Once more figures leaped from the craft and pursued the fein, who set out to climb the steep wall of the canyon.

Exploding gas grenades were hurled. Kyika inhaled some of the poisonous mixture and fell stunned to the ground.

Before Igi knew what had happened, the sky demons had gathered up Kyika's body and borne it away. Igi pursued, roaring imprecations and challenges, but the shining craft accelerated and vanished into the blue sky.

Disconsolate, Igi returned to the village and sought wisdom from the older fein, the mzees.

There were many opinions concerning sky demons, and many different remedies were suggested.

However, since sky demons were creatures from beyond the Hokkh, from out of the world itself, it was generally agreed that in reality there was precious little anyone could really do if afflicted by them.

Igi felt most definitely wronged and afflicted. But as Mzee Loberki pointed out, the sky demons were not present to be adjudged for their wrongs. Nor could their next appearance be predicted at all accurately.

"You will be lucky to get within kifket range of the creatures again in your lifetime," said old Burgugu. "Sky demons are notoriously rare manifestations. You must have committed an act of impurity to attract them in the first place."

Mzee Chalma suggested that Igi build a large beacon fire of logs, in the shape of a cross, a sign of peace and strength. This might cause the sky demons to return and explain themselves.

However, several others present thought this a dangerous idea. Who wanted the sky demons to return? They might be implacable and wish to carry off others of the fein.

Mzee Chalma said that if they did that, then surely the Arizel tki Fenrille would be aroused and would return and see to these sky demons once and for all.

Several other Mzees scorned this remark. The Arizel tki Fenrille would not return over such a small matter. Only if the unholy fire was lit, or the world was overrun by some plague from beyond the sky, would they come back. Until old Long Legs himself was dead, in fact.

On this there was more or less general agreement.

Igi decided to make a pilgrimage to the sacred glade of the Quiet Spirit of Iropo. This would involve a journey of many days, and so he wove a backpack and filled it with meat jerky, dried tubers, and tang berry sauce. He took down a braided kifket sheath and attached it to his belt.

When he was ready, he made his farewells to his mother, Nochas, and to the mother of Kyika, Noppi Inko, and he set off up the valley, heading in the direction of the sun's rise.

He traveled thus for three days. On the fourth day he

passed over the top of the ridgeline of Kanwa Ibli and entered the barren, cold valley of Nishaka Gon Koli. Upland moors, drear and bleak, stretched ahead of him. Far in the distance was the sawtoothed edge of great Iropo, white cap glistening in the sun.

All day Igi toiled across the moors, and by nightfall was halfway across Nishaka Gon Koli. He searched for a good campsite alongside a stream and was about to sit and assemble a small fire when something made him look up. In the direction of Iropo he saw red and green lights moving across the sky.

Igi shivered. These were not a natural phenomenon. The lights came closer, and soon he detected a roaring sound with a horrid familiarity. It was undoubtedly sky demons, perhaps even the same ones that had abducted Kyika.

As he watched, the skycraft swooped around to the south and came down to land, out of sight in a hollow in the plain.

Campfire forgotten, Igi moved toward the distant landing site. Briefly he pulled out his kifket, a stone knife-axe with two razor-sharp edges. He kissed it and dedicated himself to finding his Kyika. The sky demons would pay for their crime!

Randolf Flecker slipped quickly along the corridor. The lights were on in here, but Strang was still almost invisible, hidden inside a mountainous tangle of wires and leads.

The innards of two banks of computer hardware were hanging out behind him. In front of him was a smaller computer with the Fundan Made triangle on its side.

"What was it?" Strang said without pausing. He yanked down a set of blue lines and began plugging their clips to a set of connectors.

A monitor in front of him blinked to life.

"Ah-hah, progress at last."

"There were two of them. They weren't Khalifi."

"We knew that, tell me what we didn't know."

"How did we know they weren't Khalifi?"

"Size. One of them is less than 1.9 meters tall."

Flecker whistled. "You're right, one elderly Japanese, name of Hideo Tagomi, from the science program."

"The other?"

"Female, dark hair, heavy build, I don't know her."

"Get me some video on them." Strang continued shoving

leads into clips. He checked a reference manual open beside him. There was a manic look to his eyes.

Someone, most likely the Khalifi, had changed the entry codes for the *Founder* A.I. designer interface. The changes had been subtle, and he'd almost been trapped. But an instinctive yank back had cut connection almost instantly. So far no probe had lit up the boards around him.

However, the plan had to be reworked, and quickly. The *Founder* A.I. was off limits. He would have to work around it. That meant a set of protected hardware. Which meant rebuilding some of the control torus's degraded equipment.

And all this while the Khalifi were having things their own way with the passengers. Thousands had surrendered and been taken into the Purple level in chains. The fortunate would be made slaves and shipped to the surface. The rest?

Strang's fingers dove through the tangled leads for a yellow lead, which he connected above the blue lines. Every second might count now.

Flecker punched up video from the microcomputer, which was wired into the control net of the microtorus.

A view of the small room, the two people, sprang up on the micro's main screen.

Hideo Tagomi appeared in close-up, his face drawn and tight. He looked as if he were under enormous stress.

Then the girl's face appeared.

Strang froze for a moment. He swallowed and then looked away.

"Cannot go back, too late for that now."

"What did you say?"

Strang turned on him, wild-eyed. "Keep them locked up, d'ya hear me! We haven't time to deal with that now."

Flecker was startled by the sudden vehemence. Strang was back among the wires, pulling together groups of red and green leads. Flecker shrugged. Strang was a man obsessed.

35

Ibrahim lolled in a favorite chair, a Gorski comp-vu from early Mars. On screen he had Jurgen Smits, who headed up the new science team.

"The video you sent us of the alien was remarkable, but in the flesh she is even more astonishing," Smits said.

"She has arrived safely with you, good. Is it not wonderful? Is it not an experience, just to stand in front of that creature and feel the alienness?" Ibrahim's enthusiasm was unalloyed.

"Incredible. Never did I think that we should find such a treasure."

"Undoubtedly intelligent."

"No doubt at all, but technologically primitive."

"I was reminded of tribal cultures of long ago, the Africans, the Amerindians."

"In particular I see the New Guinea peoples. They were very primitive in some ways, but quite advanced in others."

"Indeed, indeed." Ibrahim was delighted. The presence of this alien race was like some immense plum added to the bounty of the New Word, *his* New World.

"Theories of evolutionary convergence have been rewarded with a vengeance," Smits said. "The creatures are very like us, perhaps a little larger."

"Tipler, Lowenstein, old Wallace, they were just as wrong as the damned religious nuts." Ibrahim giggled. This was one area of scientific inquiry that had always fascinated Ibrahim, who had never believed for a moment in any concept as fantastic as "Allah," and who had battled the religious believers in the family all his life as a result.

Smits laughed at this. "I have enough of those in my family. The New Dutch Kirk was bad enough, but then we got the Church of Christ Spaceman."

It was Ibrahim's turn to laugh.

"Ah, your Christian crazies, they are wild, I agree, but I have had to deal with Muslims my whole life. Do you know how mad the New Koran is?"

"Never studied it, I'm afraid. Had enough of all that irrationality when I was young and had to go to kirk."

"Well, of course I understand. But can you imagine, my ancestors were so besotted with this stuff that they actually lifted the Kaaba stone and put it into orbit? This was a magical rock that had fallen from space in the distant past. It had been the centerpiece of the pilgrimage to Mecca. So at the eleventh hour it was taken back to space. Imagine! But, of course, soon afterward there was no Mecca left, not after the war."

Smits became grave. "Yes, that was a time of mass irrationality."

Ibrahim sighed. Those early days had been terrible. The world had been consumed by hatreds. Small nuclear wars flashed in the hot spots.

"And once they had the Kaaba in orbit, they started the pilgrimages all over again. Only now you had to ride a spaceship to get there."

Smits chuckled. Ibrahim continued in a ruminating manner, "Of course, the pilgrims had been going by jet plane for a century or more, but to take the stone into orbit, to a place where the Prophet had never been, never imagined, never described, well, I ask you . . ." Ibrahim trailed off, shaking his head.

"Few passions have produced more bizarre acts than religion. For myself, I subscribe to the Mind-mekanik System. I have done so for many years."

"Yes, yes, indeed so," murmured Ibrahim, who thought privately that the Mind-mekanik was just another form of hokum. Ibrahim himself subscribed to the tonic effects of power.

"But this specimen, now," Smits said, returning to the object of their conversation.

"Yes, wonderful, isn't she? I look forward to reading an analysis of your dissection."

"It almost seems a pity. There's a weird beauty about her, isn't there?"

"There is, but we need to know so much, and so far she is our only specimen."

"Convergent evolution with a vengeance."

170

A small square window opened in the screen image. The face of Kierke Spreak appeared there.

"Ah, excuse me," Ibrahim murmured, "I have a security call."

"Of course, I will return to my work."

Ibrahim blanked Smits off his screen.

"Yes?"

Spreak was the security chief for the Camp One region.

"You asked to be informed when we had more information on the monster," he said.

"Yes, indeed. What have you got for me?"

Spreak was quite pale. "Final casualty toll is at least twenty-five, all dead. But there are some others missing, so they may be lost in the forest. We took four bodies out of the thing's guts. It ate them, suits, boots, and all."

Ibrahim frowned. "This lifeform was unknown from the biosurvey?"

"Absolutely, never seen until yesterday."

"Then it must be very rare."

"My own conclusion exactly."

"Fortunate for us then, eh?" Ibrahim said.

"Indeed, the thing was nearly impossible to kill. It tore the shovel right off the cab of one of our big diggers. I can't imagine how strong it has to be to be able to do something like that."

"And it attacked without any provocation?"

"Absolutely. It pursued the saw team for miles to kill them all."

"Mmm, sounds quite formidable. How, in the end, was it destroyed?"

"A guard pulled a grenade as he was being eaten. It went off in the thing's gullet."

Ibrahim giggled at this thought, then suppressed it. Spreak's face was flushed with indignation. After a momentary pause he went on.

"It fell down after that and we emptied our guns into it. Finally we took a saw and cut the damn thing's head off. That seemed to do the trick." He swallowed.

"Mmmm."

"However, the head was still alive an hour later. The eyes moved, the mouth opened and closed at least once."

Ibrahim frowned. Such stubbornness in a dangerous animal

171

was troubling. "I will put Tariq on to this, it is the kind of study that he excels at."

"Might I suggest something?"

Ibrahim looked up. "Yes, what?"

"That an immediate census of these creatures be made. We need to know where they come from. Such regions must be avoided."

"Possibly we will have to take stronger measures, culling them, eliminating them from most of their range, whatever we have to do."

"Yes, even that."

Ibrahim cut the connection and called Tariq.

36

TARIQ STARED AT THE BIZZARE THING ON THE SCREEN. THE image that Ibrahim had sent him was hard to decipher at first. When the pieces finally fit and made sense, he gaped.

It lay in the middle of a mess of broken equipment. Mud-colored fur covered a torso the size of a truck, and the long, ungainly limbs stuck out ten meters in any direction.

"This, then, is the monster?" Tariq licked his lips.

"Yes, my nephew. The head was severed. You can see it in the second clip."

The head was a cylindrical turret covered in the same fur, with glossy black eyes like buttons on top. A thing like the beak of a giant pelican projected below the eyes.

"You are to do something about these things," Ibrahim said.

Tariq sucked in a breath. This was it, the ultimate in big game. He felt as if he had waited all his life for this moment.

"Yes, of course. We will have to locate them and destroy them. Obvious menace."

"This one killed twenty-five people, apparently."

"Shaitan!"

Ibrahim waited for a second before continuing. "They were

unprepared, of course. No one had seen this type of creature before."

"Yes, obviously." At last, a worthy foe for the true Crown Prince.

"So . . ." Ibrahim hesitated.

Tariq did not. The words poured out of him. "I will not fail you, my esteemed uncle. I will make you proud of me."

Ibrahim turned away from the earnest light that shone in those troubled eyes.

. . . Merzik begat this monster . . . and wishes him to rule in my place some day . . .

The old man shivered. Tariq was babbling, "I will organize a search for them. I have some nine-millimeter ammunition that should be effective—penetration heads that explode in soft tissue. The problem will be finding the monsters. They are obviously very rare."

"Yes, well," Ibrahim murmured. "Do not disappoint me this time, Tariq."

Tariq nodded. Ibrahim wondered if it was possible that some sense might finally have entered that hard, stubborn head.

They broke contact. Ibrahim returned to a meditation on the state of things.

The new palaces were open, still far from complete, but already they pulsed with the life of the new colony.

There had been endless squabbles over the allocation of apartments, and even one duel, with antique muskets, in the courtyard of the Green Tile Palace. Ibrahim could not suppress a smile. Two young hotheads were in the emergency ward, but peace had been declared between the warring women.

One happy result had been a temporary lull in most of the other conflicts. Everyone was too shocked by the outrage. Mothers thought of the loss of sons, sisters of lost brothers; all curbed their demands for this, that, and everything else.

And, of course, peace would not last. Every Khalifi Princess wanted a palace of her very own!

Ibrahim sighed. His own quarters were to be a simple house of twelve rooms that was being built at the northern end of the Azure Sky Palace. He would be separated from the main palace by a long lawn, a garden maze, several hedges, and a grove of fruit trees. With any luck he would hardly notice the rest of his quarrelsome family.

Unfortunately, his house was far from complete. The plumbing design had proved worthless and was being redone. Until it was finished, he intended to stay aboard the ship.

Meanwhile, on a happier note, all resistance to his rule was destroyed. Ibrahim might even give praise to the Allah he had never believed in.

He reached out to check the progress of the probes on the small red moon. It seemed ideal for an orbital prison. They would hollow it out, use the waste rock for shielding material, and load it up with a few thousand unnecessary passengers.

The screen windowed to offer different shots from the orbiting modules. Close-up shots followed.

He asked for projections on completion of the first prison units. More screen windows opened. Figures whirled in them briefly and then, shockingly, they dissolved. The screen display wobbled and went off.

Then chaos broke out. For a moment the lights in the tent flickered. A slave screamed in terror somewhere behind him.

And then the lights really went out. And stayed out. The screams became general.

Ibrahim yelled for the *Founder* A.I. It did not appear on any screen. No power. No lights.

Outside, the artificial daylight was dimming rapidly.

Ibrahim began to feel a sensation not unlike panic.

What the hell was happening?

Then the screen on his antique unit came back to life, although there was still no power elsewhere in the tent. On screen, colored hash blazed a few seconds and then the pixilage solidified into a face.

Ibrahim sat up with a hiss.

"You! You are dead! You were thrown into the sump years ago, like the fool you were."

"I, we, live on, Ibrahim. You have not won the game after all."

The voice was so strange, so dead-sounding, that to Ibrahim it was as if he were hearing old Edward Fundan himself.

"Who is this? Who is speaking?"

Ibrahim's fingers stabbed at a key pad to summon up the *Founder* A.I. Nothing happened.

"I am Fundan. All Fundan," the face said.

Ibrahim scoffed. "This is Edward really, isn't it? Own up."

"I speak for all Fundan, I am every Fundan, since Emily and Talbot, who were the first."

Ibrahim stared. "This is fantastic, how did you do this, you old bastard? And to your own flesh and blood too? Or is this all just a construct? Some box full of biochips somewhere?"

The face was expressionless.

"That does not matter," it said. "It is time to negotiate an end to your depredations, Khalifi."

Ibrahim laughed, then spat eloquently into the darkness around him.

A moment passed.

"You have noticed the lack of lighting?" the face said.

It was actually growing chill in the tent. Night had fallen, hours too early.

"So what?"

"So I have control of the ship systems. It will grow cold in your quarters very soon."

Ibrahim stabbed more frantically at the controls. Suddenly a figure stumbled through the dark tent, fell on its knees beside him. He saw the oily gleam of a gun barrel; a candle was extended. His heart froze, but recovered when he saw that it was only Amesh.

"Master, it has gone dark. There is no power on the entire deck." Amesh was there, ready to die for the master. Ibrahim was slightly reassured.

"I know, old friend, I know. Keep guard at the door to the tent, there may be assassins."

Amesh moved away silently. The slaves groveled in terror. Ibrahim turned back to the screen.

"Look you, whatever you are, we will find you and then we will see who has control of this ship."

Ibrahim hammered out a secret interior code to the A.I. There was a flash of light suddenly from the tent's interior spots. Ibrahim whooped. "Now, my ghostly enemy, now we will have you!"

The lights came again and steadied. Simultaneously, a window opened on the screen. The *Founder* was back.

"I have reasserted control of the Purple level," the A.I. said in a curiously disembodied voice.

"What has happened? Your voice has degraded."

The Fundan was gone; his window blinked off.

"I am not entirely sure," the A.I. said. "But probability analysis suggests an infiltration/subvert run. There are certain codes to which I cannot refuse access. Like the interior code you just used."

Ibrahim flushed in horror. His worst nightmare come true.

"But I had you purged. The Gamei people told me you were clean!"

"They lied. They were paid to," the A.I. said suddenly.

"What?" Ibrahim felt his eyeballs distend.

"Gamei Intersyndic Corporation was owned by Tersant Bank."

"Yes, yes, of course. Tersant, it was. Good bank, used them myself on many occasions. They had an office aboard *Rimal*."

"Tersant Bank was part of the Hodoya Conglom. Edward Fundan was a founding member of the Hodoya Six."

"But Hodoya were Koreans! Of the old school. How—"

"Edward Fundan paid three billion credits for entry. He did a great deal of business through Hodoya, primarily in ice-engineering tech."

Ibrahim gave a shriek of rage. Outwitted...

"Find that construct for me!" he screamed at the screen.

In response, a design map of the ship came up on the screen and scrolled to reveal the tiny control torus that turned about the spindle, within a pocket in the particle shield.

"Oh no," Ibrahim breathed, his folly finally revealed to him. "But that was deactivated! My men did that. I know that was not left to Gamei."

"It was deactivated, but it is also the source of the infiltrations. Someone is there now, but I can exercise no control there. All systems have been insulated from central control."

"How can it be attacked, or seized?"

"It is too close to the main life hab to be destroyed with explosives."

"How can we retake it? There cannot be many of them in there."

"Through the spindle, and then through the outside skin. The guards will have to cut their way in."

37

THEY WERE COMING. THE SPECKS ON THE SCREEN WERE OBVIous enough. Floating out from the spindle like glittering insects. Five men, five trained killers.

He saw them and did not hesitate. He pulled himself around and groped for a small case on the floor. It opened to his touch and he jerked out another pair of Fundan .32 automatics, slick little gray handguns that fired smash-type disintegrator plastix with scant recoil.

He needed time. The cyberclast kit was still working its way through the *Founder*'s screen of protexture. He'd built the kit himself, programming on a microcomputer he'd pulled from a shuttle.

The clast was a cross between a virus and a bomb. It was now just a few minutes away from penetration of the A.I. interior-shell function matrix; the killers would not give him those minutes.

He grunted. Well, that had been a problem with the plan since the beginning, but there had been no way around it. His opening work with the design code had succeeded in arousing the A.I., and also in blinding it to the real peril.

Now Ibrahim was keeping it busy searching the ship for other threats.

He had planted lures, new control nodes in many of the ship's local computer units. These had to be purged, some physically, by sending in guards to turn off power to hardware installations.

The *Founder* was distracted. The cyberclast kit was too small, too delicate for the A.I.'s protex mesh, the automatic screen, the nerves in the "skin." The clast was running in picocode, trickling through the nanomeshlines.

Given the time, it would go all the way.

But now there were the killers.

Strang found Flecker in the stairwell.

"Take these." He handed over the guns. "Give them to the two you captured earlier. Tell them that this is their chance to fight the Khalifi. Their only chance. You've got to keep the guards out of this section, just give me a few minutes."

"Guards? You mean guards are coming here?" Flecker squawked.

"They'll be here in less than a minute. You have to give these guns to those two and get into defensive positions. Now. No time to waste."

Flecker stared, swallowing hard.

"How many guards?" he said at last.

"Five, get going."

"What about you?" Flecker said. "What will you do?"

"I'm either going to blow the *Founder* or I'm going to go down with the ship. A fighting bluejay either way."

"What?"

There was something completely crazy now in Strang's eyes.

"Hamilton Tiger Cat time, y'see. Then we force Ibrahim to surrender. Third-period surge, that's all."

"Yeah." Flecker looked at the guns in his hand bitterly, then back to Strang's wild-blue eyes.

"We force Ibrahim to surrender. Yeah."

And I'll be dead by then, he thought as he spun away.

Melissa saw the door open, and tried to adopt the relaxed but ready posture taught by Fundan martial-arts schools.

The red-haired man popped inside. His eyes were wild and he was chewing his lower lip. Suddenly, without any warning, he tossed a gun to her, another to Hideo, who emitted a little squeak and promptly dropped it as if it were red hot.

"Listen to me," the man said. "If you want to fight the Khalifi, now's the time to do it."

Melissa automatically checked the gun. It was loaded. She thumbed the safety.

"You'd better explain yourself," she said, ready to fire if she needed.

"Khalifi guards are coming here. The man says we have to stop them."

"Man? What man?"

"Strang." Flecker realized he had no idea what Strang's credentials were for his role. Strang was a mystery Noram, a blue-eyed echo of an ancient people.

178

"Strang? Who the hell is that?" Melissa snapped. "And who are you, for that matter?"

Flecker held his hands up in frustration. "We don't have time for formal introductions. Those guards are on their way here, we have to stop them."

"What is this Strang doing?"

"I think he's destroying the A.I. that controls the ship."

Melissa gasped. "But how? What codes does he know?"

"I don't know, I don't know anything much about all this. There hasn't been time to find out, really. If you see what I mean . . ."

Melissa stared at him.

"I'm a tree scientist, that's what I know about, you see. My dissertation was on Virginia kudzu."

Melissa wore a blank expression.

"Anyway, are you coming?" he said.

"Yes, of course." She turned on Hideo with a fierce look in her eye. "We both are."

Hideo moaned softly, but picked up the gun.

"But at least tell me your name." Melissa spun back to face him.

"Flecker, Randolf Flecker. I was in the tree-science program. I know Mr. Tagomi, of course."

A flash of recognition blinked across Hideo's face. "Yes, I know you now, I remember, Mister, ah, Flecker."

"I was in command of the Ground-Break Team Eight."

Hideo nodded. "Ah yes, I remember perfectly. Badly treated by a chitin insect nest."

There was a loud clang somewhere.

"They're here, they're in the ship. Come on, before it's too late." Flecker ran from the room.

Melissa jumped out in pursuit of him. She recalled her short training class in ballistic-weapon usage. It seemed a long, long way away, and long ago.

To his total surprise, Hideo Tagomi found himself stumbling along right behind her, clutching the little gray gun. He could scarcely believe this was happening to him. The worst thing he could have imagined happening as a result of his agreeing to put on that damned space suit was to end up in a battle with the Khalifi guards. And now he was going to battle those same guards.

They ran back toward the under-entrance to the torus office space.

Flecker was unsure what to do. He pushed open the doors of a few rooms along the way. All the doors were triple hinged, surrounded by Fundan seal.

Melissa caught up to him and pulled him to a stop.

"We have to hit them from an ambush; they're already inside."

Flecker nodded, close to a paralysis of mind and body from fear. He remembered Garmash with terrible clarity. It had been horribly difficult to kill Garmash.

Melissa pulled Hideo into a room on the right side of the corridor, just back from an intercorridor door. Flecker went in on the left.

They waited. To get to the control sections, the guards would have to come through there.

Half a minute ticked by. Melissa thought the guards were taking a little too much time, and then the intercorridor doors opened together and two men, guns ready, jumped through.

A boot knocked the door back.

She fired and dove simultaneously to her right. Hideo was already lying on the floor, beneath a countertop.

Plastic loads whopped into the walls, the guards both firing in.

Melissa rolled to her right. Something hit her left leg, and right afterward she knew she had no leg left below the knee.

The bullets were still mashing into the walls, fragments of wallboard dusting the air. Melissa got off a shot, saw it hit the door uselessly, and she looked up into the gun eyes of death.

But the guards were already toppling, falling in with bulging eyes and blood everywhere, shot in the back at close range by Flecker.

They were dead by the time they hit the floor. Flecker looked in and staggered away to be sick.

Melissa sat up, looked at her shattered leg, and felt a peculiar weakness.

"Help me," she gasped to Hideo. Then she fainted.

Hideo saw her leg and almost fainted himself. Blood was everywhere. He gagged, and then remembered the suit's built-in medpack. He ripped it open with shaking fingers, pulled out a sprayer, and coated the shattered end of her leg with wound spray.

"I have stopped the bleeding," he said. He was surprised at how calm he felt. And yet he knew that the calm was false, for beneath it he felt a sudden, strong, rising rage.

They had wounded, perhaps killed, Melissa. Hideo Tagomi was now aroused to war.

He checked Melissa's pulse. She lived yet, and now that the blood loss was stanched, she would survive, provided that the rest of the guards were stopped.

Flecker was at the door.

They stared at the intercorridor doors.

"I will take the left now," said Hideo, who slipped across and concealed himself.

A second later the doors pushed open.

"Gizmo, Blucher, where are you?" a huge, brutal-faced guard called from the dark.

Silence prevailed.

"Sounds like Giz don't hear you," another huge man said.

"I don't like this," the first said.

"Tell Amesh about it, see if he cares." The other strode in, looked left and right at the doors but failed to see Flecker or little Hideo.

The first guard edged in after him, speaking into his communicator as he came.

"Inside section doors, don't have contact yet with Gizmo and Blucher."

The receiver crackled. Flecker fired from concealment behind the door.

His shots took the man in the neck and face plate. One slipped through between cheek and jugular and removed his head.

The other guard spun and fired in one smooth movement. The bullets whanged off the steel door and mushed into the floor fiber as Flecker fell to the floor inside.

The guard jumped backward into the room where Hideo was hiding and jerked out a grenade.

Hideo saw it, a gleaming poisonous egg, the red button pulsed. Hideo lifted his gun and pulled the trigger.

Nothing happened.

The guard noticed him!

The poisonous egg!

The safety was on, Hideo knew. But he forgot how to thumb it down.

The guard was charging, still holding the poisonous egg, a huge hand outstretched to crush a frail, old throat.

Hideo dropped the gun, took hold of the charging guard's outstretched arm, and turned inside, expertly tossing the giant

181

over his hip. The man slid through the door, hand up, still holding the poisonous egg.

And then came a flash so bright that Hideo knew he would see no more as he was hurled across the room and smashed into the wall.

38

AMESH HAD GLIMPSED THE FURY OF THAT GRENADE BY THE INtercorridor door. He understood immediately, and ducked the shrap that sizzled by overhead.

Then he moved fast.

He had already made an exploratory hole in the ceiling. Now he slung a grapple and hauled himself up. The struct was light there, but he was agile; he propelled himself across the ceiling on his toes and the heels of his hands, traveling on the joists and beams.

Gizmo and Blucher, Rock and Fele—they were all dead. It was up to Amesh to carry out the master's order.

The ceiling over the central room was cut off by titan-flex security net. To cut through would take too long.

He backpedaled and came down through a detachable ceiling panel in an outer room. Dark rooms, barely lit corridors. He tiptoed forward.

The control room was circular. At the curved wall he clamped a sensor on the surface to get a reading on the inside.

One figure showed, standing near the center of the room.

Amesh pulled out explosive tape and slapped a square on the wall. Then he crawled around the wall and put up another square.

He scrounged through some office rooms and came up with a big foam pack that had once shipped a desk set.

The tape blew. He hurled the box through right after it. Bullets mashed the box, blew out the hole, and thudded through the offices.

Amesh pressed a control stud.

The second tape blew.
Amesh slipped through the hole.

Like sad music falling through cold air, the A.I.'s interior protextures peeled away into nothingness. An entire modal sleeve had dissolved in the virus generated by the picocode. Now, like dying blooms, the flexing shields were fading.

The cyberclast kit was close to detonation point.

He shrugged, shivered. Some unknown sense sent a twinge, a premonition. He glanced over his shoulder. The doors were shut, but they could be blown open; the structure was unarmored.

Had the guards come now? He was expecting them.

He'd heard the shots, the automatic-weapons fire. Then a louder blast, and silence.

Were the others dead, then?

It could hardly be otherwise, a thought that sent a tremor through his face. He had sent them to die. He had sent his own kin sister to certain death.

"But you can't go back, you can't . . ." The other voice was more insistent than ever.

His face contorted into a weird snarl.

And then, at last, the cyberclast reached its target. Instantly he lost the contact as sections of the A.I. collapsed into chaos. The internal memory structures broke up as virus codes ate into them and fissioned madly through the matrix.

He leaped into action, keying out the prepared modules he had ready in rampax.

Fresh code structs bloomed in the suddenly empty spaces. The blooms set out lines and matrix control nodes.

Strang put in a call to Ibrahim's personal monitor once again.

Ibrahim was there, eyes hooded. Behind him there was darkness.

"Once more I have control, Khalifi. You will surrender now."

Ibrahim laughed, a cold sound. "We will see."

And with a flash, a charge took out a section of the wall and a large something came hurtling through. Strang's gun ripped; the thing shattered into puffed stuff. Polypack, a feint! He moved.

The wall behind him went out with another flash. Bits

struck across the back of his legs as he slid along the floor and found cover behind the control desk.

He fired a burst through the first hole and hit a figure just as it stepped through, the plastix slapping on armor plates on the upper body.

The giant stepped back smartly and fired through the hole.

... body armor...

Bullets whopped into the wall; his monitor screen blew. But he had the keypad, still connected.

"Ibrahim, do you hear this," he whispered as his fingers stubbed hard on the keypad to send in a preset macro.

And Ibrahim did hear something, loud bangs, heavy thuds, deep in the structure of the habitat itself. Thuds that seemed to tremble beneath his own feet.

"What is it?" he said.

"Those are bulkheads going down, between you and Airlock Twelve. In three seconds the bulkheads on your section are going out, you'll be breathing vacuum."

Ibrahim's eyes bulged.

"Stop the man outside this room, order him to stop now! Or you're dead."

BANG... Thud... BANG...

Ibrahim felt the floor tremble.

"Amesh," he called out, "stop firing, stand back."

The final... BANG... did not come.

"All right, Ibrahim, time to talk."

39

Tobe Berlisher paced in his tiny cell. The light of the sun crept in through the high, narrow window for a couple of hours every day. The light was not that of the ship, so he knew he was on the surface of the New World.

He'd been drugged so long, so often, that anything was possible. But wherever he was, he was a prisoner of the Khalifi.

The air-conditioning was fierce. The gray lightweight trousers and vest seemed insufficient most of the time.

Sometimes he heard screaming and cursing from somewhere above but not too far away. Many voices, all female, participated in what he took to be family quarrels. Other than this he heard very little.

With nothing to do, he had studied the cell interior with great thoroughness. It was a small rectangle, four meters long and two wide. It was absolutely plain, soulless. Wall-toned in pale gray. The floor had a soft but resistant black matting. The mat was chemically bonded to the walls and floor and resisted all his attempts to pry up a corner.

The dim lighting came from a luminescent strip that ran around the walls about a foot below the ceiling. The light never varied, except when the sunlight came through the little window.

Every so often a heavy tread passed the steel door, and Tobe knew he was being scanned.

Twice a day a food trolley passed. A narrow slot would open in the bottom of the door and a microwave tray would be thrust in.

The food was dreadfully simple, nutrisoup thickened to a gray gel, with a chunk of bread. It was the same every meal, and it was just enough to keep him from starving, although he was hungry more or less all the time.

He slept, dozed, walked the cell.

In vain he tried to question the people who brought the food. But they never answered, although once he heard two voices raised in merriment.

He despaired. He might stay here forever; the Khalifi were notoriously whimsical. His interrogation was over. He had given up any useful information he might have had long ago, but he knew nothing of what they really wanted to know—"designer codes," "access codes," what was "English gambit"?

He heard their voices in his dreams, especially Ibrahim's, and he could no more give them answers there than he had been able to in the tank.

Most of his conscious time he wondered where Adelaide was, and prayed. The thought of her in the hands of the Khalifi drove him to agonies of fury, shame, and helplessness.

Would he see her again? Would she ever know how he felt about her?

So he would pace, for hours at a time, trying to think of a way out of the cell.

Nothing occurred to him whatsoever, and the sun came and went, and came and went.

Then one day, when the sunlight was gone from his window but the food tray had not yet appeared, there came a sudden, light step in the corridor. Someone stood outside his cell for a while, and then he heard the click of the locks sliding back.

The door opened. A slim figure, hooded in a chador, wearing leggings and black slippers, threw him a set of white overalls.

"Put those on and then follow me. Don't hesitate, if you want to save Adelaide."

Tobe gaped for a second or two. This was a Khalifi woman. The accent was unmistakable. He put the overalls on and slipped out of the cell. Who was she?

They went down a long corridor, floored in similar matting to that in the cells, except that it was marked with red lines in the corridor. There were many cell doors, and most were filled.

Then the woman opened another door and they were in a shaft, with stairs in raw puffcrete that ascended in squared staircases.

He climbed after her for three floors, then they exited from another door.

She led him to a hatch that opened onto a recess in a tiled roof. The warm light of late afternoon flooded in, along with a jungle scent and humid, hot air.

The air was so hot it was like a physical blow. Sweat glistened on his brow almost instantly when he stepped outside.

The roofed building was a long, low rectangle. It joined a more massive central turret not far away. From the central mass four graceful towers soared, clad in green tile, picked out in blue and brown with delicate patterns.

A Khalifi palace.

An alien jungle confronted him from several hundred meters' distance. Huge trees, things the size of office buildings, stood all along the perimeter of a cleared space, wreathed in dust where bright orange machines were at work.

Watchtowers and a tall wire fence were visible beyond the fields, close to the forest.

The New World, undoubtedly...

Tobe gaped at those trees. One of Earth's long extinct giant redwoods would have served as a branch for these trees.

"Hurry!"

The woman was signaling urgently. She caught his hand and tugged him along the roof and into another small door set into the vertical wall of the central building.

Here the corridors were wider, with pink ceilings and paisley-patterned matting. The predominant colors were bright greens, reds, and yellows. They ducked quickly along this corridor, through a set of rooms filled with scattered possessions, and into a small, darkened room, half filled with packing cases and foam molds.

The woman closed the door, turned on a null-zone generator, and removed her chador.

It was the Princess Leila. Tobe reeled in shock.

"Princess . . ." he began.

"Tobe."

He couldn't restrain himself; he hugged her.

She was embarrassed, but endured it for a few seconds before pushing him to arm's length.

"We have a big job to do, you and I, Tobe. Are you up to it?"

"Where is she?" he said.

"Ras Order is keeping her in his own apartments. She is in a corner room, not all that far from here."

"Is she all right?"

"As far as I can tell, yes. Ras Order is not like the rest of his brothers."

"He had better not be," Tobe said in a grim voice.

"Yes, well, listen to me."

"How can we reach her there?"

"I have a pass code that will let us in. Inside we will pose as if we belong."

"How can I pass?"

"You will be there as a slave, a castrate. There are dozens of them in all areas of the harem."

"Fucking hell!"

She said nothing.

"What do we do after that?" he said after a while.

"We will leave the palace . . . we will go to the coast. There have been great changes there."

"Like what?"

"The rest of the ship's passengers have debarked there.

There are small towns now; they are planting crops, starting farms, just like my family is here."

"Then what happened? How did they get there? I thought the Khalifi were going to keep everyone prisoner aboard the ship."

"It is a big secret, but I know that my great-granduncle lost the battle up there. He was forced out. I saw the end of it. They arrived here all at once in the middle of the night, in a rush of guards and orders and cars. I saw them arrive here from a window in the upper harem.

"Then who won? The Seats? I don't understand, it seemed we had lost everything. They hanged Kasok, did you know that? We saw it, right there . . ." He trailed off. His head hurt whenever he tried to remember anything.

"I don't know who 'won,' and don't expect Ibrahim to tell anyone soon. They've been in meetings constantly for days."

"And you say we can get to the coast?"

"Yes, we will have to steal a car, but that won't be too difficult as long as we don't raise any alarms."

"And Adelaide is alive."

"Yes, she is untouched. Ras Order has some remnants of decency left in him."

40

PRINCE RAS ORDER HATED THE ALIEN JUNGLE, AND EVEN more, he hated having to march through it on foot. He was dripping with sweat after the first kilometer.

He had never been an athletic person. He tired easily, and with all his equipment, he was soon on the verge of exhaustion. He had to struggle just to keep up with the others— Tariq, his cousin Revilkh, Johan Smits, Kierke Spreak, plus the guards.

They were all carrying guns, rifles for the Princes, shotguns for the guards, who were under strict orders not to open fire unless told to. The Princes wanted to bag this particular game themselves.

The hunt had been sent into action when a new "monster" had appeared by the roadside the day before. That morning it had ambushed a three-car convoy of techs en route to Blue Jade Palace. Eight techs had been killed before the thing had been driven off enough to allow the survivors to escape in the last workable car. Their descriptions fitted exactly the creature that had been destroyed after killing twenty-five people the week before.

A lone messenger on a two-wheel autobike had given an alarm later that day when the thing just missed him at a spot where the new road passed through a region so rocky not even the ubiquitous giant trees could grow. Only quick wits and the speed of the bike had saved his life.

And so the hunters had flown in at once to search the sector. In reserve, in case there was an emergency, they had two choppers on call at the palace.

They had clambered through the jungle for hours since then, with no sign of the beast.

Ras Order could think of thousands of things he would rather be doing, but Ibrahim had been adamant. The old man wanted a personal representative along on this hunt. He didn't want to be dependent on Tariq's own descriptive powers.

Ras Order had planned to spend the day with the new girl he'd bought at the last auction of prisoners. She had limpid blue eyes, a baby angel's face, and blond curls. She was only fourteen, but very knowing.

Alas, instead of enjoying her in his bedroom, he was here, trudging through the humid heat in pursuit of a dangerous animal.

Ras Order felt accursed. Another bulky root loomed ahead, another climb over an eight-foot-high barrier.

Even with the ladders carried by the attendants, getting over these constant obstacles was heavy work.

Ras Order sighed and started to climb.

The island was a dozen miles out, in the delta of the great river, where the shoreline was a distant gray smudge. There were no giant trees here, only stands of blue-stemmed plants which resembled sugarcane. Sand hills sparsely covered with low shrubs ringed the ocean side. In the lee, mud flats were exposed during the tides.

On a high point of the dunes a group of colonists had built a small hospital—a two-story, rectangular building of white puffcrete blocks, roofed with a solar-energy system.

Around the hospital were grouped a dozen dormitories, a warehouse, a machine shop, and a retail arcade. Beyond that were dozens of sites, with private houses rising on them as fast as the puffcrete could be made and delivered.

A small puffcreter had been set up on the landward side of the island, near the airstrip. Next to it was a glass furnace, turning the pure sand of the dunes into windows. A new road linked it to the hospital complex. Another road had been laid along the length of the dunes.

In the hospital were about three hundred people, split roughly in half between victims of the violence during the rebellion and older people, whose extended medical was in ruins because of the Khalifi misrule of the ship.

Randolf Flecker had been on the island since the rebellion. He was building a house on a stretch of gravel a couple of kloms from the hospital. To the south was a wide view of the sea, to the north, blue grass stems waved, and beyond them the waves of the delta.

He already had the walls and roof up of what would be a five-room, single-story house. A solar air conditioner was already attached to the central room.

Flecker was not the only member of the old 14th Stumpers on the island.

Im Sohn, now recovered from the worst aspects of her experiences at the hands of Garmash, was working in the hospital as a nurse assistant.

Guvek was a shift operator at the little puffcrete plant.

And in the hospital's psych ward was the mysterious Strang.

Flecker divided his time between house building and shifts as an orderly at the hospital. His major task was to help the wounded take walks in the new garden on the ocean side of the complex.

As yet, the garden was nothing but sand and clumps of short bushes with black-green leaves. Certain sections had been marked out for lawns and flowerbeds, and a dozen benches made of pressed wood had been set out.

Here the wounded liked to sit and watch the ocean. Like all the spacers, they found the ocean to be the most amazing thing in the New World. It had a mesmerizing effect on them.

Randolf, however, sometimes ignored its spell and turned northward to the distant smudge of the mainland. He always felt a familiar guilt. There was the forest he should be working in. But with the science program in complete disarray, he was out of a job. His lifetime's work was on hold. Perhaps never to be taken up again.

Worse, he didn't care. Which was the source of his guilt. He realized that the alien forest was not something he wanted to investigate anymore. He only wanted to live here, build his house here, and forget science.

In the evenings a lot of people took lines and fishing rods made from spylo tubing and cast in the surf for the plentiful fish. A few were poisonous, but most could be treated with a detoxing spray and made fit for tasty meals.

Some hospital workers had started a microbrewery, using a plankton-carbohydrate cycler to generate fermentables.

After the evening's fishing there were beach feasts, fires, and jugs of homebrew. Flecker liked this a lot better than the life in the camps on the mainland.

Since the *Founder* had begun emptying itself after the defeat of the Khalifi, the camps had become small towns, with severe overcrowding. New housing was going up fast, but they were still hampered by the fact that the Khalifi had stolen so much of the heavy equipment. They'd also taken almost all the laboratory equipment, the supplies, batteries, computers, everything.

Nevertheless, the colonists were overcoming the shortages and the crowding. More forest would be cleared soon, and more domes were going up. Much of the coastal region was targeted for clearing and landscaping, like a park.

Randolf Flecker was glad just to be alive.

At the hospital he sometimes ran into Im Sohn, who appeared little changed from her days in the stumpers. She too, however, seemed to have abandoned her role as an ecologist.

"If you look over there with binox," she told Flecker shortly after meeting him again, "you can see Prominence 46 and the cliffs near Camp Two." There was a peculiar intensity to her voice. "I never look over there now." Her eyes were like dark, blank pools.

He nodded, he understood.

On most days he ended his shift by taking a side trip to the small psych ward on the north side of the hospital.

Here, under Dr. Kathrin Villon's care, were a dozen or so

people with severe mental problems. Among them was Strang, who had become virtually catatonic since his victory.

"Split-personality effect," was Dr. Villon's diagnosis.

Flecker always said the same thing.

"How is he?"

"As well as might be expected. There is some improvement, but the basic sense of unreality is still there—he still has the two voices, the lack of control."

On this occasion he had no sooner sat down beside Strang's bed than Strang turned to him and said, "You've been away."

Flecker smiled, unsure what to say. This was unusual.

"I've made a decision," Strang said.

"Oh, and what was that?"

"It's time to build a boat. Can fish better with a boat." Strang gestured out the window to where people were casting in the surf.

"Fighting Blue Jays need boats."

There was a sudden rumble in the sky, and the white chopper that plied the route between the island and Camp Two swept past the hospital to the landing pad.

"It will cut down on the need for the choppers too."

"Boats," Flecker breathed. "Yes, of course. But how?"

"We'll turn up the puffcreter a few notches and bake the sections for the boat from grade-seven crete. That will be relatively light, but strong and certainly waterproof. Best of all, we can weld sections of it together with ceramaze."

"A boat," Flecker repeated. Why hadn't anyone else thought of this?

"A regular Hamilton Tiger Cat of a boat, that's what!" Strang said happily.

Later, Dr. Villon said the same thing. "A boat!" She smiled broadly. "That sounds like an excellent idea. What are the chances of getting the required time on the puffcreter?"

"I don't know; I'll ask Guvek, she works there."

"It's just the sort of project he needs, something to get his mind working, get it out of the rut it's running in now. He needs a purpose, I think it's vital."

"I think that's always been his problem."

In Ras Order's spacious apartments Leila moved more freely, less furtively. With Tobe behind her, she swept through a series of drawing rooms, each decorated in one of Ras Order's favorite periods. There was a room with repro Louis

XIV furniture, paintings of dogs and fruit. There was one with mid-twentieth-century Americana, with chairs shaped like cartoon cats and mice. Ras Order had excellent but eclectic tastes.

They passed occasional small groups of Khalifi, minor family members, hangers-on, ancient aunts. Leila greeted some more warmly than others, but she greeted all of them. None spared more than a cursory glance at Tobe in slave white.

Finally she knocked at a door. It opened automatically on a small dark room. A figure sat hunched up on a bed by the wall. Glaring like a dazzling jewel was a small portable screen, set in front of the bed.

Adelaide saw them and jumped off the bed.

"You found him, you didn't lie!" She gave Tobe a ferocious hug.

Tobe wept for joy.

"No, I didn't lie," Leila sniffed.

Adelaide wept, too, and laid her head on Tobe's shoulder.

"Poor Tobe, did they torture you?" she whispered.

He shook slightly. "They did everything they wanted to."

Leila wore an odd smile. "They were actually quite gentle with him. They didn't even strip his personality down. No deep-level probing. I mean, if they'd thought he was G.B. he wouldn't be able to talk, he wouldn't know who you are."

Adelaide touched his cheek, saw the love in his eyes and sidestepped it.

"Poor Tobe, how you must have suffered, and all for us." For Clan Fundan . . .

Tobe wept, clung to her.

Leila switched off the monitor, swung back to them.

"I know you two are glad to see each other, but we have to move. Tobe will be missed within the hour.

"Yes, of course." Adelaide disengaged. "What about the other prisoner? I want to free her."

"It will be difficult, it may be impossible."

"Ras Order said that they will kill her soon. We can't let that happen!"

Leila struggled with something, then composed herself. Her features became a smooth mask.

"All right, we have to do it."

"Have to do what?" Tobe said, bewildered.

193

A door opened. A servant girl came in, carrying a little boy who wore a brown spylo suit.

Adelaide stared, then looked quickly to Leila.

"This is my son," Leila said with a bitter smile. "Dane's son. His first name is Compton. Dane told me that any son we had would have to be named Compton."

Adelaide nodded, completely astonished. "Yes, of course. Compton was the son of Emily and Talbot."

"That may be, but I call him Shanur. A name from my lineage. That is his second name."

"Compton Shanur, an interesting name," Tobe said.

Adelaide felt the old rivalry again, Fundan-Khalifi, wrapped up in that tiny bundle of life.

"My son is coming with us. I can't trust them."

"They would do that? To one of their own?"

"I believe they do not regard Shanur as one of their own. He is Compton Fundan, after all."

The little boy had dark hair and blue eyes and a most solemn expression on his face. Adelaide was fascinated. What would Emily and Talbot have thought of this!

41

To ENTER THE LABORATORY WOULD HAVE BEEN IMPOSSIBLE without Ras Order's knowledge of the security system. It was sealed off from the rest of the palace.

There was, however, a way in through a delivery passage leading directly from a loading bay at the rear of the palace's kitchens. There were guards at the loading bay, but Leila got past them by simply driving up in a stolen ATV and unloading a large empty crate.

She had all the documentation required, courtesy of the Prince.

As she explained to Adelaide and Tobe, "Ras Order has a core of decency, you see. He knows that this is evil. But he's too close to Ibrahim, too close to the line of succession to dare to rebel."

She tossed her head. "But I wore him down. I knew I could reach him, even through that hedonistic haze in which he is lost most of the time."

Adelaide had faced the "haze" too closely, too recently to find much love for Ras Order in her heart. But she accepted the Prince's aid gladly in order to further this mission.

From the moment she'd seen the video in Ras Order's suite, she'd known that they had to do this. No matter what the risk.

While Leila's data chip was checked, Tobe and Adelaide, in the humiliating white overalls of slavery, manhandled the crate across the loading bay and into the access corridor to the labs.

In the back of the truck Leila's little boy and his nursemaid Ana were crouched in concealment. After the crate had been removed and the data chip passed, Leila walked over to the truck and closed the back door. Little Shanur was intent on the story Ana was showing him on a hand video. He only looked up briefly to wave a hand at his mother as she shut the hatchback.

The access way to the labs was quite bare, just raw crete toned white with a light strip on the ceiling.

Inside the laboratories they passed a couple of men in pale yellow smocks, pushing a dolly loaded with crates of equipment. Beyond that all was quiet; it was early evening, and the labs were closed for the day.

Leila knew just where to go. They opened a door with a code given her by Ras Order and slipped into a darkened room.

And then a light flared. They froze. A massive figure sauntered forward, a Khalifi guard.

Leila had not expected this.

"Welcome, what can I do for you?" the guard said.

"I, well . . ." She stumbled for a second, then recovered her aplomb. "I—I have a delivery to make here." She waved to the crate.

In her sleeve she had a gas spray; she slipped it into her hand.

The guard was one of Ibrahim's own, a massive giant with brutal features.

"I must check your identities first." The guard held out a hand for her documentation.

Leila sprayed him right across the eyes.

The guard staggered back. His sidearm came out while Tobe leaped at his arm. The giant groped for Tobe and then plucked him away and slammed him into the wall.

The gun came up. Leila sprayed the guard again and kept spraying until he finally sagged and slid to the floor.

Tobe struggled out from beneath the hulking form. He gagged, choking on the gas.

Leila bent over the guard and examined him.

"He'll be out for an hour at least. Let's get on with it."

She turned on a room light. Tobe meanwhile found himself staring into the face of an animal in a large cage.

He gaped. "What's this?"

"The native intelligent life form on this planet," Leila said.

"What?"

"Khalifi captured her. We're going to set her free," Adelaide said briskly.

Tobe stared at the alien being. It was as tall as the guard. It looked like something evolved from bears or lions. It snarled defiance at them.

"You want to free that? It might kill all of us."

"We have to free it."

Tobe still gaped. "And it's intelligent?" he bleated.

One look in those blazing eyes told him that it was.

"Come on, Tobe."

Leila was opening the packing case. She pulled out the metal cutter they'd brought, a slim, deadly steel tube with a power pack at the top and the lasers at the bottom.

Leila found it light and easy to maneuver.

"No point in touching the lock, it's computer controlled."

The creature watched her avidly. Adelaide went to the bars, stared in at the beautiful alien animal.

Her fur was silky brown, an inch to two inches long. And while she had the build of a lioness, there was no denying the "female" look of her breasts and hips.

The bars were going now as the cutter did its work.

Suddenly the alien jumped at that side of the cage. Leila darted back with a little scream of fright.

The alien seized the bars and gave a great effort and hauled two of them up into the cage while ripping the meshing away. In another moment she had squeezed through the space, heaving, grunting, and venting a stream of subvocalizations that sounded very much like curses.

Leila gave a little laugh. "My, my, such language."

The alien was free. It raked them with a squint-eyed glance and then flung itself to the doors, yanked them open, and looked up and down the corridor outside. Then she turned to them and made an unmistakable signal to them.

Follow me!

"No, wait! We brought this crate in for you!" Leila motioned to the crate.

The creature gave her a long look, then sniffed eloquently and shook its head in a universal gesture of rejection. Kyika of Yamuk would not be caged by these sky demons again!

Instead, she moved into the corridor and started walking rapidly away.

"Uh-oh, now what do we do?" Tobe said.

"We go with her, what else?" Adelaide said.

"Of course, of course." Tobe shrugged.

They crept down the corridor, with the alien moving silently in front of them.

She halted when she came in sight of some rubber-flap doors. Kyika was unsure exactly what to do next.

This place of the sky demons was enormous, like some huge underground cavern. It was cold, always cold, and Kyika could smell no way out.

Abruptly the one who had cut the bars touched her arm, motioned to her to follow, and started down the passage to the left, back to the access tube.

Kyika looked at her. Could the sky demon be trusted?

But this just started more questions running through her head.

Why had they freed her? What did they want?

Kyika did not have answers to such questions, so she followed, fighting the sense of panic that threatened to send her running blank-eyed down the passage like a startled gzan.

Would she ever get home? Kyika was sure that if she did, she would never leave her village again for the rest of her days. If anything was wanted beyond the village, she would send Igi for it while she stayed in the yard.

They came to the checkpoint. Leila and Adelaide used elaborate motions to make Kyika stop and press herself to the wall.

She understood this. Some danger lay beyond this doorway, filled with the clear, glittering stuff. Everything of the sky demons was like this, sparkling, gleaming, smooth, and cold.

Were sky demons naturally cold? They were warm to the touch, that much she knew.

She waited and watched as the demon that had cut the bars went to the doors, opened them, and spoke with another being inside.

Something was wrong! There was a fight! Hands wrestling her demon down.

Kyika reacted without thought, bursting through the doors and cannoning into the struggling group, two men in uniforms and Leila.

Leila's gas spray fell to the floor.

Kyika pushed the men back, sending one rolling into the wall with a thud that knocked him senseless.

The other gave a scream, yanked up a gun, and got off a shot before Adelaide clubbed him with the gun taken from the guard.

The shot was terribly loud. Their ears rang.

Kyika looked to the wall beside her, where a hole had suddenly appeared. Then she looked to the weapon that had fallen from the guard's hand.

What weapons these were! Kyika connected the events easily. The weapon made the noise and threw a tiny kifket with great force.

They motioned to her to come, to hurry. She ran with them down a corridor, burst into a larger space filled with more people. There were shouts, screams, and then another shot as a man in legion uniform appeared.

Adelaide fired a burst that sent everyone diving to the floor.

Leila pulled open the door to the truck and signaled to Kyika to follow her inside.

Kyika would not get in.

"Oh please, we don't have time," Leila implored.

Tobe tried to take the fein's massive paw and lead her to the ATV.

Kyika jerked back hard. Tobe was yanked off his feet. Kyika's hand seized his face.

"No!" Adelaide screamed, her gun leveled at the alien.

Kyika looked up, lost in panic for a few seconds, but the sight of the gun cooled her.

198

Sky demons surrounded her. She could die here very easily, far from her home.

She dropped the man and ran for the light she saw at the end of the docking-bay tunnel.

"After her," screamed Leila, who was helping poor Tobe to his feet. Adelaide jumped into the front seat of the truck and gunned it to life. Then they were off and moving in a shower of dirt, leaving the stunned techs on the dock staring after them.

42

THE REST OF THEIR FLIGHT FROM THE PALACE WAS A CONFUSED race through new-laid vegetable gardens, past astonished slave workers.

Then the gardens ceased and there was just a long, dusty lane wending between storage sheds and occasional piles of logs. Farther off on a flat plain, dust tossed in the air as snorting machines raked the land.

Kyika paused, chest heaving, amazed at this sight. The sky demons were extraordinarily active creatures. What did they do with all this noise and dust? She glanced back at the alien mass of the palace. The forest seemed far away.

She felt the panic return.

Where was this place, then? Did the sky demons live somewhere on the Knuckle of Delight? How would she ever get back to Yamuk?

An engine roared right behind her and the truck ground to a halt. The door opened. Once again the demons tried to persuade her to climb in.

An alarm began wailing in the palace and a bell joined in, ringing high and shrill.

Kyika stared at the truck. Was this the only way out?

She looked back to the distant trees. It seemed that it was. With considerable unease she got into the back of the truck.

Leila climbed in with her.

Kyika's presence sent the nursemaid into near hysterics, but Leila snatched up little Shanur and hugged him and introduced him to Kyika.

Kyika, who had been on the point of shirrithee, even panic, saw the little one and then broke into a chuckle. Compton Shanur was uncertain how to react, but when Kyika reached for him, Leila let her take him, trying to ignore the hammering in her chest.

But Kyika cuddled the child and chuckled some more, and Compton Shanur decided he liked the big, friendly face in front of him and the faint smell of oranges that came from the fein sweat, and he laughed and reached for Kyika's face.

"Your cub!" said Kyika in feiner, understanding the honor done her by the sky demon.

Truly these sky demons had to be friends, they would not trust her with a cub otherwise.

Kyika glanced out the rear window of the truck and stared in astonishment when she saw how they were speeding across the ground, faster than any fein had ever run.

They reached the outer fence before the chopper even got off the pad at the palace. This fence was of reinforced spylo mesh, braced every two meters.

They climbed out. Kyika handed Compton Shanur back to Leila, who held onto him while the nursemaid continued to have hysterics in the back of the van.

"Stop making all that noise, Ana," she said sharply. "The alien won't hurt you, she's only trying to get to freedom, can't you see that?"

Ana gulped and quietened.

"Better, now hand me the baby harness, I'll carry him from here on."

Ana was frozen.

"You don't have to come, Ana. I told you from the start that you did not have to come with me. As for what will happen to you if you stay, I think you need not worry unduly. You will be questioned, but you are innocent, they will see that."

Ana said nothing, her eyes so big they seemed they might burst. Adelaide finally had to go in and take the baby harness from her nerveless hands.

Tobe used the metal cutter to cut a slice down the mesh of the fence. Kyika pulled apart the two sides with a single heave of her shoulders. She slipped through and turned to say fare-well.

To her astonishment the sky demons pushed through behind her, including the dark-haired one with the cub.

Beyond the fence was some low brush and a stand of glob globs.

The chopper circled toward them.

Adelaide grabbed Kyika's wrist. "Come on, they'll shoot us if they see us!" She pulled her toward the brush.

Kyika understood that the clattering thing in the air was bad. They ran, bent over, through scrub, glob glob, and satursine vine. Then the welcoming shade of the great trees swallowed them up.

Later they heard the helicopter whirr past high overhead, scanning with infrared, but it missed them and went away south and they heard it no more.

On Hospital Island the first boat slid down the beach just as the sun began to set. All told, casting and welding it together had taken four hours, and most of that time had been spent waiting for things to cool once they were out of the creter.

Flecker, Strang, Guvek, and her friends from the creter crew did the pushing, but the boat was surprisingly light for something that was thirty feet long and nine feet wide.

When it floated, Flecker jumped and shouted and threw his billcap high into the air. It fell in the surf and he retrieved it sopping wet from the foam.

Strang had a tether which he staked to the ground before he waded out and climbed aboard.

Guvek tossed up a scaffolding pole and Strang used it to drive the boat back onto the sand.

After a moment's reflection on the boat, as if admiring its sweeping lines, Strang turned and loped back up the trail, past the creter, to the hospital.

He went immediately to the machine shop.

Flecker watched him go, then waded out and climbed into the boat and explored it thoroughly.

It had movable decking, in sections that locked together in the ship's center. Under the decking was a six-foot-deep space for cargo. In the center was a keel hole, and a socket for the mast.

The stern was squared off, with a small platform to which could be attached an outboard motor.

Flecker hadn't believed that it could be done this quickly, if at all. But there didn't seem to be anything that could stop Strang once he got going on a project like this. He knew the ins and outs of every bit of Fundan equipment. The creter crew didn't know half the stuff he'd used in casting the boat and then baking it down.

Flecker jumped down. Guvek was waiting.

"So your boat is ready. Where are you going to sail it to, Captain Flecker?"

He laughed, grimaced. "We're going to take it over to Camp Two, use it to ferry stuff back and forth, passengers too. You want to come?"

"No thank you, I've seen all I want of Camp Two. It's so crowded, lines for everything, you know."

"Yeah, we're definitely in the better place out here."

"He's full of surprises, isn't he, Mr. Strang?" Guvek said. Flecker nodded.

She drew close and whispered, "Well, I heard that you went up to the ship with him, that he did something that made the Khalifi quit the ship and let everyone go."

Flecker nodded. "Essentially that's correct."

"But he still won't speak, doesn't say a word."

"Yeah."

"You wanna come down and have a beer, we're off this shift."

Flecker shook his head sadly. "I'd love to, but I have a date, another time perhaps." Flecker parted company with the creters and headed into the hospital. He took the stairs to the top floor and made his way into the severe-casualty ward.

He found Melissa awake, reading from her monitor screen.

"Hello," he said.

She looked up, smiled, and switched off her monitor.

"Hello," she said shyly.

"What did the doctors say?"

She shrugged. "They couldn't save anything for me below the knee. But they think they can grow me something, to replace it, with bud cells. I'm still young enough."

Flecker felt a sense of relief.

"That's good to hear."

"And when they're ready, I'll go into the nutritank for three months. They think that might be enough."

"Three months."

"Sounds a long time, doesn't it? But they keep you unconscious throughout, and when you get out of it, you're well on the way to regrowth."

"I guess you won't feel a thing."

"Of course, it won't be quite the same as the old leg. Apparently they never are, they're usually a little smaller and weaker than your original limb. Bud cells can only take you so far, I guess."

"But you'll be up and walking..."

"Well, not till next year, walking, but I'll be out of this damned bed and this damned ward. I can't wait to go outside again. I've never been to the beach, even."

Flecker smiled. "I'd like to take you to the beach sometime. I could—I could carry you."

"I'd like that. I'd like that very much."

43

TOBE AWOKE WITH A START. IT WAS HOURS LATER, ALMOST dawn. He stared around himself. The nightmarish forest of gigantic trees was still there, but this was no dream. The road was still there, too, cut through the forest nearby.

Adelaide was snoring lightly beside him. He felt the warmth of her leg and buttock against his own. He shifted carefully, trying not to awaken her.

The fein was gone. Leila slept, wrapped in a parka with her son cradled to her.

Tobe crouched, still staring carefully around. He fumbled for the gun, felt the smooth shape in his hands, and was reassured once more.

There was a loud crack, a splintering sound, above him somewhere.

Something was on the tree! And something big, at that; he felt the whole thing move beneath him! He stared upward into the gloom, looking for the bulky figures of "Nachri," as Kyika had named the baboonoids. But the tree was all he could see, and that very dimly in the dark.

Where was Kyika? Had she abandoned them?

Then a chorus of animal cries began, faintly at first but growing louder as the first rays of the sun lit up the treetops.

Adelaide stirred and rolled over. Leila was awake. "What is it?" she hissed.

"I don't know," he whispered. Tobe gripped the gun tight, the breath hard in his throat. He shook Adelaide.

"Wha?" she said in a bleary voice.

The root beneath them was shuddering violently.

Adelaide was wide awake now. "What is it, Tobe?" she whispered.

Tobe was about to answer that he didn't know, when there was another loud crack. A piece of bark the size of his head came hurtling down from the darkness above and bounced off the root, missing Adelaide by a couple of feet.

"Wow!" She scrambled to her feet.

"Let's get out of here," he said, pulling her away from the tree.

"Where did the fein go?" Leila said.

"No time. The tree's shedding bark, watch out!" Another big piece came walloping down and bounced away perilously close to Leila and Compton Shanur.

Somehow they stumbled through the near dark to the roots of the next tree. Compton Shanur was crying, frightened by the sudden activity in the dark.

Tobe shone his light back to the first tree. The tiger stripes that Kyika had been so agitated about had broadened and merged, and now the bark beneath them was bulging and rippling.

The cracking sound came again, and was repeated.

Tobe saw a section of bark heave apart high up the tree.

"Look," he whispered.

The black shiny bark was wriggling, as if something were trapped beneath it. He tightened the focus on his light and turned it on the broken section of bark.

There was a movement there, something emerged for a second from the tree.

"What the hell?" Adelaide muttered. She turned her light on the same patch.

Suddenly the crack widened, and with a great grinding sound like a rusty zipper being opened on armor plate, the bark split right down the length of the tiger-striped section of the tree.

An arm broke through the crack about halfway down. Tobe blinked, scarcely crediting what he was seeing.

The arm was twenty feet long, and it had a hand that was about seven feet across. Something at the end of the fingers glittered ominously. The arm reached back to tear open the bark marked by the black, shining stripes.

The hairs on the back of Tobe's neck were standing out stiff.

Then suddenly the arm stopped its efforts and silence fell. Compton Shanur had stopped crying, and the songs of the forest animals returned, louder than before, while the light increased steadily, moment by moment.

Something large jumped at them from behind. Tobe whirled, gun ready, and recognized Kyika.

She seized his shoulder roughly, pushed him down into cover, and clapped another big hand over his mouth. She crouched in cover with them and with a long, furred finger across her lips made the universal gesture for silence.

The bark cracked open again with a loud report.

Tobe peeked around the corner.

The arm had emerged again and been joined by a leg, and both limbs were working in the cavity. More cracking and snapping came, and then bark was pushed back right down the length of the tiger-striped zipper mark. A moment later a creature slid out of the crack and stood, trembling slightly, beside its parent tree.

A sweetish smell, rather like cinnamon, filled the air.

Tobe swallowed, but his mouth was bone dry.

The thing was seventy feet high, at least! A bipedal monster, with a head like a triangular gun turret sporting tufts of fiber at the corners. For a moment he thought of an ape crossed with a giant pelican.

The body was a barrel at least ten meters in length and half that in width, and the whole thing was supported on two spindly legs which were perhaps fifteen meters high.

The head swiveled suddenly, jerked into life by unknown forces, and in the dawn's light Tobe saw a row of gleaming black disks set on the top of that head. They reminded him of the eyes of hunting spiders, and he felt a chill run down his spine.

These eyes swept up and down the road as their owner examined the world into which it had just been born.

The triangular head split open and the beak snapped a couple of times. It reached up with a giant hand and scratched the top of its head. Then it emitted a long, low, hooting cry.

After the one cry it stopped, as if listening intently for a reply.

The forest had gone absolutely silent at that sound.

Suddenly it shifted and strode down into the cleared road. It stooped over and scratched at the supermac surface with the long fingers on its giant hand. Then it crossed the road and inspected the remains of a fallen tree, cut down and shattered with explosives.

The thing laid its head down onto the tree's bark for a few seconds and then emitted several long, low cries.

Abruptly it stood straight once more and looked up and down the road with chilling deliberation. Then it turned and moved off to the south with an odd, clockwork gait that soon took it far down the road.

44

IGI OF YAMUKA HAD HAD MANY ADVENTURES SINCE THE STAR-tling moment when he had swung himself through the hatch and into the sky-demon craft. He had never dreamed that the world could be so large, or so complicated.

He had quickly won the little fight that took place inside the sky-demon craft. He'd used only the flat of the kifket blade, hardly spilling blood. The sky demons were not great fighters, not without their magic weapons, not when surprised.

Then, with the sky demons cowed, Igi searched them for weapons and found some small metal things that he smashed with the kifket and tossed out the hatch.

Satisfied that the sky demons could not attack him with magical means, he sheathed the kifket and pulled shut the outer hatch. Then he sat himself on a padded bench along one side of the central cabin and held his hands up to the sky demons, palms outward, to signify his peaceful intentions.

After a long silence the sky demons began to communicate with each other. They jabbered among themselves for another lengthy period and then came to a decision.

"It wants to come with us."

"But why?"

"How should I know, but I'm not arguing. Let's go."

Igi smiled at them. They shrank from the sight of fein teeth.

They busied themselves with the controls. Fortunately, nothing was broken except the assistant pilot's nose, which bled profusely.

The craft lifted itself into the air. Igi felt the motion and clung tightly to the padded bench. This was a terrifying moment for the fein. He knew he was rising, away from the sacred ground of the Knuckle of Delight. A sense of panic gripped him and threatened to send him leaping out the hatch to his death.

Igi clenched his teeth together and gripped the bench and fought the terror down. Kyika had gone to wherever it was that sky demons came from; to get her back, Igi would have to follow.

However, it was not to the ship that the shuttle flew, but down to the south coast and Camp Two. On their arrival the shuttle crew received another shock. The Khalifi had been overthrown. The ship was emptying.

All shuttle crews were reassigned to the mass disembarkation effort.

They landed with alacrity, opened the hatch, and motioned to Igi to step forth.

It is fair to say that Igi's sudden appearance on the airstrip at Camp Two caused a sensation.

The news that an intelligent alien life form had commandeered a shuttle and flown it to the coast raced through the camp. A crowd gathered quickly around the big furry alien.

It spoke to them in its own tongue. The crowd was astonished, drew back a few more feet.

Igi tried everything, but all he knew was feiner and gesture, and neither had much effect. The sky demons listened to him intently, then jabbered among themselves.

They offered him no violence, at least, and after his fruitless efforts to communicate had failed, he began to move around among their shining structures, seeking some scent of Kyika among the alien smells of the place. But he found nothing. The sky-demon "tents" were things without personality, cold and lacking scent. There wasn't the slightest hint of Kyika's presence. Igi was sorely disappointed.

By this time the crowd had grown to several hundred. A group came forward and motioned to Igi to join them. They held out objects, from stones to various pieces of plants, and named them, then handed them to him.

Igi soon caught on and named them in feiner in turn.

A stone; "Kush," said Igi. "Sto-an" said the sky demons; "Sto-an" said Igi. "Kush," said the scientists, recording everything.

The sky demons in the crowd clapped their hands and emitted cries of excitement.

More objects were brought out, including alien things that Igi had no knowledge of. Again panic rose within him. Igi felt a strong incipient shirrithee begin. Questions abounded.

Where was Kyika? Where was Igi? Where was this, in fact? Igi was close to despair.

He noticed then that there was a clear sex difference between the sky demons. Big hips, breasts, these were obvious symbols of femaleness to him, common to many animals of the Knuckle of Delight. This gave him a great idea. He jumped to his feet suddenly, scattering the scientists, and strode into the crowd.

They fell back in front of him with screams and shouts of alarm.

"Look out, it's moving!" went up the cry.

Igi caught the hand of a particularly curvacious woman, pulled her to his side, and hoisted her up in his arms. She emitted a prolonged shriek and drummed on his chest with her fists.

Unperturbed, Igi carried her back to the scientists, who were staring at him in numbed shock.

"Put her down, damn you!" shouted a young man who hurled himself at Igi and pulled at his arms with little effect.

"It's attacking!" someone else shouted. Further cries of unreason rang out. Hands reached out to seize Igi. Others grabbed at the young woman and began to haul her bodily out of the fein's arms.

Igi reacted wildly, letting go of the woman and tossing the first few assailants to the ground.

Then there were a dozen or more on him and he was pulled down, fortunately, before he could free his kifket. He was struck a few times, then tied up and dragged into a room in one of the white structures.

He remained there for that day and most of the next while intense arguments went on about what should be done with him.

Renee Zisch, the lady who had been seized, was demanding that the alien be put to death. She had considerable support among the most recently arrived passengers, people who had never seen an animal of any sort except on video.

The scientists called for calm. There had to be a reason for the alien's actions.

"The creature wished to slake his unnatural desires!" the hysterical Renee Zisch screamed. The crowd murmured.

The scientists suggested that the alien had most likely been attempting to signify something female when he grabbed Ms. Zisch. They observed that the alien wore an apron over his genital region, a sure indication of sex differences and gender consciousness. Many human languages were imbued with a strong sense of gender; it was likely that the alien's was too.

A stubborn third of the colonists refused to listen to such talk and maintained that the alien was "dangerous" and had to be kept locked up or destroyed.

"The responsibility will be yours if it commits further outrages!" went their shrill cry.

"What outrages?" the scientists responded. "It was only trying to show us something, it did not attack the woman!"

"Nonsense, we saw it with our own eyes!"

And thus it went, for hours.

Eventually, however, a compromise was reached. Igi was brought outside to a cleared place set between four of the white structures. He was tethered by one leg to a stake that was hammered deep into the ground, then his other restraints were removed.

The tether was two meters long and made of struct-spylo with full twist; nothing but a machine could break it. The stake was a Fundan construction spike; it, too, was virtually indestructible.

The scientists resumed their efforts to communicate with Igi, but Igi was now in no mood to learn the speech of the sky demons.

Eventually it grew dark. They tried to feed him, but he sniffed the bowl of odorless mush they proffered and pushed it back.

His belly was rumbling, however. And when they brought him a selection of wild fruits and seeds collected from the forest, he worked through the pile for glob glob fruits and ate a couple of handfuls of those. There were some unripe satursine pods, too, bitter but edible, if you spat out the white seeds.

These calmed his stomach for a while.

He pondered his situation. All that he knew for sure was that he had traveled to the shore of the ocean.

The fact that he was by the ocean told him he was far away from home; every fein agreed on that, the oceans were a great distance from the mountains on either side of the Knuckle continent.

To this Igi could add that sky demons lived on these shores. Or at least this kind of sky demon. Because it now looked as though there might be several kinds, or tribes of them, and that Kyika might be a hostage among another type or tribe altogether. Which thought depressed him tremendously.

As for the sky demons, they were a puzzlement, but Igi chided himself for his action. They had misunderstood him, he now realized. These sky demons were not particularly malevolent, by all appearances. But they were overly protective of their females, perhaps.

The night went on. Groups of sky demons came to stare at him and jabber among themselves for a while.

Most of the sky demons, however, retired into their structures. Only small crews on the puffcreter and mix master worked around the clock. A few trucks ground up and down the roads, disappearing into the forest.

The Pale Moon had risen; Igi felt his strength renewed by its rays. He went to work on the stake.

It took some time, for it was deeply set, and it was itself some magical material of the sky demons and could not be broken off. But eventually it came loose and he yanked the stake from the ground and was freed. He looped the tether around his waist and stuck the stake through it like a sword or fish club, and went in search of his kifket.

However, he abandoned the search after a little while. The kifket had been taken inside one of the sky-demon structures. Igi would have to make himself a new one.

He slipped away into the forest, heavy of heart. He still had no clue as to the whereabouts of Kyika, and he had lost the kikfet that Chumzi, his father, had given him when he was grown from cubhood.

"Keep this blade sharp, Igi," Chumzi had said. "It has been blessed by the Adepts of the Spirit for you."

Igi remembered the scene as if it had been the day before. What would Chumzi have said of him in this situation? Alas, Igi realized that Chumzi would not have known any better than he what to do; this was an entirely new situation. Sky demons were simply beyond normal fein experience.

He moved deeper into the forest and eventually decided to climb a tree and find a place to sleep.

As he climbed he noticed an unfamiliar spicy odor. Igi had learned the ways of the great forest and its guardians, but this smell he had never encountered before.

No source for the spicy scent presented itself, however, and he climbed to the first branch and made himself comfortable and slept for a few hours.

When dawn awoke him he climbed down.

Then he noticed the black striping that marked many of the trees around him.

The fur stood up on the back of his neck.

He knew what those patterns meant!

The sky demons!

It all fitted together suddenly in Igi's mind. The sky demons had landed here recently. They had performed sacrilege and destroyed trees. The sky demons were not of the Knuckle of Delight, they knew not what they had done.

Long Legs would soon hatch.

The sky demons were a blundering folk, they had made mistakes, but Igi sensed no great malevolence in them. They had not harmed him. They had even brought him glob glob fruits to calm the rumbles in his belly.

Igi felt they scarcely deserved the fate he now foresaw for them. And if they were destroyed, then how would he ever find Kyika?

Filled with concern, he turned and jogged back to Camp Two, arriving shortly after breakfast.

People were already astir.

He ran to the central place, raised his hands, and summoned the sky demons with a loud cry.

45

THE SURVIVING HUNTERS RAN FOR THEIR LIVES THROUGH THE tangled growth at the foot of the giant trees.

Ras Order was in the lead now, his equipment lost and his one-piece shredded by thorns.

Tariq and Kierke Spreak were close behind him, Rook farther back, covering the retreat.

Ras Order had run farther, faster than he had ever dreamed possible. He had dragged himself through tangles of vines to force a trail, he had crawled through slimy mud to get underneath huge roots.

He had discovered that he was prepared to do anything to stay ahead of the monster.

Tariq still had his rifle, so did Spreak, but both knew they were very lucky that the monster had not chosen to follow them. Rifles and grenades didn't seem to mean too much to it.

The screams of the others had caught up to them long before. There was no doubt in their minds about why their calls on the short-range radio had received no answer.

They stopped again, for Tariq to try and call in the chopper once more. So far they'd had no response whatsoever, and Tariq had the only unit with the range necessary to reach the palace, if it was working properly, and who among them knew?

Ras Order hopped from foot to foot, exhausted, but terribly anxious to get moving again.

Ras Order would never forget the moment when it started. It had happened with such an explosive suddenness. There had been no time to react, no time to think.

They had been on the trail, as they'd been for hours. Then a guard named Gort had spotted something moving in the jungle of vines to their left.

Everyone had turned to face the vines, but whatever it was had gone. They waited and watched for a minute or so, and then someone screamed, "Our front!" and it was upon them, coming around a tree directly ahead.

Ras Order had frozen like a Jurassic rodent gazing at a passing allosaur.

Seventy, eighty feet high, the thing moved with a strange clockwork gait. The long arms darted out in front, the huge hands reaching for the men.

Gort got off a shot, hit the thing in the chest, and then was picked up and stuffed into the giant mouth while wailing in horror.

Jaws chewed on him before their astonished eyes.

The thing smashed Porosh into a jelly with a blow from a fist the size of a door. A servant in white had fallen into a fetal ball on the ground. A foot came down and stamped the servant flat.

Their rifles were firing by then, but even as puffs of fiber and dust blew off the monster, it kept killing them. Revilkh followed Gort into the thing's snapping maw; vigorous mastications took place, a few indigestibles were spat out. In a moment of surreal madness, Ras Order had seen Revilkh's binox, slathered in saliva, go bouncing past his own head.

With a jerk Ras had raised his rifle and blazed off the clip at the thing, for the most part missing.

Then it was too late to shoot.

"Run, Master," Rook had said, pushing him ahead.

Ras Order had started to run, slowly, hesitantly, utterly confused.

"Filthy coward!" Tariq sneered.

Tariq's gun jammed. The monster reached for him, slower now. It had taken some heavy damage at last.

Tariq scrambled backward and then ran for his life.

Rook put a grenade into the monster's chest. *That* finally staggered it. It dropped to its hands and knees with an odd little cry like a short toot from a steam whistle.

Ras Order would never forget that sound.

Tariq had given a hoarse shout of elation and finally got his gun going, loosing off another clip into the thing. Fiber, brown juice spattered off its hide. Tariq's cry became a scream of triumph.

But the monster did not fall. Indeed, it began to get back on its feet, unsteadily, a little slowly, but still very much alive! And then, abruptly, the situation worsened beyond compare. A second, slightly smaller monster appeared on the scene.

Ras Order could remember his eyes bulging. Was this the monster's mate, come to finish them off?

It killed two guards immediately, stamping them flat on the ground, ignoring their gunfire.

Then it moved toward the rest of the hunters.

Most were reloading, frantic fingers scrabbling clips into their guns. Tariq was screaming with frustration and terror. Rook's last grenade fell short.

It was right among them, there was no time, no room, they broke and ran, splitting into two groups, heading in different directions.

The servants, most of the guards went one way. Tariq, Ras Order, and Kierke went another, with only Rook to protect them.

When Ras Order saw Tariq running with him, he could not hold back his bitter retort.

"So who is the coward now, Tariq?"

Tariq had not answered beyond giving him a fathomless glare.

So they'd run, despite exhaustion. Then had come the screams and shots and more screams as the other group of men were hunted down. Finally there was a merciful silence.

But the silence quickly grew menacing. They could easily imagine the monsters stalking them through the dark.

Thus they went on, staggering blindly through the jungle, praying they were traveling away from the monsters and not back to them. They had lost all sense of direction, the sun was invisible beyond the green vault of leaves, the light was dim, the forest quiet.

Ras Order felt utterly doomed. The thought of being devoured by the things was too horrible to contemplate. But if they caught up with them, what chance would they have? The things were virtually unkillable.

Tariq shook his communicator in disgust. "I cannot raise anyone, I don't think they're listening."

Dully, they stared at the slim gray radio in his hand.

"What good are the choppers now, Tariq?" Ras Order said. "Now, when we want them, they're forty kloms away, and nobody's listening to the radio!"

"Shut your filthy mouth, you coward. Your balls are the size of sesame seeds, Ras. You run like a woman."

"I'm not the only one who's running, Tariq."

"Look, shut up, the pair of you," Kierke Spreak snapped. "Give me that radio, I want to make sure Tariq's doing it right."

Tariq stared at him in shock, then handed him the radio and went to stand a few feet away. Suddenly his shoulders shook. Ras Order stared in wonder—Tariq the Terrible was crying! Tears were streaming down his face.

Flecker had anchored the boat in the shallow lagoon waters near the puffcreter complex of Camp Two. A handful of people were on hand to welcome the first arrival of the *Tiger Cat*. They clapped and cheered as the ceramic anchor went splashing into the lagoon.

Nobody but Flecker knew who had painted that name on the prow of the boat.

It was as miraculous as the rest of the boat project. Like the moment when Strang told him that he, Flecker, was going to pilot the boat, while Strang stayed on Hospital Island and built a second boat.

"We're going to need a lot of boats. We need to be able to exploit the fish resources here, since their protein is easily treatable for human consumption. So we need fishing trawlers."

Flecker shrugged. Strang was always planning something.

For this first trip Flecker had been unable to find any passengers, but the hospital had entrusted six small crates of drugs to him. These were antifungal pills, freshly made in the hospital lab. Everyone tried to take one every day.

And so Flecker found himself guiding the boat across the choppy waters of the delta. Whereupon he was extremely glad that the outboard motor had plenty of horsepower. Strang had refitted a motor from an ATV to power the boat and added ceramic propellors to it that he'd cast himself in the lab ceramizer. In the worst of the tidal race the motor had kept the boat ploughing steadily through to the headland, kicking up bow waves and leaving a boiling wake.

Flecker went ashore on the raft as it was hauled back to the beach. With him went the supplies of alvosterine.

Camp Two had swollen considerably since last he'd seen it. Dozens of small puffcrete domes had been laid out on narrow streets and twisting lanes.

The canyon road from the puffcreter where they'd dumped

Garmash's body was now graded and smoothed. Domes clustered thickly beside it.

At the top of the headland the maintenance sheds were busier than ever, but red-tag control center had vanished and been replaced by a two-story block in cream puffcrete with glass windows.

More two-story buildings had arisen in the center of the camp. The old inflatables were still there, but now they were dwarfed by the new structures.

He became aware of a disturbance; a crowd was yelling its head off nearby. In the center there.

He went on, up the slope of the spine of the headland, and soon came to the camp center, where a crowd of several hundred was standing in a wide circle around a single figure.

Flecker's eyes bulged out of his head as he saw that the figure in the center was not human.

An alien being, and one that was wearing handworked clothing and performing a series of ritualized gestures. The shock sank into him like a shot of hundred-proof vodka on an empty stomach.

"What is it? A dance of some kind?" a woman said to her friend, standing beside him.

"The bloody thing is crazed, someone get a gun," snarled another voice, a man.

"Shoot it? You can't do that!"

"You want to stop me?"

"You're an idiot, it's not hurting anyone."

"Just give it a chance and it'll be abducting people to eat in the forest."

A struggle broke out in the crowd as a man tried to aim a rifle at Igi.

The gun discharged, but into the ground.

Flecker felt the hair stand up on his neck. Their first contact with an intelligent alien life form and these people wanted to kill the damned thing!

With a shout to the alien, Flecker sprang forward, unthinking.

The alien watched him approach. It was tense, wary, balanced on the balls of its large feet.

Flecker suddenly realized that he was very close to the thing and that it was large, formidable, and very aroused. One false move and he was a dead man, he was sure.

216

But there were others running up with guns, and screams and shouts in the crowd for killing the alien.

"Come with me!" Flecker yelled, reaching out a hand, taking the other's larger hand, pulling on it urgently.

Eye contact; the creature was preternaturally alert, the big yellow eyes alive with questions.

Flecker tugged, signaled.

The alien looked at the crowd, saw the knots of struggling figures, saw a man pull out a hand weapon and fire it. The bullet whizzed past their ears like an angry insect.

Igi realized that he had enraged the sky demons in some way. They were trying to kill him. The sky demons were rather unpredictable creatures, and they were perhaps more trouble than they were worth.

He ran with Flecker, crouched over. They were in the crowd then and nobody dared shoot. Then they were out of the crowd and heading down the hill. Another bullet whined off the ground, smashed a window to their right.

Flecker pushed Igi on down the road to the puffcreter and the boat and then turned and put his body in the line of fire.

A bullet whined off the ground by his foot and he almost lost control of himself, but he kept shouting in a loud voice, "Stop it! Stop shooting!"

"Get out of the way, you fool!" someone screamed. A man with an aimed rifle forced his way out of the crowd.

Scientists threw themselves in front of the man.

Another struggle broke out.

Flecker looked down the hill to the creter. The alien was a short distance away, staring back. Flecker ran toward him, gesturing with his arms wildly.

The alien ran on, downhill. A bullet whined off the canyon rocks.

Flecker ran full tilt down the road, arms windmilling to keep his balance. The alien did something very similar.

Together they zoomed past the puffcreter while the fighting behind them progressed to a general brawl.

On the sand dunes they fell and rolled over and over down to the bottom of the beach.

Flecker and the fein waded out to the raft. Igi's face lit up. Rafts he knew about, he had built several with his father and uncles to fish from in the High Blue Lake near Yamuka.

The boat, on the other hand, was another wonder of the sky demons, although now Igi was confused. Were these sky demons he was among now, or were they water demons?

Or even demons at all, or instead, some other creature? Perhaps the old mzees had been wrong, perhaps these creatures were not the real sky demons.

Flecker hit the motor ignition and sent the boat roaring out into the lagoon at top speed, kicking up a huge bow wave while the engine noise echoed off the distant trees.

After a while he slowed, throttling the boat's engines down to a murmur.

Igi's eyes were wide with amazement. The power that the sky demons controlled! It was something to envy. Never had he traveled across water so swiftly!

But now Igi swallowed, put it all aside, and recalled his own mission. He had to tell someone; maybe this one would be more receptive.

He pulled Flecker around and mimed the process that was going to take place soon in the forest around the camp. He drew a tree in the air with his hands and then mimed taking a baby from it.

Then he mimed the Long Legs and its rage.

Flecker stared at the alien in wonder. It was desperately trying to tell him something, of that he was certain.

And on a gut level Flecker knew that it was something to do with the forest. The alien kept pointing to the land, to the distant trees, now cleared for a mile or more back of the headland and Camp Two.

The mob of struggling colonists at the top of the headland was still faintly visible. Flecker turned the murmuring boat northward, along the shore, toward the forest.

He nosed the *Tiger Cat* into an area of shallows and indicated that the alien was free to go.

The alien leaped over the gunwale into waist-deep water, reached back and signaled to him to follow. Then it splashed ashore. Flecker followed, with some misgivings, after casting the anchor overboard again.

Once under the trees he found it hard keeping up with the long-legged stride of the alien, but eventually they climbed the slopes of Prominence 46 again for a short distance until they reached the boundary of the road, which had now been widened and graded over much of its length.

Along the road every tree bore a strange mark, like a gigantic black zipper.

Flecker remembered the zigzag pattern he had seen with

Strang, the night after they'd killed Garmash. This was the same, only more developed, and it had spread to every tree.

Now the alien was gesticulating, pointing to the trees, then going through a careful, slow dance that seemed to be almost a mime. Flecker strained to understand the motions and began to feel an odd little fear, a tremor in his mind.

Suddenly he whirled to stare at the trees.

46

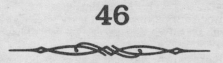

WHEN LEILA TIRED, TOBE TOOK THE BABY HARNESS AND young Compton Shanur. Adelaide then carried the gun and Tobe's share of the food concentrates and water.

Kyika didn't want to make any stops at all until she reached the ocean, which she could smell not far away. But she realized that the sky demons were not as used to long marching as she.

Still, just being in this forest was uncomfortable. The trees were screaming! The tiger stripes were everywhere. Hundreds, thousands of trees bore the marks of Long Legs in gestation.

The rage in the trees was so strong, other vegetation was wilting. The animals had fled. Kyika did not want to be in this forest when the Pale Moon rose full.

So she urged the humans on with little clucks and growls. In truth, they needed little urging. They understood the dire warning of the stripes on the trees.

To stave off hunger they had concentrates, which Kyika tried but found distasteful. So she gathered fruits and seeds as they moved along and fed herself that way.

To try and keep her awareness of the forest's anger down, Kyika threw herself into the effort to exchange words across the language barrier. Eagerly she named things, pointing to various objects and giving them the fein words. But it was a slow process. The humans had a hard time understanding whether it was the ground she meant when she pointed downward, or the moss that covered it, or the small pebbles within it, or satursine seeds that lay here and there upon it.

Yet they had made some progress, enough for the most rudimentary communication, before nightfall that day.

Eventually Leila felt she was going to drop at any moment. She begged to be allowed to sleep, for just a couple of hours.

Adelaide tried to explain it to the fein—to "Ki-ee-ka," as she now knew her to be—but the concepts of time were hard to describe with the very limited vocabulary between them.

Kyika heard her out, then bared her teeth in a smile that startled Adelaide and Tobe. She picked Leila up in the next moment and put her on her broad shoulders.

"Tired woman, ride, Kyika will carry you. Kyika is a big old gzan with six calves, she can carry a field of hay, a yard of tubers."

Kyika broke down into fein giggles at her own absurd boasting. Males were so much better at boasting!

She thought of Igi once again, and wondered how her mate was and where he was and what he was doing. Her heart grew heavy and she pressed her lips tightly together to keep from sobbing.

Kyika found the humans staring at her wide-eyed. She sniffed, then turned and pushed on, carrying Leila swaying above her.

Kyika began to think about building a raft, if there were time. The problem being that they didn't have a kifket between them, only the little weapon that made the noise that broke heads.

They continued walking. The Pale Moon rose. She could not see it clearly, but she knew it was perilously close to full, and when it rose at its fullest, then there would be many Long Legs in the forest.

Preoccupied, she almost missed the slight sounds ahead of them, but the ugly yowling of sky demons was unmistakable. She froze, held up her arm to silence the others.

A voice was raging up ahead. "I want that chopper in here now! Sooner than now! I swear I will have your blood!"

Kyika set Leila down on her feet.

Leila and Adelaide stared at each other. That voice, they knew it.

"Tariq," Leila breathed.

"Out here? Is he hunting us?"

"Possible, anything is possible with Tariq," Leila said.

Tobe felt Compton Shanur move in the harness, but the little boy remained asleep, lost in a two-year-old's dreams.

Kyika had gone, just melted away into the dark. Tobe listened carefully but heard nothing, or perhaps just a slight rustle in a bush one time, but that was all.

Then they heard Tariq yelling again, then some other voices spoke up. Tariq yelled some more.

The fein was back. She signaled to them to follow her, there was little danger of their being heard. After a short hesitation, they got to their feet and followed.

They sidled around the noisy men, at one point climbing under a root not fifty feet away.

They could see Tariq, speaking into a handheld communicator. The others stood a little farther away.

Then Adelaide glimpsed one of these other men.

"Ras Order," she whispered.

Tobe's eyes widened as he saw the Prince.

And then Ras Order broke away from the others, and using a handlight, walked off into the forest a short distance. He unzipped his spylo and began to urinate against a root wall.

A strange impulse pushed Leila forward, out of the shadows to stand at his side.

"Hello, Ras," she said in a whisper.

He jumped like a startled deer and almost lost his footing.

"What the hell!" he said when he saw her.

"Don't make so much noise, the others will hear."

"The hell they won't, and this is a hell of a place to jump out at a man when he's trying to take a piss."

"I'm sorry I shocked you, but then, I always have."

"I wouldn't be so sure of that, Leila. And just what the hell are you doing here?"

"I broke my friends out of the palace and I'm going with them to the coast."

"To the coast?"

"Look, you should come with us."

"Why? A chopper is coming here to pick us up."

"Yeah, we heard. Tariq's voice carries in these woods."

Ras Order gulped and looked around.

"Have you seen any . . ."

"Of the tree things?"

"Tree things? I don't know, they're monsters, twenty-five meters high, terrifying."

"Yes, we saw one. They hatch out of the trees. Every tree

you see that has the markings that look like a big zipper, those trees are going to hatch one of those monsters."

Ras Order felt his mouth go dry. "That's absurd. How can anything hatch out of a tree? Trees are plants. Filthy damn plants don't walk around, they don't eat people."

"I don't know, Ras Order, but we saw it happen."

There was a sudden noise overhead. The chopper had finally shown up and was circling above the canopy of leaves.

A dolly with red and white lights on it was lowered down through the branches.

"Don't go back to the palace, Ras. Come with us."

"You're crazy, the palace is the safest place to be."

"I don't think so."

Ras Order focused on the baby. "That child, is that your Fundan bastard?"

"Yes," she said in a defiant voice.

"You're taking him to the coast, too, to the Fundans?"

"If I can find them, yes."

Ras Order's frown dissolved in irritation. "I can't go there, you're crazy, the monsters will eat you. Come back to the palace, Leila, come back with us now."

The dolly was down on the ground, Tariq and Kierke scrambling onto it. Rook was calling him.

"I have to go, Leila."

"Don't, Ras, listen to me—"

But he was gone, running back, with his fly still open, to the dolly. Rook stared past him but saw nothing to shoot at, and turned and joined the others.

The dolly rose up, lights blazing, and slowly disappeared through the branches.

The chopper roared and then moved away, gathering speed.

Kyika was motioning to them frantically. The chopper noise would draw any Long Legs there were to this spot. They had to move and move fast.

222

47

THE DAWN FOUND THEM ON THE EDGE OF A VAST EXPANSE OF swamp. They had seen no further sign of the Long Legs, for which Kyika was enormously grateful. Furthermore, none of the trees in the surrounding area were marked with the black zipper marks.

But now the trees came to an end and the swamp stretched away before them, lush with blue knuckoo and pink hobi gobi. Kyika called a halt, she needed to assess the situation.

Tobe and Adelaide dropped immediately to the ground with groans of exhaustion.

Leila sank down beside them, cradling Compton Shanur, who was wide awake now and unhappy because there was nothing to drink but water.

Fortunately Leila had found that Compton Shanur liked the flavor of the citrus concentrate, which came in bars. Compton Shanur liked to simply chew the bars direct. Leila gave him another one and he went to work on it immediately with enormous concentration.

There were only two more citrus bars left, however.

Kyika squatted down for a few breaths herself. Hardened to long walks, she was nevertheless reaching her own limits.

The sight of the swamp ahead filled her with more gloom. This would be most arduous terrain to cross without a raft.

Idly she watched Leila play with the little boy. So light and fragile was that alien cub. It had the most odd skin, which both repelled and fascinated her. It looked as if it had been peeled or something equally terrible. Like the worst case of mange she could imagine. Her own fur rippled in horror at the thought.

Someday she would have to tell Igi about all this. How she had shepherded the "hooman" sky demons through the forest at night. How noisy and clumsy they had been!

Of course, she recalled with a sudden pang, this depended on her actually finding Igi again. To push away unwelcome questions she returned to the task at hand.

Toward the sun's rise there was higher ground, and distantly, a line of surf. In the other direction the swamp went on in featureless immensity.

The higher ground would provide the quicker route to the ocean. She waited a few minutes and rallied the humans. Wearily they staggered onto their feet and lurched off behind her.

The way led along the margin where the great forest faded out into the swamps. Dead trees, some drowned, some lying on their sides, were far more common here than in the deep forest.

The rotting trunks of some of the fallen giants were simply too high to climb over and they had to detour, walking inland for a kilometer or so to get around them.

Slowly, though, they made progress. By the time the sun was approaching the zenith, they were on firmer ground, climbing steadily along the flank of Prominence 46, with the headland occupied by Camp Two dead ahead.

Here they heard the sudden growl of a big engine. Something massive and green was rolling through the forest nearby.

"The road," Tobe said. "Maybe we can hitch a ride the rest of the way."

Adelaide brushed her hair back from her eyes. It was sticky and matted, like everything else.

"How's the baby?"

"Heavy, very, very heavy, if you want to know the truth."

"Better give him to me again," Tobe said.

"Thank you, Tobe."

Compton Shanur simply sucked harder on his citrus-concentrate bar, oblivious to the change of carrier.

Then they were past another giant tree and saw the road and another truck, this one a bright red, that went growling past, heading upcountry.

Soon they saw trees with the tiger-stripe markings. Kyika became very uneasy.

"I don't like the look of these," Adelaide muttered.

"I vote that we head for an island somewhere," Tobe said.

They walked on down the side of the road and soon came in sight of a tree with broken bark down the length of the black marking.

Everybody froze at the sight.

Kyika grunted. "Long Legs hatch here already."

They moved quickly away from the road, Kyika trying to get the humans to move silently. But in their fatigued state they could only blunder along, hearts pounding as they snapped twigs, tripped over vines, and crunched dry seedpods under their boots.

Kyika prayed the Long Legs would not hear them, and her prayers were answered, for they went on for another hour or so and glimpsed nothing but light and open sky ahead.

Kyika clenched her paws into fists with excitement. She had only heard about the ocean in the old fein tales. Now she would see it for herself.

They climbed another root system and abruptly stepped out into a vast empty space, with piles of tree debris mounded up here and there on a surface of bare, brown dirt. Dust rose into twists in the wind.

Kyika stared at the strange desolation. Buildings glittered on the far side. There were many sky demons in this place, and soon there would be many Long Legs thirsting for revenge.

Kyika did not know what to do. She had thought to bring herself, and the sky demons that had helped her, to safety by the ocean. There they could hide from the coming fury while she worked out a plan for returning to her home.

Instead she had brought them all to a place of even greater peril, for the moon would rise full that night.

48

On Hospital Island, Igi's appearance and Flecker's apprehensions about the forest had stirred astonishment, unease, and debate, in that order.

The sections of Strang's second boat, much longer than the first, were cooling on the sand of the landward beach.

A storm was blowing in, heavy rain likely.

An interminable meeting of the island council was in progress. It had been called initially by Dr. Villon, to discuss Flecker's news. Unfortunately, it had soon turned into a discussion of the many complaints concerning the use of the puffcreter for making boats.

The council members were generally unsure about Flecker's story. Flecker's background was murky, there was a question mark there about the disastrous Ground Team 8 expedition.

But the alien creature, "Iggy," was all too real.

No one knew what the consequences might be. Some had already raised the "native intelligent life form" problem.

"Does this mean we have to abandon the planet?"

"No way we can do that, we're here now. There's no going back."

"The *Founder* was designed to travel one way only."

"But if they're intelligent life forms, they have the right to this planet."

"Then we'll have to make 'might' more important than 'right.'"

"That'll make us the invading aliens from space, then."

"Yes, but we can't go back."

When the meeting turned back to complaints about missing septic tanks that should have been cast in the creter but hadn't because of the misuse of the machine by Strang, Guvek, and Flecker, the latter stormed out and went up to Strang's ward.

Flecker found him up on the roof of the hospital, staring out to sea where the storm front was brewing. The winds were strengthening steadily. Whitecaps flecked the ocean.

"Quite a blow coming in," Flecker said.

Strang was in one of his silent moods. Flecker noticed the signs. Strang was like that, he'd concluded. He went back and forth between brief bursts of activity and long periods of introspection, when he hardly seemed to know what was going on around him.

"I want you to meet somebody," Flecker said.

Strang gave no evidence of having heard him.

Flecker gave up after a while and started to leave. The wind was shrieking faintly about the corners of the roof.

Strang followed him onto the stairs. Strang's eyes were wide and luminous.

"We've got work to do, Flecker, got to finish the boat."

Strang collected a tub of ceramaze and an applicator from under his bed in the ward.

Then they walked down to the inshore beach.

Here, Igi had built himself a fire from knuckoo trash and was roasting pieces of a basking fish he'd speared. Igi stood up as the sky demons approached. It was the one named "Flecka" and another that Igi had not met.

Strang's face underwent an almost comical progression of expressions as he took in what he was seeing. Then he strode forward to the side of the fire, reached out a hand and clasped that of Igi, shaking it vigorously.

"Hamilton Tiger Cat, in the flesh," he said happily.

In the New Palace the Khalifi brethren heard Ras Order's report in a somber mood. Ibrahim was under criticism from Merzik and the others.

Patrols had been sent out but had reported no trace of the fugitive Fundans and the alien.

Now they listened to Ras Order's report on the disastrous "monster hunt."

"Your conclusions, Prince?" Faruk said finally.

"We need heavier-caliber weapons. The rifles barely slow them down. They can even survive grenades."

Faruk turned to Ibrahim. "What are our prospects of resuming manufacture of weapons?"

"Can't be done in less than a month. Our machine shops are all fully engaged in making machine tools and construction equipment. We would have to remodel completely."

"What are the chances that there are more of these creatures?" Feisal said.

"Limited, I should think," Ibrahim replied.

"But there may be more out there."

Ibrahim raised his hands. "There may be. It's possible."

Merzik leaned forward. "We have stupidly left ourselves without the capacity to manufacture new, heavier weapons."

Ibrahim sighed. "It was scarcely imagined that we would need anything more potent than twenty-millimeter cannon."

"How many of those do we have?"

"I don't know."

"It would be a good idea to find out, wouldn't it?" Merzik's eyes were flashing.

"We are protected here." Ibrahim was on the defensive.

"Bah, you have been out of it since the disaster. You were beaten by a damn renegade Fundan and you've lost your grip!"

There was a silence. Clearly Faruk and Feisal were close to siding with Merzik. Ibrahim viewed them all with gloomy eyes.

"My brethren, let us not quarrel now. Let us concentrate on this problem."

"Where is Tariq?" Feisal said.

Now Merzik was on the defensive. Tariq was under sedation. He had completely lost his wits.

Having Igi to help them push the sections of the new boat together had sped things up enormously. The fein was strong enough to shift one side of a boat section on his own. Finally the boat was complete, the ceramaze still bonding.

Igi clasped hands with the "hoomans" and beckoned them to his fire. The storm was a lot closer and the winds were strong. The fire restarted easily as Igi piled on bits of blue knuckoo.

Strang sat and watched the fein with the fascination of a zoo visitor. Igi busied himself with the remains of the basking fish, cutting chunks of it off the major bones and skewering them neatly with splinters of blue knuckoo.

Flecker said, "If we're gonna eat roast fish, then we need some beer!" and strode off to the hospital complex. He returned with a two-liter jerrican of the best "Hibby" and three beakers.

Igi sniffed the "beer" suspiciously and then tasted it. His eyes widened; this was like plum brew! Only lighter in flavor.

He swilled a little around in his mouth, then smacked his lips with a long, pink-gray tongue in a gesture both humanlike and comical. Flecker grinned, looked to Strang. Strang was fascinated.

"I think he likes beer," Flecker said. "I should have known he would."

Igi held out the beaker for more.

49

"LOOK, I'M AWFULLY SORRY, BUT YOU HAVE TO UNDERSTAND our position. We're elected officials here. The shuttles are going flat out, but there are still a lot of angry people up on that ship."

"But don't you understand? If I'm right, then those people will be coming down here to meet their deaths."

"And what if you're not! Then who is going to take the heat? We are. So it's our judgment call."

"This isn't a sports event, there's a terrible peril hatching in those trees. We've no time to do anything about it except to try and get off this headland."

The president of the executive council, Degalia Weers, lost her patience at last.

"Look, there's more than a thousand people in this camp. Even if we packed every shuttle on return load, we couldn't lift them all off for days. We just don't have the fueling capacity. We don't have anything like our full complement of equipment either."

"Why not?" Adelaide said. The Fundan designers had certainly planned for the equipment to be there.

"Damned Khalifi, of course. They built their own landing pads up in the woods and stole half our stuff."

Adelaide groaned. Weers continued, "So, the council is in an impossible position, don't you see? If you're just dreaming all this stuff and we call a halt to shuttle flights, we'll suffer at the next elections."

"If you don't do something, believe me, there'll not be many voters left for the next elections!"

Weers sighed. Dealing with Fundans was a royal pain in the ass. There were more than twenty Fundans in the camp now, and they all wanted treatment as it would be accorded to royalty.

"You know these monsters exist, there's the corpse of one sitting out there on the road."

"Yes, we know there are the occasional monsters, we don't know that there are armies of them."

"And besides," Jarmela Butte broke in, "we'll be ready for the next one."

"You've got twenty men and a slim barricade."

"The barricade is perfectly adequate. We had thirty people working on that barricade."

"The monster that attacked last night was killed by just five men with their rifles," Weers said smugly.

"Only after it had killed three people!"

"It doesn't matter, the council has voted on this matter and that is that," Weers said firmly.

Someone whispered, "Damned Norams, think they own the place."

"Come on, Adelaide, let's go get some coffee." Leila took Adelaide by the shoulders and helped her to her feet. "These people are as blind as the Khalifi."

"Who the hell do they think they are?" said fat-faced Bozov, representative of the puffcrete crews.

"White Norams, Bozov, that's all. Been spacers too long. Think they own the universe."

Outside the meeting room Adelaide was shivering. "We tried to warn them," she said. The racial insult had shocked her.

"You're exhausted, you need a good long rest."

"Not going to get it."

"No." Leila nodded. "I don't think so."

They wandered across the main street of the camp. There were vehicles moving up and down fairly constantly now. The first "traffic" on the New World.

And the shuttles continued to land. Every half hour another silver bird, laden with anxious new arrivals, came winging in over the ocean.

Tents had gone up all the way down the sandy peninsula, past the Khalifi-built administration block to the landing strip where the islands in the delta could be glimpsed in the distance.

On the edge of the headland, where it overlooked the sand spit and the delta, a café had been started by two enterprising women. In their residential dome they had set up a bar, with a coffee maker from a Fundan-designed canteen and a brick oven in which they baked "bread" and heated up ration packs. The First Coffee House had already been joined by the Camp Bar and Grill.

Inside, Adelaide and Leila joined Tobe and Compton Shanur at a corner table.

"I don't think they're taking this seriously enough, Tobe," Adelaide said in a mournful voice.

Tobe looked up from a plate of beans and protato fries. Compton Shanur sat in his lap helping himself to protato fries, which he particularly liked when dipped in the red stuff at the side of the plate.

"It's no good, Addy, they won't listen."

"They've got twenty men on a barricade, they don't even all have rifles."

"I think we should try and get out of here."

"The other camps will be equally dangerous."

"What about this Hospital Island, where the beer comes from?" Tobe had a beaker of Hibby in front of him.

"Well, I guess."

"I mean, where else is safe? Except the ship?"

Adelaide nodded. "That's the only place I can think of right now."

"But the shuttles are going up empty now to save fuel?"

"Right. There's not enough fuel."

"Well, Kyika intends to go to the island. I think she's building a raft to that end right now."

"A raft?" Adelaide said in wonder. She'd been in the meeting all morning—since the first, near disastrous moments when they'd entered Camp Two and one maniac had almost shot Kyika.

Now the fein was building a raft. Well, it sounded like her, straightforward, practical, active.

"That other fein they showed us the video of, he was definitely her husband, then?" she said.

"Definitely. When they showed her the video of him, she almost killed the poor guy who loaded the screen for her. She wanted to know where her Igi was."

"Monogamy, among alien lions, how about that?"

"So she made herself a kind of hand axe, I guess that's what you'd call it. Took a discarded lump of heavicrete and sharpened it up on a lathe in the machine shop. Now she's out cutting down the swamp to make a raft."

"Well, if she's going to Hospital Island, I'm going to Hospital Island," Leila said emphatically.

"I don't think we can just walk out on these people," Adelaide said.

"You heard them, they won't listen."

"But Tobe, if what Kyika thinks is going to happen does happen, we may lose everything here. Those creatures will destroy everything."

"Addy, we may even lose our entire colony tonight, don't you think I know that? But there's nothing we can do. These people are just too unimaginative to listen. And besides, you heard them, we're goddamn Norams now. We screwed up the world for everyone else, and all that old stuff from hundreds of years ago."

Adelaide's Fundan nature would never let her give up.

"The camp council is due to meet again after lunch. We have to go back and try again."

Tobe groaned.

But when they returned to the council meeting, they got short shrift. To her horror, Adelaide found that the council had invited ancient Agatha Fundan to consider Adelaide's petition and pass some kind of family judgment on it.

"You've got to listen to me," Adelaide said in a voice crackling with tension.

"No! You come in here with your alarmist views, with this nonsensical story about monsters hatching out of trees, and you expect us to believe you. You must think we're mad, touched by the forest, like you."

"She's quite, quite mad," Agatha said with satisfaction.

That was enough for the council.

Adelaide still would not let go. "Look, it will only be a few more hours before the sun sets. When the moon rises, if I understand the fein correctly, then hundreds of these trees are going to give birth to those things."

There were smiles around the meeting.

"But wait, listen to me, doesn't it make sense? I mean, what other trees survive on the land mass here?"

They stared at her.

"This species of tree has dominated completely because it protects itself, don't you see? It has an active component, which can uproot and destroy any opposition forest!"

There were more smiles.

"Poor thing, she needs some help."

"Too much exposure to the alien forest, that's clear."

Adelaide left finally, utterly dejected. She wandered down to the beach in a daze. There she found the others, all busy with the raft. The wind was rising and in the distance dark clouds were piling up on the horizon.

On the shore, watching, was a small group of scientists, intently observing the fein.

Kyika worked swiftly and Tobe sweated and struggled beside her, pulling the twenty-foot-long stems of knuckoo out of the swamp, where they fell when Kyika cut them with the "magic" kifket she'd made with the alien rock.

Kyika knew that time was running out. Her raft had to be big enough to take at least the aliens that had befriended her. And with the dirty weather coming in, it had to be much bigger than it would otherwise have had to be.

On top of her general fatigue, it was a heavy load. But at least "her hoomans," as she thought of the little group, understood the peril. They were helping her just like cubs would help their mother or father.

What the other "hoomans" were up to was anybody's guess. A gaggle of them were standing there watching her and not lifting a finger to help. Didn't they have anything better to do?

Leila sat on the sand and plaited long strips of knuckoo bark to make cords which were then twisted three ply into crude rope.

Adelaide sat down with her and began to help.

Compton Shanur was on the beach, collecting together bits of knuckoo and bringing them to Leila for inspection and approval. Compton Shanur was having a great time.

Later Kyika finished cutting knuckoo and worked with Tobe to haul it onto the beach. There they bound it up in big bunches and then lashed the bunches together.

By the time the light was failing, the raft was ready to go. The clouds, however, were much closer, and the winds were getting fierce.

Kyika had meantime cut some "paddles" from dead and dried hobi gobi leaves. She wanted to be well away from land before the rise of the full Pale Moon, despite the threatening conditions offshore.

233

50

THE DISK OF THE PALE MOON ROSE IN TAWNY FULLNESS.

The time was come. "Now" began. Deep in the hearts of the wood, where wet begat bone in slithering dark, many new lives pulsed.

As the light of the Pale Moon struck across the canopy, the bark of the mother forms began to break.

The silence of the eternal forest was shattered by the splintering and crashing of bark.

It was come, the night for revenge.

There had been tree damage, slaughter, destruction! The ultimate nightmare of sessile living things. For untold eons trees had sat in dread of the creep of insects, the tramp of animals. These trees had evolved their own way of dealing with enemies.

The bark split, the mother forms trembled, and from the long wounds in their bark came forth the "mouths" of the mother forms.

First one, then ten, then a hundred, then a thousand, all along the length of the roads blasted through the forest by the saw teams and the stumpers.

Their beaks clacked together. They rustled in a mass, touching, mouthing, understanding.

They looked this way and that, they scratched flat-topped heads. They heard the screaming of the wounded trees and the grieving for the dead.

Their eyes swiveled ominously.

There, through the trees, could be seen an alien manifestation. A hated thing of straight lines and walls and boxes.

They moved through the trees, a regiment of bipeds seventy feet high. The ground trembled.

At the edge of the clearing around the Khalifi palace they halted. Thousands of beady black eyes glared in baleful ferocity across the open space.

Many, many mother forms had died here. Their remains had been smashed. They had been desecrated, their bodies being turned into components of the alien structures.

Rage bubbled in the hearts of the "mouths."

Every animal and bird in the forest was aware of that rage; they fled as if before a giant forest fire.

On the terraces of the palace, and even more in the gun towers set up in the outer fields, the legionaries on guard felt it. A creeping sensation on the spine, a desire to run away in mindless flight, an instinctive urge, operating at a primal level, reptile brain kicking legs into frantic movement.

Men shivered over their machine guns.

Something odd was going on.

The clone guards alone knew the truth. They were on the lookout for another of the monsters. Ever since the Princes came back in a state of abject terror, the guards had been on the lookout. They thirsted to avenge their losses.

But they also felt the eerie sensation of being the focus of some enormous, unsympathetic force.

They shrugged, moved in exercise rhythms to throw off the feeling. Checked their weapons. Rook had been very specific. Everyone had frag in their clips, penetration rounds were worthless.

Then it happened, a rustle, a stamping of feet, and the mouths moved forward. They came quickly. The outer fence was ripped out of the ground and torn to shreds. The outermost watch towers went down. Guns were stuttering now, but still the men on the palace roofs were staring with mouths wide open.

An army of things had appeared, things as tall as buildings. Things that moved on long pairs of legs with long arms waving above.

The guards' guns kicked in with a clatter. Nine- and twenty-millimeter machine guns stuttered, grenades were launched. Bright flashes lit up the sky.

The army of monsters kept coming. One or two went down. The rest absorbed the damage with scarcely any lessening in stride. More watchtowers went down like bushes beneath an avalanche.

Gunfire rose to a crescendo. Men ran hither and thither through the palace with messages.

Ras Order was dragged from bed, where he had gone to

sleep, heavily sedated. He was groggy and barely able to understand the words of the messenger.

Blearily he stumbled to his feet. He heard, felt, the guns firing. A lot of guns.

Was this a dream? Or a nightmare? He pinched himself. Still the thudding of machine guns could be clearly heard.

He staggered to the balcony that connected all the apartments on the top floor of the palace's main building.

Ibrahim was called from his supper by an anxious Amesh.

"What is it?" he said as they hurried out onto the balcony at its widest point, right in front of Ibrahim's suite.

"Monsters, Master, many, many." Amesh gave him binox with night enhancement and pointed.

Ibrahim glanced through the binox. Impossibly huge bodies, covered in shaggy fur, were lurching toward him. Eyes like polished black stones were arrayed in rows across the tops of the nightmarish heads. There were hundreds of them.

The roar of weapons made it hard to think.

Ras Order was there, in a dressing gown. An injection of instastim had his eyes open, but his brain was still whirling. Vaguely he recalled Leila's warning in the forest.

Tariq had appeared now, his eyes wild.

"We must get out of here, Sire!" he bellowed.

Ibrahim stared at him with distaste.

Merzik was coming.

"We must go, now. Order the choppers!" Tariq was grasping Ibrahim's hand. Ibrahim shook him off with loathing in his voice.

"Leave me, you imbecile."

Ibrahim whirled to Ras Order. "What artillery do we have?"

Ras Order felt his brain go blank. The monsters were at the outside walls now. A new noise could be heard.

"Artillery! Where is it?" Ibrahim was shaking him.

"I don't know, I was asleep. I only just got back from hell."

The new noise was the sound of puffcrete walls being broken. The monsters were tearing them down.

Ras Order saw an ATV rise into the air outside the wall, then it was thrown over the wall as if it were no more than a rock.

Gunfire was continuous.

Ibrahim gave up on the Crown Prince, turned to Amesh.

"Find out where our bigger guns are."

"Look, Master." Amesh pointed down into the courtyard. Men in legion uniforms were pushing a pair of twenty-millimeter cannon into position.

A section of wall collapsed somewhere. Men died screaming. A terrible hooting noise had begun as the monsters scrambled through the break.

"Fire the guns!" Ibrahim shrieked.

The guns opened up on the things, but though a few of them were cut down by the heavy-caliber shells, there were too many now. The guns lasted less than half a minute.

Other monsters were already climbing the outside of the palace, reaching through windows and tearing whole galleries off the structure in crescendos of collapse.

Tariq led the Khalifi lords in headlong flight down the passage, into the heart of the palace.

"How can we get to the choppers?" Merzik screamed in Ibrahim's ear.

Ibrahim's breath was roaring in his ears, his heart seemed to be hammering its way out of his chest.

"Call ahead, to the pad, tell the pilots," he gasped.

Faruk was there, with Feisal and several women.

Everyone began screaming at once.

51

STRANG WAS CONVINCED. IGI'S MIME OF THE LONG LEGS, HIS gestures to the distant forest, roused him to action. Flecker had been right. But Flecker had missed the reference to the heavens. With dusk falling, Igi had tried again. He traced the motion of the Pale Moon. Strang understood.

"We launch the barge tonight."

Flecker gestured around them at the rising storm waves.

"Helluva night to try a new boat."

"The water will be high, it will be easy to launch. We three can do it."

"Oh yeah," Flecker said, giggling from the beer. "Just us three can do it."

And when the ceramaze had done its job, they did launch the barge, Igi shoving from behind while Strang and Flecker, soaked to the skin, worked at the sides. Flecker couldn't believe he was doing this!

The waves coming in on the landward side of the island were not the ocean breakers falling on the outer beach, but they were still rising above the men's chests before the barge was afloat.

Cables to the shore and the *Tiger Cat*, bobbing at anchor nearby, had already been attached. The barge was held just outside the breakers.

"She won't stay there long," Flecker said. "The anchor on the *Tiger Cat* won't hold it there."

"It's all right, we're leaving now."

Strang unlooped the line holding the barge onshore. He wound it up as he went and then tossed it into the water ahead of him as he waded out to the waves, dove through them, and then swam out to the *Tiger Cat*.

The fein muttered a charm to himself and then followed. He swam with the fein breaststroke, head below the surface, like some enormous alien otter.

Flecker stared after them both, then with an oath ran down the beach and dove in too.

On the boat Strang got the engine going in no time, and held it idling there while they pulled up the anchor. Then he turned over the helm to Flecker.

"You know how to drive this."

Flecker swung the *Tiger Cat* around and drove her out into the waters of the delta. The line to the barge was already taut. It twanged now as it took the strain and the *Cat* was driven down a gear, engine chugging hard. Then the barge came free of the waves and hauled out behind.

Not far away, on the sandy beach of the lagoon near the puffcreter, Kyika and her group of humans were about to push their raft out into the rising waves when they were interrupted by shouts from the dunes.

A body of men and women came down the path from the creter complex. Several of them had guns.

Adelaide quickly reached for the gun they'd brought with

them from the Khalifi guard. She held it in her hands as the people came close.

At the head of the group was Jarmela Butte, her face drawn tight with determination, her shoulder-length red hair streaming in the strong onshore wind.

"You adults are free to go and drown yourselves if you wish, but we cannot allow you to take the little boy to his death."

Leila jumped to her feet, ran to collect Compton Shanur, who was sitting amidst the big pile of knuckoo fragments he'd collected.

He gave a wail of dismay as he was plucked up and held tight.

"We won't let you take him on that thing," Jarmela said, pointing at the raft.

"With that alien animal, it isn't right!" a man next to her snapped.

Adelaide could not let this pass. "The 'animal's' name is Kyika," she said. "And she appears to be just as intelligent as any of you people. We'll be a lot safer on this raft than staying here with you."

Kyika was now watching all this with acute interest. She was standing waist deep in water near the "prow" of the raft, adding some extra lashing with three-ply knuckoo rope. Her body was largely hidden from the people on the land with the weapons.

By the tone of their voices she could tell they were under strain; violence murmured there. She had already seen similar tensions earlier.

The raft tossed, spray flew up as a big wave surged past her.

"You can go and be safe with her, the little boy is staying here with us."

"He's my son, he goes with me! How dare you suggest otherwise." Leila was beside herself, her face flushed with anger.

Compton Shanur was shocked by his mother's anger and he burst into sudden tears.

"Look at her, damn Khalifi, should lock her up," a tall man in dark robes said. "I don't know why they're letting these people run around. A Khalifi and this alien creature, it's wrong, I tell you. They should be locked up."

"Who the hell are you to condemn anyone else?" Leila shot back.

"Margave is my name, and I will be pastor for the new Kirk to Christ Spaceman that we will soon build here!"

Margave had a loud, booming voice.

"And when we have that kirk, we will work to preserve religion's place here in this new and alien realm."

"Thank you, Margave," Jamela Butte said, "but we should stick to the point. We simply can't allow this child to be put at risk like this."

She waved an arm and three men armed with rifles stepped forward.

"Give me the child," she said.

"No!" Leila shouted. "He is my son, I will take him to safety."

Leila started for the water's edge.

"Stop her, bring her back!" Jarmela Butte yelled.

The men with guns lurched down the beach. Adelaide lifted her own weapon to cover them.

"Stop!" she yelled.

The men looked up.

A gun fired to her side, a woman screamed, but Adelaide had already been knocked off her feet by the impact.

She hit the sand, felt a fierce sting in her side, in her arm as well.

Grains of sand in her mouth, pain shooting through her.

There was more screaming.

Tobe was there, "Adelaide," his arms were around her.

More screams, another shot, someone shouting.

Tobe grabbed up Adelaide's gun, opened fire. More screaming and shouts, with feet thudding on the sand.

Tobe turned Adelaide over.

"Help me lift her, she's wounded," he said.

Adelaide tried to sit up, and discovered that she really *was* wounded, there was blood on her fingers and she felt the wetness spreading inside her one-piece.

There was a heavy tread behind her, and then Kyika was there. She lifted Adelaide with a single heave and carried her into the surf.

Tobe fired again, into the air, and scuttled forward to grab the rifles that had been dropped and toss them into the water.

He waded out, still holding the sidearm and covering the dunes.

Jarmela Butte and the others watched them go with sullen eyes.

Leila and Compton Shanur were already aboard. Compton Shanur's wails had cut off abruptly when he was placed aboard the raft, which fascinated him. He tried to stand up, fell over, and giggled to himself. Gleefully he clutched at the blue knuckoo and pulled himself onto his knees. The bumpy motion of the knuckoo stalks was amusing; he laughed.

Kyika poled the raft out with a thick stalk of knuckoo. Tobe Berlisher kept the sidearm ready to fire back at the people on the mainland, should anyone else decide to open up with a rifle.

52

THE WEATHER WAS BREAKING FAST IN AN EXTRAORDINARY murk of black clouds, tinged green by the lost sunset.

The chop on the estuary had grown fierce, and the raft was tugged this way and that by the currents and waves. Occasionally a squall sent a spatter of rain over them, but the main body of the storm was still offshore. Lightning flashed and flickered.

Kyika and Tobe had paddles, but they were of limited effect. However, the tide and the flow of river water were carrying them out to sea despite the storm waves.

Adelaide lay beside Leila. Big pink med patches covered the wounds in her side and upper arm. Compton Shanur was curled up inside the curve of her body, lying quite still, staring at the tossing waves and the wild black clouds beyond.

Leila watched the mounting seas with concern. The raft was no more than twenty feet in length. Did the fein really know what she was doing?

Clouds moved in the east and moonlight broke through suddenly. Kyika saw the moon was full. She looked back to the land. Leila saw her and shivered.

Then came a cry from Tobe, "Look!"

He was pointing with his paddle. Leila strained to see, then stared. A pair of red lights was visible on the water ahead.

"What is it?" Leila said.

"It's a boat," shouted Tobe, who stood up and waved his paddle in the air.

"A boat?" Adelaide said, propping herself up on one arm.

"It's a miracle!" Tobe cried, waving frantically.

A beam of light swept across the water to them.

The red lights turned slightly, bore down upon them until they could hear a heavy motor chugging through the sound of the gathering storm.

A boat it was, red-brown sides, a motor launch, with men aboard it, waving to them and towing another, larger boat behind it.

The first boat drew closer and slowed. But then one of the figures on board gave a great cry and hurled itself into the water.

They gasped. Tobe dropped his paddle and ran to the edge of the raft.

Kyika was scrambling to the front, her weight sending the raft skittishly sideways.

Then the figure reappeared, swimming with powerful strokes. In a few seconds it swarmed up over the side of the raft like a sputtering sea monster, roaring.

Tobe sprang back. It was another fein!

And then Kyika had jumped on it with a ferocious-sounding yell and the two were rolling around madly on the front of the raft, depressing it under the water while they gave each other mock bites and tremendous hugs that would have broken a man's ribs in seconds.

"Kyika!" the invader shouted.

"Igi!" Kyika shouted.

The boat nudged closer still. A man in the prow threw a line across the raft.

Tobe grabbed it and wrapped it around a projecting bundle of knuckoo.

Leila stood up with a little scream. Her eyes were locked on that man. She took a step forward, then looked back to Adelaide, who had Compton Shanur beside her. Her hand was at her mouth.

She whirled and looked again. The man was staring at her.

He gave a great inarticulate cry.

The boat rode up close to the barge. The man jumped across and landed on all fours, got to his feet unsteadily, and wrapped Leila in his arms.

Adelaide's jaw dropped.

"Dane?" she shrieked. Compton Shanur looked up in sudden uncertainty.

Tobe staggered forward, eyes bulging.

"Dane?" he said, stunned. He dropped to one knee beside Adelaide.

It was Dane Fundan, no doubt of it.

"You're alive, my darling, I thought you were dead!" Leila wept.

Then she turned, pulling him after her, reached down, and took Compton Shanur from Adelaide.

"And this is your son, this is Compton Shanur."

Stunned, Dane took the little boy in his arms.

53

THE *TIGER CAT* HELD STEADY BEYOND THE SURF, WITH THE barge winched in close and Kyika's raft secured to the side of the barge; they knew they would need every scrap of space. They were positioned off the lagoon shore of the sand spit. The shuttle pad was close by, the old Khalifi administration block next to it, although the fence that had once surrounded it had gone.

The headland loomed up above them. The big puffcreter chuffed away on their left, busy come rain or shine. Up on top of the headland there were lights, buildings.

The Pale Moon was hidden behind the clouds. Rain was spattering down. The first drops in a downpour. The wind was whipping up fiercely, and Flecker had turned the *Cat* out to sea and was running the engine hard just to keep everything in place.

Then they heard the first shots.

"Oh no!" said Adelaide, who had been hoping against hope.

The shots increased in number, and there were other sounds, grenades detonating.

Then there were screams, distant, chilling. The shots became ragged then widely spaced, and the screaming became far more general.

Other sounds became audible, heavy impacts, detonations. Bright light flared suddenly from an exploding hydroengine. Flames licked up shortly afterward.

The shots had resumed their previous intensity, but in intermittent bursts. The cries and screams grew much louder.

It wasn't long before they saw the first figures come running down the pathway off the headland.

More flames and flashes were lighting up the sky behind them.

Dane, Tobe, and Leila went over the side. The water was up to their shoulders. They kicked off and swam toward shore.

On the beach they hesitated, trying to judge what was happening above. The winds were fiercer than ever and squalls of rain were coming in almost horizontally.

More figures had appeared at the top of the road running down into the puffcreter canyon. Soon a steady stream of people was coming that way.

The crew of the puffcreter had emerged from the control room in the waist of the machine, twenty meters off the ground. They waved and gesticulated suddenly, ran inside the machine, and slammed the doors.

At the top of the road two men with rifles appeared. They turned, knelt, and fired off entire clips of ammunition. Then, abruptly, they stopped firing and ran for their lives.

Behind them came one of the monsters from the trees. It caught them while they were still running full out, and they died from hammer blows of those huge hands.

The monster then started smashing the domes. A fire was blazing in a building directly behind it, and the thing was outlined in eldritch starkness for a moment.

The people were streaming down the beach.

Dane, Leila, and Tobe shouted to them.

"This way, we have a boat! Hurry!"

The people needed no further encouragement. They waded out to the surf, and with the aid of the fein, clambered aboard the barge.

More people were coming, from the direction of the shuttle port. A few were swimming toward them from farther up the headland.

The noise from the camp had become general now, with flames rising high amidst the sound of the utter destruction of everything brought there by the colonists.

Things were being hurled off the top of the cliffs, dimly visible giants ripping down buildings and tossing roofs, walls, foundation blocks, into the sea.

More groups of fugitives ran or scrambled down the path to the beach. Some were lucky and dodged around the monster that was still engaged in demolishing the domes.

When they reached the beach, the lucky ones ran to the water's edge.

Here Degalia Weers and Jarmela Butte found Leila and Tobe.

"Wade out to the boat, it's your only chance." Tobe said.

Weers swallowed, her face flushed with panic, her body shuddering.

"I—I—I—" she said.

"You were wrong, that's all," Leila said without bitterness. "You should have listened to us."

Jarmela Butte wept as she went past and the waves broke over her legs. She stumbled back.

"I'm sorry," Degalia Weers said.

"I can't swim," Jarmela said.

"You don't have to, it's not that deep," Tobe said.

"I'm afraid."

"So am I," Leila said with searing intensity. "We're all afraid."

And then the skies opened up and a shuttle, lights ablaze, came swooping in to land at the shuttle pad.

"No!" Flecker screamed hopelessly.

The shuttle's boosters boomed as it lowered itself to the ground.

The sound brought an immediate reaction from above. Dozens of huge bodies were in motion, coming down the path.

The waverers on the beach rushed for the boats. Jarmela Butte waded with the rest of them, screaming as she went.

Leila and Tobe moved back with them, fleeing reflexively. Then they turned and looked back for Dane, but he was sprinting down the beach, his long legs extending forward and back.

"What the hell's he trying to do?" Tobe said.

Dane had turned to climb the beach, heading for the shuttle pad.

"No!" Leila cried.

She started after him, but Tobe grabbed her. "Princess, come back to the boats, it's not safe here . . ."

Dane vanished, running past the old Khalifi block, into the spaceport.

The monsters had reached the puffcreter. Here they paused, six or seven strong, fascinated by the thing that towered over them and emitted such bright flashes of light.

Then the monsters surged forward to attack. One seized the mantle on a projecting high-pressure valve from the steamer. The mantle came off, and since the creter was in the middle of a burn, the steamer blew with tremendous force. A heavy blast of superheated steam shot out that knocked the monster down, killing it. The steam screamed like a giant whistle.

The other monsters paused for a second. Then they renewed the attack with hoots of rage.

"Come on, Leila, to the boats!" Tobe cried.

He pulled her into the water, propelled her before him. She was weeping, choking on water.

The puffcreter's combustion chamber exploded with a tremendous flash. Huge pieces of metal crashed down on the beach and fell into the water, which hissed as it boiled.

Somehow Tobe heaved Leila through the scalding waves and onto the raft. He climbed past frightened, stunned people and jumped across to the *Tiger Cat*.

Flecker had the engines roaring. He let them play, and the *Cat* tugged hard at the barge and slowly began to pull away from the shore. Behind them was a scene of carnage. The creter's explosion had killed several of the mouths of the mother forms. The others were still bent on destroying the shattered creter.

Flecker moved the boats along the sand spit to a point level with the shuttle on the pad. Its landing lights were still whirling, red and green, and the fumes from the boosters were whipping past, torn by the squalling winds.

Dane appeared at the rear of the shuttle pad, hurling open the doors to the arrivals section.

Startled passengers, still in space issue, were stumbling down the sands, rain lashing them. Dane came behind them, shepherding them forward.

More passengers came running out, along with the shuttle

crew. Dane dashed back to urge them down the beach.

When they argued, he pointed to the creter and the headland. They saw the flames, the people running on the beaches, and finally the things, advancing toward them.

They ran then.

Flecker let the *Tiger Cat* be pushed back onto the edge of the surf. The barge and the raft drifted in close. For a moment he thought they had grounded, and he revved the engines quickly to pull back a little.

The passengers waded out, clambered onto the raft and then into the mass of people in the barge.

Flecker didn't wait to see if the man he'd known as Strang was aboard before he hit the engines full and began slowly pulling out of the wave area.

The monsters were close, too close. He had the drive lever pressed over as hard as it could go, but the *Tiger Cat* was hauling a much greater load now and it was slow going.

One of the monsters went past on the beach. Flecker sucked in his breath. But it never slowed, and went on to the shuttle pad. Then another could be seen climbing into the shuttle pad. It was carrying a pylon with which it began to strike the shuttle where it sat on the pad, wreathed in lights and steam.

More monsters went past, all intent on the shining mother form of the pest things that had dared to assault the trees.

Finally the *Tiger Cat* cleared the surf and built up some momentum, pulling out from the beach and hauling the heavily burdened barge with it.

There were swimmers here, and Flecker slowed to allow as many as possible to grab hold of the raft and either pull themselves out or hang on and be towed out into the lagoon waters.

He looked back as the shuttle exploded, fuel tanks going up in a row of bright flashes. A dozen or more of the monsters were incinerated, while pieces of the shuttle were hurled in all directions.

A huge cloud of smoke blew in toward them, carrying an evil stench. But it dissipated swiftly in the raging winds. When Flecker looked up next, Strang was back.

"We're full up," Flecker said.

"Yes, have to go back now." He turned and went forward to find Leila.

54

THE RAIN HAD STOPPED, BUT IT WAS STILL BLOWING HARD when they finally beached the barge on Hospital Island. More than four hundred survivors staggered or were carried up the beach.

There were many injured; one man had a broken back.

Those who could manage the walk were given shelter in the unfinished houses on the dunes. The rest were bedded down on the floor of the hospital.

The med staff went to work at once, setting bones, fitting splints and casts.

Flecker and Tobe Berlisher meanwhile refueled the *Tiger Cat* and took it back to the beaches off the headland to search for other survivors.

Dane, however, brought Leila and Compton Shanur down to the machine shop in the basement of the hospital. It was locked and empty, but Dane had copied a key for himself. He had also stowed a cot there for times when he worked late into the night and didn't want to wake people in the ward upstairs.

Compton Shanur was already sound asleep when they wrapped him in a blanket and laid him down.

Leila had a desperate need to talk. She grabbed his hand as if she were drowning.

"I thought you were dead. For so long I have been so sad." She wept freely.

"I *was* dead," he said, feeling a curious sense of liberation as he spoke. "In a way. I couldn't live with myself then, I couldn't stand the loss of the *Founder*."

He paused, his voice tightened. "It was my whole life until then, except for you."

"It destroyed you."

"Yes, it did, in one way, but I survived. I changed, that's all."

"You had a breakdown."

"Yes, even that."

"Yes. I saw that coming. I couldn't stand watching you suffer like that."

"I'm not suffering now."

They stopped talking after that, for a long time.

Later, propped on one elbow, Dane marveled at the small body of his son, breathing slowly and softly in his arms.

He felt as if he had been wandering alone in an immense wilderness and had finally found his way home. This was how he wanted his life to continue, now that it had been given back to him. This child that was a part of him, this was the symbol of the future he would work for. He would be witness to the growth of a new generation of Clan Fundan. The line of Talbot and Emily would continue.

Dawn, when it finally came, was clear and bright, with only a few high streamers of cloud to mark the storm's passing.

In the east there were still clouds of smoke rising from the smoldering ruins of Camp Two.

Flecker and Tobe Berlisher had been up and down the coast on either side of the camp in the *Tiger Cat*. They came back with another thirty survivors, people who'd hidden in the rocks or up to their necks in the waves.

They reported that the monsters were still busy, smashing the camp and everything in it to powder.

Meanwhile, calls to Camp One and Camp Three produced no response. But later in the morning there came a call from a small group of survivors from Camp Three who had escaped by driving off in an ATV during the early part of the attack. Now they were twenty kilometers away from the ruins of their camp and calling for a shuttle to lift them off the beach.

There was no word from any of the Khalifi palaces, and indeed, not a single survivor was ever found.

The *Tiger Cat* was finally beached once more, and Tobe and Flecker helped the last few survivors ashore.

They found Adelaide waiting for them by a fire. Instacaf was brewing, and a pot of porridge and some biscuits cooking.

They sat together, afraid to speak at first. Then Adelaide gave them the news as she'd heard it.

"No survivors anywhere else."

"Pretty grim situation, I'd say," was Tobe's comment. He finished some porridge and drank some coffee.

"We've lost everything, all our equipment," Flecker said.

"Looks like it," Tobe agreed.

"Well, at least we seem to be safe out here," Adelaide said.

"Some New World, then, just a few sand islands."

"We'll find a way to survive," Adelaide said confidently. She stood up, held her side but stifled the gasp of pain. Her wounds were healing fast under the med pads, but her side was very sore from the bruising.

"We didn't get much of a formal introduction, but I gather that you are Flecker," she said.

"That's right, I was on the biosurvey, tree science."

"Yes, I heard about that. You see, I visited Melissa a little while ago. She said she wanted to see you."

Flecker brightened visibly at this. "She did?"

"Yes, she did."

"Look," Tobe said.

The two fein had appeared, stretching and yawning, from a dense thicket of blue knuckoo in which they had spent the night in each other's arms.

The fein joined them around the fire and everyone exchanged greetings, "good morning" and "bril beni" or "bril go ba." Igi and Kyika were hungry enough to even try the porridge, which they found odd but edible. Adelaide was unsure whether it would agree with them; the protein configuration of oats was surely alien to their metabolism.

But neither showed the slightest sign of discomfort, so she relaxed and assumed that amino acids were amino acids, no matter where you were, and the fein liver was capable of the necessary enzyme production.

In the early morning light the fein seemed even larger-than-life than they had in the night. Adelaide caught herself staring rather rudely at them and enjoying the obvious familiarity that existed between them. When they looked up at her with questioning eyes, she blushed and looked down, afraid suddenly of the alienness of them and embarrassed by her fear.

She heard her name being whispered, and looked up again to see Kyika trying to teach Igi to say it.

"Ad-ell-ayd," he said.

Despite everything that had happened, and the losses they had sustained, this little absurdity vaporized her depression. So what if the colony had been smashed to its knees? She felt a sense of hope for the future that she hadn't felt in a long time.

She asked Tobe to take a walk on the beach with her, and as they walked down to the water's edge, Adelaide put her good arm around Tobe's waist and hugged him.

He turned to her in surprise. "Addy."

"Shush, Tobe, I just realized something."

"What's that?"

"I love you, you idiot." She kissed him, and then burst into giggles at the absolute astonishment writ large on his face.

ABOUT THE AUTHOR

CHRISTOPHER ROWLEY was born in Massachusetts in 1948 to an American mother and an English father. Soon afterward he began traversing the Atlantic Ocean, a practice that has continued relentlessly ever since. Educated in the U.S., Canada, and for the most part at Brentwood School, Essex, England, he became a London-based journalist in the 1970s. In 1977 he moved to New York and began work on *The War for Eternity*, his first science-fiction novel. Published by Del Rey Books in 1983, it won him the Compton Crook/Stephen Tall Memorial Award for best first novel. *The Founder* is Rowley's sixth novel.